STAKE

STAKE

Kevin J. Anderson

Severn House Large Print
London & New York

This first large print edition published in Great Britain and the USA
in 2021 by Severn House, an imprint of Canongate Books Ltd,
14 High Street, Edinburgh EH1 1TE.

First world regular print edition published in 2020
by Severn House, an imprint of Canongate Books Ltd.

British Library Cataloguing-in-Publication Data
A CIP catalogue record for this title is available from the British Library.

ISBN-13: 9781780291710

Typeset by Palimpsest Book Production Ltd.,
Falkirk, Stirlingshire, Scotland.
Printed and bound in Great Britain by
TJ Books Limited, Padstow, Cornwall.

*This one, like so many others,
is for Rebecca, who got me straight
through the heart . . .*

One

A dusting of early-season snow covered the gray shoulders of Pikes Peak, and aspens splashed gold along the Front Range to the west of Colorado Springs. The clear blue sky was bursting with sunlight.

Perfect conditions for killing a vampire.

Just after noon, the Serenity Hedge apartments felt subdued, with most people off at their day jobs. Preschoolers played on the courtyard swing set or rode plastic Big Wheels along the sidewalk, while their mothers chatted.

No one noticed him as he approached with practiced nonchalance.

Simon Helsing knew how to stay invisible. For centuries, vampires had used similar techniques to move unseen through everyday society. At this time of day, a vampire's powers would be at their lowest point, but nosy observers could also pose a great threat.

Helsing wore a gray plumber's shirt and a Colorado Avalanche cap over his long brown hair. His battered metal toolkit held weapons rather than plumbing tools. Carrying fake work orders he had produced on a public printer down at the library, he walked with a casual confidence that told the world he was supposed to be there.

Helsing climbed the concrete exterior steps to the second floor of the apartments, glanced again

1

at the paperwork as if to double-check the address, though he knew full well that the creature's lair was in #220. A hand-lettered index card permanently taped to the door said *Quiet! Do Not Disturb.*

He pantomimed a polite knock, but made no noise. At the height of day the vampire would be in a deep sleep, likely having fed well the night before, and a simple knock wouldn't wake him, but Helsing didn't like to take chances. The job was risky enough as it was.

After waiting an appropriate time for an answer, he got out his picks and smoothly unlocked the door, as if the building manager had given him access. He slipped into a dark, sinister apartment that reminded him of shadows and blood. After closing the door behind him, he no longer worried about being seen, but was in danger nevertheless. He froze for a moment, assessing the threat inside. His skin tingled as he sensed the brooding evil here. Yes, this was the place.

He had adopted the name 'Simon Helsing' when he embraced his new mission, and it fit him like a calfskin glove. He lived entirely off the radar in Colorado Springs; it was important to maintain a quiet profile so he could do his work. Even though the members of the Bastion offered him support, and their leader Lucius shared the same mission of saving the human race, Helsing did his bloody work alone.

After hunting the *lampir* – the Bosnian word for vampire – in secret for years, he had decided to change tactics. No longer did it serve his purpose, or humanity's, to hide his crusade.

People needed to know that real monsters lived unnoticed among them . . .

He waited for his eyes to adjust to the apartment's dark interior. The curtains were made of a heavy opaque fabric, a significant upgrade from the flimsy dishrags usually found in cheap dwellings. The inhabitant had added light-blocking window shades to prevent any purifying sunlight from seeping through.

The front room held minimal furniture – sofa, chair, coffee table, end table, lamp – austere basics that had probably come with the apartment. No pictures on the walls, little of the clutter he would have found in any normal human home.

The place was silent as a tomb except for the faint ticking of the stove clock in the small kitchen. Helsing remained still as he peered through the gloom, discerning the door to a hall bathroom and a second mostly closed door – the room where the vampire slept during daylight.

Before moving forward, he rested his toolkit on the sofa and opened the latch with only a muffled click. He raised the metal lid and withdrew a mallet and the wooden stake he had sharpened.

Helsing had surveilled the target, studied his background. Mark Stallings worked as a nighttime clerk in a convenience store on North Academy Drive. He had filled the night shift for three years straight and never once, as far as Helsing could tell, worked during daylight hours. More telling, according to public records, 'Stallings' had not existed before he moved to Colorado Springs. No previous addresses, no tax returns, not even a driver's license in any other state. No siblings, no parents, no wives, ex or otherwise. He was alone, a cipher who drew no attention to himself so he could feed without being caught.

Over the past three years, four separate tenants in the Serenity Hedge apartments had mysteriously vanished without giving notice or leaving a forwarding address. Helsing was convinced that Stallings had killed them and discreetly disposed of their bodies. Or maybe the victims were among the unidentified corpses burned by members of the Bastion to prevent them from turning into *lampir*.

Drawing a deep breath, Helsing strengthened his resolve to move forward with his terrible work. From the kit he removed a plastic bottle of holy water filled in St Mary's Cathedral downtown. As if it were sacred cologne, he dabbed the moisture on his face and neck, then slipped the cross on its chain over his head and adjusted it. He wasn't sure how effective such religious trappings were, and he was not religious himself, but centuries of folklore had to have some basis in fact. The peasants near Sarajevo knew what worked, and he would accept any protection the cross might provide.

He pulled on a pair of latex gloves and crept to the vampire's lair with the mallet and stake in hand.

As soon as he pushed open the bedroom door, he could smell the creature's animal odor, possibly even rank blood from a recent victim. Stallings lay flat on his back, sound asleep in the darkened room, an indistinct silhouette under a rumpled sheet. The convenience store uniform shirt hung on a chair in front of a cheap build-it-yourself desk. Clothes lay strewn around a hamper in the corner, most of them on the floor rather than inside it.

Stallings was utterly quiet, not snoring, sleeping as if dead. Vampires needed to breathe less than normal humans. The creature had a beard and reddish-brown hair matted with sleep. He wore dark flannel pajamas with the shirt unbuttoned, conveniently exposing his chest. His head was turned on the pillow, eyes closed.

Three silent steps took Helsing to the side of the bed, where he loomed over the *lampir*. Stallings didn't stir.

Helsing positioned the tip of the stake directly above the sternum, and gripped the mallet like a carpenter about to pound a nail into the two-by-four. He let the sharpened point just touch the vampire's skin. 'You'll never hurt anyone else,' he whispered.

When the wooden point touched his chest, Stallings started, blinked his eyes. 'What—?'

Helsing raised the mallet high and brought it down using all his strength. The point punched through the breastbone and pierced the vampire's heart with a spurt of hot blood.

Even before the monster began to twist and jitter, as they always did, Helsing pounded a second time with a loud crack, driving the wood all the way through the back. The stake pinned the body to the bed so that it could never again rise from the dead.

Two

Alexis Tarada stared at the headline for a long moment before posting it to her website.

BIGFOOT RAPES WOMAN IN PIKE NATIONAL FOREST

It was by no means the most unlikely story she had run on HideTruth.com. Some would ridicule her for it, but there was a kernel of veracity, so she opted to include it for the possibility, however small, that it might be true.

One of these days, I'm sure to be right, she thought. By now it was practically a mantra. She tucked a lock of brown hair behind her left ear in a fidgety habit and kept researching the details.

The assault in the woods was undeniable, even if the Forest Service downplayed the sensational aspect of the story. The hiker had been attacked in the Front Range just west of Colorado Springs. Since the mystery was right in Lexi's backyard, it caught her attention.

The details of the incident were sketchy, which left room for interpretation. A single young woman, Holly Smith, age twenty-four, had been backpacking alone on the Ring the Peak Trail deep in the national forest. Several days after she was expected home, her sister had reported her missing. Word of the vanished hiker had sparked a flurry of stories on the local news.

Lexi had seen the reports, but assumed the hiker had gotten lost or injured out in the forest. When three hikers accidentally came upon Smith on an isolated part of the trail, she was bloodied and bruised, hungry, terrified. She insisted that Bigfoot had kidnapped her, held her prisoner in his lair, and raped her repeatedly. The hikers brought her to safety and shared her wild story, although the victim herself had refrained from comment.

The Bigfoot claim had piqued Lexi's interest, though, and she dug more deeply into the case. According to police records and the appended medical report, Smith had suffered numerous scrapes, scratches, and contusions, all of which signified rough treatment. Her wrists showed ligature marks where she had been bound by a rope. Her fingernails and clothing were torn from clawing her way free. A rape kit showed evidence of recent sexual intercourse, while vaginal tearing and pubic bruising strongly suggested rape, which corroborated the woman's story. Long, brown hairs from her assailant had been found on her; the strands would be tested for DNA evidence with the hope of searching for possible matches in the sexual predator database.

A Forest Service spokesman downplayed the idea of Bigfoot and deflected further questions. Journalists were reluctant to ridicule or shame a victim of sexual assault. Smith had given no public statement about the sighting or the attack. In fact, the young woman's identity would have been kept quiet, except that her name and photograph had been spread all over the news after she went missing and volunteer search parties were organized.

Lexi herself had hiked in the nearby Pike National Forest, but only on day outings. Since she worked at home from her rental house, she could go on a weekday hike whenever she liked. The scenery of the Rockies was a far cry from her native Dubuque, Iowa.

With all the information she could find, she posted the story to her site with a satisfying click and sat back in the chair in her home office, leaving the comments field open, knowing she would soon have a host of theories, supporting evidence, debates, skeptics, and with the vibrant traffic, a few more donations would appear in the tip jar.

At twenty-six, Lexi was driven and independent with a small frame and straight, shoulder-length hair, currently strawberry blond. Blair, her house-mate, kept suggesting she switch the color to auburn, but he thought about her hair color more often than she did.

Before long, comments about her post began to roll in, and she tried to maintain a sense of decorum, which was sometimes difficult with the passionate HideTruth audience. Her followers claimed to be open-minded, yet often demon-strated extreme defensiveness when anyone expressed skepticism.

As background for the Bigfoot discussion, she called up old threads about Sasquatch, a perennial favorite, especially here in Colorado. With count-less outdoor enthusiasts, hikers, hunters, and backpackers out in the wilderness, anecdotes and sightings were legion, particularly in the mountain communities around Pikes Peak. Many locals believed that something lived in the forest, but they put up with it, just as they had a live-and-let-live attitude toward it, just as they did with bears or mountain lions.

She had found persistent reports of abandoned fire circles, remnants of large camps deep in the wilderness, stories about feral homeless groups hiding from society. Were these rumors a way to explain Bigfoot sightings without invoking any fantastical elements? *One of these days, I'm sure to be right.*

As she watched, someone posted a blurry photo of what looked like a low, dark tree that had a vaguely humanoid shape. 'Proof that Bigfoot was in my backyard!' said SkyWatchr1. Many of the commenters in the HideTruth forum preferred avatars and screen names; few used their real identities.

Though she was dubious, Lexi allowed the blurry photo to remain on the site. No harm done. SkyWatchr1 was a prolific poster, endlessly hopeful, even gullible. He or she had also posted pictures of odd oil stains on the driveway, speculating that the patterns meant something. PencilNeck posted an audio clip of what sounded like rushing leaves and some kind of gruff animal undertone deep in the background, claiming it, too, was proof of Bigfoot.

Though fascinated by fantastic stories, Lexi didn't consider herself to be on the fringe. She was perfectly happy to accept evidence that

9

debunked any wild theory, but she didn't automatically scoff at strange notions either. The world held some things that couldn't be explained . . . yet.

Back in Iowa, her parents had said she possessed an overactive imagination, but Lexi called it a sense of wonder. She felt humility in accepting that she didn't know every answer to every question about every aspect of the world. Her mission statement on HideTruth said, plainly, 'There are still discoveries to be made and questions to be answered.'

Two years ago, bored with her regular online work and unwilling to admit her lack of friends – before Blair had moved in – Lexi started HideTruth to find like-minded people, interesting new friends, to discuss the unknown. She was curious to make connections, to see what kind of interesting debates she could have. She chose the site name as a kind of reverse psychology to elicit exactly the opposite response. On her website, she had no intention of hiding the truth. Would the readers?

If every curious person pulled together in a concerted search for the truth, what might they uncover? After all, a network of amateur astronomers pooled their resources to search the night sky for new asteroids; others had combined their personal computing power to run SETI searches for extraterrestrial signals. Why not pool the knowledge and resources of countless truth seekers who wanted to explain the world's unsolved mysteries? Lexi was deeply interested in the answer, for her own reasons.

She had no idea what a can of worms she was opening.

HideTruth took on a life of its own, and Lexi found some of the speculations, connections, and obscure facts to be thought-provoking (although some were admittedly silly). The more popular her site became, the more her fans donated to keep her going. And the more donations Lexi received, the more bills she could pay, and the more bills she could pay thanks to HideTruth, the fewer hours she needed to waste on regular jobs. *One of these days . . .*

Through the half-open door of her bedroom/office, she could smell the exotic spices of whatever Blair was making for dinner – Indian food maybe – and she was sure it would be delicious. He always took care of her.

The commentary about the Bigfoot assault would pick up after dinner as more users got online. While waiting, she browsed other pages on the site, individual forums that covered a wide range of mysteries and speculations. Most of it wasn't true, she knew that, but anything was *possible*. She read it eagerly, looking for the precious kernels of truth, or even a deeper mystery. That was what kept her spark burning. Even if only one bizarre theory proved to be valid, that would change the world. And she would *know*.

Monster sightings, classified as 'cryptids' by the true believers, generated less interest than conspiracy theories – dire warnings about vapor trails and microwave manipulations. The vampire thread remained particularly active, as always.

11

Vampire legends were remarkably persistent and endlessly interesting. She had presented many such claims, feeling an affinity for the passionate die-hards, rather than the curious goth blood drinkers and over-exuberant *Twilight* fans. She knew how to tell the difference.

She saw that one of the most earnest vampire believers had posted again. Despite his sometimes disturbing intensity, Stoker1897 also offered careful, rational compilations of subtle evidence. He was quite convincing.

'We can't let down our guard,' Stoker1897 had posted that morning. 'Vampires are smart and devious. They know how to manipulate our beliefs, our doubts, and our fears. Don't let them fool you into thinking they're just a superstition. That's what they want you to believe. That is how they've remained unnoticed in human society as they feed on us. I have seen them. I have investigated their vulnerabilities.'

Lexi knew the rant would go on for a dozen more postings. No, not a rant – a sermon. This man wasn't irrational. Unlike many others, Stoker1897 provided documentation, connecting dots in ways that no one else had seen. By tracking detailed inventories of blood bank supplies, studying expiration dates and disposal records, he presented a convincing pattern of lost receipts as well as untraceable paperwork that reduced hospital blood stockpiles for no apparent reason and no indication of where the supplies had gone. He also flagged suspicious suicides in which bodies were drained of blood that conveniently went down the sink. Or had it?

The answers were impossible to ascertain, leaving only questions.

Stoker1897's conclusions banked on an uncomfortable number of coincidences, yet there was a chance he was on to something, however small. When she started HideTruth, Lexi had dedicated herself to giving that 'small chance' a real chance. Let the users decide.

As she read Stoker1897's latest series of posts, she heard pots banging in the kitchen, and delicious smells wafted through the air. She knew not to ask when dinner would be done. Blair insisted that a good meal took as long as it needed to. Who was she to complain? Pop-Tarts, Top Ramen, and Checkers Pizza got boring after a while. She drew in a deep breath now, trying to identify the scent. Vindaloo?

'You need to be ready. We all need to be ready,' Stoker1897 had posted that morning. 'Here is a list of tried-and-true methods to slay a vampire, which I have compiled despite a great deal of misinformation spread by vampires themselves. If you want to save humanity, you will need to use these techniques if you should encounter a real vampire.

'Pound a wooden stake through the heart. Everyone knows that. Alternatively, cut off the vampire's head and stuff its mouth with garlic. This can be messy, but it leaves no doubt as to its effectiveness. Vampires can be burned, or drowned in running water. Though reputed to be effective against werewolves, thanks to Hollywood disinformation, silver bullets are deadly to vampires and are particularly useful because they can kill a vampire from a distance.

'Keep your eyes open to the danger around us. I am willing to do what is necessary, but I must not be alone in this.'

Lexi frowned. *Alone in this?*

He concluded with, 'I know that some of these methods work, because I have killed vampires myself.'

Three

The Rambler Star Motel was a known sanctuary that members of the Bastion could use. Helsing noted the hidden mark on the low brick planter in front of the office and knew he would be welcome here. He needed a safe place.

In an older part of Colorado Springs on South Nevada Avenue, the Rambler Star was one of several nondescript motels with 1950s architecture. The ancient sign boasted Color TV and Air Conditioning as selling points. The red shake shingle roof was faded, and the turquoise color of the doors to the outside rooms was more unsettling than cheery. Despite the half-empty parking lot, the flickering neon light insisted there was No Vacancy.

Helsing knew that wouldn't apply to him.

As darkness fell, the motel office shone with garish fluorescent lights. He lurked outside long enough to make sure there were no other customers before he went inside. The bitter smell of old coffee roiled from a glass urn on a hot

14

plate, and a game show droned at low volume from a TV in the lobby.

The night clerk sat behind a high desk that served as a barricade against disgruntled customers. The nameplate said *Daniel Gardon, Manager*. He was a thin man in his late forties with black hair and Asian features. He barely looked up when Helsing entered. 'No rooms available. Sorry.'

Helsing walked to the desk. 'Not even for the Bastion?'

The manager's demeanor changed. He looked up, met Helsing's eyes as if double-checking what he had heard. Without further comment, he reached into the cubbyholes in front of him and removed a key. 'Room forty-one is always available. Take what you need. People usually don't stay more than a day.'

'That's long enough.' He accepted the brown plastic fob. 'I'm familiar with the process.' He didn't thank Gardon or make additional eye contact, simply melted back out the door.

Room 41 was the last in the line of turquoise doors, offering extra privacy at the end of the building. An old tow trailer was propped up on a cinderblock in the adjacent parking spot, which kept other cars away from the last room. Gardon had taken care of everything. The Bastion helped its own.

Most of the people lived in a main camp out in the national forest and they moved often, like gypsies and ghosts. The million acres of remote wilderness was a safe haven right on the doorstep of Colorado Springs. Members of the Bastion

15

were off the grid and covered their tracks, and with their resourcefulness and ingenuity the group would survive the coming apocalypse.

Though the Bastion camp was self-sufficient, from time to time members made trips into the city for food, clothing, specialized tools, medicine, or other supplies. Some of the new generation had never even seen civilization and were rightfully terrified of it. Others, though, chose to make occasional visits to remind themselves of what they had left behind, and why. Many of them blended in with the homeless population in the city, people who tended to be invisible, which was what the Bastion liked. Their leader, Lucius, had worked for years to establish a secret support network at strategic spots throughout Colorado Springs. The Rambler Star Motel was one such place.

Helsing opened the door with a creak. Drawn drapes darkened the room into a safe haven, and he flicked on the light to reveal low shag carpeting, two double beds, a round laminate table, and a desk with a large old computer and a laser printer. The air held a faint undertone of old cigarette smoke, cleaning products, and air freshener. He turned up the thermostat, and the wall heater hummed loudly as the fan kicked in. This place would be perfect for his needs.

He locked the deadbolt and hooked the chain, just in case. It was dark outside, and the *lampir* might be out. He didn't think the creatures knew who was hunting them, but he always kept his guard up.

Helsing stripped out of his clothes and sorted

the ones that needed washing. The bloodstains that marked the sleeve of his plumber's shirt might not entirely wash out, but who would notice a few extra stains on a plumber's shirt? Other spots of Stallings' dried blood covered his arms and neck, and he was anxious to scrub it off, never certain just how contagious vampire blood might be.

He ran the shower so hot it steamed up the bathroom, and when he emerged afterward, he felt fresh, energized, ready to continue the fight. Helsing had known it wouldn't be easy, but someone needed to fight for the human race. Vampires were everywhere.

After he dried off with the bleached white towel, he opened the closet to find shirts of all sizes – long sleeve, short sleeve, sweaters – along with a selection of women's clothing and even some children's clothes. Eight pairs of shoes were neatly lined up on the floor. The dresser drawers contained socks, underwear, bras. Stacks of pants, mostly jeans, were ordered by size.

In the bottom drawer, a Tupperware container held neatly rolled twenty-dollar bills, almost a thousand dollars. On the lid a handwritten note said: 'Take what you need.' Helsing peeled off sixty dollars. The Bastion had plenty of resources, but its members were not greedy nor extravagant.

Next to the microwave he found a selection of canned chili, stew, and soup, and he heated chicken noodle in a plastic bowl. While the microwave hummed, he found underwear and socks, pulled on his old jeans again, and chose a warm flannel shirt.

17

This refuge was exactly like other Bastion sanctuaries he had used before. When the manager at the previous motel began to recognize Helsing after frequent visits and even tried to chat with him, he knew it was time to go somewhere fresh.

The Rambler Star manager was a former member of the Bastion who had decided to go back to the city. Lucius insisted that Daniel Gardon was trustworthy, and Helsing had no reason to doubt the assessment. Sometimes, new Bastion members just didn't adapt well to the forest, but they could still serve the overall cause. In a sense, the manager was working undercover deep within enemy territory – like Helsing was. They each had their job to do.

Through careful analysis and observation, pulling together scattered details that normal people wouldn't notice, Helsing had concluded that a powerful and manipulative king vampire resided in the city. Surprising, since Colorado Springs was the headquarters for numerous Christian organizations and missionary training centers. But vampires thrived on misdirection, and a king vampire might have chosen the Springs exactly because no one would expect to find such creatures here.

He turned on the old monitor and computer, waiting for them to warm up. Going online, he went directly to the HideTruth site, which was another sort of community for him. Helsing had an affinity for these people and their exuberant, if often irrational beliefs. It was a place where he could speak the truth, and some would even embrace what he said. But he doubted he could ever dispel the fog of confusion spread by the *lampir*. For centuries, the underground secret society of vampires had spread insidious misinformation, rumors, and ridicule, and humanity had swallowed it up.

In the earliest days of his fervor, Helsing had studied a variety of vampire exposé websites, but most were sensationalist garbage. There, vampire lore devotees shared their stories as if telling tall tales in a bar, and Helsing easily spotted the poseurs. HideTruth was different, and the site administrator accepted possibilities so long as some evidence backed them up. He saw HideTruth as a way to recruit other crusaders, or at least open a few minds.

Today he ignored the threads on UFOs, alien abductions, and an active new forum on Bigfoot; instead, he went to the section on vampires. Many of the postings were ill-informed, but Helsing knew how to sift through the deliberate misinformation to find that kernel of truth.

The site admin, a young woman named Alexis Tarada, curated the postings and added her own responses. She even posted well-considered essays on the homepage if a subject interested her enough. Her writings were even-handed, and she was not some starry-eyed convert who would go chasing a different conspiracy at a moment's notice. She winnowed out the silliness, highlighted the most convincing arguments. She confessed that she couldn't refute most of the evidence on missing hospital blood supplies that Helsing himself had presented. She wrote, 'We have to at least admit the possibility.'

Scanning the discussions now in the motel room, he was anxious to respond, but restrained himself. It wasn't safe to do anything but read from this computer. Earlier, Helsing had offered his list of proven techniques for killing vampires, hoping that others would assist in his crusade. Whenever he posted as Stoker1897, he used a public terminal at the Pikes Peak library. As a safe house for the Bastion, the Rambler Star Motel probably had solid firewalls, and Helsing was comfortable enough to search and browse, but he would never post from an IP address that could be traced.

He knew that Alexis Tarada was local to Colorado Springs, although she was careful to keep her personal details hidden. That was wise, considering some of the oddballs who frequented the site. Thinking she might be a valuable ally, he had tried to track down where she lived, but she was too adept at covering her tracks. Smart girl.

He was tired but satisfied. Today was a good day. He had this safe motel room. He felt clean, refreshed. He'd eaten a satisfying meal. And he had eradicated one more vampire.

He rinsed out the plastic soup bowl in the bathroom sink and decided to get a good night's sleep. It was dark outside, nearly midnight, and that was when prowling vampires were strongest. Right now, he was protected.

Helsing would wait until sunrise to continue his mission.

Four

Detective Todd Carrow hated crime scenes. He had seen plenty of them in his thirteen years on the force, and he would see plenty more before he retired. The intentionally gruesome ones were the hardest to understand.

He climbed the concrete steps to the external door of #220 in the Serenity Hedge apartment complex (who thought up those names?), ignoring the gawking residents. Uniformed Colorado Springs Police Department officers talked with men and women from adjacent apartments, and crime-scene techs wearing masks and latex gloves moved in and out of the door. The coroner was already inside. Everybody knew everybody, and Carrow mumbled a greeting as he passed the techs on his way into the murder scene.

Though the lights had been switched on, the place held an intrinsic gloom, an austere loneliness. Sadly, it reminded him of his own townhouse.

The main thing he noticed, as usual, was the smell. Sometimes, if the body remained undiscovered for a while, the reek could bring tears to his eyes, and he would put a dab of VapoRub under his nostrils. This time it wasn't too bad. The body had only been there for two days or so, and the weather had been cool, but the odor of old, dried blood still twisted the back of his throat.

Carrow made his way through the main area down to the bedroom. In a flurry of bright lights, techs photographed the body, collected samples, measured angles. He paused to drink in the circus, then turned his attention to the sprawled corpse. 'Crap almighty, that's something you don't see every day.'

The victim – one Mark Stallings, age forty-two, white male – lay supine on the bed, arms flopped out at his sides. His dark pajama shirt was open, the fabric stained with blood that had erupted from his chest. The techs had pulled down the blood-soaked sheet to reveal a pair of pajama bottoms. That was a relief. Carrow hated to find victims who slept commando.

A wooden stake protruded from the middle of his chest, like a toothpick in an appetizer.

'Guess I don't need to ask for cause of death.'

The coroner busied herself, humming while she inspected the body as if it were an interesting roadkill specimen. Dr Orla Watson was tall, thin, and bookish with round glasses and a detached, studious air. A hairnet covered her curly ash-blond hair, and a paper mask covered her mouth and nose. Her eyes told him she was smiling as she looked up at him. Watson truly enjoyed her job as medical examiner.

'Detective Carrow! I didn't want to move him until you got here, and I was getting impatient. The techs would have a hard time getting the body to the van while it's still attached to the mattress.' She clucked her tongue. 'It's a queen-size bed, so I suggest taking them separately. Nothing bigger than a double will fit in the van.' She looked up at him. 'Don't ask how I know that.'

The coroner often spoke to herself in the morgue and did the same when she was around live people.

Carrow stepped closer to the bed. Blood had spread across the man's bare chest, then soaked through the sheets. He regarded the victim's wide-open eyes, the grimace on his face. 'Looks like he was surprised.'

Watson snorted. 'Wouldn't you be surprised if someone pounded a stake through your heart?'

He gave her an annoyed look. 'I mean it happened fast. No torture. No ligatures. Wasn't tied up and toyed with, which is what I might expect with this methodology. Somebody prone to this much violence, and probably anger, often likes to stick around and enjoy himself, but . . .' Carrow shrugged. 'Killer slipped into the apartment in broad daylight while the victim was sleeping and hit him fast. Wham, bam, thank you, ma'am.'

Mel, the lead evidence tech, came up and glanced at his notepad. He had kept his porn-star mustache long enough for it to come back into style. 'This guy worked the night shift, slept during the day. Had all the blinds drawn, curtains closed. Nobody would have seen anything.'

Carrow saw Stallings' work shirt draped over the desk chair, a red, short-sleeved uniform from a chain convenience store. The embroidered name patch said: *Mark.*

He looked around. 'Broad daylight. Neighbors would have been awake, kids outside playing.

Nobody noticed a stranger lurking around? Parents tend to spot things like that.'

Officer David Amber, who had found the body, stood just outside the bedroom, shifting uncomfortably. 'We haven't finished canvassing all the apartments, Detective. This is an old complex, high turnover of residents. Nobody seems to have known Stallings very well. Kept to himself.' The officer cleared his throat, clearly shaken at having come upon such a jarring scene. 'I suppose it's hard to be a friendly neighbor when you work from dusk to dawn every day.'

'There's always weekends.' Carrow looked at the stake through the man's heart. Dusk to dawn . . .

Stallings' boss had called in to ask for a welfare check, concerned when his employee failed to show up for work two nights in a row and didn't respond to phone calls. The boss, who seemed more annoyed than worried, reported that Stallings was always reliable. In Carrow's experience, the explanation was usually nothing more nefarious than an employee going on a bender and sleeping through a hangover. Officer Amber had received no response to his knock on the apartment door, and the manager had let him in. There was always a chance the tenant had suffered a heart attack, fallen in the bathroom, or just skipped town. Amber certainly hadn't expected what he found.

In the nine years since Carrow had gotten his detective shield, he had seen a lot of ugly deaths. Gangland mutilations, overdosed junkies, kinky autoerotic sex acts gone wrong, crimes of passion that were as violent as the perpetrators were

24

stupid. A stake pounded through the chest was a first, but not the worst he had seen.

Before moving to the larger city of Colorado Springs, Carrow had served for five years in Pueblo. It was thirty miles south, a town with the highest crime rate in the state, and was home to one series of horrific torture murders that had ultimately been tracked to an overly territorial meth kingpin. Carrow had been very happy with his transfer to the Springs.

This city still had enough murders to keep any detective busy – fifteen to twenty-five a year – but most were run-of-the-mill, the killers so painfully obvious that they wouldn't make an interesting episode of any cop show. This one, though, was just plain bizarre.

'Plenty of ways to kill somebody. Why use a stake?' he asked aloud. 'To send a message or a threat? Revenge?' He scratched the curve of his cheek, feeling the stubble there. 'The violence certainly makes this one stand out.'

The coroner lifted her chin like a bird spotting a shiny object. 'Maybe the killer is implying that this guy's a vampire.'

Carrow frowned. 'Or he likes pounding pointed objects. Need to know more about the victim. Was Stallings involved in gang activities? Did he sell drugs? Was he late making a payment to a dealer or a loan shark, and this was a warning to other customers?' He breathed slowly, calmly, to mitigate the smell. 'Saw scenes like this in Pueblo.'

'Chop Chop!' Watson said with a knowing nod. 'Wish I could have worked those cases. Seemed really interesting.'

Carrow's throat went dry. 'You have strange interests.'

He would never forget the four victims of the sadistic drug lord: a rival small-time meth dealer who had infringed on the wrong territory, two customers who had racked up impossible debt, and a young woman who had attempted to turn evidence against the thug who liked to call himself Chop Chop. The killings were graphic and memorable. Chop Chop used a hatchet to cut off the hands and feet of his victims, then turned them loose in the middle of the night, letting them hobble or crawl on their stumps trying to find help before they bled out. Just in case any of them did manage to reach medical attention in time, Chop Chop dosed them with slow poison that would kill them in half a day regardless.

Carrow supposed a stake through the heart wasn't all that much different.

Only a few days earlier, a notorious penny-ante meth dealer had been decapitated in the watershed scrub of a park downtown. His head hadn't been found. Considering that incident and this staked body, Carrow feared they might now be seeing another round of bloody gang violence.

Happily fascinated, Watson bent over to inspect the wooden stake that protruded from the corpse's sternum. 'Did you ever put butterflies on a mounting board when you were a kid? Stick a pin right through the thorax, then spread their wings, upper and lower, so that when they dry out, they look beautiful, just like in life?'

Carrow frowned at her. 'Missed that part of my

childhood. My dad always wanted me to collect stamps.' He turned around, but found little to see in the bedroom. 'No sign of an incriminating coffin.'

The coroner heard him. 'Vamps can also sleep on a bed of dirt, their home soil if possible. I think that's their preference actually . . . not that I'm an expert.'

Carrow frowned at her. 'Neither am I.'

She pressed down on the sheets until the frame creaked. 'However, I can confirm that this is just a regular mattress and box springs.'

The crime-scene techs finished gathering data and samples, dusting for prints. Carrow was done with staring at the body, the rough wooden stake, the blood spatters, the expression on the victim's face. The details were indelibly burned into his mind.

Watson called, 'Mel, get the gurney and take the body out of here. Time to wrap up.'

Mel grumbled. 'Great. It's an old apartment complex. No elevator. We'll have to carry it down the stairs.'

'Have fun with that,' Carrow said. 'I'll have a look around.'

Stallings worked in a convenience store at night, didn't seem to have any friends. His boss had been the only one who even noticed when he went missing for two days. The man must have had a dark side to his life, something really twisted to warrant a death like this. From someone like Chop Chop?

It was a small apartment, but Carrow wandered from room to room, searching for anything that looked out of place. The furniture was plain, and the victim had no artwork on the walls. The refrigerator surface was devoid of personality – no magnets, coupons, takeout menus, or photos of kids. The apartment seemed not just empty of possessions, but of a life.

Carrow worried that his own life would look this empty if he didn't watch out. He had an ex-wife, and two daughters that he didn't see often enough, but at least he kept pictures of the girls on his cubicle wall. He looked around the victim's place. An empty life . . .

'No pets?' he called out. 'No dog or cat?'

'Not even a goldfish,' answered one of the techs.

Carrow nodded. 'Most places like this don't allow pets.' He knew from experience. He wished he could have a dog, even a small one, to keep him company in his townhouse.

Mel and another tech came through the door after hauling the empty gurney up the exterior stairs. In the bedroom they studied the corpse, forming a plan of action. The body seemed to sag as they lifted it from the red-soaked mattress, careful to leave the stake in the body for more careful analysis. The coroner helped them wrestle Stallings into the body bag.

Meanwhile, Carrow poked around the small kitchen. The refrigerator had eggs, butter, moldy cheese, yogurt that was past the expiration date, a head of iceberg lettuce more brown than green, and a six pack of India pale ale from a Colorado craft brewery.

Carrow worked his way through the cupboards.

In one he found coffee mugs, plates, glasses, everything neatly arranged. The next held canned soup, dried pasta, tuna, jars of spaghetti sauce. In the third cupboard he found salt, pepper, and miscellaneous seasonings – including two large bulbs of garlic on the bottom shelf.

Carrow picked up the garlic, sniffed it, and put it back. 'Pretty sure we can rule out vampires,' he muttered. Gang violence seemed the most obvious answer, and that meant it probably wasn't over yet.

Five

Some people would believe anything, absolutely anything. Lexi saw it every day.

Other than her work for HideTruth, she free-lanced for fraud investigation websites and helped debunk silly conspiracy theories for PRUUF, a competitor to Snopes. She worked for several different services that dealt with internet scams, phony accounts, and fake emails. She erased imposter profiles and helped websites eliminate phishers. When small business sites were hijacked, malware could send out chainmail that spread as swiftly as the Ebola virus. Somebody had to stomp on them.

Lexi felt embarrassed by how obvious some of the scammers were. Was it possible that any human being on Earth was unaware of the Nigerian prince looking to transfer millions of dollars, but only with a sucker's help? Or the lost uncle trying to unload ten ounces of diamonds and you were his only hope? How could anyone fall for such things?

Some people must get duped, though, or the scammers wouldn't keep doing it. How could people be so gullible? Why didn't they bother to do any research? Anyone feeble enough to fall for the Nigerian prince scam shouldn't be allowed to have a social media account.

Or email.

Or a toothbrush.

Even after Lexi purged the scammers, they would pop up on another server within minutes, like a kudzu infestation in the south. It was a hopeless task, but it paid well. She could work as many hours as she liked from the luxury of her own home, which wasn't all that luxurious.

Be your own boss! It sounded better than it was. She could take a day off whenever she liked, but she didn't have a social life. Alexis Tarada was young, pretty, smart and resourceful – and spent her days and many evenings in her room delving into conspiracy theories, debunking nutty myths, and drawing attention to the ideas she felt were most intriguing, secretly hoping to find one that was *real*.

One of these days, I'm sure to be right.

PRUUF was a hotbed of rumors and urban legends, pervasive and titillating stories that occasionally had some basis in fact, though most of them went woefully wrong. In most cases, the explanations weren't difficult to track down, but some crazy stories had fascinating, unlikely answers.

She had spent the past two hours compiling a dossier on the persistent and astonishingly stupid theory that the Moon did not exist, but was instead an elaborate hologram projected by aliens to hide their invasion base.

Another rumor claimed that a vast FEMA death camp was hidden beneath Denver International Airport.

And that the CERN high-energy particle accelerator in Switzerland was actually designed to reawaken the Egyptian gods.

Enough people actually *believed* such theories that people like Lexi had to debunk them – not that the believers would ever look at the evidence, because it was all part of the larger conspiracy.

Every once in a while, though, Lexi ran into something she couldn't easily disprove, and that was what she lived for. She wasn't necessarily *convinced* by the proffered explanations, but she could accept that the real explanation had not yet been found. Some stories were just damned mysterious. She held on to those and savored the sense of wonder.

Those were the ones she posted on HideTruth.

She heard a quick knock on the bedroom door, and her housemate poked his head into her room. 'Time for a break, Lex. I insist.'

She had been so engrossed in holographic moons and FEMA death camps that she didn't realize it was already 8 p.m. 'Got a better suggestion? I'm all ears.'

He grinned. 'Spend time with me. It's part of my project to socialize you into a human being.'

Blair September was tall, handsome, erudite, and completely uninterested in her. Nevertheless, he was the ideal housemate. His brown hair was neatly combed, his clothes far too stylish for lounging around the house, but he refused to lower his standards.

'Happy hour has been extended due to popular demand. You need one of these.' He held up a martini glass filled with a cloudy green concoction. 'They're very popular at Olive U.' He extended it as if it were a magical cure, coaxing her to emerge from her room. 'Come on, join me in the living room.'

Lexi dutifully rose from her chair, stretching her legs. 'I'll bring my laptop.'

'Absolutely not. You're going to enjoy this basil martini.' He backed away from the door, taking the martini with him like bait.

Lexi followed him into the main room. He set the martini glass on the coffee table next to his identical drink and plopped on the sofa beside her. Playfully resigned, Lexi sipped from the delicate glass, tasted grapefruit, vodka, saw the stem of a floating basil leaf. 'Why did you say I need one? Do I look like I've had a bad day?'

'No, you look beautiful, but *I've* had a bad day, and I don't like to drink alone.'

She clinked her glass against his. 'That's as good a reason as any.'

A couple of years ago, Lexi had recruited a housemate to help pay the rent. Blair worked several nights a week at a trendy downtown martini bar, Olive U, and days at a vintage clothing shop.

For her own part, Lexi was the responsible one in the household. The lease was in her name, she did the paperwork, paid the bills, and kept the accounts. That was a good thing, because 'Blair September' didn't show up on any credit reports – she had used her extensive online resources to check.

She had raised the question before accepting him as her housemate. 'That's not your real name.'

'It is now. It's my identity. I'm a caterpillar that emerged from a cocoon to become a beautiful butterfly.'

'Moths come from cocoons. Butterflies come from chrysalises.'

Blair had huffed. 'Then, switching metaphors, I'm an ugly duckling who has become a swan.' He gave her a warm, sincere look. 'Look, I promise I'll pay my share of expenses, do whatever housework you don't want to do, including all the cooking, and I'm generally charming, as you can see. Before you know it, you'll consider me indispensable.'

Following her instinct, she had taken him in, and had never regretted it. To her surprise, even now that she knew him well, he kept his personal information completely off the radar, saying that he valued his privacy. If Blair had some dark secret in his past, she hadn't been able to find it. He seemed so casual, easy, relaxed, and he had rapidly become her best friend.

Lexi spent much of her time as a recluse, but

Blair was gregarious. He insisted on talking about his day, his customers, sometimes even his dating dramas, and he elbowed Lexi for not having enough similar stories of her own. He won even more brownie points because he read the HideTruth site and often commented on the discussion threads.

Now he sat on the sofa beside her, relishing his drink. 'So, shall we talk about UFOs and anal probes? Why exactly are aliens so fascinated with the—'

'No, I don't want to talk about anal probes.' Lexi took another slow sip. 'It would ruin a perfectly good frou-frou martini.'

'Glad you like it.' He took a much bigger sip of his own. 'Or we could talk about lizard people. They always make for good conversation.'

'Not lizard people either, please.' She shuddered at the caustic memory of her past stalker. HideTruth did attract more than its share of tinfoil-hat crazies, as well as those genuinely fascinated with possible wonders and mysteries in the world. 'The people who believe in that nonsense can be intense, maybe even dangerous.'

Blair swirled the stainless-steel shaker before pouring himself a second (or third) martini and topped off her glass, too. 'UFOs, then. If aliens are really visiting us, why aren't we flooded with crystal-clear flying saucer pics now that everyone has a phone camera?'

'We *are* flooded with UFO shots, but everyone also has super-high-resolution image-manipulation apps, so you can't tell real from fake. None of it counts as proof. It's easier for the general public to disbelieve in everything so they don't get fooled again.' She sighed. 'Remember when a blurry shape walking through the woods was proof of Bigfoot? Nowadays *anything* can be convincingly faked, so how can anybody know what is really true?'

The world was an entirely different place from the 1990s when *The X-Files* had turned millions into starry-eyed believers. Before that, countless grainy flying saucer photos had inspired a generation to believe in UFOs and Erich von Däniken led a movement of devotees to ancient astronauts. Today, inundated by a flood of information and misinformation, people had given up trying to sort it all. They believed in what they chose to believe and scoffed at everything else, including settled science.

Russian bots, alternative facts, foreign governments placing disguised political ads, absurd claims about one candidate or another. With so many rampant conspiracy theories, so much fake news, so many silly but trending memes, people turned a blind eye to it all. How could anyone sort the signal from the noise?

Halfway through the second martini, Lexi realized that Blair was excited about something, like a kid with a surprise. He was holding back some juicy information.

'All right, what's up, Blair? There's no point in keeping it secret. I'm good at rooting out mysteries.'

'Ha, you caught me.' He picked up the TV remote and switched it on. 'I recorded something on the local news while I was cooking us dinner.'

He scrolled down the menu of recorded programs and selected the one he wanted. 'You would have found this on your own, but I'm so glad I get to be the one to share it with you.'

Lexi savored the warm buzz of the martini as she watched the news story about a local man who was found murdered with a stake pounded through his heart. 'Wow. That *is* right up my alley.'

'What are friends for? I know you so well.'

Death by wooden stake. Lexi knew she had to investigate this further. Vampires in Colorado Springs? The TV station's website should have further information, and she had other back channels that would provide more details. She set down the half-finished martini. 'Wait right here. I'll get my laptop so I can stay halfway sociable.'

Blair gave her a frown of disapproval. 'I'd rather you were *entirely* sociable.'

Not rising to the bait, she brought her laptop to the sofa and called up HideTruth. Before she could look into the discussion group, she found a delightful admin alert. 'The tip jar runneth over!'

'Your patron again?' he asked.

'Hugo Zelm. He really wants to believe – to the tune of a thousand dollars. Same as last month's donation.' Zelm was an eccentric local philanthropist who had been a fan of her site for more than a year now and offered regular contributions to keep HideTruth afloat.

Blair raised his martini in salute. 'If it keeps going like that, you'll be able to pay your own expenses and won't need a housemate anymore. Then where will I be?'

'Don't pout. I'll always need a housemate so long as you cook dinner and make me martinis.' She patted his hand.

'You'd miss me the moment I was gone.' He drained his drink. 'But if Mr Zelm is going to subsidize us, then I'll switch to that most excellent Breckenridge vodka instead. It's the cost of business.'

'You're allowed.' Lexi took another sip, distracted by her laptop. In the vampire thread several people had already posted about the stake murder. It was time to dig into the gruesome details.

Six

In the autopsy room, Detective Carrow watched as the medical examiner went about her work. Bright lights illuminated the cold, pale body of Mark Stallings who lay on the stainless-steel table, his pajamas cut off with sharp clothing shears. Watson hummed as she approached the corpse like a gourmand about to tuck into a multi-course feast.

A man on the table with a stake through his heart wasn't the only thing strange about the situation. With the election coming up, Dr Orla Watson had commandeered part of the room as headquarters for her campaign to be re-elected as El Paso County Coroner. Lawn signs were stacked in a corner, and neat piles of bumper stickers covered part of her desk next to a brown sack lunch and bottle of iced tea.

Watson noticed Carrow's attention. 'You can take a bumper sticker and a lawn sign if you like, Detective. You're satisfied with my work as ME, right?'

'Not sure your approach is the best way to get votes,' he said. 'But I'll grant you points for originality.'

'Oh, Walter gets all the credit for the jokes.'

Dr Watson's husband fancied himself a stand-up comedian and managed to book a few gigs at local clubs. Instead of a dry and straightforward *Vote Orla Watson for County Coroner*, Walter had decided to add a little humor. *People are dying to vote Watson for County Coroner!* And *Don't be a stiff! Vote Watson for County Coroner.*

'You know how hard it is to get anyone to put up lawn signs and show their support for this office?' she grumbled. 'Medical examiner isn't one of those big publicity elections. I wish someone would tell me why I have to spend time on a campaign. I've got work to do.'

'Power of democracy,' Carrow said. 'The people get to choose.'

'It's all rigged.' Watson snorted as she paced around the autopsy table. 'People are easily duped by a shiny new story or some scandal. Explain why it makes a difference whether the coroner is a Democrat or a Republican?' She pressed a finger to the shoulder of the corpse, testing the pliability of the skin. She nodded down at the body. '*He* certainly doesn't care.'

'Better wrap this one up soon, in case you don't get re-elected. I hate loose ends.'

Watson had already filled out the victim's vital statistics, as well as the core body temperature which determined the time of death at between one and three p.m. on Monday. CSPD officers were knocking on the doors of the Serenity Hedge apartments, asking if the residents had seen or heard anything suspicious in that timeframe. One harried Air Force mother with three kids thought she'd seen an electrician or cable TV guy around the complex, but couldn't be sure. An old apartment building like Serenity Hedge had no security cameras.

Dr Watson bent close to the dead man's face as if she intended to kiss him. Still humming, she pried open his eyelids, looked at the lifeless eyes, then pulled up Stallings' lips to show his teeth. 'I wanted you to verify this, Detective.'

Carrow looked down at the dead man's mouth. 'And I'm seeing . . . what exactly?'

'Nothing, which is exactly the point. No fangs. I just thought we should make sure.'

He rolled his eyes. 'Very funny.'

'My husband's the comedian.' She picked up the left hand, then the right, inspecting his fingertips. 'Note also, no monster claws.'

'I applaud your thoroughness. You're sure to win the election.'

Distracted, she looked up at the ceiling, considering. The fluorescents were bright, supplemented by movable floodlights above the table. With a long-legged stride, Watson went to the wall switch and flicked off the lights, plunging the room into shadows, leaving only glimmers of daylight through the closed blinds. She tugged on the cord to open the blinds, releasing a flood of bright sunshine.

Carrow held a hand in front of his face. 'What's that for?'

After looking at the body on the table, the coroner directed a long-suffering sigh at him. 'Don't you know *anything*, Detective? We needed to make sure he doesn't crumble to ash under the purifying rays of the sun. More proof he's not a vampire.'

'Good thing it's just me and you in here. You actually going to write that in the report? People will think we're crazy.' He didn't mention the garlic he had found in the victim's cupboard.

'Could be, but I guarantee you somebody's going to ask about vampires.' Watson's lips quirked in a smile. 'Besides, it's good to take precautions before I pull out the stake. What if he comes alive again?'

'I'm more convinced about the gang angle. Still haven't found the head of the drug dealer killed the other night. Seems like the same sort of message.'

He felt tired, although the coroner seemed to be having a grand time. Watson's good cheer weighed on him. He never thought anyone would brag they were 'born to be a coroner', but he knew Watson was fascinated by the human body.

Watson wiggled the wooden stake like a child playing with a loose tooth. 'It's wedged in there good and solid.' She rocked it harder, twisting the wood until it finally came loose with a wet pop. Dark, sticky blood clotted the end. 'Nice, sharp point.' She laid the stake aside for tagging and collection in an evidence bag. Again she paused, counting to ten. The sunlight covered the body's chest and the gaping wound in the sternum. Stallings didn't twitch. She let out a sigh. 'Good. Wanted to make sure he wasn't going to lunge up and attack me before I made my Y cut.'

Carrow wasn't particularly squeamish – not after seeing the mangled stumps and horribly tortured victims of Chop Chop early in his career. Watson cut open the body, removed and weighed each internal organ. Her work was time consuming but thorough.

'Not really any question about the cause of death is there?' he asked.

She looked up at him, distracted. 'If I don't perform and document every step, some conspiracy nut will claim we're covering something up.'

She removed the liver and the heart and made notations while she engaged in small talk. 'Are you going back down to Pueblo for the Green Chile and Frijoles Festival? It's that time of year. Get yourself a bushel of fresh, charred green chiles?' She held up her blood-drenched gloves and smiled as if savoring an imaginary meal. 'Walter and I shuck the skins off, then freeze the peppers in individual packages so we can make *chile rellenos* or green chile stew all winter long. You should take your daughters to the festival. They'd love it.'

'I doubt that beans and chiles would be the most exciting activity for a parental visit. I don't see the girls often enough as it is.'

41

After the divorce, his ex-wife LeAnn had voluntarily moved back to Pueblo, which proved – in his mind, at least – that she was batshit crazy. He felt sorry for the girls, but with the dreary townhouse he lived in now, he couldn't do better for them up here. It wasn't as if he could charm them with stories about finding dead bodies with stakes through the heart. He visited his daughters whenever he could, but the forty-five-minute drive was just enough of a chore that it required actual planning instead of a spontaneous drop-by, a fact that LeAnn appreciated very much.

When Watson finally finished the autopsy, she looked down at her notes, clicked her tongue against her teeth. 'It's all perfectly routine, Detective. The blood work showed no obvious abnormalities. High cholesterol, remnants of statin drugs, ibuprofen. Basically normal.'

'Except for the stake through his heart,' Carrow said.

'Sure, except for that.' Watson bent close to the wooden stake in the metal tray beside the body. She turned it over to look at a feathery fringe of bright green paint just visible in one of the cracks. 'This might be something, though.'

Carrow had noticed it before. 'Paint from a lumberyard. They all use it.'

'Not bright green. Most use orange or red. I'm pretty sure D&R Lumberyard off West Fillmore uses green paint. I remember because Walter used them a few months ago when he tried to build a deck in the back.' Her lips quirked in a smile. '*That* was funnier than any of his comedy routines. I told him he should work the material into his next set.'

'D&R . . . I know the place.' Carrow shrugged. 'At least it's a starting point.'

'You should come and see my husband's act sometime,' Watson said. 'He's doing an open mic this Saturday.'

'Sorry, can't make it. If I'm going to the Green Chile and Frijoles Festival, I better keep the schedule open.'

She clearly didn't believe him. 'Don't forget to take a lawn sign when you go. Show your support for my campaign.'

'A sign on a wooden stake? How about something a little smaller?' He chose a *Don't be a stiff!* bumper sticker and left before she could talk him into taking more.

Seven

Sitting on the sofa with her laptop, Lexi kept Blair company as he cooked dinner. He liked having her there.

'Stir-fry tonight. Chicken and shrimp.' His hands were a blur as he peeled carrots, chopped bok choy, celery, and green bell peppers. He threw minced ginger and garlic into the wok where it hissed and sizzled in hot peanut oil.

If Lexi hadn't already been sitting down, the delicious smell would have made her knees weak. 'You take good care of me, Blair.'

'Only because you don't take care of yourself. If you don't stay healthy, then I'll have to move and find a far less appealing housemate.'

'Let's keep things as they are.'

'Good. I'd prefer that.'

She continued to dig for information on the stake murder. The Colorado Springs Police Department had been very cagey about releasing details on the victim, but Lexi had back doors and gray-area resources. Her followers on HideTruth had already plunged into a frenzy of speculation and theory-based conclusions, which generated a smattering of new donations. Although the exotic murder weapon was intriguing and carried a lot of cultural baggage, Lexi guessed that this was probably some sort of horrific revenge killing intended to send a message. *Mess with me, and this is what you get.* Or was the killer really suggesting the victim was a vampire?

Remembering what Stoker1897 had posted in the HideTruth forum, she ran a search through national law-enforcement databases and found two other stake-through-the-heart murders, unsolved, both in the greater San Francisco Bay area more than five years ago. She didn't see any obvious connection to the victim in Colorado Springs, but the stories were provocative gems and she posted them in the thread under the title 'How Widespread Are Vampires?' Because her followers could be both enthusiastic and gullible, she also obtained, and posted, the old autopsy reports of those victims to show that there was no biological evidence that any of the bodies had actually been vampires.

When she widened the parameters in the national database, the number of potentially suspicious murders was overwhelming. The case reports demonstrated a wide range of writing skills among police detectives. In particularly sensational murders, such as a stake pounded through the heart, detectives often avoided adding gruesome detail. In fact, they often obscured the truth with bland language. She discovered one murder in Texas with the cause of death listed as 'the insertion of a foreign wooden object through the sternum and into the chest cavity, resulting in a fatal puncture of the cardiac wall.'

She searched more thoroughly, but knew it would be a challenge to clear away the obfuscation. Were other supposed vampire killers out there, or only one killer with a wide range? Were the victims connected in some way – San Francisco, Texas, and Colorado Springs?

Building on the stake murder in Colorado Springs, Lexi reviewed other local deaths over the past year or two, but found no explicit instances of stakes as a murder weapon. She did come upon the case of an alleged meth dealer, Patric Ryan, who had been found decapitated in the watershed of Monument Creek in old downtown. That had been a few days ago, and the head hadn't yet been recovered.

Beheading was one of Stoker1897's suggested vampire-killing methods.

She read reports of three other bodies found badly decomposed in waste land around the city, unidentified and presumed homeless. Another corpse had been dumped and burned beyond recognition, again without identification. Burning was another effective way to deal with vampires. No detailed investigations had been conducted in those cases because the victims themselves were of no importance, and no loved ones were demanding answers. CSPD had labeled the deaths 'gang- or drug-related', although the headless man was the only one actually associated with the drug trade.

Lexi collated the information and submitted her summary to the CSPD tip line, being a dutiful citizen. In her message she pointed out how the other suspicious deaths might be connected to vampires, at least peripherally. Being detailed, Lexi included Stoker1897's list of effective ways to kill vampires. She flagged the decapitated meth dealer and sent a note. 'If you ever do find the head, check for garlic in the mouth.'

She submitted the tip, expecting no response.

As he made the stir-fry, Blair was like an orchestra conductor at the wok. With the burner turned up high, he stirred with a long wooden spoon in each hand, adding the hard vegetables after the garlic and ginger had caramelized, then the soft meats – chicken and shrimp – and finally the mushrooms, snow peas, and bean sprouts. 'Extra ginger and red pepper flakes give the stir-fry a good burn. You'll like it.'

She looked up from her laptop. 'Are you asking me for permission?'

'I'm informing you.'

'And if I don't like it, does that mean I don't have to do the dishes?'

He sniffed. 'Doing dishes is part of our bargain,

my dear. Cleaning up is the least you can do to show your appreciation for a good meal.'

She inhaled the divine smells. 'No complaints.' Blair called himself a nurturing person, and he called her driven, distracted, and obsessed. In other words, they made a good team.

He paused in his stirring. 'You're far too interested in vampires.' He added more garlic, as if to protect her, then turned the burner off and moved the wok aside. 'Personally, I prefer the sparkly ones.'

He dished up two plates and set them on the table, calling Lexi from the sofa. He placed chopsticks on folded cloth napkins – he was horrified by paper napkins as being too low class.

She got herself a soda from the refrigerator. 'Should I bring the soy sauce?'

'Not if you want to keep me as a friend.' He gave her a withering look. 'I prepared it with exactly the right seasoning. Taste it first.'

She closed the refrigerator door and sat beside him. 'Lesson learned.'

As they ate, Blair chatted about one of his coworkers at Rags to Riches, the vintage clothing shop, or oddball customers at the martini bar, including a handsome olive-skinned young man named Cesar who was obviously interested in him. They already had a date set up for the following night.

When Blair ran out of his own anecdotes, he kept the conversation going with questions about Bigfoot and vampires. 'You really want to believe, don't you?'

'I admit the stories and witness reports are more

47

entertaining than convincing,' she said. 'But there's always a chance. I leave the door open a crack. What if one of the stories actually turns out to be true?'

He gave her a serious look. A few strands of his perfect hair had fallen out of place across his forehead. 'I know you, Lex. You're smart and intense, and I would never call you gullible, but I can't figure out why you take all this stuff so seriously.'

'Not all of it – in fact, most of it isn't even worth a second look. But I've learned not to brush aside each incident because it seems hard to believe. One of these days, I'll find the right one.'

She twirled her chopsticks, picked up a shrimp and popped it into her mouth. 'Just about every-thing has a rational explanation if you look closely enough. Every so often, though, I come across things that I can't debunk, no matter how hard I try.'

Blair listened with rapt attention, resting his elbows on the kitchen table.

'I'm not interested in regular crimes or cover-ups, and certainly not political conspiracies. But sometimes . . .' She paused and stared off into a blank place in her own thoughts. 'I never told you this, Blair. In fact, I haven't told many people at all, but two times in my life I've personally experienced real, inexplicable events that rocked my world. They weren't tall tales from a friend of a friend – I experienced them myself. *Me.*'

Blair was intrigued. 'Do tell.'

'Each time I was a thousand per cent convinced

that something genuinely unreal had occurred.' She lowered her voice. 'Turns out that one of them did have a rational explanation after all, but I would have sworn down to my marrow that I'd had a supernatural encounter.'

'But you solved it?'

Lexi nodded. 'I felt relieved and foolish when I did, but before that I would have bet everything I owned . . . See if you can figure it out.'

Blair set down his chopsticks so he could give her his full attention.

'A few years ago after I moved from Iowa and started exploring Colorado, I collected stories of weird ghost sightings, local legends, haunted places. There's a speck on the map called Alma in the middle of nowhere, an old mining town with a handful of leftover buildings – vacation homes, a general store, a saloon, coffee shop, and legal pot dispensaries.'

'Ah, tourism,' Blair said.

'There was an old flophouse from the 1800s with a bunch of little rooms for rent, a shared bathroom at the end of the hall, a bar downstairs, antique furniture. One of the rooms at the Alma Inn was supposedly haunted, so I asked to stay in that one.'

'Of course you did.'

'The bed smelled like something had died in it. The room had one window with a roll-down shade, a wooden chair, a wobbly nightstand with a lamp. I had my overnight bag, my computer case, laptop, remote keyboard, and some notes. I thought I might write in the sitting room off the lobby, but it reeked of cigarette smoke.

49

Instead, I worked in the cozy little room, even though it didn't have a desk.

'I took out my laptop, dumped the computer case in the corner, tossed my duffel up against it, and sat on the bed. I opened a new document to write down the details about Alma and the ghost. But before I could type anything, random letters started to scroll across the screen, gibberish. I lifted my fingers from the laptop. I wasn't touching the keys at all, but the letters kept coming, nonsense and random, typing faster and faster.'

Blair remained silent, his brow furrowed, fascinated. 'Were the keys stuck?'

'I hit *delete* again and again. I hit *return*. I rubbed the keyboard, loosened the keys. But the letters kept coming all by themselves, pouring across my screen, line after line. They filled a whole screen.

'I tried to figure out what the message meant. Was it a message from the ghost? What was it trying to say? My thoughts went cold. By now half of a second screen was filled with babbling keystrokes. I could not explain this.' She looked down at her stir-fry, but didn't feel hungry.

'Finally, I forced Word to quit, then restarted and opened a new blank document – and the gibberish started spilling across the screen again. I shut down the laptop entirely, rebooted it. Same thing. Nonsense typing itself, line after line. My pulse was racing. I didn't know what to do. I didn't feel threatened, but it was disorienting, so detached from reality.' She skewered Blair with her gaze. 'I couldn't stop the letters, no matter what I did.'

He rocked back in his chair at the table. 'You just gave me a chill.'

'I was willing to believe, Blair. I *wanted* to believe! I'd had an encounter in high school, something I couldn't explain and still can't. I'll tell you about that in a minute. As I sat there in that musty, creepy room, I had no way to understand what was happening, no matter how hard I tried.' Her eyes burned as she remembered the terror and fascination of that moment.

'So I decided to leave. I snatched my duffel, grabbed my computer case from the floor, and threw it on the bed next to the laptop.' She paused, looking at Blair.

He waited. 'You said there was an explanation?'

Drawing out the moment, she took another bite with her chopsticks before she continued. 'In my computer case, I'd stuffed a small wireless keyboard. I prefer using that if I have to type for long stretches, but since I didn't have a desk, I had just taken out my laptop and tossed the computer case against the wall, then set my duffel against it.

'And that squashed some of the keys. The Bluetooth connected automatically and sent signals from all those random keys being pressed. That's what showed up on my screen.' She laughed nervously. 'Perfectly simple explanation, but under the circumstances my imagination went straight to a supernatural occurrence. If I hadn't figured out what was going on with the separate keyboard, I'd be convinced to this day that some ghost was trying to communicate with me.'

51

Blair chuckled. 'I can see how you'd be fooled. It would have creeped me out.'

Lexi nodded. 'That's why I'm always willing to admit there might be a normal explanation, whether or not I've found it yet. I really want to believe, but I maintain a healthy skepticism.'

Blair finished half of his stir-fry, as if to gain energy before she told her second story. 'But your other experience was even more convincing than that?'

'I'm not even sure I want to tell it.' Her throat was dry, and Blair reached over to pat her forearm reassuringly. 'My best friend in high school was Teresa Marillo. We had known each other since seventh grade, both nerds and we didn't fit in with the usual social circles, didn't really know much about fashion or flirting. No surprise, neither of us dated all that often.'

Blair laughed. 'You just needed some coaching.'

'We both did. I thought Teresa was prettier, and she insisted I was. In fall of our senior year, we tried to decide where we wanted to go to college after we graduated. We had dreams for our future to see new places, have some adventures. And we wanted to stick together. Dubuque was the biggest city either of us had ever seen, but Dubuque, Iowa, is still just a small town with bigger buildings. We swore we would get out of there, do something important with our lives, but the odds were against us.

'Teresa had an older sister, Melanie, who had made the same kind of vow that she was going to leave as soon as she graduated, but she got pregnant, married the guy, and stayed in Dubuque.

So many people were like that, and Teresa and I swore it wouldn't happen to us.'

'Small town tar pits.' Blair shook his head. 'You're trapped and you just can't pull yourself free.'

Lexi paused for a long moment, reliving that night in her mind, hearing every word of her last conversation with Teresa. She *knew* it had happened, even though it wasn't possible.

'We were supposed to go to a party, a big one. Teresa and I were thrilled to be invited with all the popular kids. But I got the flu with a bad fever. It broke my heart to cancel, but I insisted that Teresa go without me. All alone at home, feeling queasy and achy, I lay in bed for a miserable Friday night. I was going to watch *Ghost Whisperer* and *Medium* on TV in my room.'

She paused to gather her courage before continuing.

'I went to the bathroom, and when I came back, Teresa was there in the chair by my desk, waiting for me. I was surprised to see her, but I figured my parents must have let her in. By now, the party should have been in full swing, so I thought she decided not to go. Teresa said that she had to see me, that she had something important to say. She gave me this look, a really deep look.' Lexi paused as her voice hitched. 'We were best friends, remember. Teresa and I could talk about anything. No secrets.

'She said she was worried about me, made me promise I wouldn't throw my life away. The way she said it was really deep and serious, a little scary. She made me *swear* that after high school I would leave Dubuque and see the world, find work I was passionate about. She was so intense! I made the promise, laughing a little since she and I were going to do those things together anyway. I shooed her out of my room, told her to go to the party and have fun on my behalf. She got up and left. I never saw her again.'

She stared at Blair. 'I looked right at her. I heard her words. I swear she was right in front of me!' Tears stung Lexi's eyes. 'The phone rang fifteen minutes later, Teresa's mom sobbing. She was sure that I'd been with her, that we'd both been . . .' Her voice halted, and she had to force the words out past the lump in her throat. 'That we'd both been killed in the accident. Teresa's car was rammed by a truck when she was on her way to the party – an hour before.' Lexi clenched her fist. '*An hour before*, Blair!

'I remember Teresa there, and I know damn well what time it was. I remember Patricia Arquette on TV working on a murder mystery. I could probably even identify the episode of *Medium* if I had a list. I remember looking at my clock at the bedside.

'But Teresa was already dead. The police knew the exact time of the accident. The ambulance records showed when they arrived at the scene – and Teresa came to my room after that.'

She heaved a deeper breath.

'My parents said they never let Teresa in, that she hadn't come to visit me. They thought the fever made me hallucinate. Was that it? I have no evidence that she was really there. Nobody else saw her, but I know she was with me.

'I've tried and tried, stretched my imagination

54

into every possible crackpot theory, but nothing makes sense. I just can't explain it. Was it my heightened emotional state? My fever? Did that make me more susceptible?'

Lexi felt shaken and wrung out after she finished. 'So, all those years later when I saw the letters appearing on my computer screen in the haunted room, I thought it was another ghost, maybe even Teresa trying to communicate with me. I wasn't terrified so much as hopeful. I really wanted to believe!' She wiped her eyes with the cloth napkin.

'That's the thing with the people on HideTruth. Some of them might be crazy, but they cling to that spark of hope, that desperate need for wonder and mystery in the world. I *know* something happened to me. I *know* I wasn't imagining it.'

Blair got up from his chair and wrapped his arms around her shoulders, pulling her close to him. 'Oh, Lex, I believe you.'

'There's got to be a chance, you know?' She leaned against him. Blair felt solid and good and safe. 'And I don't care if other people think I'm a nutcase, because there's that chance in a million. One of those stories is going to be proved true.'

Eight

After three days of resting and planning, Helsing left the Rambler Star Motel, not because he was no longer welcome, but because the Bastion members were only supposed to take what they needed and only for as long as necessary.

Outside, he waited among the down-on-their-luck homeless in front of the soup kitchen near St Mary's Cathedral. Since it was a nice day – clear blue skies and a crisp autumn chill – many of his fellow misfits and outcasts chose to eat outside, lingering in the park under tall oak trees. Joggers ran the paved paths along Monument Creek.

Helsing held a paper bowl of split pea soup with a slice of white bread soaking up the broth. In his other hand he carried a Styrofoam cup of weak black coffee. He fit in among these people. He knew some personally, recognized others, but didn't strike up a conversation. Most of the homeless caused little trouble, kept to themselves except for the occasional panhandling. Those who didn't choose beds in the shelter found places to live outside in the marshy watershed around the creek.

Helsing visited the soup kitchen when he needed food or just wanted to be around other people who would not judge or threaten him. They wore old clothes in layers for all weather. Many were military vets, as he was, and some merely wore military surplus clothing. Some were hustlers who accosted pedestrians on the street corners. Helsing didn't like those, because they ensured that the quiet homeless couldn't be as invisible as they wanted to be.

Other unfortunates were genuinely disturbed, muttering to unseen companions, reliving ancient arguments in their heads, indignant about past injustices. Helsing had been that way for a while, still at war with the world after he left the California VA hospital, but that was years ago. Since then he had built up a lifetime of experiences, and he had adopted a real mission for his life.

From eye contact he knew that some of the homeless were also members of the Bastion, men or women who came briefly back to Colorado Springs to observe, scavenge, or just reminisce. Some wanted reminders of civilization and reaffirmation of their decision to leave it.

A middle-aged woman wandered close, obviously wanting his company, maybe quiet conversation, but Helsing turned away. Company and conversation were not what he needed.

Here among the homeless population, Helsing detected a general undertone of uneasiness. Rumors spread as swiftly as if they all had cell phones. He knew that some among them had been killed, the bodies found drained of blood, their throats mangled. Helsing himself had disposed of those bodies by quietly burning or dismembering them before they could transform into *lampir*. By now, dozens of victims had been quietly swept under the rug. The police were all too willing to write off missing persons, especially among the homeless.

But Helsing fought the enemy directly. Recently, he had decided not to hide anymore. He would kill vampires in plain view so that the public could understand the extent of the infestation, but it was a lonely battle. Even Lucius and the Bastion were unwilling to go on the offensive,

57

and there was so much more going on than the sheep in the city understood.

Maybe they wanted to be unaware. These normal people had happy lives, families, careers, stable homes. He'd once imagined that was the life he wanted, back before it all changed.

He had tried to do the right thing, serving in the military because that was his duty. When he enlisted back in the 1990s, he had never even heard of Bosnia or Herzegovina and certainly couldn't have found the country on a map of Eastern Europe. Then the complicated chaos of the Bosnian War broke out, small subdivisions of the country that had once been Yugoslavia splitting along historical and ethnic lines, boundaries so deep and so shrouded in obscure history that few could understand alliances, feuds, or shifting loyalties.

In 1995 NATO launched Operation Deliberate Force, and the United Nations sent peacekeeping troops into unknown territory – a blur of Bosnian, Serb, and Croat family lands, villages hammered by indiscriminate shelling, rebel forces engaged in ethnic cleansing, religious wars, and the mass rape of women who belonged to a different heritage.

Back then his name was David Grundy, according to his dog tags and his military service record, but that whole existence had been lost after the ordeal. He was just a young medical corpsman trying to follow a family tradition of military service, hoping to make his parents proud. He had no idea what he was stepping into.

Grundy had plenty of work helping injured

villagers outside of Sarajevo, treating burns and cuts, brutal amputations. Although he didn't speak the language, he fumbled to console women who had been sexually assaulted after seeing their husbands murdered in front of them. Each day was horrible.

One night under a full moon, he rode in a Red Cross ambulance truck on a winding road in the rugged mountains outside of Sarajevo. Rebel armed forces (he wasn't even sure which army) had been shelling the outer villages. He accompanied a battlefield surgeon and their UN driver, a German man who believed he spoke English better than he actually did.

The unpaved mountain road was dark, with precipitous drop-offs. Towering black pines and beech trees clung to the slopes, and the moon shone down. The ambulance headlights fanned out ahead of them in yellow pools, and those lights made the ambulance a target. The clear Red Cross and Red Crescent markings should have protected the vehicle, but that was a naïve assumption that only journalists and politicians believed. The Bosnian War followed none of the usual rules.

Grundy sat in the back seat behind the doctor. The German driver toiled along, downshifting as the road became steeper. Gravel spun under the wheels. No one heard the popping of the first sniper shots before starburst holes appeared in the windshield. One bullet smacked the driver in the center of his face, and in his dying spasms he twisted the wheel. The ambulance careened to the left.

The road had no guardrails, no dirt berms, nothing to keep the vehicle from plunging down the mountainside. Even though the ambulance was already falling down the steep rocky slope, the sniper fire continued.

Belted in, the surgeon – a man named David Lee – clawed at his shoulder as a bullet slashed through the meat of his upper chest. Grundy heard the shot impact the flesh and go all the way through into the seat just in front of him. Both he and the doctor were screaming as the vehicle struck rocks and rolled down the terrifying slope, smashing, tumbling. It slid down into the darkness until it slammed to a stop at the bottom of a ravine far below.

He lost consciousness for an unknown time and when he woke up he smelled blood and gasoline. The truck had crashed through trees, splintered pine boughs. The wall of the ambulance was crushed in. The windshield was smashed out, and the side windows lay in glittering debris all around. The full moon shone down like a cataract-covered eye. Grundy felt blood on his face.

His seatbelt held him like a straitjacket as he dangled. After silently inspecting himself, he guessed that some ribs were broken – he could feel it when he drew in a deep breath and coughed out blood. He flexed his fingers, left hand then right hand, then checked his legs, saw that they were not broken. He would have to crawl out of there.

'Doctor Lee?' His voice came out in a croak that sounded loud amid the quiet ticking of the wreck. 'Doctor?'

The seat in front of him had been torn aside. The roof of the ambulance had caved in. As Grundy fought to free himself from the seat-belt, he saw the doctor's shoulder in front of him. There was so much blood.

When he finally disengaged the seatbelt and dropped free, wincing, he reached forward to shake Dr Lee's shoulder. The neck ended only in a bloody stump. The doctor's head lay on the seat staring at him, eyes open, lips parted as if about to make an insightful comment about his decapitated state.

Pinned by the steering wheel on the other side, the German driver slumped back, a red wet bullet hole in the middle of his face, a larger exit wound out the back of his skull. Grundy had seen countless wounds like this when he tended the injured among the Bosnian villages.

The confined air in the ambulance stank of blood. His cracked ribs made it impossible to draw a deep breath. He found himself hyperventilating.

Then he heard the wolves howling. Under the full moon, the sound was primal and terrifying, one long mournful howl joined by another and another.

He turned to look at Dr Lee's head resting on the front seat. The dead man's expression seemed to have changed, his mouth open in a mocking leer. The lifeless eyes inexplicably shifted toward him. With a shudder, Grundy told himself it wasn't real, just a trick of the moonlight. He was letting his imagination get away with him, and he was aware enough to realize he was in shock.

His shirt was soaked with sticky blood, like an entire bucket poured across his chest and shoulders, enough that he would have died if it were his own. It must have come from the doctor.

Were the wolves closer now? He didn't know that wild wolves existed in Bosnia, but the army had left out a lot of details. Grundy had to get out of the ambulance. Drawn by the scent of blood, the animals would come here to feed.

Suddenly, the German driver let out a gurgling, inhuman sound, a hungry moan. His body twitched, but he was trapped in place by the broken steering wheel. Grundy screamed. The driver turned the bloody crater of his face toward him, one eye bulging like an overripe fruit. The wet mucus sound bubbling up from the undead man's throat grew louder.

Grundy thrashed, desperate for a way out, not caring how much more he cut or bruised himself.

The nearest side window had been shattered, and he had to squeeze through it. He had to! As his panic rose, he wrenched his leg free, still hearing the stir of the mangled driver. He thrust his head through the window opening and clawed the rocky ground outside, pulling himself out. Sharp edges of glass bits sliced his shirt, his skin.

Once free of the wreck and the bloody horrors inside, he could hear the wolves drawing closer. Grundy dragged himself away, leaving his two dead companions behind. His father would have excoriated him for the very idea of abandoning his comrades, but he needed to get out of there.

After he managed to get to his feet, Grundy began to run, following the line of least resistance, just going as far as he could. Finally, with enough distance that he could risk catching his breath, he slowed and felt his body for major injuries, but all he found were bruises. He spat blood from his mouth. He could have ransacked the ambulance for medical supplies, but he didn't dare go back there, not after what he had seen.

The terrifying howls echoed through the mountain wilderness, the thick beech forest, and he ran faster.

Desperate to get to safety, to civilization, he turned in one direction and another, searching for any sort of twinkling light, home windows or headlights on the forest roads. But every direction was dark, with only the eerie moon for company.

Grundy limped onward, ignoring the pain. When he treated people in the isolated villages, he had heard them whisper, knew that this old land was soaked with superstitions and lore. Considering how strongly they believed, and in his current emotional state, he thought there might really be monsters abroad in the night.

He had no idea where to find help. He didn't speak the language and didn't look like any of the local clans, but he was certain he had frequently seen something in the peasants' haunted eyes, a shared secret and a common fear. He understood that they *knew* something terrifying about their own country . . .

'Cigarette?'

The voice jarred Helsing out of his memory and back to the present. He turned to see a man with a ragged beard, brown hair below his ears, and a faded Texas A&M cap.

'What? I'm sorry.'

'Cigarette?' the man asked, pressing closer. Other people from the soup kitchen milled around.

'No, I don't have any.'

The man sounded exasperated. 'Buddy, I'm *offering* you one. Just trying to be friendly.'

Helsing looked at his half-finished bowl of pea soup. 'No thanks. I don't smoke.'

'Suit yourself. Bad habit anyway.'

The man walked off.

Helsing thought he recognized the man as a member of the Bastion, but he wasn't sure. These days he saw too many things, made too many connections, and not all of them were real.

Part of David Grundy had died that day in Bosnia, but he had awakened to the true dangers that lurked in the modern world, insidious monsters that disguised themselves as normal people and kept their existence very quiet.

For now, he was alone in his crusade, but someday there would be others to fight the great enemy. He would find an ally out there. Somewhere.

Nine

On bargain day at the second-hand store, Lucius decided to stock up on supplies, not just for the emergency caches and safe houses in the city, but also for the main camp. Members of the Bastion had to be self-sufficient in these dire times, and he needed to make sure that anyone who risked visiting the city had access to the necessary emergency supplies.

He'd already made several purchases at Goodwill, but this veterans' charity store had better prices. Lucius gathered a stack of shirts in various sizes, mostly men's but some for the children, too. Joshua was growing like a weed. A couple of women's outfits rounded out the purchase, particularly warm winter wear. He took special pride in finding a fleece jacket for Mama. She deserved it.

He paid in cash, carefully counting out the bills and taking every penny in change. The clerk thought nothing of it.

Carrying his bags, Lucius went to the rundown Volvo in the parking lot. The car's body had seen better days, but its engine worked like a charm. The back seat was already filled with bags of groceries, canned goods on sale from the dollar store. His people collected fresh berries and wild vegetables from the forest, but he bought a sack of clementines that they would consider a treat.

The Volvo started right up, and he drove to the Rambler Star Motel listening to the news, verifying that civilization continued to careen toward self-destruction in one form or another, but it was important for him to keep up with world events for the defense of the Bastion. The apocalyptic dangers made Lucius uneasy, but he had more immediate concerns as well. Recent reports on the local news about 'Bigfoot' assaulting a female hiker had rocked the Bastion.

Lucius was a large-statured man with caramel-colored skin, a thick head of blue-black hair and eyebrows to match. He had trimmed his thick black beard for this visit to the city, but he would grow it full and shaggy as winter set in. Before leaving the forest, he changed into a sturdy pair of blue jeans and a khaki jacket over his buffalo-plaid shirt. Despite his broad shoulders and big hands, he kept his voice soft and knew to look clean and civilized so that he drew no attention. When he went about his business, he didn't want anyone to feel threatened. Or to notice him.

Reaching the motel, he sauntered into the empty lobby, and Daniel Gardon quickly sat up behind his desk. 'Lucius!'

'I'll be in and out quick. Just need to restock the room.'

He reached for the key to room 41. 'If you need any supplies in particular, let me know. I can always buy them myself. I take care of the room when no one's using it.'

'You do enough for us already, Daniel. Your job is to keep the computer and internet available. That isn't something I know how to do.'

'Not a problem. How . . . how is everyone?'

Lucius paused and looked at the man. 'Surviving. And we intend to keep it that way. You know where to go if things get bad.'

On the television set, loud celebratory bells chimed and a giddy contestant jumped up and down, having correctly named the price of some kitchen appliance. Lucius felt sad and tired. 'Are you sure it was worth giving up everything for this?'

The motel manager looked guilty. 'Not always. I had concerns when I left the Bastion, but I'm still loyal. You can count on me when you need to.' Gardon handed him the key on its plastic fob. 'Still, each night when I go home to my wife and help her cook dinner, or when we go out to a movie or to a restaurant, I get convinced all over again. No regrets.'

'Suit yourself. It is what it is.'

Lucius knew the man had his doubts. While he and the rest of the Bastion saw the end of the world coming at them from all directions, the motel manager questioned what he called their alarmism. He said he couldn't buy into all of their doomsday scenarios and he wanted to try out a normal life. He had never rejoined the isolated camp, but even though he was skeptical, Gardon's heart remained with the Bastion, of that Lucius had no doubt.

Having a trusted man at the Rambler Star Motel gave them certain advantages. Two other local motels also offered safe havens, in case of emergency. All in all, Lucius preferred the peace and security of the wilderness.

When he entered room 41, he could see that one or two people had used the resources since his last visit. He restocked the canned goods, added warm socks to the drawer. The motel manager had laundered any dirty clothes left by the previous occupants, folded them and put them away. Lucius checked the cash stash and added another hundred dollars. After he finished, the room looked safe and complete.

Lucius returned the key to the motel manager and

drove off with a full load of food, supplies, and clothing in the back of the Volvo. He would head west into the foothills and wind his way through the forest roads. There were eight other nondescript cars parked in strategic places around the city – off on side streets, in parking lots or in front of auto repair yards where no one would notice them. Members of the Bastion knew how to find them. Each car had a scratched letter 'C' under the rear passenger door handle.

As Lucius drove away, he headed toward the hunched buttress of Cheyenne Mountain with its array of communication antennas on top and its underground NORAD complex from the Cold War days. The government had known how to hide people back then, too.

But nuclear war wasn't the only thing that Lucius and his people worried about.

He felt a weight leave him as he drove through the upscale Broadmoor district, heading into the Front Range. The Pike National Forest was a pristine wilderness above Colorado Springs laced with a maze of numbered Forest Service roads, old logging tracks, private roads, and vast acreage marked with faint and forgotten hiking trails. Only the Bastion knew all its secrets. With good tires and all-wheel drive, the Volvo traveled a dirt road rutted by recreational off-highway vehicles.

Lucius drove past private lanes leading to empty vacation cabins or loners who lived off the grid. Chain barricades and *No Trespassing* signs kept the curious away. He passed the graffiti-marked ruins of long-abandoned army bunkers, nothing more than concrete walls, remnants of a military presence that had withdrawn shortly after World War II.

At a rough drive blocked by a chain and a *Private Property* sign, Lucius stopped the car, climbed out to remove the chain, then rolled the car through before hooking the chain again. He drove farther, passing several blind tracks and diversionary turns that went nowhere. The Bastion knew how to keep their presence hidden.

He parked the car and waited in wary silence, gripping the steering wheel until figures stirred out of the trees. They came to greet him, even children. Recognizing Lucius was alone, they bounded closer, smiling.

He felt like Santa Claus bearing gifts. Men and women helped take the groceries, eager to make a fine feast while the perishables were fresh. They would place the canned goods in stockpiles for winter. Right now, teams were hunting deer, rabbits, and squirrels, which they would preserve. He tossed a bag of hard candy to the children, who snatched it and ran off with their treasure.

A sturdy woman with a heartbreakingly beautiful face approached with a smile. She tugged a gray-streaked brown lock out of her eyes. 'I'm happy you're home, Lucius.'

'There's nothing like home, Mama.' With a dramatic flourish, he presented the fleece jacket. 'You never had a wedding dress, but this may serve you better.'

'Beautiful and practical.' Taking it from him, she stroked the fabric. 'I thought it was *your* job to keep me warm over the winter?'

'It is, but that's for when I'm not next to you.'

He picked up the last bag of groceries and closed the Volvo's back door with his hip. He wished they didn't have to rely on civilization, but it was the best solution for now in order to survive. Lucius would make sure they did what was necessary.

He followed his people into camp.

Ten

The invitation surprised Lexi. The fancy, elaborate envelope stood out prominently in the mailbox among the grocery flyers, charity solicit-ations, and the utility bills. Stepping back inside, she tossed the junk mail in the conveniently placed recycling bin and looked at the embossed envelope, the fine crimson paper, the return address.

Hugo Zelm.

As he emerged from his room, Blair picked up a lightweight khaki jacket from the wall hook, ready for his day job at Rags to Riches. 'Looks like a sophisticated invitation. Who's getting married?' He stepped closer.

She pulled out the engraved folded card inside. 'Not a wedding. A charity benefit gala in the Broadmoor Hills.' She inspected the invitation, front and back. 'Hugo Zelm personally invites me to join him. I didn't know he even had my address.' The thought momentarily disturbed

70

her, but then Zelm was a man of substantial resources.

The dark blue ink of the handwritten note stood out against the red paper: *'I would very much like to meet you in person, Ms Tarada. You make me want to believe.'*

Blair peered over her shoulder. 'Well, then, he is one of your biggest supporters. You have to go.'

Zelm was eccentric, reclusive, and generous. His patronage of HideTruth made an enormous difference to her, even if it was no more than a blip in his petty-cash fund.

'He must make hundreds of donations, but maybe he does pay attention to HideTruth.'

Blair skimmed the invitation. 'You'll definitely need a plus one, Lex. Don't forget your favorite wingman.'

She didn't have to think about it. 'How could I? No one else even comes close to being my first choice.'

After Blair left for work, seemingly more excited about the invitation than she was, Lexi spent the afternoon researching another eye-rolling conspiracy theory for PRUUF – a mind-altering chemical contamination in a freak snowfall across northern Georgia. Apparently, the clouds were seeded via poisoned vapor trails in a specific attempt by the oil companies to cast doubt on climate-change science so they could avoid environmental regulations.

She could find no kernel of truth in the story, and most of the evidence was easily debunked. The people who were convinced, however, would not likely change their minds.

Despite her absolute certainty about what she had witnessed during Teresa's spectral visit, Lexi had never posted that story, hadn't told anyone but Blair in years. She wondered if other people would place her conversation with a dead friend in the same category as contaminated vapor trails and freak snowfalls. Nobody believed her – certainly not her parents – and Lexi knew what that felt like.

You make me want to believe. Hugo Zelm's comment resonated with her. Lexi wanted to believe as well, but she also didn't want to be fooled.

She leaned back in her desk chair, staring at the screen. At least debunking urban legends and eradicating fake accounts paid the bills. Was that what Teresa had meant with her insistent message from beyond the grave, urging Lexi to make something of her life, to find something she was passionate about? She supposed it was better than flipping burgers somewhere.

One of these days, Lexi would stumble across that incontrovertible piece of evidence, an incident compelling enough to make others want to believe. Then all of her work would be justified.

When her phone rang, she answered automatically, assuming it was some business call, but when she saw the caller ID – her parents – she braced herself for a longer conversation. 'Hi Mom and Dad.'

She listened to a brief, startled pause. 'How do you always know it's us before we even say anything?' her mother asked.

'Caller ID. Every phone has it.'

'Ours doesn't,' her father said.

'That's because your phone is from the 1980s.' Hearing the sting in her tone, she quickly added, 'Love you.' That was enough to derail the argument.

'We haven't heard from you in a while, so we decided to call and check up on you,' her mother said.

'And because we heard about that murder in Colorado Springs,' her dad added. 'Are you safe?'

'We have murders in Colorado Springs,' Lexi said. 'Half a million people live here, so it's bound to happen. It's ten times the size of Dubuque.'

'You'd be safer here,' her mother said.

'Yes, I'd be safer . . . and probably bored.' Lexi fingered the delicate gold cross necklace they had given her for a graduation present. She wondered when they would ever stop trying to get her to move back home. Certainly not today.

Having grown up in Iowa where the farmland fringes of the city were called the 'incorporated area' for tax purposes, Lexi had always felt frustrated there. She was too much of a free spirit to thrive in the rural Midwest. Teresa had known it, too. After only two years of college, Lexi found a job as a contractor for PRUUF and several internet security services. She had traded cornfields for the mountains and rarely turned her gaze east. She had promised Teresa she would leave Dubuque.

Her father, Perry, had his own small insurance agency in Dubuque. Her mother, Sharon, did clerical work for the State of Iowa. Lexi cringed when her mother called herself a secretary. Perry and Sharon Tarada were strait-laced and conservative, and they firmly believed in an America that matched what they saw all around them. But they had never seen any other part of the country. They promised to visit Lexi out in Colorado someday, though the thirteen-hour drive intimidated them.

'So how are things back home?' Lexi asked, which released a stream of stories about people she barely remembered from high school: who got married, who got arrested for drunk driving, who got injured in a tractor accident. Apparently, the senior class president was running for mayor, the youngest ever, but Lexi's mother was sure he would never win because he had 'gotten that girl pregnant and had to marry her'.

As Lexi listened and made appropriate noises, she distracted herself by going on HideTruth. She scrolled through the comments, looking at more discussions about vampires hidden in society. She found one more posting about the Bigfoot rapist, though that thread had mostly died.

When her dad finished talking about his latest fishing trip, Lexi interrupted with a more serious topic. 'And how are you feeling, Mom? How's the chemo?'

'Oh, you know, mostly finished. I have good days and bad days, but at least I'm losing some weight.'

'You didn't need to lose any weight. What did the oncologist say?'

'He said it's doing fine. I go in for another scan in a month, then I can give you all the details.'

Lexi knew she would never get the details. Her mother was being treated for breast cancer, and Lexi had no idea how serious it was because her parents brushed aside any explanations. They thought talking about breasts was inappropriate, and neither of them had much medical knowledge. They trusted doctors too much, assuming they were all like TV show doctors; they accepted whatever the oncologist said, without asking for more information. Lexi kept sending them links so they could do their own homework, but she doubted they followed up on them.

'Please take care of yourself,' she said, knowing it was the best she could do. 'Eat healthy and let me know whatever you find out.' She put an edge in her voice. '*And* get details.'

'Since when did you become a doctor, dear?'

There was no point in pursuing that argument. Her mother had never had an independent opinion in her life. Her gruff father had enough opinions for both of them, and that turned any conversation into a minefield. He and Lexi had gotten into plenty of arguments when she still lived at home – another reason she didn't want to move back. Now, they kept their safe distance and trod carefully in conversations.

'Are you dating anyone yet?' Sharon asked. 'You're such a smart, pretty girl.'

'Oh, no one special.' The answer was just plain 'No', but her careful phrasing left enough doubt in her parents' minds that they didn't pester her. 'You sure there's nothing going on with that

75

handsome Blair? He's always very nice and polite.'

'He certainly is,' Lexi said. 'But no, there's nothing going on. He's just a housemate, helps to pay the bills.'

When he had first moved into the small house, her parents had been convinced the two were living together as a couple, that Lexi wasn't telling them everything. Perry and Sharon struggled to be understanding, but they didn't believe her reassurances. Being from rural Iowa, they had no gaydar whatsoever. Lexi couldn't explain *that* to them either, because her parents would have even more of a problem knowing there was a gay man in the same house.

She did try to date, but her success rate was not inspiring. She was attractive and had varied interests, but once the men found out about HideTruth, they treated her differently. Most became condescending, and she questioned the judgement of the ones who thought the conspiracy stuff was cool, the ones who believed everything posted on the site. She had enough to worry about without throwing another stalker into the mix.

While she studied the potential mysteries in the world, with an open mind and jaded eyes, the true believers could be just plain scary. Some items were clearly gags – 'Bat Boy Gets a New Puppy' for instance – but other conspiracy fanatics spread violent memes. They attacked random targets, often celebrities, attempting to destroy careers with doctored and easily disproved evidence about white slavery rings or murderous pedophilia. Some trolls were truly vile, harassing the parents of school-shooting victims and claiming that their dead children were a hoax.

Lexi wanted nothing to do with those people, and she refused to post such stories on HideTruth. This frustrated some of her followers, because they wanted to believe in their pet conspiracies, and then they wanted to argue about them . . .

After ten minutes, the conversation with her parents petered out. They admonished her to be careful. Lexi was surprised the staker had gotten play on the Iowa television news, and then she smiled. 'Are you reading my website? I posted the story there with all the details.'

'Not regularly,' her father said. 'It seems pretty far out.'

She didn't point out some of the crazier things her parents blithely swallowed from the fringe cable news they watched. 'I'll watch out for Bigfoot and vampires – as long as you do, too.' They chuckled, but the joke was strained.

Lexi hung up, tired, but the phone call was a weekly obligation, now fulfilled. She would never admit this to her parents, but she knew she had to be careful. HideTruth's core audience could be vicious junkyard dogs, scrappers fighting against anyone who ridiculed them. Lexi walked a fine line because they were *her* junkyard dogs. She was skeptical, but they knew that she was honest and open-minded. They respected that, but she didn't doubt for a minute that they would turn on her if she took a wrong stance.

She had already learned that once.

Her stalker had been a cruel, faceless man named Richard Dover, an intense believer who objected to the fact that she had mocked a particularly asinine conspiracy theory about lizard people. He had been indignant, argued with her, insulted her, and Lexi made the mistake of fighting back.

Since his public name was Richard Dover, she shortened it to Dick Dover, which quickly degenerated into *Dicked Over*. She meant to be sarcastic, but it just looked immature on her part. Dicked Over didn't take it well. He had harassed her mercilessly, trolling her website. Each time she deleted his profile, he reestablished it within minutes. He was smart, too, and dodged her IP address searches.

Even though Lexi was careful never to make her home address public, such information was impossible to hide from a true conspiracy theorist. She understood how resourceful they could be, especially a maladjusted cyberstalker like Dicked Over. When she pinged and found that some of his postings came from Colorado, Lexi grew worried. She spent so much time home alone, and even when Blair was there, she didn't think a bad guy would find him very intimidating.

For a couple of weeks she convinced herself that Dicked Over was probably just a fat thirty-year-old virgin living in his parents' basement, but his harassment didn't stop. In fact, his comments escalated. Finally, Lexi posted on her own site, seeking advice. 'I'm considering buying a handgun for personal protection. I hope I never have to use it at all, but I want it handy in case some dick threatens me.' She used the word 'dick' on purpose. 'Any suggestions?'

Now *that* had engaged her fans! She foolishly expected clear recommendations, maybe some comparative discussion, but the boards exploded with comments, vehement advice and outright verbal brawls. If she'd asked for suggestions about fishing poles, she would have gotten a couple of responses, but this!

After a day of endless debate, Lexi typed, 'You guys sure are obsessive about your guns!' She stared at the screen for a long moment, then deleted the comment without posting it, since it would only throw gasoline on the discussion.

Ruger, Beretta, Smith and Wesson, Glock, Sig Sauer, model numbers and calibers that meant nothing to her. After the debate wound down, then wound in circles, she narrowed her choices, went to one of the many local shooting ranges, and finally settled on a .38 Special Revolver. It worked, and she needed something she could get out of her nightstand drawer if Dicked Over came to the house.

Lexi hoped never to fire it, but she damn well wanted to know how to use it. After buying the gun, she'd gone to the shooting range twice, went through two boxes of bullets, enough to get herself comfortable with the weapon. She'd chosen the revolver because she needed a gun she could grab, point, and shoot.

The third time she went, to test herself in a worst-case situation, she gulped four cans of Mountain Dew, ate two candy bars, then walked at a fast pace four blocks to the shooting range. By the time she arrived, she was in the right condition for a real-life scenario – jittery, sweaty, out of breath. It had been great practice.

After her extensive public discussion on handguns, though, Dicked Over dropped off the site and never harassed her again. She kept the weapon at her bedside just in case. Yes, there was a murderer in Colorado Springs who had pounded a stake through his victim's heart, and yes, she covered stories about UFO abductions and Bigfoot and lizard people.

But Lexi was far more afraid of crazy stalkers, because she knew for a fact *they* were real.

Eleven

The noisy D&R lumberyard was surrounded by gravel mounds and vacant lots. Forklifts moved lumber around, loading big deliveries on flatbed trucks for home construction projects or dropping smaller loads in pickup beds for DIY enthusiasts.

Detective Carrow didn't have many leads, and he hoped he might at least find some hint about the origin of the stake. If it was a gangland killing, like Chop Chop in Pueblo, gang members often worked in construction. He hoped to find a viable clue, but that was a long shot. It wouldn't be difficult for anybody to find a scrap piece of wood.

He pulled his beige Ford Taurus into the gravel parking lot near the office trailer. On stacks of two-by-fours and islands of plywood sheets, he easily spotted the lime-green marker paint used to identify lots. Construction workers in dark jeans, sturdy work boots, and gloves moved boards off a neat stack and clattered them into another pile. Carrow wore slacks, a dark gray jacket, and a nice shirt per CSPD policy, but he felt overdressed. He did not look like a customer as he sauntered toward the lumberyard office.

The temporary trailer looked as if it had been there long enough to become a permanent part of the landscape. He stepped up the metal grate stairs and popped open the flimsy door, which swung wide with surprising ease. The lumberyard manager sat at an old desk with a ten-key adding machine punching in numbers from a handwritten ledger book. Three calendars from various insurance companies were thumbtacked to the plywood walls, each one showing a different month.

The manager looked up. 'Here to pick up an order?'

'Here to ask a few questions.'

The man looked disappointed. 'Sure, I'm a regular answering service.'

Carrow opened his badge wallet, got the man's attention. 'Some wood from your lumberyard was found at a crime scene, and I hope you can help me out. It's my only lead, so any advice would be appreciated.'

'What kind of crime?' The man sounded eager now. 'And how does my lumber figure into it?'

Deciding the startle reflex might gain him cooperation, Carrow removed his manila folder and opened it to a color printout of the bloodstained stake and the line of green paint on the wood. 'It was used in a murder.'

'Holy shit, the stake guy?' The manager picked up the photo. 'Yeah, that green paint is ours. You're a regular Sherlock Holmes.'

'Sherlock Holmes has more of a fan following,' Carrow said. He'd never gained much recognition on his job. No one looking for fame and fortune would join the police force in a mid-sized city. After he caught the stake killer, he would probably end up on the TV news, but the publicity would blow over quickly enough, and public affairs would draw most of the attention. He had no delusions of making the talk show circuit or *Dancing with the Stars*, and he certainly wouldn't attempt writing a book about it; he hated just typing up police reports.

At forty-two, Todd Carrow realized whenever he looked in the mirror and saw his hair thinner than it used to be, the few extra pounds he had put on, the lines on his face starting to show 'character', that he could no longer pretend he was an up-and-coming guy. His 'great future' had divorced him and taken the two girls back to Pueblo. He was already who he was ever going to be, dancing on the edge of middle age, living alone in a sparsely furnished townhouse. So much for the *Leave It to Beaver* American dream scenario he'd expected.

Well, shit happened and he had a job to do.

The lumberyard manager held on to the photograph for a long time. 'I bet it was pretty disgusting.' He seemed to want more details. Carrow didn't offer them.

Even after a couple days of digging, he had found little information on the victim himself. Stallings had almost no connections in society, no known friends or family, no email account. The violence of the pounded stake suggested that the killer was malicious and furious, like Chop Chop. Did that mean Stallings had a well-hidden secret life? Gang or drug connections?

The manager stood up from behind his desk, closed the ledger as if afraid someone might look at his penciled numbers. 'Even if this is the right lumberyard, that won't do you any good. D&R doesn't have a special section for vampire stakes.'

Carrow followed him out of the trailer. 'Didn't think so, but I have to take a look.'

They walked across the hard-packed ground where heavy tires had pressed the dirt into cement. The smell of resiny sawdust mixed with the oily odor of diesel exhaust. The manager led him around islands of two-by-fours and two-by-eights until they reached the scrap pile, a mound of broken boards, marker stakes, and split posts – an endless supply of raw material that could be sharpened into stakes.

'Take your pick, Detective. We have truckloads of scrap. If someone stole a few stakes from this pile, I'd never know. And there are dozens of construction sites and other scrap piles around the city using our lumber. Your murder weapon could have come from anywhere.'

Carrow's heart sank. 'Don't suppose you have security cameras?'

'We do in the main yard, but this is just the garbage pile. Nothing worth watching here, and we reset the recording every two days. We'd know pretty damn quick if there were vandals from the night before.'

Carrow stared at the wood, hoping some brilliant revelation would occur to him, but he saw only a mound of scraps. The murderer wouldn't have any shortage of stakes if he decided to kill again.

Twelve

Nobody noticed the nondescript Honda where it was parked. It could have sat there for months without being reported as abandoned, but Helsing located the vehicle in a poorly planned residential area constructed in the early 1970s. Oak trees had split the sidewalks, roots slowly erupting from the concrete. The street's gutters were filled with dead leaves.

Half a century earlier, these cookie-cutter duplexes must have made great starter homes for young families, but now they were run down with a high turnover of renters. The tenants had better things to do than pay attention to an old-model car left on a side street near no particular driveway.

Members of the Bastion knew how to find such available vehicles left there for their use. Helsing walked casually along the sidewalk, glancing at the parked cars until he found one with a clumsy letter 'C' scratched beneath the back-passenger door handle. The mark looked as if some half-hearted vandal had keyed the paint but had run out of anger.

Helsing opened the driver's door, ducked to feel under the mat where he came up with the loose key. The engine coughed and then warmed up. The Honda still had nearly half a tank of gas, certainly enough for Helsing's purposes.

He drove through the residential streets with a list of addresses, potential targets he had collected through long research. This was part of the 'stakeout' process (and he acknowledged the irony of the term).

In these days of working at home or online, it was far easier for the *lampir* to work a camouflage job that did not require venturing out during daylight hours. The options were dizzying to consider, and it had taken Helsing quite some time to narrow down the list of potential targets. Bartenders, hotel desk night clerks, third shift nurses or ambulance drivers, security guards, custodians, warehouse workers, department store shelf stockers, taxi drivers, online anything . . . It was a challenge to weed them out. Vampires were very skilled at hiding, but Helsing's careful research winnowed the possibilities. He knew what to look for, and he would be a fool and a coward if he denied the evidence of his eyes.

He had survived that horrific night in Bosnia for a reason. Drenched in blood that was not his own and aching from uncounted injuries, he had been dizzy, in shock as he fled the wrecked ambulance.

Hearing the distant howl of wolves spurred him

faster. His vision was blurred, doubled, and his head pounded. The silver light of the full moon provided enough illumination for him to pick his way down the slope to where he heard trickling water. A stream whispered and hissed over rocks.

He, David Grundy, had stood motionless for a long moment, unable to decide whether or not to cross. Even thinking was such an effort. He dropped to his knees and splashed water on his face, washing away the blood that caked his eyes and forehead. The snowmelt water was as cold as death. He heard something move in the forest behind him, branches cracking, pebbles stirring, noises loud enough to be heard over the rushing stream. Some dark predatory presence hovered in the air.

It might only be deer, but he had also heard wolves howling. The violent opposing factions in the turmoil of the Bosnian War were the greatest danger he'd ever expected to face over here. But what Grundy felt moving in the dark forest, slowly closing in, did not feel like enemy soldiers. It was definitely something else stalking him. His skin crawled, and he kept moving.

He stumbled along the bank, then splashed across the stream on large rocks. On the opposite side he found a flat area, a game path where animals came to drink. The bushes along the stream clawed at him, and he thrashed his way through. The dark beeches towered overhead, creating ominous shadows in the moonlight.

Grundy could see no lights anywhere, no houses, no campfires, but if he followed the running water he might eventually find a hunter's cottage, a mill, even a village. He kept going for hours, hiding, creeping over a carpet of fallen leaves, dashing across moonlit clearings. The pain from his injuries grew more sharp-edged, and he felt the warm stickiness of blood on his skin, though he had washed much of it away in the stream. Every breath brought an electric shock of jagged ribs.

At last, long after midnight, he came upon flat stumps of sawed trees, an open area cleared by woodcutters. Ahead he saw darker shadows with sharp angles, stone walls, roofs – buildings of some sort. The sight gave him the energy to keep moving.

He stumbled up to a cottage made of fieldstones and a tile roof covered with moss. Crosses hung on the outside walls near every opening. The door was closed and the windows shuttered for the night, making the cottage look abandoned, but he saw a garden patch, a nearby shed or barn. The people inside must be sleeping. A cottage out here, especially in war-torn Bosnia, would have no electricity, and poor peasants wouldn't waste fuel burning lanterns long after everyone was asleep.

But there were people, and they could help him.

He lurched toward the door and collapsed to his knees. He pounded on the door and called out, 'Help! Is anyone in there? Help!'

He heard stirring inside, muttered voices, then a hushed and terrified silence. Though he nearly fainted, he hammered even harder. 'Help! There's been an accident. I'm an American.' Isolated peasants in the mountains far from Sarajevo might not understand English, but they would hear the desperation in his voice.

A flare of light glowed through cracks in the window shutters, a lit candle that made a profound difference in the darkness. He heard children whimpering, a gruff man's voice grumbling in a foreign language.

'Help,' he croaked. 'Please help.'

The male voice came again, then a woman's voice, both sounding frightened. Grundy rattled the latch on the door, and he heard a gasp inside, then the scraping noises of furniture, perhaps a cabinet or a chest of drawers being dragged across the door. The man yelled from the other side of the door, threatening.

'Please! My name is David Grundy. I'm a medical corpsman with the NATO troops.'

More candles were lit inside, but he remained locked out in the darkness. Beyond the clearing around the cottage, he could still hear stirrings in the forest, branches rustling. He thought he saw bright eyes – maybe wolves, maybe worse.

He started sobbing. 'Please let me in!' He pounded against the door, too afraid and too weak to leave this cottage and seek other salvation. He didn't dare.

Unable to forget the staring head of Dr Lee in the front seat of the ambulance, the wet metal smell of blood everywhere, the groan of the driver who seemed to come back from the dead, he sank to the ground and drew his knees against his chest, leaning back against the solidity of the cottage door. The huddled people inside kept him out, leaving him vulnerable to whatever lurked in the darkness.

It was full sunlight when the door finally creaked open, and Grundy slumped backward over the threshold, unconscious. He woke groggily to a gasping and muttering family. He found himself drenched with fresh blood and knew he must be bleeding from multiple injuries. The peasant couple chattered, having some kind of an argument while the children stared.

'Please . . .' Grundy said.

The Bosnian man pointed at him, at the blood, at the bright daylight, and seemed to insist that the family had to tend to him. The peasant man dragged him inside, sending a fresh burst of pain throughout his body.

Grundy went in and out of consciousness for some time. They bandaged him, fed him soup and hot tea. The man spoke only a handful of English words, enough to be frustrating but not enough to communicate. He kept saying the word *lampir*, over and over again. Grundy held up his dog tags, pleading for help before he fell back into unconsciousness.

The peasant family tended him for two, maybe three days. Exhausted, traumatized, he couldn't be sure how much time had passed. When he awoke, he saw them speaking in hushed voices, using words they knew he couldn't understand. He ached everywhere. He developed a fever and vomited twice, which terrified the peasant family even more, as if they feared he carried some kind of plague.

After stumbling aimlessly through the night,

traveling miles and miles, he had no idea where he was. No one knew what had happened to the ambulance. He, the German driver, and Dr Lee were missing, and search parties must be looking for them, but even if they found the ambulance halfway down the mountainside, he was no longer there.

One afternoon, a loud pounding on the door woke Grundy, startled the family. The father pulled open the door and let fresh sunlight pour into the house. An orthodox priest with a thicket of beard stood outside in a plain robe. A heavy cross hung on a beaded chain around his neck. The priest and the peasant father spoke quickly, and the priest locked eyes with Grundy as he lay under his blanket in the main room.

The bearded man strode forward and loomed over the pallet. Grundy could feel the man's charismatic presence, saw the blaze in his pale blue eyes. The priest held the wooden cross in one hand like a weapon, while he reached out to press his other palm against Grundy's cheek.

'What are you doing? I—'

He winced as the priest pushed his head to one side then the other, exposing the sides of his neck. The man roughly yanked down the blanket, revealing the bandages on Grundy's chest and shoulder, and stared at him as if dissecting his soul. The priest straightened, heaved a sigh of relief. 'No *lampir*.'

The family chattered and nodded. The mother wept. The peasant father asked numerous questions, but the bearded man faced Grundy and spoke surprisingly in English. 'I told them they

90

did a good thing in saving you. If they hadn't intervened the monsters would have had you, turned you into one of them.'

'You . . . speak English?' It was a stupid question, but the first one that came to his mind. 'My name is David Grundy. I'm with the NATO troops. I—'

The priest interrupted him. 'We know what you are, and now I know you are human. You were out at night. We are sure the *lampir* tracked you, hunted you, but you reached this house in time.'

'The people wouldn't let me in at first,' Grundy groaned. 'I pounded on the door. I heard things moving out in the forest.' The terror struck him again, and he closed his eyes to block the memories.

'I had blessed this house, and the family has crosses and icons. They take the proper precautions. It was enough to scare them away.'

'I know I heard wolves,' Grundy said.

'Maybe wolves, maybe not,' the priest said. 'I went to school in London for a time, so I know that too many of your people don't believe. They scoff at the existence of *lampir* – you would call them vampires. That is exactly what the monsters want, so they can feed with few people guessing the real danger.'

The priest came back for the next three days, teaching Grundy about the *lampir*, showing him ways to protect himself, how to kill vampires, how to find them where they hid in society. Gradually, he came to realize how narrow his escape had been. As the priest described the ways of the *lampir*, Grundy began to remember details of his flight, shadows he had seen in the forest, the sound the creatures made as they stalked him.

He was lucky to be alive, but he had to get back to his people so he could report what had happened. He was recovered enough now. At his request, the priest managed to get a message to a town that had a working telephone line. After more than a week of being lost – and being saved as well as educated – David Grundy was rescued.

The wrecked vehicle had been found several days earlier, along with the two bodies inside. As he recovered in a UN infirmary, Grundy learned that the two corpses had been mangled, torn apart by predators. Maybe they had been drained of blood . . .

As he told his unbelievable story again and again, the listeners were at first fascinated, then impatient with him. He repeated what the priest had said about the *lampir* until it was clear that his comrades lost respect for whatever else he had to say. His superior officer even reprimanded him.

So he learned to keep his mouth shut, to hold the night terrors inside as the certainty grew darker and darker in his mind. After he failed several psychological evaluations, he was declared no longer fit for duty. The Bosnian peace accord happened some months after that, and all the peacekeeping troops were withdrawn anyway. At least he didn't receive a dishonorable discharge.

But David Grundy was never the same. Part of him died that night in the ambulance crash, and another part had awakened to what was going on.

Now, in his nondescript Honda, carrying the notes and addresses he had compiled, he drove around the city, on the hunt for vampires.

Thirteen

Lexi was dismayed when the Bigfoot rapist thread flared up again on HideTruth, this time hijacked by trolls. Disgusted by their comments, she was reminded that the worst parts of human nature could be found on the internet.

Blair had concerns of his own that had nothing to do with the website. He stood at her bedroom door, eyeing her with disapproval. 'I'm not saying that I ransacked your closet, Lex, but I don't believe you're planning properly for the occasion.'

She looked up from her screen, still preoccupied by the vile comments. 'What occasion?'

He rolled his eyes. 'Hugo Zelm's gala! Did you even read the invitation? It's an evening event, very formal, very high class.' He ran his gaze up and down her form as she sat at her desk in casual clothes. 'You're like a fish out of water and a thousand feet up in the air. What are you going to wear?'

She hadn't thought about it much. The event was still two weeks away. 'A dress, I suppose. I've got a few.'

'I'll be the judge of that. When was the last time you wore one?'

Lexi considered. 'I used to go to church back in Iowa. I'm sure one or two of them still fit. I keep myself in shape.'

'Yes, you do, dear girl.' He crossed his arms over his chest. 'But just because you can *fit*, doesn't mean that it's appropriate for such an event.'

'Church dresses don't go out of style.' She paused, having never thought about it. 'Do they?'

He looked wounded. 'This is a genuine tux and cocktail-gown event, and it requires you to have jewelry, high heels, and a tasteful amount of cleavage.'

Lexi didn't want to talk about it. 'I haven't even said I'm going to go. I didn't return the RSVP card yet.'

Blair was like a drill sergeant. 'Well, you'd better! Hugo Zelm wants to meet you in person, so I insist that you make a killer impression to ensure he keeps making his donations to your website. Besides, I plan to look dashing, and I don't want you to seem out of place as I escort you to the party.'

She sighed. 'Getting all dressy isn't my thing.'

Blair finally looked in control of the conversation. 'Leave it to me. Rags to Riches has a fine selection, and I'll make it my quest to find something perfect for the occasion. I'll get something that looks classy.'

'I thought your store just sold old clothes? If I'm going to have an old dress, why don't I just wear something from my closet?'

His exasperation was plain. 'Not old – *vintage*! I recall a beautiful dress on the rack, tasteful and elegant, just perfect for you. You'll look spectacular.'

Lexi knew Blair would do exactly as he said, and she was relieved to hand off the responsibility. 'I place myself in your hands.'

He sauntered off. She knew she had brightened his day as much as the Bigfoot thread had soured hers.

The assaulted hiker had dropped off the radar, hunkering down and waiting for the attention to fade, and the trolls came out like hyenas to attack her.

'I bet she likes the wild hairy sex.'

'Does Bigfoot have a big cock? Inquiring minds want to know!'

'Did she take pictures? Pics, or it didn't happen!'

Some asshole even posted Holly Smith's home address in Colorado Springs and encouraged big hairy guys to go surprise her with another thrill. 'She likes it!'

Luckily, within minutes of the posting Lexi deleted that comment and permanently blocked the user. Wondering if Holly was in imminent danger, she tracked down the troll's location from his IP address. The creep lived in South Carolina, too distant to be a threat. He was just a troublemaker, an internet anarchist – and no longer welcome on HideTruth.

The police didn't reveal the identities or addresses of sexual abuse victims, but the search for Holly had received so much news coverage there was no way to restore her privacy.

Lexi remembered being harassed by Dicked Over, when she had learned that US law did almost nothing to protect victims of internet stalking. Wouldn't want to infringe on some violent turd's right to free speech.

Angry, she deleted all the troll comments on the thread. She tended to have a high tolerance for volatile opinions, but not on this one, not with a woman who had been assaulted – whether or not Bigfoot truly was the culprit. The young woman worked as an office assistant for an accounting firm, was unmarried and had family in the city, but she lived alone.

Though she had deleted the thread, Lexi was still worried that Holly Smith might be exposed to danger. Since she had the victim's local address from the deleted posting, she decided to go make a polite visit, hoping Holly might appreciate a friendly ear, someone who wouldn't mock or disbelieve her.

She went to her closet, wanting to dress professionally. She had to look compassionate and trustworthy. She chose nice slacks, a green blouse, black leather jacket. Seeing her old church dresses hanging at the back of the rack, she realized that Blair was right. Those wouldn't do at all for a fancy soiree.

By the time she reached Holly Smith's ground-floor apartment in a new development off Powers Drive, Lexi still hadn't figured out what to say. She would offer support, but Holly probably just wanted to be left alone. Lexi would have a challenge.

It was two o'clock in the afternoon when she rang the doorbell. After a long moment, the lock clicked and the door opened to reveal a thin young woman with short brown hair, a loose

T-shirt, and baggy pants. Her eyes were dark blue, and the heavy shadows beneath them gave her a haunted look.

Lexi smiled. 'Are you Holly? I don't know if you want to talk, but I'd like to offer you support and friendship.' She extended one of her business cards.

Holly was instantly suspicious. 'What do you want? Are you a reporter?'

'Absolutely not.' It was mostly true, and she didn't intend to post any details about this interview. Whatever happened, Lexi just needed to hear the answers for herself. *One of these days, I'm sure to be right.* 'I'm someone who wants to believe, and I'm willing to listen.'

She and Holly were about the same age. Since Lexi had come alone, non-threatening, speaking in a soft voice and showing compassion, the young woman hesitated. 'Another therapist? The rape counseling center talked to me for an hour, and that was all the time they could spare. Real therapists are a hundred dollars an hour or more, and they're backlogged. I'll just have to deal with it.' She sounded angry, but not at Lexi.

'I don't charge at all for my time. And I listen just as well.'

As if in a daze, Holly opened the door and let her inside, still holding the business card, although she gave it only a quick glance.

Despite the bright afternoon, the small apartment was dim with the blinds drawn. 'I've read the police report and done some additional research, but I'd like to hear your version. I promise I'll listen with an open mind.'

Holly seemed reticent but detached, kept her gaze averted. A part of her was probably still lost out in that forest, trapped in memories of whatever had happened to her there. The young woman sat on the corner of the sofa, implicitly inviting Lexi to take the adjacent chair. She clutched her hands together in her lap.

'I told them everything. Search parties were combing the forest looking for me, and the police and the rangers promised they would catch the man who did this.' She let out a bitter laugh. 'But who can find Bigfoot?'

'There've been sightings in the area for a long time,' Lexi said. 'Many people around here believe in Sasquatch, and some of the national forest is deep, deep wilderness.'

'I was naïve and stupid.' Holly looked up, and her mouth twisted into a frightened grimace. 'I've hiked with friends countless times, but most of them can't keep up with me. I've been doing the Ring the Peak trail in segments, never thought twice about hiking alone. I had my pepper spray, and I was more worried about mountain lions and bears. Those are the real dangers, right? What hiker worries about Bigfoot?' She put her face in her hands and began to cry.

'I'm so sorry. I can't imagine . . .'

The young woman didn't seem to hear her. 'He came right out of the trees, down a hillside, long matted hair, big hairy chest. I think he was seven feet tall and strong. What was I supposed to do? Where could I run? I was miles from anything, and I hadn't seen another hiker all day.

'I screamed and ran, but he bounded after me.

Each of his strides was worth two of mine, and I had already done eleven miles that day.' She breathed harder, faster. 'I was losing ground. I stopped and fumbled for the bear spray in my pack, but I couldn't get to it fast enough.' She blinked. 'I was so stupid. What would I have done if a mountain lion attacked? I should have kept the spray in easy reach.'

Her voice hitched. 'Then he grabbed me, hit me so hard on the back of my head that my ears rang and I couldn't see straight. He punched me in the stomach and my legs went weak, and he dragged me off. I'll never forget the look on his face, in his eyes. Why would he do that? Why would he take me?'

She looked at Lexi as if expecting answers, but in all her research she'd never read anything about an assault like this. In other Bigfoot sightings, the skittish creature always fled.

'He took me deep into the forest, far off the trail. There was a rock overhang and some kind of lean-to with a fire pit. I guess it must have been his home. He held me there and he . . . he . . . When I fought too hard, he hit my head against a rock so that I couldn't resist. He didn't say anything, just forced himself on me whenever he liked. He kept me tied up.'

Lexi didn't need to see the distraught look on Holly's face to know that something truly had happened to her, something violent and soul shaking.

'On the third morning, he left at dawn, maybe to go hunt. Once I was alone, I fought and twisted and managed to break the rope around my wrists, untied my legs. I threw on my pants and T-shirt, shoved my feet into my hiking boots, and I just ran. I left my backpack behind. I left everything. I didn't yell for help because I knew it wouldn't do any good. Who would hear me out there, other than . . . him? I didn't even know where I was going.

'I stumbled on to a trail after a few hours, and I just followed it. A while later, I bumped into other hikers, and they had cell phone reception. They called in a rescue party.' Holly shuddered. 'I could never find that place again, and I don't want to.'

She shook her head, and her shoulders slumped as she sat on the sofa. 'But in some ways it's just as bad being back home. Some people think it's a joke. They laugh at what happened to me. But it was Bigfoot! I saw him, all covered with hair. I felt his big hands hitting me. I felt . . .' She hitched a deep breath and looked down at Lexi's business card. She seemed to be coming back from a distant place. 'Who did you say you are again?'

'Just someone who will listen.' Lexi felt as shaken as this woman looked.

Curious, Holly pulled out her phone and went to HideTruth. When the screen came up, her face darkened. 'I'm so stupid. Get out of here!'

Lexi held up her hands in a placating gesture as she stood from the chair. 'I don't mean any harm. I promise I won't post any of this, if you don't want me to. I'm just trying to understand.'

'Get out!' Holly screamed.

Lexi retreated quickly. 'I swear I won't post

this or give any details. I just wanted to know if it was real.'

'You're asking me if it was *real*!?' Her face was red and outraged. 'Fuck you. Fuck all of you!'

Lexi retreated through the front door. She spoke in her sincerest voice. 'I believe you, Holly. I really do.'

When the door slammed and she heard the lock click, Lexi felt like shit.

Fourteen

The bitter smoke of campfires hung among the trees. The man stood shaking in terror as the people muttered, uneasy about what they knew he had done.

Lucius hardened his heart. This was the difficult but necessary part about leading the Bastion. 'It is what it is.'

Roland was a big brute who normally inspired fear, towering nearly seven feet with long, tangled brown hair, a bushy beard that had never seen comb or razor. His eyebrows sprouted like feathers above his big brown eyes. Roland's neck, shoulders, and arms were covered with a pelt of wiry brown fur, enough to keep him warm even in the autumn chill so that he needed to wear nothing more than an old brown pair of overalls. The hirsute man groaned deep in his throat, shook his head from side to side, swaying his long locks.

'No . . . No . . .'

The settlement was scattered among the trees. Tarpaulins covered piles of cut firewood and crates of supplies, stockpiles that would be used throughout the winter. Tents and lean-tos formed the homes of the numerous families. Pots of coffee or soup hung over cook fires, while some preferred to use small butane burners or camp stoves. Bastion members who desired less social interaction had their own tents out in the surrounding forest. The entire camp could pack up and vanish in the space of an hour, should they be exposed.

Lucius stood before the prisoner, as implacable as a statue. Though dwarfed by the hairy giant, he showed no fear. He was the leader of the Bastion, and all the people had gathered around in judgment.

'We took you in, Roland. We helped you. We put up with a lot.'

'No,' the big man said in a low phlegmy voice.

'You were one of us.'

'Bastion!' Roland said. 'I am one of us.'

'Not anymore. Not after what you did.'

The giant dropped to his knees, crackling dry leaves on the forest floor. He sniffled and sobbed. Around the camp, people shuffled their feet, sad and sickened. But they had voted. They all agreed.

Roland was one of those outliers who made his home on the fringes, a man who liked to be left alone, yet craved company every week or so. Now the towering man had put them all in danger.

'What is the Bastion about?' Lucius asked the audience.

'Safety,' the people muttered in unison.

Roland groaned. 'I want to be safe!'

In one of the campfires, a knot in a log cracked and popped like a gunshot, startling them. Roland bowed his head, clawed dirty fingernails through his matted hair.

Lucius continued. 'We have to stay hidden. The outsiders can't know about us. We are the only ones who will survive whatever comes, but we only survive if we stay safe! You exposed us, Roland. You found a hiker, you grabbed her, and you hurt her.'

'No . . . didn't hurt her,' Roland said. 'She was my mate.'

'She was not! You hurt her. You raped her.'

'I was lonely.'

The hairy man's depths of abject misery almost moved Lucius, but he steeled himself.

He glanced over at Mama. She looked beautiful in her new fleece jacket. If Lucius didn't do what was necessary, he knew Mama was strong enough to do it herself. 'If you were lonely, then come to us for company.'

Roland had always been a misfit, unlike the better-adjusted members of the Bastion who could make trips back into the city if necessary. The hairy man was born to be isolated in the wilderness. He could never survive in a complic-ated, civilized world. He was slow-witted, gener-ally friendly, and wore his emotions right out in the open. But he had never before exhibited violence.

103

Whenever Roland was angry or frustrated, he would run deep into the forest and just scream at the top of his lungs until he felt better. Lucius had taught him that, and he had thought it was enough to keep him stable. Afterward, Roland would return to the Bastion, smiling as if all had been forgotten.

But this . . . this couldn't be forgotten.

'You hurt a young woman, Roland, and she will never be the same – because of you. Worse, you brought attention from the outsiders. For days, rangers and search-and-rescue teams combed the forest . . . We are lucky that someone didn't stumble upon remnants of one of our camps.

'I don't want to be lonely,' Roland said.

'Because of what you did, you will be more lonely than ever,' he answered in a hard voice. Parents placed consoling arms around their young children. They stood with intent gazes.

Roland was well liked among the Bastion. They sympathized with him, as if he were a family pet or a mascot, but no one questioned Lucius's decision. He could have taken an even harder line. *It is what it is.*

Mama came up beside him and took his hand to give him strength.

Lucius pronounced, 'You are exiled. You need to go far away. Leave the camp, leave our home, go into the far hills. Live by yourself, with no contact from any of us until spring. You get no help, no supplies, no conversation. You're alone.'

The other members of the Bastion stepped closer to Lucius, standing together to present a united front, leaving Roland on the outside.

'What am I supposed to do?' he said.

Lucius didn't let his heart melt. 'Take your supplies, find a cave or build a shelter, but go far away. You know how to hunt. If you are desperate, you know where we've hidden emergency caches in the woods. Take them if you need them, but you may not ask us for help.'

As the shaggy man rose from his knees, he seemed to keep growing as he stood until he was enormous, dangerous looking. No wonder a mere glimpse of him would make people think of Sasquatch.

But now Roland was broken by what he had done. 'No,' he groaned again.

'Yes! And if we see you again before spring, the sentence will be harsher. We'll kill you if we have to.'

Gasps went around the camp, but again the people didn't argue.

'I have to keep us safe – and you are no longer part of the Bastion.'

Stumbling as if he were drunk, paralyzed with grief, Roland crashed out of the camp. At the outer fringe of Ponderosa pines, he turned back, as if hoping they would change their minds.

The members of the Bastion remained silent. Lucius took Mama's arm.

Finally, the hairy man stalked into the forest, devastated. Come spring, Lucius would track him down, but for now he felt shaky with relief.

Fifteen

Working online at home detached Lexi from clocks, calendars, and normal human routines. Some entrepreneurs called it freedom, the ability to set her own hours, to run her own business, to take a day off whenever she didn't want to work. But if she didn't complete her work, she didn't get paid.

Thankfully, Blair kept to a regular schedule, and that grounded her. He worked his day job at Rags to Riches three or four days a week and served cocktails at Olive U on weekends and other nights.

Tonight, though, Blair had the Happy Hour shift, so he had to leave before dinner. He dressed in a trim blazer and a pewter-colored raw-silk shirt. Sometimes on Fridays he liked to party after he got off work.

'You'll feed yourself, Lex?' he asked, more to reassure himself than to remind her. If he didn't check on her, she would subsist on granola bars, cold cereal, and microwaved dinners. And he did not find that acceptable.

'I'll order a pizza or something. Don't worry about me.'

She went back to her room to work, spending hours for PRUUF and more hours pulling up the weeds of phishing addresses. She remained unsettled by her clumsy and disastrous conversation with Holly Smith. What had she been thinking? Her heart was in the right place and she wanted to be understanding, but the young woman would never believe that now. Lexi wasn't trying to profit from a victim's misery, didn't see herself as a predatory reporter. But her actions were – she had to admit – creepy.

After spending so much time with social misfits and fanatics on her website, had she lost all of her own social skills and common sense? Had she forgotten how normal humans interacted, especially in a tragedy? By claiming to be a sympathetic ear and saying that she was open to hearing more about Bigfoot, Lexi had hoped the other woman might see her as a friend. Not too bright.

She shook her head and felt the hard weight in her heart, the twisting of guilt and dismay as if she had scorpions instead of butterflies in her stomach. No matter her innocent intentions, she had certainly put her foot in it. She hoped Holly didn't file a harassment complaint with the police.

Later, she was shocked to see that it was 1:45 a.m., and the growling in her stomach reminded her that she hadn't, after all, called for her pizza. Knowing Blair would scold her if she admitted that, Lexi picked up a flyer for Checkers Pizza, which delivered 24 hours. She placed an order for a large pepperoni and black olives so she would have leftovers in the fridge.

Even when she was home alone, Lexi left her bedroom door mostly closed, a habitual concession to privacy that came from living with a housemate. She had been in her room for so long that the rest of the house was dark, the lights off in the hall, kitchen, and living room.

Waiting for her pizza, she went back on HideTruth and was annoyed to find even more offensive, crude troll postings about Bigfoot sex, and in disgust she deleted them all. 'Enough of this shit.'

Annoyed and unsettled, Lexi switched to the vampire thread to read what was new on the stake killing. Stoker1897 had again posted his theories – lists of mysterious deaths that might have been vampire victims, missing persons that could have been drained of blood and conveniently eliminated.

Lexi compiled and posted a summary of related materials she had found in addition to Stoker1897's evidence – not just the details on the Mark Stallings murder, but the possible other stake killings in California and Texas from years past, as well as the decapitated meth dealer in Colorado Springs whose head had not yet been found. She organized the list, made connections, and presented a compelling argument.

'It's all circumstantial,' she typed, 'but it's still evidence. I've submitted this to the Colorado Springs Police Department tip line, but they have not yet responded. If vampires do exist in our society, infiltrating night jobs, feeding on innocent humans and then erasing all sign of their presence, how can we prove it? We certainly won't know if we don't look.'

One of the trolls on the deleted Bigfoot thread popped up, accusing her of censorship, of hiding the truth, calling her a patsy for the puppet masters. She deleted that comment too, knowing there would probably be more. What if one of those trolls turned into a sick stalker like Dicked Over? It was her site, dammit!

By now it was after two in the morning. She was so intent on her work that she was startled to hear a noise, the click of the door, someone moving furtively inside the house. A chill went down her back and she froze, listening through her half-closed door. Hearing no sound for a long moment, she wondered if she was just jumpy from all the mysterious things on her site. Then she heard a thump as someone bumped into a chair. The living room was dark, and the bright light in her own room reduced her ability to see in the shadows.

She backed to her bed, dreading that this was finally the day she had feared. Another stalker tracking her down? She slid open the nightstand drawer and removed the loaded .38. Ready to go. Damn, she wished she had gone to the range more often, but she had never intended to shoot anyone. The point of the big revolver was to serve as a threat, but she wasn't sure she had it in her. She calmed herself. The reason she had chosen this weapon was because she could just point it and shoot. She wrapped her fingers around the grip, held the gun firmly in her hand. The revolver felt alien, dangerous, yet comforting. With her thumb, she cocked it so she could pull the trigger more easily.

She heard someone stumbling around in the dark front room; there was no doubt about it now.

Lexi yanked open her door, flooding the hall

and the main room with light, and lunged out, barely able to see. 'Who the hell are you? What are you doing in my house?'

The light shone upon Blair in his rumpled blazer and pewter shirt. He shielded his eyes, wearing a foolish grin. When he saw the gun she held, he recoiled, raised his hands and took a step back. 'Jesus, Lex! Welcome home to you too.' She quickly uncocked and lowered the revolver, shaking. His words were a little slurred, and he walked toward her with an unsteady gait.

So relieved she wanted to laugh and cry at the same time, Lexi set the weapon safely back on the desk in her room. 'You scared the crap out of me, creeping around in the dark! Why didn't you just announce yourself?'

'Didn't want to turn on the lights, didn't want to bother you.' As if he had forgotten about the gun, Blair appeared happy, even giddy, and much more tipsy than she normally saw him.

'You're out late,' she said.

'Late . . . or early. Maybe, just maybe, I got lucky.' He laughed and started humming. 'I think I need to go to bed.' Again, he gave her a wolfish smile. 'The most wonderful, amazing guy. He's come into the martini bar six times, and he just couldn't resist my charms. Cesar.' Blair inhaled a long breath and let it out. 'Isn't that just the most charming name? *Cesar.*' He dropped his voice to a scandalous whisper. 'I may be late a lot more often, if things keep going well.'

Humming to himself, he strolled down the hall with alarmingly liquid footsteps, and closed the door to his room.

Still unsettled, Lexi returned the .38 to her nightstand drawer and closed it safely out of sight. She decided to just go to bed. Yes, tomorrow would be a better one. Enough drama for one day.

She had just pulled off her socks and found the oversized T-shirt she slept in when the doorbell rang. Lexi groaned, remembering the pizza she had ordered. She turned on the living-room light, dazzled by the brightness, and opened the front door to find a thin, thirty-ish man in a Checkers Pizza shirt and cap. He held a flat cardboard box that smelled amazingly of pepperoni. She realized how hungry she was after all.

'Late-night pizza.' The man had a ragged brown beard, long straight hair, and intense blue eyes under the bill of his cap. Checkers wasn't the best pizza, but it was the best pizza at two o'clock in the morning.

'Thanks.' She took the box with her left hand and dug into her jeans pocket, pulling out a twenty-dollar bill.

'It's twelve dollars,' said the delivery man. 'I'm afraid I don't have change.'

That was odd. She set the pizza box on the small table beside the door. 'Let me get my purse.'

The pizza delivery man stood awkwardly on the porch, just on the threshold. He looked into the empty house, and when he saw no one else there, his demeanor changed. 'Can I come inside while I wait? It's cold out here.' His voice had an odd accent. Russian? Eastern European?

In an automatic polite gesture, Lexi was about to invite him inside, but she paused. A chill went

111

down her back. It was a cool autumn night, but pleasant, not frigid. The delivery man stared, waiting for her to say the words and invite him in. What kind of pizza guy carried no change? Wore no jacket and then complained about the cold? Her skin began to crawl after a long awkward moment. 'I . . . no, I wouldn't feel comfortable with that. Just wait there.'

He kept staring at her with intense blue eyes. 'I am no threat, I promise. All my deliveries are logged by the company. It would just be nice if—'

'Keep the change.' She thrust the twenty-dollar bill into his hand and closed the door in his face.

Her pulse was racing. What was going on? She was jittery because of reading about hidden vampires, stake murders, and Bigfoot assaults. She'd seen too many movies, knew too many superstitions. Vampires couldn't enter a house unless they were invited in. Wasn't that what the legends said?

She locked the door, threw the deadbolt, wondering if the pizza man was still standing out there, inches from the door and waiting for her to change her mind. Lexi realized she was spooking herself.

She picked up the pizza box, no longer hungry after all. She put the entire thing in the refrigerator.

Sixteen

Detective Carrow felt little sympathy for a scumbag meth dealer. Patric Ryan was a known quantity, slimy enough to slip out of any significant jail time because evidence disappeared and charges were dropped – usually because his victims were also his customers, and preferred to remain customers rather than see Ryan in jail. Carrow knew he was a bad man.

Still, seeing the partially decomposed head tangled in the weeds made him feel a little sorry for the creep.

The steep bank of Monument Creek was rocky and cluttered with scrub brush and urban flotsam. Carrow worked his way down from the bike path above, grumbling. From the greenway trail, a jogger had spotted feasting crows in the underbrush at the bottom of the incline, thinking it was an odd piece of washed-up garbage. Patric Ryan was a different kind of garbage, but that was Carrow's opinion.

By the time Carrow arrived, the crime-scene techs had already worked their way down the embankment to the muddy drainage. Monument Creek and the greenway trail wound through downtown Colorado Springs on the east side of the Interstate. At this time of year the water was mostly a trickle, though a late-season storm a few days ago had increased the flow – enough to wash a severed head downstream.

Planting his left shoe on a stable boulder and his right on the gravelly mud of the bank, Carrow bent closer to the bloated head. After the decapitated body had been identified by fingerprints, he had seen Ryan's face on his rap sheet. The decomposing face bore little resemblance to his mug shot. The jellied eyes were mostly gone, pecked by scavenger birds, and teeth showed through drooping lips. His shaved head was still wrapped in a tight skull-and-crossbones bandana.

'Drug dealer,' Carrow muttered. 'Call central casting.'

Beside him, Mel let out a deep chuckle and grinned with his big porn-star mustache. 'Good one, Detective.'

A second crime-scene tech strung yellow police tape around the vicinity, even though no casual curiosity seeker would wander down the embankment to have a look. Carrow looked up and down the watershed, heard the trickle of the stream, the rustle of dry weeds. Crows cawed in the bushes, impatiently waiting for the humans to leave so they could get back to their feast. The head was far from where the rest of the body had been dumped, and enough time had passed that he didn't expect to find any peripheral evidence.

With gloved hands, Mel pressed against both sides of Ryan's head, careful to keep the bandana in place as he rocked it back and forth to loosen it from the mud, grimacing. When he lifted the head free, it made a slurping sound. 'Ewww.'

The second tech came forward with a plastic

evidence bag. 'Trick or treat.' Mel dropped the head in and sealed the bag.

Carrow listened to the hum of traffic from I-25 not far away. Cyclists whizzed past on the greenway path above, but he saw no one else down by the water. Groups of homeless sometimes camped out of sight in the weedy barrens on land that no one else wanted.

Whoever had decapitated the meth dealer had dumped his body among the weeds. Either the head had been washed downstream or someone had moved it. Carrow decided to canvas some of the homeless downtown, see if they had witnessed anything, but they would probably be afraid if a thug like Chop Chop was murdering people like Ryan and Stallings. The brutality of the act left Carrow uneasy. Maybe the next victim wouldn't be such a scumbag.

In the autopsy room, the coroner removed the head from the plastic bag and propped it in an empty plastic tray the size of a litter box. Orla Watson hummed as she regarded the specimen. 'Want me to remove the rest of the body from the refrigerator? Just to make sure the stump ends match up, Part A and Part B?'

'Don't make my life more complicated. Is there any doubt the head belongs with that body? Do we have other unidentified headless corpses lying around?'

Watson gave him a thin smile. 'Just want to take care of every detail, especially right before the election. I'm the best coroner El Paso County's ever had, and I want to keep my job for a few more years.' A few of her campaign lawn signs remained in the corner of the room.

He tried to sound enthusiastic. 'You've got my vote.'

'Stupid politics,' she muttered. 'Is a coroner supposed to shake hands and kiss babies on a campaign? It seems ridiculous. Walter was even going to write a catchy little jingle to run on the radio.'

What an awful idea, Carrow thought. 'Can't wait to hear it.'

Watson bent toward the head and used forceps to peel back the bandana, removing the fabric from the discolored skin and setting it aside. She took photos, poked and prodded the scalp. Shifting position, she looked at the ragged neck. 'The killer used two different blades, which I already determined by analyzing the opposing stump on the torso. His throat was sawed with a large sharp knife, but the spine was probably too hard to cut through. Looks like a hatchet was used to finish the decapitation.'

'The right tool for the right job.'

With her gloved fingers the coroner pulled back the lips, tapped the teeth, then pried open the jaw. The tongue was swollen, but Ryan's mouth was not entirely empty. 'Maybe something interesting.' She inserted her narrow forceps into the mouth cavity and probed around. 'What is this, *Silence of the Lambs*?' She withdrew a soft, yellowish object about the size of a hazelnut. 'Several of these in there.'

Carrow came closer. 'What is it?'

Intent on her work, Watson used the forceps to

remove three more pale lumps. 'I believe they were inserted post-mortem. Not likely he kept them in his mouth as his head was chopped off.'

Carrow felt a chill as he thought of the violent message the killer might have been trying to send. 'Like a mobster stuffing a severed penis in a victim's mouth.'

'Might be the same sort of thing, Detective.' She poked the objects with the tip of the forceps. Despite the sickly smell of decay, she leaned closer and inhaled deeply. 'It's garlic, I think.'

'Garlic? Who would stuff garlic in a victim's mouth?'

Watson turned to him with her owlish eyes. 'You know what that means, of course.'

'A mouth full of garlic? Is it the Italian mafia?'

The coroner rolled her eyes. 'Cutting off the head and stuffing the mouth with garlic? Doesn't that sound at all familiar, Detective? It's purported to be an effective means of killing a vampire.'

'They teach you these things in coroner school?' He looked at the head and the garlic cloves at the bottom of the tray. 'I won't deny that beheading is effective. Sort of an all-purpose solution.'

The coroner paused impatiently, then prodded, 'Hello, Detective? *Vampires*?'

He thought again of the severed hands and feet of Chop Chop's victims, who had been forced to stagger and crawl on their bleeding stumps before they finally died. 'A sick drug lord is easier to believe.'

'Even after the stake through Stallings' heart? I think the message is that the killer believes in vampires. Or at least wants someone to think he does. Run an internet search and brush up on your vampire lore. You might need to know it.'

Her words triggered a connection in his mind. 'Wait – after the Stallings murder, we did get a crank call on the tip line. I think the caller even mentioned the beheading, trying to draw a connection between the two cases. She said to look for garlic if we ever found the head.' He looked over at her desk. 'Can I use your computer?'

'Just don't play games on it.' She went back to studying the head, which seemed to fascinate her.

Carrow accessed his CSPD account to review his case records and the logged tip-line reports. 'Here it is, someone offering a handy list of ways to kill vampires.' He had skimmed the tip when it came in, but dismissed it. 'Alexis Tarada, a vampire enthusiast who wants to be a helpful citizen.' Tarada had even included a link to her website. He clicked on HideTruth.

When he saw the home page filled with conspiracy theories, his shoulders slumped. 'Crap almighty, you've got to be kidding me.'

Seventeen

So many targets to choose from, but Helsing had to hunt carefully. He needed to be sure.

After leaving the VA hospital in the San

Francisco Bay Area, he wandered from place to place. Making his way down across Arizona and Texas, then up to Colorado, Helsing had killed *lampir*, disposed of the bodies, wiped everything clean, and moved on. For a long time, he called no attention to his work. The fact that his vampire killings had caused no uproar made him certain he was right. When no one reported the disappearances, to him that meant the vampires themselves were helping cover it up in order to maintain their low profile.

From the start, Helsing had considered this his private war, but now he wanted other people to know about the threat. Change of tactics. He had left the staked body of Mark Stallings where it would be found, as well as the decapitated drug dealer, an insidious monster who addicted his prey so he could feed on them more easily. Once the vampire threat became obvious to the public, the sheep in Colorado Springs might awaken to the danger lurking among them.

Unfortunately, by making his crusade more obvious, he also let the *lampir* know that someone was hunting them. They would be wary, which would make them more and more difficult to kill. Helsing doubted the vampires knew his identity. Yet.

He'd gone back to the Rambler Star Motel as his base, though he was careful not to grow too comfortable there. He didn't mind sleeping in the homeless camps, but he needed certain tools and resources to do his work. Searching on the room's old computer, he had narrowed down his leads. Next, he set about conducting careful in-person surveillance to focus his list of potential targets even further. Using the creaking laser printer, he had assembled a large file of evidence and potential targets in a manila folder. He had eliminated more than a dozen possibilities already, which only made him more certain about the names that remained on the list.

As dusk set in outside, he sat on the corner of the bed with the wastebasket propped between his knees. After collecting several pine stakes taken from the scrap pile of the lumberyard, he sharpened them with his large knife. He sat in absolute silence, not turning on the television; he didn't care about the news or any kind of entertainment.

Each stroke of the long blade curled off a ribbon of wood, honing the stake to a deadly point. The smell of the fresh pine reminded him of learning woodcraft with Lucius out in the forest.

Before joining the Bastion community, Helsing had survived for a long time on his own. He knew how to find food and shelter, day by day. He had panhandled, harvested dumpsters, found help among other down-on-their-luck people. Members of the Bastion, though, were not unfortunate, but rather a network of like-minded people who had chosen their way of life in order to survive any number of imminent catastrophes they feared. Helsing was part of that extended family, but he worked solo. Ever since his ordeal in Bosnia, he realized how few people understood the magnitude of the *lampir* threat.

He scraped with the knife again. The edge was razor sharp, and the soft pine was like butter. He finished one stake, rolled it over in his palm, and concluded that the wicked tip would penetrate a vampire's heart. He set it on the bedspread and picked up the next piece of wood.

That afternoon he had gone to the Pikes Peak Library and taken advantage of their public internet access to post as Stoker1897 on HideTruth. Though he found the site users interesting, he placed little stock in them. Most were lunatics who believed in nonsensical conspiracy theories, but he only needed to convince one or two to help him on his mission.

Alexis Tarada seemed sympathetic to his postings and unlike many people she actually had an open mind. She had even defended him in a couple of flame wars when other users disputed his conclusions. She was skeptical herself, but out of caution, not foolishness. Helsing was keeping an eye on her. If he could convince the right people, he might even encourage government action and maybe the FBI would begin an all-out vampire eradication program.

Unless there were already vampires inside the FBI, and other branches of government . . .

From his research and observations, Helsing suspected that a highly influential king vampire had a lair in Colorado Springs, manipulating his minions, pulling puppet strings. Helsing had to be careful about trusting anyone.

He had been mocked too much because of his experience in Bosnia. He had learned the true nature of the threat, the *lampir*, but when he tried to discuss the danger with his superior officers, he'd only received looks of patronizing sympathy, even scorn. His case was transferred from person to person, until he was diagnosed with post-traumatic stress disorder and paranoid delusions. A nutcase. The military considered him an embarrassment and didn't want him telling his vampire story to anyone, so they did what they could to hide him from sight.

Around the same time, another American serviceman, Captain Scott O'Grady, had been shot down in the Balkans. He had survived for a week in the dense forest, eating bugs, running from enemy Serb fire. After Marines rescued O'Grady, *he* was welcomed home as a hero.

But poor David Grundy received no compassion, no hero's welcome, no crowds clamoring for his story. He'd come home a mess, bounced from one VA hospital to another.

He had grown up in a military family, and his parents were not warm people. His father was tough as nails, an officer who never missed a chance to point out his son's inadequacies. His mother was also judgmental, without a maternal bone in her body.

Just before Grundy was sent to Bosnia, his father was diagnosed with colon cancer and tried to tough it out, insisting that he was going to beat the disease, but he died even sooner than the doctors predicted. Soon thereafter, his mother got herself a new husband along with two more acceptable, full-grown children. When Grundy came back from Bosnia damaged from his terrible experience, she abandoned him – filing her son in the same memory drawer as her first husband – and moved on with her new life.

The VA hospital's universal solution was to treat returning soldiers with plenty of drugs, prescription after prescription. In California, they gave him therapy to deal with his nightmares. When the doctors insisted that his convictions were just delusions, he had snapped at them, 'Your therapy assumes that there's nothing real to fear. But what if there is?'

Sitting face to face with one psychiatrist, he hoped to make a compelling argument when he told the story of Herbert Mullin, a serial killer who murdered thirteen people in the San Francisco area in the 1970s. The killing spree had garnered a great deal of media attention. Mullin hadn't launched the killing spree out of any sort of sadistic pleasure; rather, after receiving a 'vision', he was absolutely certain that a devastating earthquake was about to strike northern California, which would destroy the Bay Area and kill hundreds of thousands. The only way to prevent the quake, according to his vision, was to make thirteen sacrifices. Mullin blatantly murdered the appropriate number of people, making little effort to cover his tracks. And when he was done, having accomplished his purpose, he surrendered himself to the authorities. He had done what he felt was necessary.

The VA therapist researched Mullin and came back with a counter-argument. 'Mullin was sentenced to life imprisonment, Mr Grundy. He was found to be insane.'

Grundy leaned forward, jabbing a finger toward the man's sagging face. 'Maybe, but no earthquake devastated northern California, did it?

What if Mullin wasn't crazy? What if his vision was a true premonition? What if he was *right*? Yes, he was a murderer, I don't dispute that. He killed thirteen people. But what if he saved countless thousands by doing so? We'll never know.'

The exasperated therapist wrote something down. He did not look convinced.

Grundy was institutionalized for several years, received countless psychiatric evaluations. They covered up his story – probably because he knew the truth about the *lampir*. Eventually, he was released from the VA hospital when there was no more funding and no more interest in treating him.

That was only the start of his crusade.

In his mind he became a new person, Simon Helsing, and began his real life's work. After wandering and working for years, one day while eating lunch at the Colorado Springs mission, he had met Lucius, and a new doorway opened for him. He told Lucius his fears and his mission. He found the Bastion and his calling.

The knife scraped down the pine, finishing another sharp point. He set the completed stakes aside, five of them. He would also hone the edge of the hunting knife, in case he decided to cut off another head.

Brushing pine shavings off his jeans and tidying around the wastebasket, Helsing went to the desk, opened the manila folder, and reviewed possible *lampir*.

It was time to get rid of another one, before they killed again.

Eighteen

Lexi opened the front door only to have a badge flashed in her face. It was more startling than intimidating.

'Detective Todd Carrow,' said the man in a gruff voice. 'Looking for Alexis Tarada with some questions.'

She felt as if she were in a scene from some cop show. 'That's me.'

She kept him standing on the porch, just as she had with the pizza delivery man. The detective was less impressive than his badge, only a few inches taller than Lexi. He wore a dark gray sport jacket, slacks, white shirt, tie. His dark brown hair was dusted with gray, and a few extra pounds rested heavily on his face and belly.

'What is this about?' With a sick feeling in the pit of her stomach, she wondered if Holly Smith had filed a complaint. She tried to keep a poker face.

Carrow said, 'I'm here to follow up on a tip you sent after reports of the stake murder.'

Surprised and relieved, Lexi let him in. 'Yes I did. Always happy to help.' She suddenly frowned as another thought occurred to her. 'Wait, I left my email and cell phone, not my home address. How did you find me?'

Carrow attempted a wry smile in response to the question. 'I'm a detective. They teach us those kind of things. I feel obligated to track down all possibilities.'

'Good to hear. I always advocate keeping an open mind. Did you find any other evidence of vampires?' She led him inside to the living room, where he took a seat on the sofa. She went to the adjacent kitchen. 'I don't have any coffee made. You'll have to put up with my meager skills as a hostess.' She could easily brew a mug for herself and the detective with the single-cup machine. Blair was sleeping late, exhausted from having gone out with his new flame Cesar every night since their first date. He was walking on air . . . whenever he wasn't sleeping in.

The detective pulled out a notebook. 'As you might guess, we received a lot of crank calls and tips after the stake killing. I'm checking up on all of them.'

She bristled and replied with brittle sarcasm, 'And I was one of the crank calls?'

'You did tell us to look for other vampires rather than the killer himself.' He shrugged as if the conclusion was self-evident. 'I looked at your website and found it . . . imaginative. You have a lot of followers who believe extreme stuff.'

'I'm skeptical of most of it, but I won't dismiss everything outright.' Lexi found it hard to warm to him. 'And yet you're here, so maybe something rang true in my message? Did you find anything suspicious about the stake victim? Are you sure he was human?' She knew she was going over-board, but she wanted to push him to think out of the box.

'No, Miss Tarada. The victim was perfectly

normal in every respect, except for the pointy piece of wood in the middle of his chest.' Carrow flipped a page in his notebook. 'I'm here because yesterday we found the head of a previous murder victim, Patric Ryan. Your tip to us – long before we discovered the head – was to look for garlic in the mouth.' He leaned toward her. 'That's exactly what we found. How did you know about the garlic? Want to tell me why you suggested that detail? Do you know something about the two victims? What made you think the cases were connected?'

Lexi placed her hands on her knees. 'I didn't say they were connected. I suggested that you *check*. One guy is murdered with a stake through his heart, another guy has his head cut off. It's only natural to wonder if there's garlic in the mouth.'

Carrow paused with his pen and he looked at her, raising his eyebrows. 'Natural? My instinct was to think they were gang mutilations, meant to send a message and incite fear.'

'And vampires wouldn't even occur to you,' she replied, not making it into a question. 'I have a unique perspective. You've seen my site. I think about these things every day.' She felt her cheeks flush. 'I sent you the list of commonly known methods for killing vampires. If there's a severed head, of course you look for garlic in the mouth. But you probably weren't thinking about real vampires.'

'Not one of my concerns on a regular basis. It was our first severed head.'

'And so you have a hard time connecting the

dots. It's the reason I called in to the tip line – and I was right, wasn't I? You need to think about vampires more often, or you won't solve this case. It'll give you an entirely different perspective. And if the victims were real vampires, then the man who killed them might be a hero, not a murderer.'

Carrow seemed taken aback. 'A hero? You clearly didn't see the crime scenes, Miss Tarada.'

Lexi pressed. 'Now that you know, maybe it'll help you think outside the box. Did the blood analysis show anything . . . unusual?' She wasn't sure exactly what kind of test would identify a vampire by blood type, but surely there would be some anomalies. 'Any possibility that either victim might have been a . . .' It sounded silly as soon as she said it. 'A real vampire?'

The detective struggled to maintain his composure. 'Don't be ridiculous. We did standard tests, but the cause of death seemed pretty obvious. Headless victim was a drug dealer, and his blood samples showed traces of crystal meth in his system, no big surprise. Stake victim was clean, nothing unusual. We're trying to figure out if he was connected to drugs or gangs in any way.' He huffed. 'To the best of our knowledge, neither was a real vampire.'

Lexi wondered why Carrow had even come here. 'I'm not sure standard tests would be sufficient.' She remembered all the arguments Stoker1897 had made, trying to establish a compelling case. 'If vampires do exist, they've hidden in society for quite a long time, so any differences would be very subtle.'

'R-i-i-i-ght,' said Carrow.

Lexi persisted, even though she saw he wasn't actually open to possibilities. 'Have you looked into the activities of the two victims? Imagine that they might have been vampires – or at least *looked* like vampires to the person who killed them. I suspect that neither one had any close family. They probably worked entirely at night, were never seen during the day.'

Carrow was clearly put off-balance by her unexpected line of reasoning. 'Yes, on both counts. But drug dealers often have business hours after dark, and Stallings was a night-time clerk at a twenty-four-hour convenience store. I'm sure if I dug through his employment records, I could find a day shift here or there, but doing that would take a lot of hours and manpower, and for what purpose? I'm trying to find a killer, not raise suspicion about the victims.'

'Unless they really were vampires,' Lexi said. 'The victims are what connect the killer. Why did he pick them?'

Carrow was growing impatient with her. 'And maybe I'll run tests for werewolves next time I pull over a drunk driver during a full moon.'

Lexi hardened her voice with sarcasm. 'If it's a werewolf, then he wouldn't be driving during a full moon. He would be fully transformed.'

Carrow clearly shut down. 'Write all you want about monsters and ghosts and aliens on your website, but I'm dealing with a real murderer who's killed two victims so far.'

'Maybe more.' Lexi reminded him of the other suspicious bodies she had found listed in the police database. 'And you might want to have a second look at your missing-persons list. A real vampire hunter might not leave all his kills out in the open.'

Carrow changed the subject and pressed, 'Did you have any personal contact with Mark Stallings? Or with Patric Ryan? Were you one of Ryan's customers?'

'I don't do drugs, though my housemate makes an excellent basil martini.' Seeing his expression, she answered him definitively. 'No, Detective. I never met Stallings, never purchased drugs from Ryan. I don't have any connection to either victim. On the tip line, I was pointing out what seemed obvious to me but something I thought might not occur to you. I'm glad I did.'

Frowning, he shifted on the sofa. 'You're not going to convince me that vampires are walking among us.'

'I didn't think so, but at least I raised the question. Now it's on you. And remember, even if you don't want to believe in vampires, the killer certainly does.' She rose, signaling that the interview was over. 'Let me know how the investigation turns out. I'd be happy to post an interview with you on HideTruth.'

He looked as if he had swallowed a pickled onion whole. 'Don't think so, Miss Tarada. CSPD policy.' He rose to go. 'I will grant you the possibility that some nut job *believes* in vampires and is choosing victims based on what he considers to be suspicious nocturnal activities.' He closed his notebook and headed for the door. 'Vampires don't have to be real, but the killer certainly is.'

Nineteen

Branches snapped and twigs whipped in his face as Lucius charged through the forest, pursuing the eleven-year-old. He carried a menacing cudgel and bashed it against a pine bough, a loud threat that rattled the branches.

The terrified boy sprinted ahead in his wild and unplanned escape. His shoes scuffed the carpet of brown pine needles, and he slid down an embankment, catching his heels on a speckled granite boulder. The boy sprang up again and changed direction, following the terrain, choosing the path of least resistance. He had dark hair, almond eyes, and a face filled with fear.

Lucius roared after him, 'You know what I'll do when I catch you, Joshua!'

The kid ran with greater energy. When he screamed again, Lucius barked, 'That's a useless waste of breath. Unless you're near people, unless you're close to the Bastion camp, nobody can hear you scream.'

The boy fell silent, but kept running at breakneck speed.

Lucius bounded over a fallen tree, and when his hiking boot cracked down on a rotten limb, he stumbled, caught his balance, and ran after his quarry. Lucius kept his body toned, and his leg muscles were hardened from regular hikes. Joshua would burn out soon enough, but Lucius could keep going all day. It was only a matter of time. The energetic boy had a lot to learn about survival.

Joshua sprinted along a dry seasonal streambed choked with rocks and deadfall.

'Run and dodge!' Lucius called. 'If you don't stay ahead, if you don't get away, then you'll die.'

The boy came upon an overgrown hiking trail, a forgotten path that threaded through the national forest. No longer needing to fight through underbrush and boulders, he put on a burst of speed, but wasted time by repeatedly looking over his shoulder. His skin was flushed and red with exhaustion, his brown eyes wide with terror.

He pulled ahead, but only for a moment. As soon as Lucius reached the trail, he also picked up speed. He raised his voice in a taunt. 'The trail might look like a good idea, boy, but my stride is longer than yours.'

Joshua kept running, but he was panting hard. He couldn't continue at this pace for long. Lucius closed the gap within seconds. The boy glanced over his shoulder, reeling with fear.

'Each time you do that, you lose half a second!' Lucius snapped.

Joshua plunged along the straight path, when he should have dodged into the underbrush, since his smaller form could slip among branches and trunks that might hinder a bigger man like Lucius. He would have to hammer his lessons into the children. 'I've got my eyes on you. I'm fixed on you – and I won't get distracted.'

The kid screamed again. Lucius was growing

impatient. Time to end this. He drew upon his reserves, extended his stride, and reached forward with a swift surge. He grabbed the collar of Joshua's shirt and yanked him to a stop. The boy struggled and thrashed, but Lucius had him now.

He raised the ominous wooden club, leaned closer to the terrified face. Pine needles and dry leaves studded Lucius's wild hair and beard, and his eyes were fierce. He pressed his face close, curled back his lips to show imaginary fangs. 'Boo!'

Joshua laughed, and Lucius let him go. Heaving deep breaths, the boy sat down on a fallen log. 'I did better this time, didn't I?'

'But I still caught you. If I were a real monster, I would've torn open your throat to drink your blood.'

The boy didn't look afraid at all. 'You'd protect us. I know you would.'

'Believe whatever you want, but never let down your guard. In the end you are responsible for your own survival.' Lucius tossed the stick into the trees and pulled Joshua to his feet. 'Let's get back to the camp. Hurry, now. Mama should have the midday meal ready.'

The boy's expression fell. 'Can't we just rest for a while?'

'If I hear you say anything like that again, I'll make you *run* all the way back.'

Without further complaint, Joshua straightened and walked along the trail. Lucius kept pressing him. 'Were you paying attention as you ran? Can you find your way back?'

The young man frowned, insulted. 'I can always

find my way back! Even if I have to spend a night or two alone out in the forest, I know how to take care of myself. I know how to build a fire, and I know how to hunt.'

Lucius grinned. 'Good. I don't want to teach those lessons all over again.'

Together, they made their way through the trees. Before long, they could hear the sounds of cooking, low conversation, an axe cutting firewood in the Bastion camp. Resplendent in her new fleece, Mama was adding noodle soup packets to a large pot over the campfire, then burning the wrappers in the coals. Several other children ran about the camp, playing or helping with chores. Their ages ranged from toddlers to Joshua, the oldest. Two young men, fourteen and fifteen, were considered adults in the eyes of the Bastion, and they had normal duties. Many of the younger ones had never been to the city, which they viewed as a scary place infested with apocalyptic dangers, not to mention the more mundane terrors of civilization.

Mama saw Lucius and Joshua emerge from the trees and raised her spoon in greeting. 'You're back! How did he do?'

The other children came running. 'Is he dead?'

'Did the monster eat him?'

Lucius responded to the children with a grave nod. 'He's dead, alas, but I think some good soup will revive him.' He tousled Joshua's dark hair with a big hand.

'I got farther than last time.' The boy couldn't keep the pride out of his voice.

'But you're still running wild and acting on

panic,' Lucius scolded. 'We face many threats from the outside world, and we have to be ready for them. For instance, vampires are not wild beasts. They're intelligent – and so are you. You have to *think* if you're going to get away from them. And stop wasting time looking behind you. Look ahead!'

All the children listened, and Joshua nodded.

He looked at an eight-year-old girl helping Mama with the soup. 'Tomorrow it's Lily's turn. This will be your first monster chase.'

The girl's eyes were huge. 'Am I ready?'

'You're ready to start.' Lucius gave her a hug.

Mama ladled up a plastic cup of soup. Lucius stepped forward to take it, but she handed it to Joshua instead. 'He needs the nourishment, since he's dead and all.' Mama gave the boy a maternal smile. He took the soup and slurped it from the edge as he shuffled off toward his family's tent. The other children followed him, jabbering with questions.

Watching them, Lucius felt a genuine spark of hope. Mama said, 'You've made sure they're raised right.'

'I do what needs to be done. It is what it is.' Lucius was determined that all members of the Bastion would survive whatever holocaust mankind might inflict upon itself.

The world outside was a dangerous place with myriad threats, and his people were the only ones to see it. Like vampires, for instance. For the most part, they would remain in the cities, an easy feeding ground, but Simon Helsing's brash activities would have raised an alarm through whatever communication network the monsters had. Some of the *lampir* knew about the Bastion, and sometimes vampires even ventured into the deepest forest.

Lucius made sure his people were ready. The cost of failure was unthinkable.

Twenty

The Sarka Imports warehouse was surrounded by a chain-link fence topped with barbed wire, like a military installation. At night, garish floodlights illuminated the premises but also intensified the shadows. Helsing knew that artificial light did not have the purifying qualities of direct sunshine and had no effect on a vampire. This one maintained his camouflage as a night security guard.

Douglas Eldridge. Helsing had chosen him as his next target.

Sarka Import Specialists was in a rundown, half-empty business park just off Fillmore. The Sarka warehouse kept its windows covered, its doors locked even during the daytime. Other than the name on an unobtrusive sign, the building gave no information about the company or the business conducted inside.

Helsing knew that Sarka Imports brought in unmarked crates labeled with only code numbers or SKUs. Most of the crates originated in Eastern Europe, which in itself was a red flag, but he had plenty of other evidence. He wasn't able to access the company's shipping manifests, though he could imagine what sort of materials might benefit a secret society of vampires. Native soil perhaps for when they bedded down during the day? Coffins dug up from unhallowed graveyards and shipped to a new home? Maybe they just wanted their favorite pastries from Transylvania?

He still didn't know which legends were true and which were part of the disinformation campaign spread by vampires over the years. He had laid out superstitions and 'common knowledge' about vampires, some of which was obviously false. According to one tale, if a vampire was pursuing you, a wise victim could throw a broom or scatter a handful of grain in his path, and the monster would be compelled to count the strands of the broom or the number of grains. So, *lampir* were insufferably OCD? Helsing didn't think so, and he wouldn't count on that as a defense.

Religious symbols – crosses, holy water – purportedly worked, but that may have had more to do with the core faith of a victim rather than actual supernatural powers. He had seen photos of some of his prime candidates, including Eldridge, which called into question the rumor that vampires did not show up on film. Or did a digital photo have entirely different rules? And mirrors . . . He had seen some of his own targets reflected in mirrors, so maybe they had a defense against that as well.

Helsing would not let doubts get the best of him. The shadowy investors behind Sarka Imports were beyond his reach, at least for now, so he set his sights on an achievable goal. The night watchman was in there, hiding behind the imagined safety of his fence.

Avoiding streetlights, Helsing made his way to the back of the warehouse. He could hear something rustling through the dumpsters just outside the chain-link fence, probably a raccoon or a rat. After being moved outside the gate for trash pickup, the dumpsters had been left right up against the fence. Helsing could have climbed on top of one, thrown a jacket over the barbed wire, swung himself over. But he wouldn't make his move yet. Vampires were strongest in the dead of night. This was just his initial surveillance and confirmation.

At half past the hour, the office door opened, and the night watchman emerged to make his regular rounds, leading a chocolate-and-tan German Shepherd on a leash. Standing in the pool of light from the open door, Eldridge fiddled with the collar and unclipped the leash to let the dog roam free. The German Shepherd bounded back and forth on his nighttime romp, letting the guard pat him on the head before he raced off to explore the grounds.

Helsing watched from the shadows behind the rear fence. He had learned everything possible about the man, which wasn't much. Eldridge was Helsing's age, and he also had a military service record in Bosnia. Eldridge had been stationed west of Sarajevo during the peacekeeping mission, but he had not distinguished himself in any way, nor had he suffered any similar ordeals in Bosnia.

Eldridge had merely put in his time and come home.

But when he returned from Bosnia, the man's personality had suddenly changed, so much so that it stood out when Helsing began to investigate. Eldridge had changed his schedule, working only nights. He left very few clues about himself. Like many of the other potential targets, Eldridge was single, lived a solitary life with no friends, no family connections. For the past seven years, he had worked as a night-time security guard for Sarka Imports.

It required very little imagination to guess that Eldridge was a lackey for the invisible businessmen who brought secretive objects back from Eastern Europe. In all likelihood, he was directly in thrall to the king vampire himself. Some nights, Eldridge mysteriously failed to show up at his job, perhaps the times when he went out hunting. He owned the guard dog, which implied he was a higher-ranking vampire, one allowed to have an animal familiar.

The guard had a broad chest and a solid belly that made him look like a barrel with arms and legs. He wore a dark uniform and openly carried a sidearm, probably a Glock. He stood on the concrete steps and lit a cigarette; the bright orange ember glowed like a demonic eye in the darkness. After taking a few drags, he ambled down the sidewalk to the chain fence in a casual circuit. Under the bright security lights, Eldridge didn't have a care in the world. No doubt, the vampire was confident he could defeat any human opponent who dared to challenge him.

Helsing watched the predatory grace of his movements and wondered what the man would be like in the stupor of midday sleep.

That was when Helsing could easily take care of him. He knew where Eldridge lived.

He was so intent on watching the guard make his rounds that he didn't hear the click of claws, the heavy panting breaths. The growl started deep in the German Shepherd's throat as it sprang out of the shadows from the corner of the building and charged toward him. The dog let out a ferocious snarl as it slammed against the fence.

Startled, Helsing stumbled back into the shadows. The dog kept barking, growling. Saliva dripped off its fangs in silver droplets. Its eyes flared with pure evil. It scrabbled on the chain link, trying to tear apart the wires.

'Hey!' The guard ran closer, huffing breaths and pumping his arms. 'You kids better get out of here!'

Helsing scuttled into the shadows of the alley, cursing the dog under his breath. 'Spawn of evil.'

The German Shepherd kept barking as it clattered against the fence, unable to climb over. Eldridge ran up to the chain link and peered out into the darkness, but he couldn't see beyond the well-lit grounds.

Helsing kept moving. He had seen what he wanted to see. Now he just needed to wait until the light of day.

The vampire's daytime lair was a small two-bedroom home with a tiny fenced backyard. The house had seen better days, but apparently

Douglas Eldridge couldn't afford anything better on a security guard's salary. Either that, or it was part of his clever disguise.

Helsing waited until the autumn sun was highest. He had already scoped out the home, knew that the neighbors on either side worked regular jobs during regular hours, never guessing that their reclusive neighbor was a vampire.

Under the clear sky, Eldridge's house was dark and silent, as if cringing from the light. The blinds and curtains were drawn, darkening the interior to shelter the creature inside. A sidewalk and a square-cut hedge of dying juniper shrubs graced the brick front of the house. Feeling exposed, Helsing walked down the driveway and slipped around the garage to the back, where a gate led to the backyard.

Helsing carried a satchel with his sharpened stakes and also a Taser, which should expedite his work. These old houses usually had woefully inadequate doors and security systems. There was always a chance a *lampir* could have installed strong barricades, but Helsing doubted it. Most of them were arrogant, unwilling to accept their own danger.

He opened the gate and slipped inside, closing it behind him. He held the solid mallet in his right hand, ready for work.

The German Shepherd galloped toward him, snapping its jaws like a bundle of fur, claws, and fangs. The attacking beast sent a primal chill down Helsing's spine, but he was ready. He assumed that Eldridge kept the dog to guard him while he slept during the day. Merely another kind of monster. Helsing had to be swift and sure.

The German Shepherd lunged toward him, slavering to tear out his throat, but Helsing swung his right arm and smashed the heavy mallet against the dog's skull. He heard a solid, satisfying crunch of bone. The animal's yelp of pain fell silent as it dropped. He left the bloody mess on the patchy grass of the backyard.

Helsing stepped up to the rear porch, swung open the screen door, and made quick work of the lock. Carrying his satchel with stakes and the red-spattered mallet, Helsing entered the kitchen as quietly as possible. Unzipping the satchel, he donned the crucifix necklace, splashed holy water on himself, then removed the Taser.

The house was filled with gloom. On a small hall table not far from the bedroom door, Eldridge had left his holstered Glock right out in the open. His security guard jacket hung on a hook on the wall.

Helsing heard someone stir in the bedroom. So, not yet the sleep of the dead . . . Roused by the loud barking of his dog, Eldridge yelled, 'Shut the hell up!' He blundered out of his room, half asleep, and saw Helsing standing there with the bloody mallet in his hand. His eyes widened, and his mouth dropped open.

Helsing brought up the Taser just as Eldridge lunged for the handgun on the table. Before he could grab the Glock, the Taser wire spun out and the electrodes pierced the vampire's chest with a cracking, popping sizzle. Thrown backward, the guard jerked and jittered.

Helsing hadn't been sure whether a Taser would be effective on a vampire, but Eldridge flailed, dropped to his knees. The crackle of the discharging electricity continued through the long spooling wire until the single charge drained.

When the guard fell to the floor, Helsing roughly rolled him on his back. Barely in control of his muscles, Eldridge blindly swept up a hand to fend off his attacker, but he was too weak to have an effect.

Moving fast, Helsing snagged the duffel and produced one of his sharpened pine stakes. He placed it against Eldridge's chest, easily finding the right spot. The man's eyes were bloodshot, confused, but when he saw the stake, he tried to scramble away.

Helsing brought the mallet down hard and fast. With a wooden crack, the stake plunged into Eldridge's chest and pierced the heart with a bubbly splash of dark blood. His hands jittered upward, grasping at something, then dropped back.

Helsing struck a second time, pounding the stake all the way through his chest. The man slumped into death, as if his bones had turned to jelly – but that was all. No flash of light, no crumbling to dust. Disappointing. It seemed to minimize the threat the *lampir* posed.

In all the times he had slain vampires, rarely did the dying creatures sprout fangs and claws. In a few spectacular instances, the victims became howling monstrosities, thrashing and fighting for their very lives with all the supernatural powers they possessed . . . and yet they always perished in the end. Most, though, died just like this, a bland and pitiful end. He guessed it was because they were too weak during the daytime.

Breathing hard with the effort he had just expended, Helsing looked down at the body with a warm glow of satisfaction. Another vampire dead, another success. Sprawled out on the linoleum floor, Eldridge lay in a pool of blood, no longer a threat to the human race.

The stake had killed the *lampir*, but Helsing decided to burn the body, for added security.

He had brought a bottle of charcoal lighter fluid in the duffel, and he doused the corpse, drenching the loose pajamas, the hair, the skin. Then he lit a match and set the body alight. It wasn't a huge blaze, but enough to ruin the body. The vampire was dead. That was all that mattered.

Leaving the stake in place as the blue and yellow flames licked upward, Helsing packed up his Taser and mallet, and zipped the satchel shut before darting out the back door past the dead dog. He became invisible again in the daytime streets of the city.

Twenty-One

Working late again, disappointed by Detective Carrow's dismissive attitude that afternoon, Lexi reviewed her own summary of the vampire evidence that Stoker1897 had compiled: the mysterious bodies, inconclusive reports of missing blood supplies, missing persons. Every curious point had a rational explanation, but the cumulative weight of suspicious little details was compelling to anyone willing to consider it.

Detective Carrow clearly was not.

One of these days, I'm sure to be right. She heard the words in Teresa's voice, as if her friend had encouraged her to keep up the search.

Because of the stake murder and the decapitated head stuffed with garlic – a fact now made public – the HideTruth vampire thread remained active. She wanted to lay out the ideas bullet point by bullet point and let the detective try to argue his way out of them. But she doubted he would take the time to read her site again.

Feeling defensive sharpened Lexi's concentration, and that was when she did her best work, even late at night during the black hole of 2 a.m. She still felt guilty about drawing attention to Holly Smith and the Bigfoot assault, so she was glad the online discussion had quieted to nothing.

The house was dark and sleepily silent, and she heard the front door open, but realized it was just Blair coming in. She let out a small sigh of relief, glad to have her friend home. No Dirty Harry response this time, no guns drawn. He had worked an earlier shift at Olive U, then gone out – again – with Cesar. She hadn't actually expected him to come home at all. His love-struck happiness seemed to linger in the air like a pervasive perfume. She enjoyed seeing her friend like that, though she was a little envious, trying to remember the last time she'd been so goofy. He deserved it.

145

In the gloomy loneliness of the quiet house, Lexi wanted his company. She stretched the stiffness out of her arms as she emerged from her room. Blair had kept the front hallway light off, trying not to disturb her. He moved slowly in the front room, keeping his head down, probably tipsy again. She went out to offer him help.

As she stepped closer, she saw his silhouette, realized his shoulders were shaking. She heard a sniffling sound. 'Blair! What's wrong?' She flicked on the light, and he covered his face with a hand. Even before she saw his distraught expression, his tear-streaked cheeks, she was already hurrying toward him. His left eye was smashed and swollen; blood welled up from his lower lip. His shirt hung askew.

He winced, turned away. 'It's fine. I'll be fine.' The swollen lip distorted his words.

She grabbed his arm and led him to the couch. 'Tell me what happened.' She wrapped her arm around him, sat him down. 'Were you mugged?'

'No. This was self-inflicted, you could say.' His voice held both despair and disgust. 'He said he loved me. It was Cesar. He . . .' He cradled his swollen eye in the palm of his hand. 'He said he loved me, Lex!'

'Oh, I'm so sorry.' She wrapped her arms around him, pulling him against her. 'So sorry.'

He shuddered, pulled away. 'Don't. I just want to go to bed. Even nightmares would be better than staying awake right now.'

'No, you're going to have to put up with a hug for a few more minutes.' Lexi just held him, and he laid his head on her shoulder. 'Just stay here with me.'

After a minute, he got up the courage to talk. 'I was kidding around, flirted with someone a few nights ago. I didn't think anything about it, but the same guy came in tonight. It was just a joke, but Cesar got jealous . . . violent.' His fingers pressed down hard on her arms. 'And when he started hitting me, I couldn't get away. I didn't know what to do, couldn't even believe it at first. And then I was down on the ground.'

She rocked him back and forth. 'I'm so sorry.' She stroked his hair. 'It'll be all right.'

'I'm not a fighter, Lex – you know that. Never hit anyone in my life. I've been beaten up three times by redneck homophobes.' He sniffled. 'But never by someone like . . . like Cesar.'

Restless and miserable, he pulled away and stood up, swaying. Lexi took her place at his side, propped him up. 'You're right, let's just get you to bed. You always take such good care of me. Now it's time for me to do my part.'

She guided him into his room and held him steady with one hand while she yanked back the bedspread with the other. 'Here, sit down.' He collapsed on to the bed, hanging his head. 'Shoes off.' She untied and removed each one, then unbuttoned his shirt and helped him fall back on to his pillow. He seemed like a marionette with the strings cut, as she lifted his legs and swung them on to the bed. 'I'll take care of you. I'm here. You're safe at home.'

He lay on his back, staring at the ceiling. He seemed so broken.

147

She wet a washrag in the bathroom and came back, kneeling beside him as she dabbed his face, cleaned away the blood as gently as she could. Her heart ached for him, and she felt a flare of anger toward Cesar. How could anyone do such a horrible thing to a good man like Blair?

'Stay here. I'll be right back.' When he reached out for her, she touched his hand. 'I'll just be in the kitchen.'

She felt fiercely protective of Blair. She had hoped he had found real happiness with his new flame. For days she had experienced the halo effect of his giddy romance, and now she felt the anguish of what Cesar had done to him. That guy deserved to have a stake pounded through *his* heart!

She dug in the freezer, looking for a bag of frozen corn, frozen peas, anything she could use on his bruised face. Back in Iowa, her parents had kept a large vault freezer in the garage filled with every imaginable frozen vegetable from their own garden, but Blair September wouldn't be caught dead using frozen produce. Deep at the bottom of the drawer, she found a bag of shredded Swiss chard covered in frost. That would do. She pounded it on the counter to loosen the frozen leaves, then took it back to press against Blair's cheek. 'Here, hold that.' He grimaced and sighed at the same time.

Back in the bathroom, she opened the medicine cabinet, dumped three ibuprofen in her palm, added an aspirin, and poured a glass of water from the sink. She made him take the pills, and he didn't complain.

'Thanks for pampering me,' he mumbled. 'But I want to be alone for a while. Please?'

She hugged him again, and he turned away, covering his face with the cold sack. Tears stung her eyes. She could sense his shame and despair, but she also understood that he just wanted to curl up alone without her hovering too close. 'I'll be right here, just across the hall.'

When she stopped at the door with her hand to the switch, he asked her to leave the lights on. 'Now I know there are real monsters in the world,' he said.

She stared at him for a long moment, heart-broken, but he quickly drifted off to hide in sleep.

Furious and wanting to *do* something, Lexi channeled her anger. She left her door open to listen for any sound from Blair's room, then sat at the keyboard. Maybe she could compile a solid enough case to make the unimaginative detective reconsider.

One of these days . . .

She had outlined her logical argument, engaged in a silent debate using Carrow as her foil. Over the next hour, she wrote an impassioned blog, edited it, toned it down, doing her best not to sound crazy. After her experience with Teresa, she knew that the impossible could happen.

Rather than focusing on the murders them-selves, she looked at the evidence. What if there were vampires? What if this crusader was actually saving lives? He certainly must believe that.

The only way to stop a bad guy with fangs, is a good guy with a stake.

She recalled how Carrow thought HideTruth

was preying upon the weak-minded. Sometimes her followers were overly enthusiastic, too credulous, but they were good people and earnest.

Like Blair. He kept many details of his personal life private for his own reasons, and although Lexi was disappointed that he didn't confide completely in her – did she even know his real name? – she understood his need to protect his details. Countless people refused to divulge their social security number, their phone number, their address. Where was the exact line between caution and paranoia?

Worked up by what had happened to Blair – *Now I know there are real monsters in the world* – she posted 'The Case for Vampires'. Displaced frustration, maybe, but it was some of her best writing. It was more than a blog post, more than an essay. It was practically a manifesto.

Now that she had accomplished something, Lexi decided to call it a night, though she was still shaking. She had vented and made her case, but she didn't have the gratification of a lawyer summing up, crossing her arms and finishing her closing argument. She doubted Detective Carrow would ever read her essay anyway.

Even in her own mind, the debate remained unresolved. Despite her passion, she wasn't convinced even by Stoker1897's evidence, but that was no different from any other forum on HideTruth. Still, she admitted the *possibility* of unusual things, as she always did. That was the point.

She saw it was nearly 4 a.m. and the blanket of night outside could hide many sinister activities. What if some vampire was out there now? What if he had already read her post and wanted to silence Lexi because she drew too much attention to the threat? She rubbed her eyes. Now who was being paranoid?

By her own rules, she had to accept the possibility . . .

She checked on Blair and found him lying asleep with his face huddled against the pillow, his back to her. The pack of frozen chard had slipped aside.

Even nightmares would be better than staying awake, he had said.

In her T-shirt and sweatpants, she climbed into bed next to him and carefully wrapped her arms around his chest to drive away the nightmares.

'I'll keep you safe,' she whispered. 'We'll keep each other safe.' Just being close to him made her feel like she was protected from the vampires as well.

The next morning, a cowed Blair, ashamed of his swelling black eye and bruised face, cooked her a special frittata with spinach and feta cheese. He avoided conversation, talked about painfully mundane things, and she finally interrupted him. 'You know you can always confide in me if you want to talk, right?'

His smile looked real and out of place on his discolored face. 'I know that, Lex. I always do. Right now, I need a free pass. No judgment.'

'You always get a free pass from me,' she promised. 'I'll try not to think about it and concentrate instead on this delicious frittata.' He kissed her on the top of her head and retreated to his room, leaving her there to eat her breakfast alone.

As she drank her coffee, wrapping both hands around the mug, Lexi remembered how incensed she'd gotten when writing 'The Case for Vampires'. Now, in the bright autumn morning, she began to reconsider what she had posted in the middle of the night. Her angry essay had been aimed at Carrow, but distributed for all the world to read. Maybe it made her seem silly.

After she finished her frittata, she did the dishes, trying to occupy her mind, then opened her laptop, ready to face the fallout from her blog. She was surprised to find a private message from Stoker1897. Her brow furrowed as she read.

'Alexis Tarada, it's time we get in touch. I have much more evidence than I posted publicly, and I will share it with someone I trust.' She was both excited and wary. 'Like you, I live in Colorado Springs. I will provide you with a complete dossier if you agree to meet face to face, in broad daylight in a public place.'

Lexi was shocked to learn that he was local. He signed his message as 'Simon Helsing', rather than his screen name, but she couldn't possibly accept that 'Helsing' was his real name. That only reinforced how strong his convictions – delusions? – must be.

But she wondered what information he might possess, what details he was unwilling to post on HideTruth. She pondered her decision, reticent. But if proof existed, she needed to see it. *One of these days . . .*

Did she dare risk meeting with one of her most active followers? Especially after Dicked Over, she kept a wall between herself and the crazies. Was Stoker1897 one of the crazies? Or did he have information even more compelling than what she had already seen?

Lexi realized she was bound by her own words. She had to at least consider the possibility. She should hear him out with an open mind.

'Yes,' she replied to Stoker1897 – Simon Helsing. And she set up a meeting.

Twenty-Two

Once inside the victim's fenced backyard, Carrow felt the bile rise in his throat. He looked down at the dead animal. 'Beautiful dog. Didn't deserve this.'

The coroner had arrived at the same time, both of them called when the fire department discovered the burned body of Douglas Eldridge on his kitchen floor.

The German Shepherd was young, no more than three or four years old, with a sleek, rich pelt. The skull had been shattered above the right eye. The dog's mouth was open, the brown eyes glassy and staring upward.

'Damn, I hate to see that.' Carrow felt a lump in his throat. He'd had his own German Shepherd when he was a boy and still regretted that he didn't have a dog now.

Orla Watson gave him a clinical frown. 'Why is there always more sympathy for dead animals than for dead human beings? In a disaster movie where hundreds of people die, the audience cheers because the puppy gets rescued.'

'I don't like seeing dead human beings either,' Carrow said. He turned away, not wanting to look anymore.

Mel opened the screen door. 'Body's in here, Detective. You're going to want to have a look.'

'Go ahead, make my day.' Carrow gestured in an awkward gentlemanly fashion for the coroner to precede him.

The house smelled of smoke and roasted flesh, along with the oily stink of burned plastic. A neighbor from across the street had called the fire department after noticing smoke coming from one of the windows. Knowing that Eldridge, a night-time security guard, slept during the day, they had assumed some casserole had been left too long in the oven. When the fire department broke down the front door, they did indeed find a kitchen fire, though the flames hadn't spread far.

A man's charred body lay in the middle of the ruined linoleum, his blackened skin covered with greasy soot. There was no mistaking the wooden stake in the center of his chest.

'I'll take a wild guess and say this is connected to the other two murders,' said Watson. 'But you're the detective.'

'Not going to argue with you.' Against his better judgment, Carrow inhaled deeply, tried to identify the smell. 'Is that lighter fluid?'

154

The coroner leaned over the roasted horror and took a long, slow sniff, like a gourmand savoring a delicacy. 'No mistaking the fresh smell of aliphatic petroleum solvent.'

Powdery fire-extinguisher residue lay like faint snow across the body, the dark and bubbly linoleum floor, and the soot-stained laminate cabinets. 'If the killer meant to burn down the house and destroy the evidence, he did a piss-poor job of it,' Carrow said.

From beside the body, Watson looked up at him. 'Oh, I don't think he was trying to burn the house down, maybe not even trying to destroy evidence. Lighter fluid is a stupid accelerant for that purpose. He was just making double damn sure. Fire is supposed to be effective against vampires.'

Carrow groaned. 'Now you're sounding like that website.'

'No, I'm sounding like someone who looks at the evidence,' said the coroner. 'And I'll run a full blood test to see if any anomalies crop up.' She raised her eyebrows at his obvious surprise. 'Just to make sure.'

Carrow began assembling the pieces and clues in his mind. He walked down the hall. Inside the dim bedroom, the drapes were closed, the bed rumpled, blanket and bedspread covering a mattress. On a chair, he saw the dark jacket with the insignia of a private security company. He turned back. 'Crap almighty. Didn't the neighbor report that the victim was a security guard? Worked at night, slept during the day? That fits the pattern. Our nut job convinced himself the guy was a vampire and killed him.' He would look into where the victim worked, see if any suspicious activity had been reported there. Maybe there was still a drug or gang connection, but it was sounding more and more doubtful.

'If he slept during the day, the victim probably left his German Shepherd outside.' He looked down at the charred stake in the middle of the dead man's chest. 'Perp must have used the same mallet to kill the poor dog.'

The fire truck was still outside, and the captain was filling out his report on a clipboard, waiting for the police to release them. Carrow stepped outside through the smashed front door to see two firefighters, neither of whom belonged on a pin-up calendar. The men were shaken, not accustomed to finding murder victims on a routine call, especially not a corpse with a stake through the heart.

'Is it a serial killer, Detective?' asked one of the firefighters. 'I heard on the news about someone else being killed like that.'

'Could just be a coincidence,' Carrow said, then added a serious tone. 'Look, I know everybody likes to talk, especially with something as unusual and exciting as this, but I'd really like to keep the sensational aspect out of the news, at least for the time being. I'll have Public Affairs report this as just another murder, without giving details. I'd appreciate it if you'd keep this to yourselves. I'll double my donation to Toys for Tots this Christmas.'

The firefighters seemed disappointed, as if they had been looking forward to sharing the salacious story over beers. 'I have my First Amendment rights,' muttered one of the men.

'Yes you do, and I'm asking for a favor. Let me have a little elbow room to do some investigating, just for a few days. OK?' Embarrassed, the man fidgeted with his helmet, and the others reluctantly agreed.

Carrow walked around the garage looking for any sign of an obvious break-in, but the back gate had been unlocked. With the dead dog, he assumed the murderer had entered from that direction. He looked down at the German Shepherd, feeling a heaviness in his chest. 'This guy's a sick bastard.'

Alexis Tarada had pointed out the possible connection between Mark Stallings and Patric Ryan, and she seemed to know a lot about how the killer's mind worked. He didn't want Tarada posting any ridiculous theories on her UFO conspiracy site.

She saw vampires under her bed, too. What if she had her own connection to the killer? A shared delusion?

He used the radio to call in a plainclothes detail, providing Tarada's name and address. 'Do me a favor and keep an eye on her – but from a distance. Could be she's had contact with the stake murderer. I want a report on where she goes, who she meets.'

He knelt beside the sprawled dog and awkwardly placed his palm on the fur, patting gently. 'I'll get him. I'll find who did this.'

Twenty-Three

Simon Helsing, aka Stoker1897, was eager to meet. Lexi felt a chill, wondering if he knew where she lived, if he was watching her, stalking her. He seemed rational in his postings online but he was also intense, which might be a bad sign. She would be as cautious as possible, but she needed to know what he wanted to show her.

Lexi arranged to meet him downtown on Tejon Street, a line of boutique shops, wine merchants, bistros, a wood-fired pizza place, a deli, a sushi bar. She chose a 'definitely not Starbucks' coffee shop as a place to meet, at one of the outside tables, in plain view.

Though she hated to leave Blair alone at home, no matter that he lied that he was 'just fine', Lexi arrived half an hour early. She would not have been surprised if Helsing did the same, just so he could watch the place. Was he paranoid? Was *she*? Lexi didn't have anything to hide, not with him. They were on the same side, right? Especially if he had evidence that was even more compelling than what he had already shared online.

But after seeing Blair pummeled by a man who supposedly loved him, she knew not to be so naïve and open. *Now I know there are real monsters out there.*

Ever since Cesar beat him, Blair had stayed

158

home from both jobs, kept to his room in the dark, hurt and ashamed. Lexi made sure Blair knew he could talk to her if he needed a friend. He had said he would go back to Rags to Riches today, though she wasn't sure he would get up the nerve. She hoped she would make it back home in time to wish him luck.

Lexi treated herself to a large cappuccino, though she was nervous enough without any extra caffeine. She looked around. Tejon Street had plenty of pedestrian traffic and she drew energy from the activity around her. Because of the unseasonably warm autumn day, she wore only a light jacket. She sat at one of the outdoor tables, trying to be as obvious as possible.

Compared to Dubuque, Colorado Springs was a stunning and vibrant city. From where she sat, she could look west beyond the tall downtown buildings and see the imposing slopes of Pikes Peak framing the old Antlers Hotel. In 1895 Katharine Lee Bates had been inspired by that same view to write about the 'purple mountain majesties' in 'America the Beautiful'.

The heart of downtown also had its share of homeless. On the corner a block away stood a large man with a shaggy beard and black hair wearing a flak jacket. He panhandled the pedestrians, but seemed quiet and polite about it.

Lexi sipped her cappuccino, looked down at her blank notebook, waiting. The minutes ticked by, and a man suddenly sat next to her unannounced, moving the metal chair with a loud scraping sound. Though startled, Lexi forced herself to be calm. She regarded a plain-featured man with long brown hair tucked under a baseball cap. He wore a Broncos jacket, which made him practically invisible in Colorado despite the bright blue and orange colors.

'You're Alexis Tarada,' he said.

She didn't hear a question mark at the end of the sentence. 'And you're Stoker1897.'

'Helsing,' he corrected her. 'Simon Helsing. No need for the screen name here. The whole reason for this meeting is so we can be honest with each other. Too many damn secrets and cover-ups, political dealings and dark financial transactions.' He spoke quickly, articulately, but each word seemed to have a broken glass shard attached to it. 'I don't care about politics and money.' He shifted on the metal chair. 'No, I'm more interested in the survival of our race. You've read my postings, and I read your post, "The Case for Vampires". A very good summary, but you don't know everything.' Helsing's eyes were dark blue, not at all bloodshot.

'We're both on the same page,' Lexi said. She decided to let him guide the conversation. 'On my site, I promise to keep an open mind, because I know through personal experience that not every-thing can be explained. A lot of it is nonsense – I think you know that, too – but not all of it. You offered some very interesting evidence, posted a lot of details about the recent murders. You're right, there does seem to be something fishy.'

'Murders?' Helsing sounded cagey. 'Depends on your perspective. If vampires exist, then is it murder to stop creatures that feed on people, drain their blood, and cover up the killings? You could call it self-defense.'

'*If* vampires exist.' Lexi felt gooseflesh on her arms. 'You seem to know quite a bit about the victims.' Could she come right out and ask him directly if he was somehow involved? Her eyes flicked from side to side.

'I know a lot about vampires.' He slid a manila folder across the table next to her cappuccino cup. 'This is vital information, and I want to help you understand. Vampires are very skilled at keeping themselves hidden, and no one takes their existence seriously. People just laugh at you if you even suggest it.'

Lexi remembered Detective Carrow. 'Yes, they do.'

He leaned closer, dropping his voice to a whisper. 'I think that's been carefully orchestrated for decades, even centuries. Native superstitions in Eastern Europe kept the vampires – the *lampir* – contained over there. There, the locals believe in them, and they know how to defend themselves. It's been a silent war for a very long time.'

She scribbled down notes so he would know she was paying attention.

Helsing kept talking. 'Vampires thrived behind the Iron Curtain during the Soviet era, especially in the Stalinist years. People vanished, but everyone was too terrified to report the victims, assuming the secret police had taken them away as political prisoners. Vampires took advantage of that and proliferated. I think vampires may even have infiltrated the Communist government. I gathered evidence of that, too.' He paused, suddenly wary. 'Sorry. That makes me sound like a lunatic.'

161

Lexi guarded her expression. 'Frankly, most of the stories on my website sound unbelievable, at least at first. But I did agree to come here and listen to you, didn't I?'

He relaxed just a little. 'You did.' Helsing seemed high strung, full of energy, but she didn't think he was on drugs. 'In the Bosnian War, I saw things that changed me forever. Vampires used the turmoil there as a way to spread over here in earnest. Some of the returning UN peace-keeping forces were turned, which allowed the vampire infestation to grow in America.'

'You make it sound like vampirism spread the way Vietnam veterans brought giardia home from South East Asia.'

His expression darkened. 'I'm not comparing the infestation of vampires to the spread of a stomach bug.'

'Sorry, didn't mean to make light of it.' She worried that he might bolt.

'That's exactly what real vampires would do,' he said. 'You have to know their techniques, their misinformation, how they hide their existence by exposing rumors, just enough to make the idea seem frivolous. They constantly sow doubts, use ridiculous Hollywood movies and fake news as camouflage. They spread outrageous memes so no one will ever take the existence of vampires seriously. They hide on the fringe, where they can remain safe and anonymous.'

'I spend a lot of time researching things like that,' Lexi replied. 'Most of the memes and fake news are designed to muddy politics, smear campaigns to destroy an opponent.'

In a perfectly serious voice, Helsing said, 'Vampires are smarter than politicians.'

Lexi chuckled. 'That's a true statement.'

Helsing paused, as if trying to understand what was so funny. 'Vampires spread melodramatic stories to make sure that any serious discussion about their existence is dismissed. They have succeeded so far.'

Lexi looked away, suddenly reminded of the 'Bigfoot Rapes Hiker' story – how Holly Smith had been assaulted, yet her story was given little credence because of what she had said. 'I believe you.'

'Vampires hide in plain sight. They live among us, because no matter how blatantly they kill their victims and dispose of the bodies, the public is just numb to it. Every time you look at the news, some absurd story makes you roll your eyes in disbelief, then an hour later you hear something even sillier. It's one whopper of a story after another, and people believe or disbelieve depending on which news network they watch. Some people believe anything they read on the internet, and others believe nothing – which means our entire society no longer has any basis in fact.'

He tugged down the baseball cap to shade his face. 'But those of us who *know* the truth have to do something! I didn't ask for the responsibility.' Helsing skewered her with his intense blue eyes, and she felt as if he had pounded a stake right through her. 'I have to keep the *lampir* at bay.'

She saw Helsing fidget, move his hand as if looking for a weapon. Even though they sat outside with a constant stream of pedestrians passing by – talking, shopping, some even helping the panhandler on the corner – she felt uneasy. Lexi began to realize that something wasn't quite right about this man.

But she was accustomed to that after interacting with so many HideTruth followers. Even if Helsing was dangerous, she doubted he would do anything to her, at least not here, and not while he considered her a potential ally.

'You have more knowledge than I do,' she said in a calm but firm voice. 'I spend my days debunking crazy stories, but I am *willing* to believe. But first it has to pass the smell test.'

'Exactly.' Helsing nudged the manila folder even closer to her. 'I've done my research and tracked down where some of the vampires are, right here in the city. Yes, there were countless false leads, and I have to be careful. Sometimes an odd lifestyle choice might make a person falsely appear to be a vampire. But I've got a solid list of candidates, and many others that are likely vampires. Check them out yourself. See if you agree with my conclusions.'

Lexi opened the folder to see printouts, observation logs, names and addresses, work records. She was impressed. 'It takes a lot of skill to get this kind of information.'

'It takes a lot of skill to fight vampires. They are smart and they are deadly.' He nodded to the folder. 'Look at the evidence. With your help, maybe we can expose vampires for what they are.'

'With my help? You want me to post these

names on HideTruth?' She instantly worried about legal issues. Even with the nice monthly donation from Hugo Zelm, she couldn't afford a lawsuit.

'It's the only way to bring them out into the light of day – if you know what I mean.' Now Helsing really smiled. 'We can't let the *lampir* hide anymore. They are everywhere.' He lowered his voice. 'I think there's a king vampire here in the Springs, and that makes our job even more difficult.' The intensity in his eyes increased. He reached forward and grasped her wrist, startling her. It was like a vice clamping down. 'I can't do this alone, Ms Tarada. You can help me. You are the only one who really understands.'

'I . . . I'll take a look.' She swallowed hard, drew her arm back. 'Please let go of me.'

Alarmed, he released her hand like a rattlesnake that had just struck. 'Sorry! I don't want to scare you. Look at the list. Look at the evidence. You'll see what I mean. You understand.'

Scraping the metal chair back, Helsing bolted, slipping into the flow of pedestrian traffic and heading away from the coffee shop. He managed to vanish in the crowd.

Twenty-Four

Standing at the corner of Tejon and Cascade, Lucius kept a kind and hopeful smile on his face as people walked by. He held out a plastic cup half full of coins and low-denomination bills, many of which he had added himself, but even while he interacted with the pedestrians, his main focus was elsewhere.

Years of living in the forest had trained Lucius to stay attuned and alert for any potential threat, even from a distance. Most people assumed he was a down-on-his-luck military veteran who had seen enough horrors to last a lifetime. Because of his large size, he had learned how to appear innocuous, just another scruffy panhandler with a distant stare.

His attention was focused on Alexis Tarada.

She sat outside the coffee shop, meeting with Simon Helsing. Lucius wished he could hear their conversation. Though he called little attention to himself, he was a big, distinctive man, and Simon had certainly spotted him standing on the corner. The two had a special relationship, although the other man was fiercely independent, even obsessive. They'd had their disagreements before.

As the leader of his people, Lucius didn't want publicity for what the Bastion was doing. The only way they could survive was to remain invisible. Exposing the danger too blatantly might provoke the *lampir* to retaliate, resulting in an all-out war with the undead. Lucius would never bring that on his people, but Simon would not be convinced. His crusade was too fiery, too personal.

Lucius also knew who Alexis Tarada was. He had begun studying the young woman even before Helsing took an interest in her. Lucius knew where she lived, had researched HideTruth.

166

Frankly, he was surprised that Simon had suggested this open meeting with her. He was zealous, desperate to find an ally, since he no longer agreed with the Bastion's approach to survival.

Lucius had a nagging feeling inside that perhaps – just perhaps – Simon was right in his dangerous, provocative approach. Was the Bastion wrong to shrink away from the crisis? But Lucius was suspicious of civilization – and of people like Alexis Tarada. Was she an ally or an enemy? A scam artist? An opportunist? HideTruth asked for donations and sponsors, and bored or unstable followers were eager to believe any conspiracy theory, any monster that went bump in the night, any spaceship that abducted middle-aged women from laundromats. Alexis Tarada posted all of the nonsense, although she did try to differentiate between the ridiculous and the truth.

Yet she was here meeting with Helsing, listening to him. Maybe she was for real.

She was clearly uneasy as he made his earnest pitch, gave her his manila folder. Hunched over the metal table outside the coffee shop, Simon spoke with animation, tapping on the pages of his dossier.

To her credit, she took notes, paid attention. Lucius studied her body language, her expression, and she seemed confused and concerned, rather than afraid.

'Spare some change?' Lucius rattled his plastic cup as three college students strolled by with backpacks slung over their shoulders.

An angry-looking student turned his head the

other way, aggressively ignoring him, as many people did, but the young woman beside him dug into her pocket and pulled out two dollars. The other young man with her did the same, offering a five-dollar bill. 'Hope your luck improves, man.'

Shamed into competing, the angry student dropped a bill into the cup as well. The three strolled on down the street, looking in shop windows, walking past Alexis Tarada.

When Simon slid from his chair, he ducked in behind the students, moving quickly, dodging the crowds. He turned down a side street and vanished, using skills Lucius himself had taught him. The members of the Bastion knew how to disappear.

Alexis remained at the table, hunched over her large coffee cup and flipping through the manila folder. She appeared unsettled as she read the documents.

Lucius made up his mind. Still holding the big plastic cup, he made his way down the sidewalk.

Often people would shun the chattering and disheveled homeless who clearly needed the most help, but Lucius wasn't one of those. He wore clean clothes, smiled, nonthreatening. He sauntered up to the coffee shop where Alexis sat, still pondering the folder. She didn't look up at him, didn't even notice him, until he stepped close to the table.

When she glanced at him, Lucius gave her a somber nod. 'It's all true, you know.' He tapped the manila folder, then kept moving down the sidewalk without looking back.

He could feel the young woman watching him with countless questions, but he reached a corner and turned in the opposite direction from the way Simon had gone.

Sometimes people had to take a chance. Maybe this woman was worth considering. He would keep a personal eye on Alexis Tarada from now on to see how she reacted.

Twenty-Five

On the drive home from the coffee shop, Lexi couldn't stop thinking about the bearded homeless man. *It's all true, you know.*

Was he watching her? Spying on her? Did the man have some connection to Simon Helsing and the supposed vampire scourge? Or was he just some mentally ill man who managed to survive at the fringes of society.

It's all true, you know. Why had he said that?

When she got home, Blair was still in his room, getting ready for work that afternoon, but she was happy to hear him bustling about. She pulled up a chair and sat at the kitchen table, engrossed in studying the documents in the folder. The information Helsing had given her was both fascinating and disturbing.

The first pages showed other victims that real vampires had supposedly killed – grainy photographs of pale corpses with notations that the bodies had been burned and sterilized to make sure they wouldn't turn into vampires. She didn't know where Helsing had gotten the photos. He could have faked them or culled them from some sick website, but she wasn't sure. The pictures were graphic, sickening, showing unrivaled violence. Many of those 'vampire victims' were purported to be homeless men and women whose disappearance would have remained unremarked.

When meeting her, Helsing must have assumed that Lexi believed in vampires, so he hadn't spent extensive time making that part of his case. Rather, hoping to enlist her as an ally, he presented evidence of specific people whom he suspected to be vampires hiding in society. Looking forward, not backward.

Lexi flipped the pages, and when her stomach growled, she realized she hadn't eaten lunch. Maybe later. She still had some leftover pizza from the other night. She wondered if Blair had eaten, but he would never consider that an acceptable lunch. After he'd been hurt, Lexi made up her mind to take care of him, cook for him, but she wanted to do better than leftover pizza for him. She could always get takeout food, which would certainly taste better, but wouldn't come from the heart.

As a fallback, if she took over the cooking chores, it might give Blair the incentive to get better faster.

Now, she turned to the next page in the dossier. Helsing had been thorough, even obsessive. Because of HideTruth, he had confided in her, delighted to find a kindred spirit at last. He believed she shared his concerns. That made her uneasy.

She remembered the similar case with Richard Dover, Dicked Over, her original stalker, though Helsing was more measured, more rational. She looked at his carefully curated list of potential vampires.

He highlighted a night-time security guard, Douglas Eldridge, who worked at a secretive Eastern European importing firm. He was always accompanied by a vicious German Shepherd, assumed to be a 'demon familiar'. Lexi frowned at the idea, but read through the surveillance, Eldridge's movements, his work shifts, his home address. She found it all a little creepy.

Then there was Tom Grollin, a night-time cab driver, and MaryJane Stricklin, a third-shift ambulance driver with records of accident victims who suspiciously died during transport when she was the lead EMT. Helsing claimed that the death numbers were higher than average.

The listings included three hotel night clerks, a pizza delivery man named Frederik Lugash, and a pair of after-hours stock clerks in the local warehouse store. She turned page after page, and the last name in the folder surprised her – Hugo Zelm. Lexi smiled at the suggestion of Zelm as a vampire. Though quirky and reclusive, her benefactor was seen quite often, even if Helsing was unable to find any photos taken in broad daylight. He did fit the clichéd wealthy Nosferatu profile, but Lexi didn't believe the idea for a second. In the margin, Helsing had written a note to himself, 'King vampire?'

Disturbed by all this, imagining what this dossier might signify if Helsing's observations were true, Lexi had an idea for a post on her homepage, 'Hiding in Plain Sight'. Just for the sake of argument . . .

Without giving any specific names, because Lexi had no desire to be sued, she decided to lay out the details of Helsing's research, the criteria he applied and the questions he raised. How could a person never be seen during daylight hours?

She also knew about confirmation bias. Helsing only found information that tended to reinforce what he already believed. Even celebrities weren't watched twenty-four hours a day. Who kept track of whether or not someone walked to the end of the driveway in the morning to pick up a newspaper? Or went to the park alone on a sunny afternoon? Just because the people on Helsing's list weren't commonly out during the day, that didn't mean they *never* ventured into the sunlight. Given Helsing's thoroughness, though, when she posted 'Hiding in Plain Sight', maybe others would search, investigate the data – and find other information. She wanted nothing more than for someone to disprove his claims.

At first, Lexi had greeted the idea of vampires with a thrill of mysterious excitement, her sense of wonder returning. Like when Teresa had appeared to her. Later, when Lexi realized that she had seen her friend *after* her death, she believed Teresa had come back to give her a message, to help guide her life. That was one reason Lexi had left Iowa and moved to Colorado, why she had accepted a job tracking down myths

172

and fake news. And why she had created HideTruth, to gather more evidence of things that simply couldn't be explained. *One of these days, I'm sure to be right.*

Helsing was serious, but in a different way. He saw a threat that the public willfully ignored. Lexi considered presenting the entire folder to Detective Carrow, letting him investigate all of these potential vampires, but he would probably dismiss the idea out of hand. Even to her, the conclusion of a vampire infestation was a stretch, unless she could find something more definite.

Rather than embarrassing herself in front of the detective, Lexi would do some investigation on her own, see what else she might find.

Blair opened the door of his room, startling her. 'Lex, I could use your help before I go to work.'

She was glad to know he had decided to go back out into the world, even if he wanted to stick to the shadows and hide his bruises. 'Anything you need.' She had been on edge about him, about everything. She hurried into the hall and grimaced to see his puffy lip and bruised face, which looked even worse after two days.

Seeing him that way made her angry, but Blair had refused to file charges against his abusive boyfriend. Now she felt her face flush. 'I can go directly to Detective Carrow and demand that he pull strings. If he wants my help on the stake killer case, then he can help me. It's his job.'

'The police won't do anything,' Blair insisted. 'A domestic quarrel. They'd get a kick out of two gay lovers hitting each other.'

'You weren't hitting *each other*. He hit *you*. Don't start gaslighting.'

Blair sighed. 'No lectures please. Free pass, remember?'

She blinked away tears. 'Free pass. What can I do for you? Just name it.'

'It's time for me to face the world, but I don't want anyone to see me like this. I need some help putting on make-up.'

She let out a surprised laugh and turned him by the shoulder, guiding him into her room. 'I'm not very good at it, but I've had to look pretty on rare occasions.'

After she sat him on the corner of her bed, he winced as she applied foundation, making do with what she had, hoping the color matched well enough. 'It'll hide the worst of the bruising. I'll do my best for you, you know that.'

He dabbed at the tender purple circle around his eye. 'You'll do great. Pretty soon it'll all be back to normal, like nothing ever happened.' He let out a wistful sigh.

He remained stoic as he endured her ministrations. Unable to keep her anger inside as the discoloration gradually disappeared, she asked, 'You're not going to see him again, are you? He might kill you next time.'

'He won't.' Blair tensed as she lifted the brush, ready to scold him, then he lowered his eyes. 'No . . . I won't see Cesar again. I've had it with him. I learned my lesson.'

'Good. If you date him again, I'll drag you to counseling.'

'If I dated him again, I would certainly need

174

counseling.' He seemed to be trying to lighten the mood.

'Don't get amnesia.' She wasn't convinced he was strong enough, but she had pushed the matter as far as she could. She knew Blair had shut down, but she would never stop watching out for him.

He tried to smile, but flinched when it stretched the scab on his lip. 'Thank you for everything you've done for me, Lex. You're the best friend. I promise I'll find you the absolute perfect dress for the gala.'

The comment came out of nowhere. 'A dress? The gala is the last thing on my mind right now,' she said, finishing up the make-up. *Hugo Zelm – the king vampire?*

'Well, it's not the last thing on mine,' Blair said. 'If I'm going to be your plus one, somebody has to worry about it.'

Twenty-Six

One of the cable channels was playing a 'Bloodsucker Marathon', though it was a month before Halloween.

Working for hours in the motel room, Helsing played the vampire movies in the background. They provided imaginary thrills, silly monsters that posed little danger, nothing at all like the real threat of the *lampir*. Peter Cushing, the brave vampire slayer, battled a snarling Christopher Lee

175

in *Horror of Dracula*, one of the better offerings from Hammer Films. Cushing was a true hero who pounded stakes without sympathy, making the sign of the cross with a pair of candlesticks to drive Dracula into a blaze of purifying sunlight, which roasted him to ash. Cushing's Van Helsing was an inspiration.

Simon Helsing, though, battled the real threat and destroyed true evil. He didn't have to be dashing, merely effective – as he had already proven to be. If Alexis Tarada agreed to be an ally, together they could be twice as effective. Once she reviewed his dossier, she would understand the scope of the threat, he hoped.

While the movie's screeching soundtrack built to a crescendo, he sat calmly at the table making preparations to destroy the king vampire, the most powerful monster in the city.

On the bedspread, which bore stains that Helsing didn't want to contemplate, lay the used camera he'd found in a thrift store, a large Canon 1D X. He had bought it dirt cheap, and when the clerk warned him that the camera no longer worked, Helsing said he just needed it as part of a costume. The long lens had cost much more, but all he cared about was the casing. When screwed on to the front of the camera, the lens looked like a grenade launcher.

With the drapes drawn against the afternoon sunlight, Helsing sat at the desk and looked at the glass jar that held chopped-up bits of silver that reminded him of dental fillings. He had haunted pawn shops, buying up old silver rings, silver coins, silver chain, silver flatware, silver earrings. It didn't matter, so long as it was silver. Helsing had spent several hundred dollars of the Bastion's money intended for emergencies, and Helsing considered this an emergency.

It had been a tedious process to hammer the earrings and silver wire into jagged lumps. With a fine jewelry saw and a clamp, he had cut up the rings and flatware one fragment at a time. He sawed the coins in half, then quarters, eighths, and even smaller, sharp-edged bits. It was an uneven assortment of shrapnel, but he had enough.

On the tabletop, he had mounted a five-stage reloading press for .410 gauge shotgun shells. He had to create his own ammunition. Although it would be intensely satisfying to stand over the king vampire and hammer a stake through his chest, Hugo Zelm would never give him that chance. Helsing's only chance might be to kill him from a distance.

With the Taurus Judge revolver he had also purchased, he would have five shots. The Judge could fire .410 caliber shotgun shells as well as .45 bullets. He would pack the shells himself, make them deadly to vampires.

Helsing had read plenty of lore about making silver bullets. There was quite a debate, including one that went on for weeks on HideTruth, whether silver bullets were even possible or ballistically advisable. Helsing would have preferred to load the revolver with solid silver bullets for greater range, accuracy, and penetration, but silver melted at 1,800°F. Melting down all this scrap silver, casting it in a mold, and machining each bullet with enough precision to prevent a jam that would cause the gun to explode . . . that was simply beyond Helsing's capabilities in his motel room.

His best option was to load the small shotgun shells with silver fragments like birdshot, but far more deadly to vampires. The .410 shells wouldn't be terribly accurate and the pellets would rapidly lose their effectiveness with increasing range, but silver itself was the deadly ingredient. Helsing hoped he could get close enough to the king vampire.

Helsing lined up the first empty casing on the initial stage of the press, and divided his cut-up silver shrapnel into five equal parts. He would have five shots. If he got close enough, the first one would do the job. Even if the shells did not blow a hole through the king vampire's chest, the silver should still prove fatal.

The orthodox priest in Bosnia had taught him that silver was deadly to the *lampir*. In common legends, silver was primarily effective against werewolves, but the pure metal worked just as well on vampires. The werewolf story was misinformation, more of the web of lies spread by vampires over the years. Werewolves did not exist.

He methodically worked through the process of filling the small shells with silver fragments, step by step, one at a time. He crimped the last of his shells, then placed the big revolver on the desk. Feeling a great sense of anticipation, he inserted the five shells into the Judge.

Now he had a weapon that was deadly to vampires – not as personal as a stake through the heart or a decapitation, but it would do the job.

Helsing imagined how much the situation would change once he killed the king vampire. And he would have his chance soon. Normally, Zelm hid behind fortress walls while he worked his nefarious influence among the upper crust of society. Helsing would be prepared when Zelm let down his guard, just a crack.

But not soon enough.

Helsing's previous three targets had been so satisfying that he wanted to keep in practice. There was more than enough time to kill one more and keep the city safe. He began to choose the next target.

Twenty-Seven

Murder victims generated a lot of paperwork. Detective Carrow sat at his desk in the downtown CSPD station, hiding behind the flimsy cubicle walls that did not keep out the sounds of conversations, ringing phones, whirring printers, and general background chatter.

Pinned to the cubicle wall was a photo of his two daughters smiling and posing with their new puppy. Another photo showed them at their dance lessons. He made a note to himself that he would see them soon, call them sooner. Maybe the Green Chiles and Frijoles Festival wasn't such an awful idea after all. He'd even kept a picture of LeAnn for a while, before he realized that it was just too depressing. The rest of his office décor consisted of sticky notes, a dry-erase board, a computer, a file cabinet, two chains of paperclips linked together, printouts, calendar reminders, and a distressingly pink mug that showed kittens doing ballet with the caption 'You're Tutu Sweet'. The girls gave it to him last Christmas to remind him of them. When the handle broke after only a few weeks, he couldn't bring himself to part with the mug, so it now served as a pencil holder on his desk.

And paperwork.

He looked back down at the case files. He still had to fill in a lot of details about the Douglas Eldridge murder, though the autopsy wouldn't be complete for a while. He also had the files on Mark Stallings and Patric Ryan, which cried out for connecting tissue that would help him solve the case. Maybe some detail from the Eldridge crime scene would make the pieces fall into place.

Maybe all three of them were really vampires. He snorted to himself.

So far the salacious Eldridge details had not leaked, but he didn't know how long the fire-fighters would remain quiet. Once the news broke about another stake victim, Public Affairs wouldn't be able to deflect all the publicity. His days would become a circus. He almost looked forward to a good old jealous husband with a gun. At least those murders didn't make his head spin.

'Hey Detective, I've got a report for you.'

He looked up to see a tall plainclothes officer standing behind the cubicle wall, tapping his fingers on the metal rim. Lieutenant Nathan

180

Dodge was an older officer within a dart's throw of retirement age. Dodge was soft-spoken, pleasant to everyone, and somehow had not become jaded even after decades of working as a cop.

Carrow closed his half-finished report on Eldridge. 'Sure, what is it, Nathan? Buy you a beer if you get me out of doing more paperwork.'

Dodge smiled. 'You asked us to keep an eye on that young woman, Alexis Tarada.'

Carrow perked up. 'Anything interesting? She scare a vampire out into the sunlight?' When he saw the blank look on Dodge's face, he waved his hand. 'Never mind. What did you find?'

'She did meet a man for coffee downtown earlier today. Furtive demeanor, bulky jacket and a baseball cap pulled low. He sat next to Tarada and they talked for a while. He gave her a folder, grabbed her arm, then bolted.'

'You mean, he ran away?'

'He tried to be discreet about it, but it was clear he wanted to get out of there, and in a hurry. He had done what he needed to do.'

Carrow tapped his desk. 'So she met someone for coffee and he gave her a folder . . .'

Nothing illegal about that. Tarada ran her oddball website and also had an active freelance career working online. She could have been meeting a client. Thanks to her conspiracy website, many of her clients might be nuts to start with.

'Anything else?'

'She talked to a panhandler, then just drove

181

home.' Dodge tapped the metal cap of the cubicle wall again. 'Seems to have a pretty dull life. Was that what you're looking for?'

'Not sure what I'm looking for, but it's better than searching for wooden stakes in a lumber-yard.' Again, Dodge's expression went blank, waiting for the punchline. 'Never mind. Thanks, Nathan. Owe you a beer, as promised.'

Carrow liked the guy, considered maybe going out of his way to socialize more with his coworkers after a shift. The other choice was to go back to his bleak townhouse, which reminded him too much of the solitary murder victims.

Carrow decided to go talk with Tarada again tomorrow, before the details of the Eldridge murder went public. Maybe she would slip up in conversation, reveal something that no simple website moderator should know.

He could finish the paperwork later.

Twenty-Eight

After perusing the folder full of information that Simon Helsing had provided, Lexi wrote her energetic and – she hoped, compelling – essay, 'Hiding in Plain Sight'. After posting it, she waited for the response from her followers, knowing they were already inclined to believe in the impossible.

When she first started HideTruth, Lexi would have rolled her eyes at the suggestion of vampires living undetected in society, but Helsing made an unexpectedly strong case and raised many disturbing questions. Could any objective person deny the possibility that it *might* be true, that the answer was at least worth considering? What would her friend Teresa have said?

Or was it just the equivalent of ghostly typing on a stuck keyboard?

She answered the doorbell and was surprised to see Detective Carrow again.

'Got a few more questions to ask you, Miss Tarada.'

'Did you find any other connection between the victims? Evidence of vampires?' She felt cocky. She had been having a silent inner debate with him since his last visit a few days ago. 'I just posted something on my site that you may find interesting.'

He scoffed, and she couldn't tell whether or not he was joking. 'What? The Loch Ness monster flying a UFO?'

She sighed. 'You aren't very skilled in making people want to cooperate with you, Detective.' She gestured him inside and led him to the kitchen table where she had been reading Helsing's dossier and fact-checking online.

He took a seat and got right down to business. 'This is serious, Miss Tarada, and I want to ensure your cooperation. What else can you tell me about this supposed vampire killer? Has he contacted you in any way?'

She closed her laptop, reluctant to tell him about her recent meeting with Helsing. 'I have a lot of activity on my site, because I'm willing to consider things you won't. To some of my followers, it's obvious that the victims might be vampires.'

'With Halloween coming up, it's probably hysteria,' Carrow said. 'Feeding into the killer's delusions.'

She felt a sudden dread. 'Has there been another stake murder?'

He pointedly didn't answer. 'What can you do to help me find this serial killer? You sure you aren't withholding information from me?'

Something about Carrow made her feel defensive. 'And are you sure you shouldn't be worried about *vampires* instead? If they are secretly killing humans, then the hunter is saving people.'

Apparently realizing she was serious, Carrow hardened his expression. 'I have dead bodies, Miss Tarada, and the coroner assures me they are human. I have no evidence for vampires.'

Lexi brushed the manila folder on the table in front of her. 'But are you willing to look for evidence that doesn't fit your preconceptions?' Speaking from memory because she had just read the entire dossier and written her blog, she coolly laid out a pattern of behavior and suspicious activities. She listed what she knew about Mark Stallings and Patric Ryan, information she culled from public records and her own detailed searches. She said nothing about Simon Helsing.

Carrow was surprised by her knowledge, but he remained skeptical, challenging her. 'I find it difficult to believe that the victims were never once seen during the day. Loners, maybe, but otherwise normal, according to their neighbors.'

Lexi appreciated healthy skepticism, but he didn't seem to have his mind open at all. 'According to legends, vampires can withstand brief exposure to sunlight. Maybe they ventured out on cloudy days, just often enough to allay suspicions.'

'Convenient. So anyone could be a potential vampire, in your point of view.'

'Not only my point of view.'

Carrow seemed to know something she didn't. 'You're working with other people, aren't you? Has the killer made contact? I know you met somebody at a coffee shop yesterday. Who was he? What did you talk about?' He looked down at the folder. 'Is that what he gave you?'

Lexi straightened, flushing. 'You're following me? On what grounds? Don't you need a warrant for that?'

'We don't need a warrant to watch what's happening in plain sight. The man you met seemed nervous, disguised. Was he another paranoid conspiracy nut?'

Lexi realized it would be foolish to deny the meeting.

'He was a vampire enthusiast, someone who wants to expose them, if they exist. He's done a lot of research, and in my mind he's pretty convincing.' She rested her hand on the manila folder. 'Have you actually looked for any other vampire *victims*? Bodies drained of blood and disposed of? Missing homeless people never reported, never investigated. If you find a pattern of victims, maybe you should think more about the vampires themselves instead of a vigilante vampire killer.'

Her comment derailed him. 'There are always missing people, nothing special about that. You see a bunch of speckled dots on a countertop and connect them into some secret grand pattern. But it's really just a bunch of dots.' He disoriented her by changing the subject. 'What do you know about Douglas Eldridge? A night security guard who worked at a warehouse for Sarka Imports. Had a German Shepherd.'

Lexi couldn't conceal her surprise. She had just read the man's complete file. 'Eldridge? He's someone that my . . . contact considers suspicious, a possible vampire. Someone worth looking into.'

Carrow's next words stunned her. 'Douglas Eldridge was murdered, along with his dog. We have kept it quiet, entirely out of the news.' His expression hardened. 'But somehow your guy knew about it.'

Lexi felt as if her bones had turned to water. 'How? How was Eldridge murdered?'

'A stake through the heart, then the body set on fire. He'd been stunned with a Taser first.' Carrow leaned over the kitchen table, uncomfortably close to her. 'The sick bastard bashed in the poor dog's head with a mallet.'

Lexi felt sickened. Helsing had been watching the man, gathering information. Had he actually killed him? 'Douglas Eldridge might have been a hidden vampire. His behavior and history fit the profile, but it was just circumstantial evidence . . . I didn't really believe he would . . .' Stoker1897 had been intense, obsessed, convinced. Eldridge had been one of his primary suspects, but Lexi balked at the thought he would genuinely *act* on his suspicions, pound a wooden stake through someone's heart. She flipped open the manila folder and pulled out the top sheet filled with Helsing's notes and records on the night security guard. 'He's right here.'

Without being asked, Carrow pulled the whole folder toward him. He flipped through the other records, his eyes widening. 'So you knew that Eldridge was a potential murder victim? That he was in mortal danger from some nutcase who believed in vampires, and you did nothing?'

'Nothing? What did you expect me to do? When I offered you information and suggested leads to track down, you ignored it and mocked me. I didn't know anybody in the file might be killed. If I called to tell you that Eldridge might be a vampire, would you have rushed over to check it out?'

Carrow continued to press. 'Who is your contact? Who gave you this information?' He held up the folder. 'This man could be the killer, or at least allied with him. We have to find him.'

'I . . . I don't know. He posts on my website under the screen name Stoker1897. I was surprised to learn he's local.' Her thoughts spun. She remembered sitting across from Helsing, looking into his intense eyes. She had listened to his convictions, just like so many of her most intense followers, but she hadn't really thought he was a crazed murderer.

One of these days, I'm sure to be right.

Now who was being stupid and gullible?

187

'What's his name? Not his screen name,' Carrow asked. 'How do I find him?'

'I . . . I don't know. He said his name was Simon Helsing, but that's obviously fake.'

The detective looked confused. 'Why? What's so special about that name?'

'Helsing? Like Van Helsing?' When his expression remained blank, Lexi groaned. 'You really don't know anything about vampires, do you, Detective? You need to read *Dracula*.'

'How else have you been in contact with Helsing? He posts on your site? I can get a warrant for your computer and search through every one of your files. Did he give you a way to contact him?'

Lexi felt a chill. 'I've already tried to track him down, to do my own due diligence. Believe me, my resources are as good as yours.' He obviously didn't believe her. She knew that if she wanted to avoid being brought in for formal questioning, she would have to give him everything she had. 'He only logs on at public terminals, uses different ISPs each time, nothing that can be traced. I only received one private message from him, and I'll forward it to you. Everything else is public, right on HideTruth. You can read the forums yourself.' But she knew he wouldn't do that, so she offered, 'I'll compile them for you, send you everything that Stoker1897 has posted.'

'That's a good start.' He turned the pages in the folder. 'And these are all targets he's identified? Potential victims?'

'Possible vampires,' Lexi said.

'Potential victims. They're not safe.'

Lexi tried to dredge up her confidence. 'Helsing said he found suspicious activity around the warehouse where Eldridge worked, mysterious shipments from Eastern Europe. You should at least investigate that. What if he's right? There might still be something nefarious going on.'

'He pounded a stake through two victims, and he cut off another guy's head. My priority is to stop him from killing again.' Carrow stood up, keeping the folder. 'I need to take this as vital evidence in the case.'

Lexi was too disoriented to think of any objection. Could he do that? She wanted to argue, but she knew she was on thin ice. He could easily confiscate her desktop computer and her laptop, bring her in for a lengthy interrogation.

He tucked the manila folder under his arm. 'We'll be talking further, Miss Tarada. Be sure to send me all the information you have, so I don't need to ask again. And call me the moment he contacts you again.' He strode toward the door and opened it. 'Vampires or not, this Simon Helsing is a killer – and I'm looking for monsters that I know exist.'

Twenty-Nine

Out in the forest camp, the members of the Bastion gathered around because Lucius had called them to witness. They were terrified.

The men and women stood by the tents and

lean-tos, cowed into silence. Campfires burned, the smoke nearly invisible in the gathering dusk. Bright battery-powered LED lanterns spilled out harsh white light, making the event more like a spectacle.

A battered young woman with torn clothes huddled on the ground, sobbing, shaking, mindless with fear. Mama wrapped a camp blanket around the girl's shoulders, stroking her tangled hair. 'Shush now. It'll be all right.'

The woman slipped an arm out from under the blanket and wrapped it around Mama's leg, holding her in desperation. 'Thank you,' she muttered. 'Thank you for saving me.'

Tall and hairy, Roland made a dejected lowing sound like a cow caught in barbed wire. The big man's arms were extended high above his head and his wrists were tied together, with the rope thrown over a tree branch so that he dangled with his feet barely touching the ground. His reddish beard was full and tangled like an animal's mane; his russet hair hung in tangled locks. Tears poured in rivers through the hair on his cheeks.

Lucius had undone the man's overalls and pulled down the front flap to leave Roland exposed and vulnerable – just as they had found the young woman he'd held prisoner and repeatedly abused.

'Sorry,' Roland groaned. 'Sorry! Pleeeease.'

Lucius felt only steel inside him. He was the leader of the Bastion. He had to protect his community. And this man was a threat to them all. 'I should not have listened to you the first time, Roland. I should never have felt sorry for you.'

The hairy man's knees buckled as he collapsed

190

in despair, but the ropes suspended him, letting him hang like a dead weight. The abrasive bonds had rubbed away the skin on his wrists, and blood trickled down his arms. 'Please! I was lonely.'

'You hurt her, just like you hurt that other girl. We can't let you hurt anybody else. Never again.'

'No! I'll be good.'

'It is what it is.'

Thirty members of the Bastion had gathered, sickened by what Roland had done. They stood around the main camp, a silent but unanimous jury.

Mama placed her arm around the victim's shoulders. The poor woman didn't seem to know what was going on. She rocked back and forth, in total shock, withdrawn into herself. 'Shhh. It'll be all right. He won't hurt you again, but I need you to look up now. My Lucius is going to ask you a question.'

The children stood with their parents, wide-eyed and still; they could feel the import of what was happening. Young Joshua stood tall as if he considered himself an adult now. He watched the hairy prisoner with hard eyes.

After the recent cold snap, the perfect autumn weather drew day hikers and backpackers. This young woman – Lucius didn't even know her name – had been out on the trail alone. He could only assume that Roland had spotted her, tracked her, seized her.

After the assault on the first female hiker, the Forest Service had conducted bothersome searches for days. But since the victim could not find the place where she had been held captive, and because the Forest Service had limited resources, the search parties had dwindled to nothing. Even if searchers did find Roland's old dwelling, he had moved on after the Bastion exiled him.

And then Roland had taken another victim, another mate. Lucius could not allow that.

He stepped up to the hairy man suspended from the rope. 'I hoped exile would be enough of a punishment after the first time.' Lucius held a sharp hunting knife in his hand, a blade that was made for killing, for butchering . . . for what Roland deserved. 'I know the only way we can be certain you will never do it again.'

'I won't,' Roland groaned. 'I'm sorry! Never again.'

Next to Mama, the girl clutched the camp blanket around her. She turned away from the shaggy brute, but Mama forced her to look at Roland.

Lucius growled his words like razors. He didn't allow the remotest hint of sympathy. 'What you did to that poor girl can never be forgiven. Your fate is her decision.' Ignoring the whimpers and moans of the hairy man, he turned to the young woman. 'Will you forgive him? Should we turn him loose?'

The victim cringed and would have dropped to her knees if Mama hadn't held her up. 'No! Don't let him loose! You can't!'

Lucius regarded her with his deep brown eyes. 'Only you know exactly what he did to you. Should we let him live?'

The woman shuddered, and the words ripped

out of her throat. 'No! Kill him!' She curled into a ball, rocking back and forth as Mama comforted her.

Lucius turned to Roland. 'It is her decision, and it is my decision. You cannot be allowed to live.'

A muted gasp rippled around the crowd, but no one objected. Some took a step closer.

In the light of the camp lanterns Roland dangled from the rope that bound his wrists high over his head. 'No . . . no . . .'

Young Joshua stood next to little Lily, whose eyes were wide. Looking at Lily, Lucius felt an acid taste of anger rise in his throat. What if Roland had attacked an innocent young girl?

'What you did to them . . .' Lucius focused on the guilty man, the rapist – the *monster*. The Bastion tried too hard to protect themselves from outside threats, but this dangerous man had been right among them. 'What you did!'

Without thinking, he tore down the already loose front of Roland's overalls exposing his large penis hanging there in a forest of red pubic hair. An assault weapon.

The battered young woman buried her face against Mama's leg.

Lucius didn't need any more convincing. He slashed low and sideways with the razor edge, lopping off the flaccid flesh. Hot blood spouted from Roland's crotch. The blade was so sharp that the despairing man didn't even feel it at first, then he let out a bellow of shock and pain.

The spectators moaned, and some covered up quiet screams.

Lucius supposed Roland might bleed out eventually, and part of him wanted to let that happen, long and slow, but he wasn't cruel. He wasn't a torturer. He just had to mete out justice.

Roland's knees had buckled, and he hung on the rope with his arms nearly wrenched out of their sockets. Lucius grabbed his shaggy head, tugged his face up. The big man blinked his eyes, and his mouth hung open in a pleading expression.

Lucius made a quick slash across his hairy throat, and another fan of blood spouted out. He stepped out of the way as Roland twitched and bled and swiftly died.

The sobbing victim turned her head away. Mama tried to comfort her. The rest of the Bastion stared in silent approval.

Still holding the bloody knife, Lucius walked over to where the young woman shuddered. Mama stroked the girl's cheek, turned her face upward.

Lucius stood over her and spoke in a soothing voice. 'I'm sorry for what happened to you, and I'm sickened by what he did. Roland was one of ours and we take care of our own. We never meant to hurt outsiders.'

'You killed him,' the young woman said, hunching over and clutching her stomach. 'I want to go home. I can't be here!'

He leaned closer to her. She blinked at him, her eyes swollen. Snot ran down her face as she sniffled. 'Do you truly believe that justice was served?' he asked. 'That Roland deserved the punishment I gave him?'

She nodded, at first uncertain and then more vigorously.

'Good, that was important to me,' Lucius said. 'I did what I had to do, but I wanted to be sure you understood as well.' He walked around behind her.

The exhausted young woman was barely aware of her surroundings, horrified and relieved at the same time. 'I want to go home.'

Mama said, 'The poor dear is out of pain now.'

After what she had been through, she thought the ordeal was over. She didn't suspect a thing.

Lucius was as swift, decisive, and painless as he could be. She deserved that. In a flash, he drove the point of the heavy hunting knife into the base of her skull. The blade severed her spinal cord, and he shoved it up into the lower part of her brain faster than even a nerve impulse could travel. She didn't feel a thing, and she was dead in an instant.

He yanked the knife out, and her body collapsed on the ground.

'There is justice, and there is safety,' he said. The rest of the Bastion stared at him. 'We had both until Roland brought attention upon us all. She saw me kill him. If we had let this woman go, she would have told others about us. I couldn't allow that. This way she'll just be missing.' He looked down at her sad, fragile body. She reminded him of a young doe killed by a hunter. 'Maybe they'll say Bigfoot did it.'

He instructed four of the men to carry the bodies away from camp so the Bastion could begin to settle in for a calm but guarded night. The next day they would dispose of the bodies in the most rugged wilderness, where they would never be found.

After years of keeping the Bastion safe, isolated, and in the shadows, Lucius felt that everything was spiraling out of control. By his actions, Simon Helsing was also exposing them to danger. He was growing much too blatant, drawing the police, the media. Lucius feared for his people.

He also knew what Alexis Tarada was doing. From a public library terminal he had read her recent post, 'Hiding in Plain Sight', and he agreed with what she was saying. Alexis was still naïve, but better than most.

Lucius might have to talk with her, give her more of the information she needed to know. And soon.

Thirty

The folder he'd taken from Alexis Tarada contained a great deal of information – creepy information. Carrow had not expected much when he decided to meet with her again to ask about her meeting at the coffee shop. In fact after reading her crackpot website, the vampire-conspiracy blogs she posted, he hesitated about stepping into that funhouse and buying into a collective insanity. He couldn't tell if Tarada really bought into it, or if she was just playing her followers to milk them for more donations.

But now he knew that she had met with the man who was likely the stake killer. Finding this unexpected treasure trove of information made everything worthwhile.

'Simon Helsing' was certifiably crazy for believing this stuff, and he stalked potential victims. Gullibility did not constitute a crime – good thing, because half the people on social media would be in jail – but Carrow had no doubt that this man had killed Douglas Eldridge, whose name was right there in the dossier. He had also almost certainly killed Mark Stallings and Patric Ryan.

Tarada might not be directly involved with the murders, but she did have contact with Helsing, and she hadn't reported the meeting or the dossier to the police. If Carrow gave her the benefit of the doubt, maybe she hadn't actually aided and abetted a serial killer. Granted, he hadn't been especially warm and fuzzy to Tarada when he investigated her tip line report, but he gave her his card. The moment she saw this dossier, why hadn't she called again? Was she protecting Helsing? Dodge had seen her tense meeting with the man at the coffee shop. He had grabbed her arm. Was she afraid of him? Maybe, maybe not. It would be hard to make charges stick, but maybe he could use it as leverage.

After taking the folder from Tarada's house, he had slipped it in a plastic evidence bag. The techs had dusted each page for fingerprints, but the killer had left no trace. Now Carrow studied the information from a set of copies while the lab searched for fibers or other evidence that might lead to the man's whereabouts.

He commandeered a meeting room down the hall which offered more space than his cubicle provided. Working under the bright lights, Carrow spread out the papers on the table, organizing them in neat stacks so he could look at them all from a bird's-eye view.

He had done his homework, as Tarada asked. 'Helsing' was the great vampire hunter in the novel *Dracula*, written by Bram Stoker and published in 1897 – which also explained the man's screen name. Van Helsing had appeared in countless other books, movies, comics, a veritable pop-culture icon.

The top set of papers were Helsing's speculations and notes about Douglas Eldridge, and that alone would be damning enough to charge him with the murder. The sheer amount of detailed information Helsing had obtained was alarming: employee files, tax records, driver's license, bank accounts. Most chilling was a log of careful surveillance. Simon Helsing had been stalking his victim for a long time.

Because the killer wanted to convince or dupe Alexis Tarada into believing there were more vampires in hiding, the dossier listed many people of interest. He had killed Eldridge before giving her the folder. Before anyone could have known . . . But the other targets were still alive.

The next name in the stack was an EMT, an ambulance driver named MaryJane Stricklin. Helsing had obtained her employment record, which showed that Stricklin hadn't served a single daylight shift in two years. Carrow rolled his eyes. 'Doesn't mean she never stepped outside in the daylight.'

The killer laid out his evidence that led to the desired conclusion. As a paramedic Stricklin had ready access to fresh blood, whether by snacking on some hemorrhaging accident victim or by accessing hospital blood supplies. Through obsessive records searching, Helsing determined that Stricklin's ambulance logged significantly more fatalities than other ambulances, DOAs that should have survived, based on the nature of the injuries. She had received a reprimand in her personnel file, but no one had ever proved that Stricklin was responsible for the additional deaths.

The next set of papers included the photo of a middle-aged man with rounded cheeks, heavy eyebrows. Tom Grollin, a night-time cab driver who claimed to have a day job, but the killer could find no record of it, no other employer – which raised Helsing's suspicions, although it could simply mean that Grollin worked online, or sold junk on eBay, or did odd jobs off the books. Carrow would not have assumed 'secret vampire' to be the first explanation. He doubted any cab driver would willingly choose the midnight-to-dawn shift, transporting drunks who puked in the backseat and forgot to tip. Helsing also listed twelve Uber and Lyft drivers who logged only late-night hours and 'warranted further investigation'.

Carrow walked around the meeting room table. The next profile in the folder was laughable.

Hugo Zelm, well-known reclusive philanthropist. Although cops did not move in those social circles, Carrow knew who he was. Zelm appeared in the news whenever he made some spectacular donation or embraced a particular cause. The dossier noted that Zelm made a regular SupportMe contribution to HideTruth.

Interesting.

'Should give the guy a free pass in the vampire department,' Carrow muttered. If Zelm was really a vampire, why would he assist a conspiracy website about vampires and UFOs? Unless that was what vampires did to deflect attention, making their existence look like mere fodder for crazies?

Zelm lived in a mansion in the Broadmoor Hills on the western edge of Colorado Springs, up in the foothills. Unlike the other suspected vampires in the folder, the philanthropist was too obvious. The man hosted a large public event at least once a year. *King vampire?*

Carrow rolled his eyes. Wasn't there *always* a king vampire? From the photos in the dossier, Zelm was a bald man with an aquiline nose, close-set eyes, and leathery skin, about seventy or so. Certainly not the suave Bela Lugosi type. Still, he had acquired much of his wealth from investments in Eastern Europe. His grandparents had fled the Balkans with stolen treasure during World War II, and Zelm apparently still had family blood ties in the old country. Helsing's notes speculated that if the man had been alive for centuries, routinely changing his identity, he could have acquired extensive wealth.

200

Considering the prominence of the 'king vampire', Carrow decided he should talk with him first. The people in the dossier might indeed be at risk.

He flipped through several other candidates – nightclub bouncers, delivery truck drivers, hotel night clerks. The last one that caught his eye was Frederik Lugash, thirty-two, an immigrant from Hungary who had lived in the US for seven years. Lugash worked nights as a delivery man for a 24-hour pizza place. Helsing found other details that aroused suspicions – at least in the mind of someone wearing a tinfoil hat.

In the past several months, three of Lugash's customers had suffered strange fates. One disappeared entirely, simply abandoning an apartment and leaving no forwarding address, no trace. One neighbor said she thought the woman had moved to a new temporary job, leaving her possessions there for when she returned, but that had not been verified. No missing persons report was filed, so the CSPD had never checked into the woman's situation.

One customer died in an extraordinarily bloody single-car accident late at night, the body mangled. Helsing had noted, 'How much blood was taken from the body, unnoticed?' A third young man on the verge of graduating from Colorado College had slashed his wrists in the dorm room sink and bled out with no one around. 'No telling how much blood actually went down the sink,' Helsing wrote. 'Or how much was otherwise consumed.'

Deeply troubled, Carrow shook his head. So the great vampire hunter was suggesting that one of the powerful bloodsuckers worked as a *pizza delivery man*?

The very idea of obtaining records of all of Lugash's deliveries and cross-matching them with every customer in hopes of linking them to strange deaths implied a level of imagination and obsession that Carrow didn't want to consider.

Simon Helsing, or whatever his real name was, was disturbingly convinced about vampires, enough that he was willing to kill anyone who fit his imaginary checklist.

Carrow was sure that Alexis Tarada swallowed it all. Was everybody looking through crazy glasses?

This folder – which the killer didn't know the police possessed – was an excellent starting point. Beginning with Hugo Zelm, he would investigate these potential targets, tell them to keep their eyes open. No, Carrow corrected himself, not just *investigate* – he had to protect them.

A vampire hunter was on the loose.

Thirty-One

Though the bruises were still visible through the make-up around his eyes, Blair's genuine smile warmed Lexi's heart. He came home from Rags to Riches with enough exuberance to startle her.

'Tah dah!' From a bulky cloth bag, he pulled out a waterfall of white fabric embellished with lace, pearlescent buttons, and ribbons. 'This dress

is beautiful, and you'll look like an angel in it.'
He shook out a creamy, elaborate Victorian gown
and raised it up to shoulder level. 'I checked the
other dresses in your closet, so I know your size.'
He held it up, urging her to come closer.

Lexi was intimidated. 'I've never worn anything
like that.' The long gown was trimmed with ivory
silk, and had a faux corset of floral-pattern
damask around the waist.

'There's always a first time. You'll look so
spectacular that TMZ will wish they were there.'

'How do you know they won't be? Hugo Zelm
wants plenty of media. But I do like to keep a
low profile. I'm not comfortable about going to
this gala in the first place. Could be vampires
watching . . . or overboard fans.'

'But you are going, and you'll revel in the
attention.' He fluttered the dress like a matador
waving a red cape. 'Let me see this on you.' He
pressed it against her shoulders, looking her up
and down. 'It'll emphasize your shape, but won't
show any cleavage. Much too prim for that. Very
proper and virginal.'

'Cleavage? I don't have much, but the lace
collar goes all the way up to the neck. Looks like
a wedding gown.'

Blair snorted. 'Bride of the king vampire? You
look classy and *classic*.'

She held the dress against her, saw how the hem
fell down around her ankles. 'You better help me
get dressed when it's time. I feel like I'm going
to prom.' Lexi felt a sting in her heart. She had
not gone to her own senior prom; the pain of
Teresa's death had been too heavy on her heart.

'It's better than prom, my dear. You're an adult, and you're going with me, which guarantees none of the drama of a real prom date.'

She touched the gold chain of the necklace she always wore. 'I'm not sure this is adequate.'

'It's not, but I have the perfect accessory.' He reached into the bottom of the bag and pulled out a crimson velvet choker. Several rhinestones glittered like fallen stars on a field of blood. Blair could barely contain himself. 'Oh, this will look beautiful.'

'I hope you didn't pay too much, because I'll never wear the choker or the dress again. What do I owe you?'

He made a dismissive gesture. 'I told my boss you were taking it home to try it on . . . until after Saturday's gala. I'm sure you'll find some reason to return it.'

She frowned. 'I don't want you to get in trouble.'

He touched the bruises around his eyes. 'I have my own ways of getting in trouble. Believe me, you don't even make the list.'

She was pleased to see his mood. This was the happiest he had been in days. The black eyes would heal, but Lexi knew that his heartache would linger much longer. Cesar had called and texted Blair, abjectly apologizing, making excuses. She could tell Blair was wavering, but every time he mentioned how much he missed Cesar, how good the good times had been in their brief relationship, Lexi made him take a hard look in the mirror. That quieted Blair, at least for a while.

Having provided the dress for the gala, he loved

the role of white knight, using his own special talents to help her. Now that she looked at the beautiful ribbons, the silk trimming, the damask patterns around the waist, she realized how woefully inadequate her old Iowa church dresses would have been. She promised to try it on later.

Blair had a shift at the martini bar that night, but he would be home for a few hours. 'What do you want for dinner? Hungry for anything in particular?'

'Whatever you'd like to make. You never let me down.'

'Right answer.' He went into the kitchen.

Lexi was still preoccupied with Detective Carrow's news from the day before, the shocking stake murder of Douglas Eldridge. She kicked herself for not having made a copy of Helsing's folder, so she only had her memory to go on. Once Carrow revealed that the murdered man was listed right there in the dossier, she couldn't deny that Helsing was clearly connected with the killings. A homicide detective was allowed to seize crime evidence, wasn't he? But what if that evidence also showed that the victims were themselves vampires? Would Carrow even give that a moment's consideration?

One of these days, I'm sure to be right.

Two days had passed since she'd met Helsing at the coffee shop, and he had made no further contact. Stoker1897 had made no postings on her site, though her 'Hiding in Plain Sight' essay, based on his own speculations, had caused a general flurry.

Still no news about the second stake victim in

Colorado Springs, and she restrained from reporting the story herself. That would infuriate Detective Carrow, and it would reveal too much to Helsing, so she decided to hold off for now. Whether or not he posted or participated, she was sure Helsing kept an eye on her. Had he seen Detective Carrow come to her house? That would not be good. He would not have wanted her to share his secret research.

Then the second question fell harder. Did Simon Helsing know where she lived? Lexi shuddered.

She had sat right next to him while happy pedestrians walked by; he had grabbed her arm. The man was quite likely involved in the brutal killings, but his report had revealed so many dots in that random speckle pattern . . . dots that no one else had identified, or would identify. They made a damned compelling case.

What if Simon Helsing was right?

Even if there were real vampires, even if she came face to face with one herself, Lexi doubted she would have the nerve to place a sharpened wooden point against his chest – a human looking chest – and strike with a mallet. But Simon Helsing did.

She tried to understand what type of person would be so methodical and ruthless as to track down those potential targets. What had convinced him so absolutely that vampires were real? Would she ever be that certain?

Then she thought of her last conversation with Teresa, alone in her bedroom, suspecting nothing. Lexi believed in what she had experienced, without a shadow of a doubt. The incident had changed her life forever.

Had Helsing experienced something comparable to give him his unshakable convictions about vampires? She had so many questions she needed to ask him, but she had no way of getting in touch.

As Blair rummaged in the kitchen, she went out to the mailbox at the curb. Weeds grew up between the concrete partitions in the driveway. Neither she nor Blair bothered with yard care, but fortunately the small lawn didn't look any worse than her neighbors' swatches of grass and unenthusiastically manicured hedges. She sorted the mail from the box, grocery flyers, bills, credit card solicitations, coupons from Checkers Pizza.

And a folded note. Initially, she assumed some local kid was offering to do odd jobs, but it was a letter, personalized to her.

'Alexis Tarada, I have more information that you need. Proof. Witnesses. Please meet me. In your heart you already know the truth. Afterward you will have no doubts – Simon Helsing.'

Detailed instructions told her how to find an isolated meeting place up in the Front Range, dirt roads in the national forest that led to a set of abandoned buildings from US Army training exercises during World War II. He gave a time for *that afternoon.* Damn, no one had gotten the mail the day before. How long had the note been waiting there?

'Nothing like planning ahead.' She studied the letter as she walked back into the house. He couldn't just meet in a coffee shop again? This was practically in Outer Mongolia. What did he want to show her?

The drive would take her an hour or more into the mountains, definitely off the beaten track, and the sun would go down fairly early. She might have expected werewolves out in the forest, or even Bigfoot, but she had always assumed vampires were city types. If she was going to make the meeting, she'd have to leave soon.

What did Lexi actually know about him, for certain? Helsing had been determined to find every detail, every clue. He had already found remarkable things that had a nagging ring of truth, or at least raised uncomfortable questions about vampires.

Now Helsing promised proof, actual proof. What if the vampire story – however unlikely and absurd it might seem – was real? At least in part? She knew in her heart that it might be no more real than a stuck keyboard sending spurious signals . . . but what if it was? What would Teresa think?

If Helsing had proof, how could she not go? *One of these days . . .*

Thanks to Detective Carrow, Lexi now knew the man was genuinely dangerous. But was he a murderer of humans, or a killer of vampires? If Helsing considered her an ally, then she had nothing to fear from him. Right? In fact, she was the last person he would consider to be a vampire.

But why would he pick such an isolated place for a meeting? Unless there was something he needed to show her at a remote location. It felt like a trap. Common sense screamed at her not to go, but would he really concoct such an elaborate ruse just to get her alone? She could think of easier ways.

Forewarned is forearmed. Her dad had always said that.

Speaking of armed, she made up her mind to bring her handgun. Lexi hadn't been to the shooting range in months, and she doubted she would have the nerve to point the weapon at Helsing and pull the trigger, but if it got to the point where she actually had to fire the .38, then she had already lost. She would bring it, use it as a last resort.

She just couldn't believe that Helsing intended to attack her. It didn't make sense. He wanted her on his side, and he thought he could convince her. One in a million chance . . . She would give him that chance to make his case.

Was she obligated to report this letter to Detective Carrow? She had promised to pass along any attempted contact. If she did so, the CSPD could set up an ambush to arrest Helsing when she went to meet him, using her as bait. Everything by the book.

But that would never work. Isolated in the forest, Helsing would see them coming, and he would easily slip away – and then he would know Lexi had betrayed him. The man would never contact her again, and he would continue his private war against the vampires.

And she would never see the evidence he promised.

Though torn, Lexi wanted – *needed* – to have the proof, to convince herself and also to show

Carrow. If Helsing could provide incontrovertible evidence that the staked victims were real vampires, then the entire investigation would take a different turn. Was there any way she could ever convince Carrow?

Was there any way Helsing could ever convince *her*, beyond a shadow of a doubt, that vampires were real?

Lexi had to see for herself. If Helsing's 'proof' turned out to be bogus, then she could turn him in.

Blair was setting out frozen chicken breast filets on a cutting board to thaw. 'I already know what you're going to ask. Chicken piccata.'

'Sounds great. That's exactly what I was going to ask.' She gave him an apologetic frown. 'But I've got someplace to go. A meeting, and I'll be gone for dinner. Can you save some for me? I'll warm it up later.'

His disappointment was palpable. 'Not the same as fresh.'

'Your food is always delicious, even reheated.' She paused, turned to give him a serious look. 'It's the man who believes in vampires. He says he has proof, wants to meet me out in the middle of nowhere.'

He paled. 'I don't like the sound of that at all.'

'I'm taking my gun for protection.' Even as she spoke, the words did not sound reassuring.

'That doesn't make me feel any better. Do you want me to go with you? Wingman? Moral support? Intimidating bodyguard?'

'No, you'll spook him. I . . . I have to do this. Just to see. I've got to be sure.' She smiled at him, looking brave, and he reluctantly conceded. 'I might be late. Don't worry about me.'

'I'm going to worry about you.' He turned back to his chicken, apparently not wanting her to see his expression.

As Lexi went to get ready, she thought of another reason why she had to go to this mysterious meeting. The letter had been placed in her mailbox.

Helsing did indeed know where she lived.

Lexi had driven these roads a few times when she took local hikes, the short trail up to St Peter's Dome or out to a small waterfall in Emerald Valley. As she left the city proper into the foothills above the Broadmoor district, she drove past mansions, then isolated cabins and rustic trailers. Following the directions in the note, she left the main route and traveled on forest roads. Fortunately, the dirt, gravel, and washboard ruts were not too severe for her Toyota. She watched her odometer, found a turnoff at the appropriate spot, and parked at a chain blocking the feeder road. No road sign, nothing to indicate where she was. But this was the place.

She wore a jacket in the cool autumn afternoon, and the revolver felt heavy and awkward in her pocket. Colorado had extremely lax gun laws, and getting a concealed-carry permit had involved little more than filling out a form and taking a class at the firing range. Her gun was legal, but she wasn't in the habit of carrying it around. She wished it made her feel safer.

She checked her phone: no signal. Leaving her

car unlocked – who would break in out here in the middle of nowhere? – Lexi worked her way around the chain and followed the dirt road on what must have been private property, puffing as the incline grew steeper. The surrounding forest was thick, quiet, and peaceful. Tall Ponderosa pines rose on either side of the road, and scrub oak filled the gullies. She thought of how Holly Smith had been assaulted out in this forest by a big hairy creature she called Bigfoot.

In half a mile, she saw the abandoned concrete structures ahead. The old ruins had gray walls with caved-in roofs. Rusted rebar rose out of the ground like the ribs of prehistoric creatures. Chunks of cement lay around as the buildings crumbled in on themselves. Illegible spray-painted graffiti marked the walls. She remembered reading conspiracy conjectures that gang graffiti was actually secret messages from aliens. This, though, looked as if it had been done by bored kids.

'Hello?' she called out. 'Simon, are you here? It's Alexis.' She waved the letter in her hand, kept her other palm near the handgun in her pocket. 'I came as you asked. I'm anxious to see this proof. If it's what you say it is, I'll get the word out. It'll be a game changer.'

No response.

Lexi approached the old bunker and walked around the walls, poking her head into one of the darkened door openings. Inside, she found beer cans, snack wrappers, and a twisted pair of discarded panties.

She could sense that someone was there. 'Hello?'

The brooding forest pressed in on her. She kept exploring the abandoned buildings, her feet crunching on concrete fragments.

'Look, I'm not here for hide and seek. I came a long way. Let's get on with this!' She spoke loudly so that her anxiety would not show. She slipped her hand into the pocket with the .38.

She entered the next bunker, saw more crumbled cement, more beer cans, an old sleeping bag that had been ripped to fluff and scraps by rodents. 'Hey!' she called out again, impatient and annoyed. Was Helsing toying with her? Or had he bolted?

She paced the echoing room, looked up through the collapsed ceiling to see the sky, and strode back through the open doorway. She had to find him somewhere.

As soon as she emerged, Lexi heard a rustle of movement. Before she could pull the revolver from her pocket, someone dropped a cloth sack over her head and tugged it down tight. She screamed. Rough hands grabbed her arms, but she managed to draw the gun, fumbling to fit her finger through the trigger guard. She kicked out, yelling, but no one would hear her this deep in the forest.

Someone pulled the gun out of her hand.

'You'll be fine,' said a deep male voice. 'We just can't let you see.'

Something wet was pressed up against the sack covering her mouth. A wad of soaked rags. She kept fighting, trying to get free. Flashes of vampires, Bigfoot, and other deadly creatures rolled through her mind. Then she remembered

Blair's sad statement. 'Now I know there are real monsters in the world.'

She gasped in a deep breath, and strong chemical fumes entered her mouth, her nose. Each time she inhaled, her brain filled with fog. Dizzy, Lexi lost control and felt herself falling. But that wasn't possible because people were holding her arms. Her legs turned to water, and her vision faded to black.

Thirty-Two

After repeated phone calls, it was late afternoon by the time Carrow got through Hugo Zelm's assistants, schedulers, and other human roadblocks and arranged to see the philanthropist in his mansion.

He drove past the exclusive gated communities in the upscale Broadmoor district, searching for the address. Zelm's estate fit right in with the other ostentatious homes, each on an acre or more of rugged mountainous terrain overlooking the city.

Carrow parked his Ford at the curb on the steep street just beyond the mansion's black wrought-iron gates. As he stepped out of his car, he tugged down his dark sport jacket, unconsciously brushing the front. He felt woefully underdressed just standing in the street. When he took a deep breath, he thought the air seemed thinner here.

The gates were closed in front of him, metal

spikes like medieval defenses. The property was surrounded by a red brick wall, also topped with iron spikes. Carrow found an intercom box on the brick post beside the gate and pressed the button.

As soon as he did, a storm of barks and growls erupted from inside the walls, followed by the clatter of galloping paws. Carrow thought that a werewolf was charging toward him – which showed how much this ridiculous case was getting to him – but instead it was a pair of Dobermans with long snouts and sharp fangs. They streaked to the gate, snarling and panting like furnace bellows.

Carrow jittered back, cursing to cover his surprise. Blocked by the gate, the Dobermans trotted back and forth, as if ready to squeeze between the bars so they could rip his throat out. 'Nice dogs,' he said. 'I like dogs.'

The Dobermans didn't seem to believe him.

A deep male voice came over the intercom speaker, startling him almost as much as the dogs had. 'Can I help you?'

'Yes.' He cleared his throat to keep his voice from cracking. 'This is Detective Carrow from CSPD. I have an appointment to see Mr Zelm, but there's a couple of hellhounds in the way.'

'Please wait.' The speaker fell silent.

Carrow faced the two intimidating dogs that kept barking and growling at him behind the bars. He felt braver with the gate closed and locked.

After a few interminable minutes, two men in dark security uniforms walked down the drive. One man carried two chain leashes, and he grasped the collars around the Dobermans' necks, unconcerned about being mauled. He clipped the leashes in place, never taking his eyes off Carrow through the bars. Without saying anything, he yanked on the chains and pulled the dogs away. The second guard opened the gate and ushered Carrow inside, not even pretending to smile.

According to public records, Hugo Zelm had no wife, no children, no significant other, just an extensive staff. Maybe that was why he needed such a large house. The mansion had two wings, a sloped black roof, and tall windows. Carrow paused to take in the breathtaking view of Colorado Springs below and the rugged Front Range behind the house. The sun had already set behind the hills, and long mountain shadows spilled across the development like an ominous blanket.

'This way please, Detective Carrow.' The guard led him up the drive to the imposing house and climbed the steps to the front entrance. He opened a door that was high and wide enough for a mounted knight to ride through.

Inside, the staff had turned on all the house lights. A sparkling chandelier lit the high-ceilinged foyer. Carrow looked at the sweeping staircase, decorative marble columns, the polished marble tile floor, the framed paintings on the walls. Rooms full of lavish furniture extended in every direction.

'Huh, reminds me of my own place,' he said to the guard, who merely frowned at him.

Hugo Zelm entered from a side room, a bald man with liver spots on his scalp and hands, just like in his photographs. He wore a white dress shirt, black dress pants and gleaming patent-leather shoes. His thin, pale face looked like parchment stretched over his skull, and his aquiline nose could have been used as a weapon. He wore a heavy gold ring on one hand and a heavier gold Rolex on the opposite wrist.

'Detective Todd Carrow, so very, very pleased to meet you.' His smile came straight out of a vinegar bottle. 'I have been following your cases.'

That surprised him. 'My cases?'

'I am alarmed that such violence could exist in our serene city.' Zelm led him into a drawing room that was larger than Carrow's entire townhouse. 'I am happy to answer your questions, and I hope you will indulge my own curiosity.'

The fifteen-foot-high windows in the large room would have offered a breathtaking panorama of the city below, especially at sunset, yet the philanthropist had covered every window with dark, heavy curtains. 'Considering how much you must have paid for this place, why would you block the view?'

Zelm pursed his lips. 'The sunshine bothers me.' He rubbed his fingertips over the back of his opposite hand. 'The doctors say I am very, very susceptible to skin cancer, and I must avoid all exposure to direct sunlight. Fortunately for me, the night view is stunning as well.' He drew in a deep breath and let it out in a sigh. 'This is where I find my greatest peace.'

His eyes grew more intense and he leaned close as if imparting a secret. 'I also keep the curtains drawn because the paparazzi spy on me, and I will not let them leer inside my home.' He tugged on a heavy pull rope at the side of the window, drawing aside the curtains to reveal the sunset shadows across the hills and the city to the east. 'There, you see. I love to enjoy a glass of wine and just watch the busy activities of the little people down there.'

'Some might consider the curtains evidence of you being a vampire.'

Zelm chuckled. 'If you are inclined to believe things like that. Are you, Detective?'

Carrow scoffed. 'Not me, but I'm surprised the media hasn't made a scandal out of it.'

The philanthropist clucked his tongue. 'The more I value my privacy, the more they want to take it away from me. And that is one reason why I host such a large open house every year, where I invite in all sorts of media, allow the reporters and the general public to see me for one night in hopes they will leave me alone for the rest of the year. It is a vain hope, I know.' He sighed again. 'Now tell me, Detective, what brings you here?'

'Your name has come up in connection with a series of murders.'

'Oh dear, am I a suspect?' His eyes went wide. 'I'm a little old to be wrestling people with mallets and stakes.'

'I didn't mention the stake killer.'

Zelm's thin lips formed a smile. 'Is there another series of murders I am unaware of? I have my own sources of information.'

'Good sources, apparently,' Carrow said, though he wasn't surprised the details of Eldridge's murder had started to leak. 'But you're not a suspect, sir. In fact, you might be in danger. We obtained a list of potential victims from the possible killer, people he thinks are actual vampires. Your name was there.'

Zelm snickered. 'I know my behavior is unusual, eccentric, but I never thought it was *vampiric*. I suppose a madman can convince himself of whatever he wants to believe.'

'He is a madman,' Carrow agreed. 'I've been to the crime scenes.'

Zelm's eyes lit up. His pale lips drew back as if someone were stretching the skin on the back of his neck. 'I hear there is a second stake victim, and a decapitated man. Do describe the cases for me. I am fascinated by such things.'

Carrow was disappointed but not surprised the man knew so much. 'At least three victims so far, each one murdered in a way supposedly effective on vampires. At first I thought it was gang activity, excessive violence to scare rivals, but it seems the killer really believes in vampires.'

'Ah, excessive gang-related violence, like Chop Chop down in Pueblo.' Zelm's eyes glittered. 'I told you I have been following your cases, Detective. But I agree with your conclusions. This deranged individual truly must believe he is killing vampires.' He chuckled. 'Have you read HideTruth? It is filled with remarkable information. Did you know that the site is based right here in Colorado Springs? I am one of their supporters.'

'Yes, I'm familiar with the site,' Carrow said, cautious. 'I've already spoken with Alexis Tarada.'

'Oh, I very, very much look forward to meeting her! I have invited her to my gala this weekend.'

'It might be wise to cancel the party, sir,' Carrow said. 'You could be in danger. It's a golden opportunity for the killer to make his move.'

Zelm gave him a patronizing smile. 'I assure you I am in no danger. Have you seen my wall, my gate, my dogs, my guards? I am quite capable of protecting myself. I have had to do it for some time.'

Carrow didn't want to be brushed aside. 'Still, I could provide an additional police security detail, station officers on the property. I'd like to be here myself, just to observe.'

'Is that a subtle way of requesting an invitation? Why of course you are welcome to come. Will it fit into your social calendar?'

The man had a distinctly mocking tone, but the invitation was serious. 'I'm sure I can clear it.'

'I could send over a list of etiquette rules to your CSPD office, if you need them?'

'Thank you. That would be helpful,' Carrow said, then realized the comment might have been a jab. 'I'll be here. Just keep your eyes open in the meantime. Alert your staff about the murderer still out there.'

Zelm gazed at the shadows spreading across the city. 'Instead of viewing the open house only as a threat, can you look at this as an opportunity to trap the killer?' His dark eyes took on a new sparkle. 'In fact, since you know Miss Tarada, maybe you should accompany her as a bodyguard.

I would not want anything to happen to her.' He rubbed his hands together briskly. 'Yes, that would do nicely.'

The philanthropist locked his hands behind his back and stared out the window as the lights began to come on in the city.

Thirty-Three

Helsing had done his research and made his choice. He was ready for his next target.

Alexis Tarada would study the file of evidence he had given her, but he did not intend to wait for her. Even if the young woman shared his certainty, he wasn't sure she would participate in the violence. Even Lucius and the Bastion refused to join him in his bloody work. That was Helsing's fight alone.

Tom Grollin, late-shift taxi driver, lived in a small flat on the second floor of an old building on Cascade Avenue downtown. The shops and restaurants at street level drew a lot of pedestrian traffic, but Grollin worked at night – hunted at night, Helsing was sure – and slept during the daytime, hiding in his protected lair.

Because the door to the stairwell leading to the upper apartments was on a public street, Helsing would not break in during daylight hours to make his kill. His chance to get inside would be in the dead of night, when the streets were silent and when Grollin was out hunting. Once in position, Helsing would lie in wait and attack the vampire while he was awake.

Feeling a thrill, Helsing approached the street entrance in the sullen darkness before dawn. The taxi driver was still out on his rounds, and Helsing had plenty of time to set his trap. When the vampire returned, sated and sluggish from his evening prowl, Helsing would strike. He had already proved that the Taser was effective.

The door to the upstairs flats was just off the sidewalk, sandwiched between an upscale clothing shop and an art gallery. At this hour, even the restaurants and bars on the street were closed.

The door was locked, accessible only to the tenants, but it wasn't a very secure lock. He huddled in the portico dressed in dark clothes and a gray trench coat, nothing that would be recognizable on surveillance cameras. He would appear to be just one of the homeless seeking shelter in the doorway. He worked quickly with the lock picks, opened the door to the entryway and slipped inside. A well-lit staircase led to the second floor, and he hurried up, though no one would likely be wandering the hallways at 5 a.m.

Grollin's apartment was one of four doors upstairs. The vampire had installed a deadbolt to supplement the lock on the doorknob, and Helsing had a few bad moments when he couldn't get inside. Though he made little sound, he was taking too much time. Finally, he clicked the deadbolt aside and ducked into the darkened apartment.

The retractable window shades were raised to give Grollin a full view of downtown Colorado

Springs at night. Helsing was surprised a *lampir* would let himself be so exposed, but he imagined Grollin rising after full darkness and raising the shades to look out at his hunting territory. He would prowl during the night and return in time to draw the shades before dawn.

This time, though, Helsing would be waiting for him.

He closed the door securely behind him, locked the deadbolt again. With the streetlights shining through the window, he didn't have to use a flashlight as he slowly assessed the area.

The taxi driver's studio apartment had a Murphy bed that was already folded down from the wall, the sheets and blanket rumpled, as if he never tidied his place. There was a tattered old recliner that might have been through several tenants, and a tiny kitchen with dishes piled in the sink. Tom Grollin was a complete loner, understandably so.

The lowered Murphy bed filled most of the open space, leaving little room to maneuver. Helsing found the best spot for an ambush, just behind the door and next to the recliner. He set down his satchel and slid out of his trench coat. He sprinkled himself with holy water, then removed the long hunting knife, the hatchet, and the jar of fresh garlic cloves.

It was now 5:30 a.m. according to the illuminated clock in the kitchen. Less than forty-five minutes to sunrise, and Grollin needed to return home before dawn.

Helsing removed the Taser from the satchel and crouched, ready. With his vampire senses, Grollin would know something was amiss the moment he entered, so Helsing would need to strike instantly. He wouldn't have a second chance. Freshly fed, the vampire would be strong, capable of tearing out Helsing's throat – unless Helsing killed him first.

The minutes ticked by. His grip was sweaty on the Taser. He was sure he would detect footsteps coming up the stairs, certainly the key in the lock.

But a faint glow of color suffused the eastern sky, visible through the windows. Something wasn't right. What if Grollin had more than one place to go to ground? Helsing's research had found nothing, but what if he was wrong? How could a vampire be out in the sun? Did he need to change his plan?

Slanted golden light came through the windows, full sunrise, before he heard footsteps plodding up the stairs. Grollin didn't seem to be in a hurry, no frantic rush to reach his dark daytime shelter; he just sounded tired.

No. Helsing touched the cross around his neck. By now the holy water had dried to a faint dampness. He could not let himself doubt. He was doing the right thing.

He heard the jingle of keys, a rattle in the lock, and he tensed, made sure the Taser was ready to fire. He aimed toward where the man would step through the doorway.

The deadbolt clicked, then turned, and Tom Grollin pushed open the door with a grunt and a grumble. The taxi driver sounded weary and unhappy as he stepped inside.

When he saw Helsing standing in front of

him, his mouth dropped open, and his eyes went wide.

Helsing fired the Taser before the vampire could make any sound. The electrode wires spun out and the barbs dug into Grollin's chest. The cartridge discharged with a zapping, popping rattle of electricity, enough to make the man jitter and flail. His legs gave out.

Helsing was already moving. He got behind Grollin, used his shoulder to knock the man forward into the small flat. The taxi driver staggered ahead two steps until he crashed into the Murphy bed.

Helsing quickly swung the door shut, clicked the deadbolt. Grollin lay groaning on the rumpled sheets, clawing at the electrode prongs in his chest. With a vampire's recuperative powers, Helsing knew he had only a few seconds.

He tossed the Taser aside, grabbed the long knife, and jumped on top of the Murphy bed, pinning Grollin on his back. With his left hand, he pushed the vampire's chin upward, then made a hard, swift stroke with the blade in his right. He cut into the neck, sawed through blood vessels and tendons. A fountain of red showered Helsing, soaked his hair, his shirt. He worked swiftly, cut, sawed, severed all the soft tissue.

Grollin's struggles ended quickly. The Murphy bed was a swamp of blood. Daylight streamed through the open windows and spilled over the bed, across the victim. But just cutting a *lampir's* throat wasn't good enough. He set the knife aside and grabbed the hatchet. He brought it down as if he were chopping kindling. Two swift, sharp blows cleaved the vertebrae and the remaining skin until the man's head rolled free from the body.

Still not good enough. He pried open Grollin's mouth, separating the teeth. The fangs were hidden now, reverted to the natural state. He dumped several cloves of garlic into the open mouth and pressed the jaws shut again.

Blood was everywhere, sprayed on the walls, the mattress, the sofa, even a fan pattern across the window glass. He looked down at what he had just accomplished. The mess always disgusted him, but it was necessary. Decapitation with garlic was the most thorough method Helsing could imagine.

Pounding a stake through the heart was far less messy, though, and quicker. That would be his preferred method from now on, except for the silver-filled shotgun shells, which he would use against the king vampire.

He backed away from the Murphy bed, glad he had brought his trench coat. At the kitchen sink he washed the obvious blood from his hands and face, letting the red trails trickle down among the dirty dishes. Through the walls, he heard a radio alarm in the apartment next door, someone no doubt waking up to get ready for work. Helsing had to get out of there before anyone saw him.

He hadn't expected to be here so late, never imagined the vampire would return after sunrise. Hoping to remain unnoticed, Helsing pulled on the trench coat to cover his blood-soaked clothes, enough to let him get out of the building and through the side alley to where he had left the car.

Once he made it back to the Rambler Star Motel, he could clean himself up and take a well-deserved rest.

Thirty-Four

Arriving at his downtown CSPD office the next morning, Detective Carrow collected the eighteen names from Simon Helsing's dossier and knew it was going to be a long day. He had arranged for added manpower to talk with the other potential targets. Hugo Zelm hadn't seemed worried, but he had his own security army. The others in the dossier seemed like normal, everyday people who happened to have nocturnal schedules.

One of the first individuals, Tom Grollin, lived only a few blocks away on Cascade, and Carrow headed there first thing. It seemed the best place to get started. He doubted he could convince the chief to provide police protection for all the names in Helsing's dossier. Fortunately, the suspected killer didn't know that Carrow had his list, unless Alexis Tarada had told him – and she claimed to have had no further contact since the first meeting. If he found out that she had been communicating with Helsing in secret, aiding and abetting a murderer, he would arrest her so fast her feet wouldn't even touch the ground.

At Grollin's address Carrow found the locked street-level door and a set of intercom buttons for the tenants upstairs. He pressed the button marked *Grollin* several times, but received no response. The taxi driver had probably worked a long shift and might have fallen asleep. Carrow buzzed again and again, enough to wake someone who slept like the dead.

Still no response. Maybe Grollin wasn't home? Maybe the intercom button was broken? Or it could have been something else. A chill went down his spine as he recalled Eldridge smoldering on the kitchen linoleum with a stake through his chest.

Unexpectedly, a woman pushed open the door, and he grabbed it before it could close. She wore a navy-blue pea coat and looked startled to see him there. He fumbled out his detective shield. 'Detective Todd Carrow, CSPD. Looking for Tom Grollin. He doesn't respond to the buzzer—'

The woman pointed up the stairs. 'He's in number four. I don't see him much. Sorry, I've got to get to work.' She hurried off, letting him slip inside.

Upstairs at the door of Grollin's flat, Carrow rapped hard, but heard no response. He pounded harder. 'Mr Grollin? Colorado Springs Police Department.' He heard no noise, nothing stirring inside the apartment. In the small flat, no one could be very far from the door. Maybe Grollin was in the shower? On the toilet?

He smelled a distinctive flat copper scent, which prickled the hairs on his neck. 'Hello, anybody home?' He looked down and noticed a smear of red on the all-weather carpeting, like blood, maybe wiped from the sole of a shoe.

'Mr Grollin!' He tried the doorknob and

surprisingly found it unlocked. With his hand on the butt of his revolver, he pushed his way in.

Morning sunlight streamed through the windows, but the stench of spattered blood struck him even harder. 'Crap almighty!'

The scene was horrific, far worse than the two staked bodies he had found. The taxi driver's head lay on the Murphy bed, his slack face staring upward. The headless body sprawled beside it. The sheets were pooled with deep red blood. Spatter covered the walls, the ceiling, the windows.

The blood on the dead man's face sparkled, wet. His cheeks were rounded, stuffed with something, and Carrow guessed what he would find if he probed inside the dead man's mouth.

His gaze tracked to the wall, to the glass of the windows. The droplets were still wet. Even with the morning sun shining on them, the blood hadn't dried, which meant this killing had happened very recently, probably within the past hour . . . not long after sunrise.

He drew his weapon and slowly turned, alert, trying to sense if anyone was still there. The cramped apartment offered few places for a killer to hide. He listened, but nothing stirred. 'Just missed him.'

Carrow immediately called in backup, knowing they would arrive within minutes. Considering the blood and violence of the scene, the killer had to be a dripping mess – easily spotted if he was still in the vicinity. Helsing would be running, hiding, trying to get away.

Carrow peered through the red specks on the

window glass to the street below. The thick smell of blood in the air nauseated him, and he felt claustrophobic in the small flat. The furniture filled almost every square inch.

He went back to the body on the bed, saw marks on the shirt and chest, and realized that Helsing must have used the Taser again. As he turned slowly, absorbing the murder scene, he imagined Helsing lying in wait and pouncing as soon as Grollin walked through the door. If he'd been fast enough with the Taser, the neighbors might not have heard much of a struggle.

Carrow looked at the rolled-up window shades. Blood was on the glass, so the shades had been open during the murder. Had Helsing tried to stun the alleged vampire with bright sunlight? Then why use the Taser?

And why was he applying logic to an obviously insane man?

Two squad cars rolled up minutes later, sirens wailing. When he let them in through the tenants' door and led them to the apartment upstairs, one of the men retched.

Carrow was eager to turn over the scene to the coroner and the techs. He knew that the serial killer, the 'vampire hunter', was responsible for at least four deaths, possibly more. The other potential victims had to be warned before it was too late. How many others had Helsing killed already?

He felt a sense of urgency. It was broad daylight in a clear blue sky – exactly the right conditions for a vampire hunter to kill again.

Thirty-Five

When Lexi began to return to consciousness, she smelled wood smoke and heard muttering voices. She recalled trying to wake up several times before dropping back into a drugged stupor. A surge of fear purged the fog of grogginess, and she snapped her eyes open.

She had a splitting headache and a foul taste in her mouth. Blinking several times, she saw trees. Filtered sunlight. Blurry people.

Lexi remembered the abandoned buildings – and the sack over her head, the pungent sweet rag pressed against her mouth and nose, her deep, panicked breaths. Now she shivered, and her body wouldn't quite function. She turned her head and groaned.

As her vision sharpened, Lexi found herself sitting in a canvas camp chair, with a blanket draped around her shoulders. She was surprised to find that her hands were unbound.

'Lucius!' a boy's voice cried. 'She's waking up again!'

She was outside in the forest, in a camp of some kind. She saw cook fires, weathered picnic tables, colorful nylon tents as well as camouflage tarpaulins. She tried to lift herself out of the camp chair. Some vague flight instinct in the back of her mind made her want to run away, but her legs wouldn't work. She couldn't even stand.

When Lexi shook her head, pain throbbed inside her skull. She coughed, worked up a mouthful of saliva, and spat, but the horrible chemical taste only intensified. She fumbled for the jacket pocket where she had put her revolver, found it empty.

A big man loomed in front of her in a buffalo-plaid shirt and a fleece vest. He peeled off grimy canvas work gloves and tucked them into his jeans pockets. She thought she recognized him – big beard, blue black hair, and dark eyes – but the context was all wrong. She couldn't place him.

'I'm sorry about what we had to do, Miss Tarada. We didn't think you would be unconscious for quite so long, but it's not an exact process. You'll feel the after-effects for a while. It is what it is.' He gave her an apologetic smile. 'We did not intend to hurt you, but we needed to talk. We couldn't let you see where we really are or how to find us again.'

Now she remembered him: the homeless panhandler who had approached her at the coffee shop right after she met Simon Helsing. *It's all true, you know.* Were they partners? They must know each other; it was too much of a coincidence.

'My name is Lucius. I lead a group that we call the Bastion, off the grid and deep in the forest where it's safe. In particular, where the vampires can't find us.' He lowered his voice. 'We will survive whatever destroys mankind.'

Her voice was just a raspy croak, and she couldn't form words.

'Here, dear,' said a matronly woman in her late forties, thick around the waist and hips from a life of hard work. She offered a speckled blue metal cup filled with water.

Lexi took a cautious sip, then drank several gulps. 'What did . . . what did you do to me?' She tried to put her thoughts in order, tried to remember. With a shock, she realized it was already morning. Had she been unconscious all night? Here in this place? 'I came to meet . . . Simon. Simon Helsing.' She fumbled for her gun again, came up empty-handed.

'He is part of our group, though an outlier,' said Lucius. 'We know he's been in contact with you, and I'm watching you, too. I read HideTruth.'

The thought of anyone following her site from a wilderness camp that relied on cook fires and battery lanterns seemed as strange as any story she posted. But Lucius had also been in the city, and she guessed he could easily have used public-access terminals or a phone browser.

Lexi saw several dozen people in this camp, but she didn't know how many more might be scattered in the forest. A crow cawed in the pine trees overhead. Morning sunlight filtered through the dense forest.

A dark-haired boy with Asian features stood next to Lucius, staring at her with wide eyes. He seemed afraid of Lexi. 'Is she going to stay here with us? Or will we have to—'

Lucius put a large hand on the boy's shoulder to silence him. 'None of that, Joshua. We invited her here to talk, and we want her to listen. She should be on our side.'

'I'm not staying here.' Lexi tried to manage a threatening tone. 'You drugged me, abducted me. You can't hold me against my will.'

'We could, but we won't,' Lucius said. 'We want to talk with you. That's why we sent you the letter.'

She calmed herself enough to think clearly. Of course they wanted to talk. They had lured her here for some reason, pretending to be Helsing. And she had come here to listen.

'All right.' Lexi took another sip of water, found herself waking up, her thoughts clearing. 'You've got a lot of explaining to do.'

'Yes we do,' Lucius agreed.

'You promised me evidence about the vampires. Witnesses.'

'We have evidence, if your eyes are open to see it,' he said.

The matronly woman went to a cook fire where a large pot sat on a grate, and she stirred some sort of savory-smelling soup or stew.

Lucius said, 'The members of the Bastion are out here because we intend to survive. We see the dangers ahead. We know about the coming apocalypse.'

'What apocalypse?' On HideTruth and in her work for PRUUF, she was familiar with dozens of end-of-the-world scenarios, some of them scientifically valid, others ridiculous.

'Should we prepare for only one? Humanity has already invented a dozen ways to destroy the world. Some disasters are instantaneous, some more subtle. You've heard them all. I know you have.' He stroked his thick beard. 'There are predators lurking in the world, Miss Tarada – many different kinds. They've been quiet for centuries, while humans developed their own ways to make themselves extinct. Civilization is unstable, naïve, oblivious. Something is going to happen. The dark ages are coming.' Lucius leaned closer to where she sat in the camp chair. She instinctively pressed her back against the canvas and drew the blanket around her.

'But the Bastion is going to survive.' He gestured to the people who helped Mama prepare to serve the morning meal. 'Groups like the Bastion exist in many places, all of them with disparate fears but a singular purpose. To survive.'

Lexi also knew about paranoid survivalist camps, and here in the huge Pike National Forest, the lack of any phone signal was just the smallest part of their isolation. In her research on Bigfoot and the assault on Holly Smith, she had read rumors of homeless camps deep in the woods. These people could pack up and vanish if they felt threatened.

Lucius nodded to a slouched Hispanic man tending a small campfire near his own tent. 'Armand escaped from a FEMA camp and lived in hiding before he finally joined us, and the Bastion has protected him ever since.' He turned his attention to a remarkably thin African-American woman, but the skittish woman ducked into a tent, as if she didn't want to be noticed in any way. 'Joy was part of a secret government breeding program, forced to bear five children from different fathers, all for some kind of experiments. But the last birth damaged her uterus, so

235

they turned her loose to wander the streets. We found her, and we protected her.'

'*They*?' Lexi asked. 'Who are *they*?'

Lucius scoffed. 'There's always a "*they*".'

Lexi wanted to leave, to go back to her safe home, her own bed, a hot shower, clean clothes. Blair must be worried about her. 'I came here on the promise of evidence about vampires. What do you have for me?' She tried to put steel in her voice. 'You faked that letter from Helsing, made me come out here. This better be good.'

Lucius showed a hint of an amused smile. 'We didn't *make* you come. We invited you.'

She shrugged the blanket off her shoulders and rose to her feet, bracing herself with the wobbly camp chair. Her legs were unsteady, but she was determined to meet him eye to eye. 'The letter promised me proof and witnesses. After all this, I need to get something.'

'I'll give you the best proof I can offer. Maybe it will convince you, maybe it won't. It is what it is.' He turned to the woman by the cook fire. 'Mama, is the soup ready? I'm sure our guest is hungry.'

Joshua and a young girl came on either side of Lexi, steadying her as if she were an old woman. They led her to a picnic table, and she sat down on the rough bench. Mama brought her a bowl of thick bean soup with minced meat and set another one in front of Lucius. Breakfast?

The others came forward, bringing their own cups, bowls, and utensils for the morning meal. As Bastion members crowded the picnic table benches to listen to Lucius's story, others stood holding cups in their hands, slurping soup or coffee in the morning chill. A basket held small wild apples.

'The Bastion has many other settlements around the country, people hiding from the cities to make a life for themselves, back to nature. At first it sounded idealistic and utopian, but others went into hiding for different reasons. When Simon joined us, he told us about the *lampir* – vampires. They've preyed on humans in Europe for centuries, and now the things are spreading across America. He was a fiery crusader, and he convinced a lot of us.' Lucius swallowed hard. 'And some of us didn't need convincing. We thought we were safe out here in the woods.'

His gaze took on a troubling intensity. The fire behind his dark brown eyes reminded her of the obsession she had seen on Simon Helsing's face. His voice grew strange and raspy.

'I already knew Simon's warning was true, had known it for years. I remember the night it happened, when that *thing* attacked our settlement. I was barely twenty. I remember when he – it – tore into one of the tents on the outskirts of camp. The woman inside, a lovely lady who gathered honey and shared it with all of us – she screamed. It was long after midnight, and we lit our lanterns, grabbed our hunting rifles, shotguns, handguns, knives, baseball bats, what have you, and rushed to defend her. Her screams fell silent before we could even get to her tent. I'll never forget that wet gurgling sound.'

Lucius shook his head. 'I had my rifle slung over my shoulder, and several other men and women closed in. The vampire tore his way out of the honey woman's tent, using clawed hands to shred the fabric. He lunged out, howling.'

Lucius turned pale and closed his eyes. Lexi watched him shudder as he relived the memory. 'I will never forget it.' He kept his eyes closed, crystallizing details as he spoke. 'Its eyes were a demon's – sharp, slitted, and red. I saw fangs, blood covering his lips, running down his chin. I unslung my rifle, slammed back the bolt. Two other people got off shots, and I saw a bullet strike the vampire. It spun, staggered, but recovered itself and kept charging toward us.

'I shot at it, but I missed.' He heaved a long shaky breath. 'I missed! But the Bastion stood together, and when the vampire saw us with our lanterns and our weapons, closing in on it, the thing fled into the forest like a shadow. The night was dark, and there was something . . . *jagged* about him.'

The other members of the Bastion ate hunched over, listening with rapt attention. Lexi finished her soup and just stared at Lucius, moved by the passion and sincerity in his words.

'The honey woman was dead in her tent. I'll never forget her wide, dead eyes. Her throat was ripped open. Blood everywhere.' He turned to Lexi with a haunted expression. 'That is how I know there are vampires, Miss Tarada – even before Simon came among us. I've seen them with my own eyes. I know they're out there. I, myself, have disposed of bloodless bodies we discovered, people with their throats mangled, usually homeless men or women with no ID.'

Though engrossed in the story, Lexi was thinking clearly now. 'It sounds like a terrible ordeal, but that's not proof. It's just a tale. You could be making it all up.'

Lucius looked annoyed. His dusky complexion turned ruddier. 'I could be. You'll just have to believe me.'

'I have proof,' said a gruff voice.

A tall man with dark skin and intense eyes came up to the picnic table. He wore a high-collared hunting jacket, a cap with ear flaps, and a thick gray sweater. Lexi turned to him and he leaned closer, defiant, intimidating. 'I fought them, and I have the scars to show for it.' He tugged at the collar of his sweater, spread open the camouflage jacket. 'Look!'

He tilted his head, baring his throat like a submissive animal. Lexi saw uneven, mangled scars on his neck, rows of them, where his throat had been torn open. But he had somehow survived. 'Two vampires killed the rest of my family, and they almost got me, but I got away.' His voice cracked, and he looked at Lexi as if he could barely hold in a scream.

'This is Nolan,' Lucius said. 'He came from a different Bastion camp, but we welcomed him.'

'Look at the scars!' Nolan jabbed at his throat.

'Very convincing.' Lexi kept her voice quiet and did not point out that the scars could have come from another injury.

Nolan insisted, 'The Bastion saved me, stitched me up, and at least I didn't turn.'

Lucius crossed his arms over his chest, looking at her. 'You see, Miss Tarada?'

239

Lexi gathered her thoughts, chose her words carefully. 'On HideTruth I ask people to keep an open mind about impossible things, and I really mean that. But you can't just state that vampires or Bigfoot are real and expect people to accept it on your word alone.'

'Bigfoot is not a problem. He's been taken care of,' Lucius said.

Lexi frowned. 'What do you mean?' He refused to answer.

Mama set another speckled enamel cup next to her. 'Here you are, dear. Some tea. We make it from the forest, pine needles and special herbs.'

Preoccupied with the bearded man's story and with what Nolan had showed her, Lexi sipped the tea, tasting pine needles, pungent herbs, a bitter under taste that was not entirely unpleasant. 'So, you help Simon find possible vampires? He showed me his list. Are you saying I should just take his word that it's all true? That those names really are vampires?'

Lucius drew his dark brows together. 'We are concerned about Simon. This should be a quiet war, or none of us will survive. The general public will never accept the real threat, and Simon's recent . . . activities are drawing far too much attention.'

'I think that's what he wants.' Lexi took another drink of the tea. 'He's trying to expose the vampire threat so that other people join his crusade. That's why he came to me. He's trying to enlist me as an ally.'

'The Bastion does not want the attention. We know the police are after him, but we will take care of our own.' He drew a deep, satisfied breath. 'I've told you what I wanted you to hear. We will watch Simon, and I'll attempt to rein him in, to minimize our exposure. He is our problem.'

'If you truly believe in vampires, why would you let them continue to prey on innocent people? Why not join Simon and expose as many of them as you can?'

'Vampires will always prey on people. It is foolish to think we can defeat them. In the Bastion, we just want to survive this apocalypse, and we have our best chance out here. I hope you understand.'

The sun had risen high by now, and Lexi wanted to go home. 'What was the point of bringing me out here? To show me your camp? Why did you tell me that story?' She looked around. 'None of this is incontrovertible evidence that I can present to doubters. At best, it's hearsay.'

She felt the headache throbbing even harder, and her vision grew blurry. Lucius leaned closer. 'Because we need you to *understand* us, Miss Tarada. And because you are safe, as far as the Bastion is concerned. We know how most people view your site. If you ever decided to reveal our secret and spread our story, nobody would believe you. But at least you know we're out here.'

Her instinctive response was indignation, but she felt sluggish. Her ears began ringing and she looked down at her empty speckled cup of special tea. Glancing around the picnic table, she noticed that no one else had taken a cup of tea. The Bastion members were staring at her.

'What did . . .?' She swallowed hard, felt that

241

intense under taste, and the world began spinning. They had drugged her again. 'Bastards!' she managed to croak before her eyelids drooped shut again.

Lucius caught her as she slumped forward on to the picnic table.

Thirty-Six

Arriving at the Rambler Star Motel, Helsing felt soiled with death. Though the long trench coat covered his red-soaked clothes, the blood had seeped through his shirt and pants, making them stick to his skin. The residue from the slain vampire seemed to throb with evil, trying to penetrate his skin.

He felt nauseated as he parked the old Honda in the parking lot, away from the door to number 41 so no one would associate the car with that room. Several guests were busy packing up their vehicles, checking out of the motel mid-morning.

He had decided not to decapitate vampires from now on, even though the brutality appealed to him. The first time had been a satisfying experience in the dark shadows of the Monument Creek watershed, when he'd killed Patric Ryan. The vile drug dealer had lured his victims into the quiet privacy of the park by promising them cheap crystal meth. Helsing assumed the vampire fed on them after addicting them. Such a man certainly deserved such a bloody death.

With Grollin, though, Helsing had taken an unnecessary risk. Normal people were stirring at that time of the morning, going about their business, and he could not be as unobtrusive as he wanted. Someone might see him. Still covered in blood, he had driven away from downtown as quickly as possible, heading to where he could hide, but the traffic was bad. An accident had blocked part of the interstate, forcing him to exit early and use side streets to make his way back to the motel.

Now he needed to get into the room, quickly. As he climbed out of the car, he pulled the trench coat around him, ducking low and pulling up the collar. Luckily, no one gave him a second look as he hurried to the turquoise door, turned the key, and slipped inside his safe room. The heater thrummed on the wall like a faulty jet engine.

As his eyes adjusted to the light that filtered through the drawn curtains, he looked around, hyper-alert. Nothing had been disturbed as far as he could tell. The manager generally left the room alone, checking it only occasionally to replace towels and to clean if necessary.

Helsing pressed his back against the door and let out a long sigh of relief. He was shaking. Then he smiled. It was over, another vampire dead.

He flicked on the yellow nightstand lamp and tossed the satchel on the end of the bed. He opened it, removed the long knife and hatchet, both crusted with sticky blood, and set them on the desk next to the shotgun-shell re-loader press that was still clamped in place. They would have to be thoroughly washed. He took the time to rewind the electrode wires in the Taser, replaced the charge, then returned the stun gun to the satchel, tucking it next to the Canon 1D X.

He had four unused wooden stakes and the mallet. The holy water was almost gone, but he still had garlic left. He removed the cross from around his neck, wincing as he pried it loose from drying blood, and dropped the chain into the bag. A vampire killer always had to be ready.

Despite the mess and the risk, Tom Grollin had posed very little challenge, but the gruesome murder would cause an uproar. Worse, after killing so many vampires, Helsing knew that the rest of the city's undead would be incensed, especially Hugo Zelm.

He took out the Taurus Judge and obsessively checked the five small-caliber shotgun shells he had filled with silver fragments. Five shots – reserved for the king vampire, by far the most difficult target. Even with his plan, Helsing wasn't certain he could escape after killing Zelm, but bravery and audacity might give him a better-than-even chance.

Helsing's pulse was racing. He wanted to scrub himself clean in a hot shower, and change into a fresh set of clothes from the closet. Then he would pass as perfectly normal again, ready to hunt the next target on his list.

He looked at the dried blood on his knuckles, under his fingernails, down his wrists. He felt as if he had just emerged from an orgy at a slaughterhouse. He peeled off the trench coat and draped it on the bed next to the satchel, and now his clothes felt cold and tacky. He plucked at his shirt, pulled the blood-soaked fabric from his ribs. He would have to burn these clothes. He could never ask the manager, even a former member of the Bastion, to launder them. It would raise far too many questions.

He whirled as he heard the doorknob rattle, a key in the lock. The door swung open with a swift and casual turn, and Daniel Gardon barged in without knocking. He flicked on the light switch.

Helsing stood there in the flood of daylight that spilled into the room from the open door, his body covered in blood. The red-slick butchering knife and the bloodstained hatchet lay on the desk next to him.

Gardon stared, aghast. 'My god, all that blood!'

Helsing lurched toward the manager. 'Wait! It's not human blood. It's vampire blood. You know—'

Gardon raised his hands as if to protect himself. 'What did you do?'

He turned to run, and Helsing instinctively lunged for a weapon. This man had left the Bastion, questioning their beliefs, their tactics. He was a danger, a vulnerability.

Helsing seized the revolver, swung it up, and pulled the trigger hard.

Gardon had just made it out the door as the gunshot exploded. At close range, the blast caught the man in the neck and the side of the head, blowing him into shredded meat. Thrown by the impact, he sprawled on to the cement doorstep.

In the parking lot two rooms down, a family was loading their hatchback with gift bags from the Cheyenne Mountain Zoo and the Garden of the Gods Trading Post. Standing by the open passenger door, the mother watched the bloody body crash to the ground after the loud gunshot. The kids screamed in harmony.

Helsing's wrist throbbed from the recoil. Throwing the revolver in the satchel along with the stakes, mallet, and other tools, he bolted from the room. Too easy to get trapped there. No time to get anything else. He didn't even take time to don the trench coat and cover himself.

He sprang over Gardon's body on the cracked concrete. More people had emerged into the parking lot and were panicked by what they had just witnessed.

Helsing bounded toward his car, grabbing the keys, which thankfully were still in his pocket. He threw himself into the driver's seat and started the Honda's engine even before slamming the door shut.

The tourist family crouched down by Gardon's mangled body at the open door of room 41. A big man in a trucker cap was already shouting into his cell phone.

The Honda's tires spun and spat loose gravel in the parking lot, and Helsing raced away from the Rambler Star. With so many witnesses, he was positive someone would note the license plate. Other motel guests could identify him; his cover was blown. He had to move fast if he wanted to have any hope of salvaging his plans.

Simon Helsing was on the run, and he knew exactly where to go.

Thirty-Seven

After leaving the Grollin murder site, Detective Carrow wasted no time going down the list of potential victims.

He turned over the crime scene as soon as the coroner arrived. As he met her at street level, heading out the door, Orla Watson was bright eyed and exuberant, which Carrow found odd. 'You seem altogether too eager for another murder scene,' he said.

Watson blinked her owlish eyes. 'I love my job, Detective. That's why I'm working so hard to get re-elected, and all this work helps increase my visibility.' She hurried up the stairs, as if she was afraid of being late.

Next name from the folder was Frederik Lugash, the pizza delivery man. Lugash lived in a small rundown home in a small rundown neighborhood, not far from the county jail and innumerable bail bond offices, lumberyards, and fenced storage areas for building supplies.

Carrow drove to the south part of town. The neighborhood was a cluster of ranch-style homes with white aluminum siding, black shingle roofs, concrete driveways, and broken-down cars on cinder blocks that served as lawn ornaments. Lugash's driveway had a Volkswagen Rabbit with a plastic Checkers Pizza delivery sign still hanging from the passenger window. His house was quiet, closed up as if it had been mothballed for the day. Lugash worked the night shift and came home to sleep, much like the vampire killer's previous victims.

Carrow hoped he wasn't too late again. Unless Helsing, or whatever his real name was, had rushed straight here after chopping off the taxi driver's head, he couldn't have had time to kill this man.

Unless he had murdered the man the previous day, when Carrow was with Hugo Zelm.

He pulled open the scrolled aluminum screen door and pounded hard on the door, rang the doorbell three times, then pounded again. After several minutes of knocking, he grew concerned, especially after what he had just seen at Grollin's apartment. He dredged up his inner macho in preparation for either shouldering or kicking the door open. Considering the circumstances, the action was justified.

Just as he braced himself, he heard movement inside: someone shuffling up to the door, locks clicking, a chain rattling. The front door opened to reveal a gaunt man in his early thirties, wearing boxer shorts and no shirt. His chest was pasty white, almost cadaverous, and his ribs showed. He shrank away from the bright daylight, rubbed his eyes, and ran a hand through his disheveled hair. 'What do you want? I'm sleeping.'

'Frederik Lugash?'

'If you don't know who I am, then why the hell are you pounding on my door? It's only ten o'clock! I just got to sleep.'

'I know you work the night shift, Mr Lugash, but there's a possible threat to your life. We have reason to believe a serial killer may have targeted you. Good enough reason to disturb you, right?'

Lugash blinked, still in the hallway shadows. 'Me? Why the hell would someone want to kill me?'

'He believes you're a vampire. You sleep during the day and work all night.'

Lugash shook his head, as if trying to absorb the words through the fog of a deep sleep. 'That's what the night shift does, man. A vampire? Asshole! Let me go back to bed.' He turned away in annoyance.

'It's not me you need to worry about, sir,' Carrow said. 'There was another murder this morning – four that we know of, so far. Killer seems to think each one was a vampire. We have his list of potential targets, and your name is on it.'

The pizza delivery man looked uneasy. 'Well, what do you expect me to do about it? I'll keep the door locked.'

'Be alert for anything unusual. Going to authorize an unmarked car here in the neighborhood for your protection, but they'll be as unobtrusive as possible.'

'As long as they let me sleep. Why the hell would he target me?'

'He's gathered what he calls evidence, but I'm not saying it's a rational theory. Do you recall any suspicious customers, someone who might have been stalking you?'

'Suspicious customers? They're all suspicious.' Lugash rubbed his eyes again. 'Shit, you know how many I see? How many houses or apartments I drive to every night? I remember the tips and sometimes the addresses, not the faces.'

Carrow tried to placate him. 'I had to ask. Rest easy. The security detail will watch over your home, keep you safe.'

'You do that, thanks.'

Carrow looked at the scrawny, half-naked milk-skinned man and handed him his card. 'Here's how you can reach me. Call if you see anything suspicious.'

'I'll do that.' Lugash tucked the card in the waistband of his underwear. 'Now I'm going back to bed.'

He closed the door in Carrow's face.

The next person on Helsing's list was MaryJane Stricklin, the night ambulance driver. She answered the doorbell on the first ring. Stricklin was in her early forties, had a rounded face freshly scrubbed of any make-up. Her thick blond hair hung in a low-maintenance perm, which complemented her lounging pants, sweatshirt, and fuzzy slippers. A news channel with nonstop inflammatory 'breaking headlines' blared on the TV.

Carrow showed her his ID. 'Looking for MaryJane Stricklin.'

'She's right in front of you. MaryJane is legal in Colorado now.' It took a moment for Carrow to understand the joke. 'I was just about to eat dinner, Detective. Come in.' He smelled marinara inside the house. A plate of spaghetti, two slices of garlic bread, and a glass of red wine sat on a small table in front of the television.

Carrow looked pointedly at the wine. 'It's ten-thirty in the morning.'

'Dinner is when you decide it is. I had a long night, lost a customer. A car accident victim, DOA. So sad. Just a kid, probably eighteen. All that blood . . .' She sounded defensive as she stepped back to her dinner for one. 'I try to enjoy my own life because I see so much death. I'm going to have a nice pasta meal, garlic bread and a glass of chianti, probably two. Is there something illegal in that, Detective?'

Carrow smiled. 'Don't actually care about the wine. More interested in the garlic bread. In fact I'm relieved.' She looked puzzled until he explained about the vampire killer and his intended victims.

'So he's suspicious of me because I drive an ambulance at night?'

'Also because of your access to blood supplies, not to mention the availability of blood from the injured victims you transport. Statistically, there's an unusual number of fatalities among your passengers.'

'Fatalities?' Stricklin sounded even more defensive. 'There are *fatalities* because people *die*, and more people die at night. Car accidents, drunk drivers, bar-room fights, drug deals gone wrong. I hate it! Maybe your vampire killer should look at my personnel file and see how many times I've requested transfer to the day shift. I'd rather handle broken bones on a playground.' She seemed angry, and Carrow understood why.

He got an idea. 'It would keep you safer if you were out and about during daylight hours, make

251

it obvious you aren't afraid of the daylight.' He nodded toward her drawn drapes. 'Can't say that the killer is actively watching you, but if you changed your work shift, he'd know he was wrong about you.'

'That's all I have to do?' She defiantly tugged on the cord and pulled open the curtains across the front window. 'I won't be able to see the TV very well, but it's just talking heads anyway.' While Carrow remained standing in the hall, she sat down, took a bite of spaghetti, then a sip of the chianti. As if showing off, she tore into a piece of garlic bread and let out satisfied sounds. 'I'll stand in broad daylight in the middle of a parking lot and eat a whole loaf of garlic bread if that will help.'

'Only if he sees you,' Carrow said.

The woman got a calculating look on her face. 'Detective, if you write me a note that my life may be in danger because I have the night shift, my supervisor will have to transfer me. He's ignored my previous requests.'

'I can make some calls,' Carrow said. It would be cheaper than assigning a plainclothes protective detail.

'Thank you!' She lifted her glass to him in a brief salute and took another gulp of the red wine. 'You saved my life in more ways than one. In fact, when I finish dinner, I'll sit out in a lawn chair in the front yard and read a magazine.'

'Sounds like a good plan,' Carrow said.

Alexis Tarada was the best option for him to spread the word about Stricklin in a way that

Helsing would see it. Even if she wasn't in direct contact with the man, as she insisted, Carrow hoped he could convince her to post something on her crazytown website. He should also tell her about Zelm's suggestion that he join her at the gala, which he doubted she would be thrilled about.

Since Tarada's house was only fifteen minutes away from Stricklin's, Carrow decided to pay her a visit before he continued down the list of targets from Helsing's dossier.

A handsome man in his early thirties answered the door. He had well-styled hair and his shirt seemed too formal for relaxing around the house. Yellowing bruises around his eyes were poorly covered by make-up. He squinted in the light and stepped farther back inside.

'Can I help you?'

Carrow ran his gaze up and down the man. 'You must be the housemate.'

The man seemed cautious and amused. 'I am indeed a housemate. Are you selling vacuums or cleaning products?'

'Detective Carrow, CSPD. Need to speak with Alexis Tarada.'

'Oh, you're the detective Lex complains about. Blair September, pleased to meet you.' He extended his hand, as if they were meeting at a cocktail party.

Carrow shook it automatically. 'She complains about me? What do you mean?'

'She says you're closed minded.'

'Because I don't believe in little green vampires?' He frowned, reset. There was no point in arguing with this man. 'Let me speak to Miss Tarada, please. I have further information on a case.'

'I wish I could help you, but she's not here.' Now Blair looked worried instead of aloof. 'She went to meet somebody yesterday afternoon and stayed out all night.'

That surprised him. 'You mean, like a boyfriend?'

Blair seemed affronted. 'That's none of your business, but no, not a boyfriend. And it's not like her.' He made no move to let Carrow inside.

Maybe Tarada was there after all, maybe hiding Helsing somewhere in the house. Was the house-mate covering for her? Was he an accessory?

Blair hesitated, seemed almost ready to blurt out something, and then he changed his mind. 'Lex knows what she's doing. She told me not to worry about her, and I'll respect that. For a little while longer.'

'Have her contact me when she gets in.' In order to make sure she wouldn't avoid him, he added, 'Tell her there's been another murder.'

Blair raised his eyebrows again, regained his aloof demeanor. 'I'm sure that'll pique her interest.'

Thirty-Eight

When Lexi awoke, she found herself behind the wheel of her Toyota in the forest. The midday sun shone through the trees. The details were so incongruous and confusing that she closed her eyes again, trying to reset reality and wake up from this bizarre hallucination.

Her head pounded and her throat felt thick. Sinister trees towered around her car on the isolated dirt road, and a chain blocked further access in front of her.

She gripped the steering wheel and pressed her back against the driver's seat, taking deep breaths, exhaling slowly. With a sudden, irrational fear of vampires, Bigfoot, werewolves, and any other frightening creature – including crazed human beings – she locked the car doors.

She tried to focus, tried to remember. Her thoughts were all fuzzy, as if Blair had given her too many basil martinis. But this wasn't a hangover. She hadn't had anything to drink . . . except tea!

She remembered it all now: Lucius, the camp deep in the forest, the survivalists who feared the end of humanity. Vampires! The story Lucius had told, the other man with the scarred throat. They meant to convince her, wanted her on their side. To join them, or just to understand? Lucius had shown her his 'evidence', which turned out to be nothing more than a campfire tale. And then they had drugged her again to bring her back to her car.

'Bastards,' she muttered under her breath and tried to strangle the steering wheel. 'That's not the way to make me sympathetic to your cause!'

How long had it been? It was early morning when she'd regained full consciousness the first time. She had talked with Lucius for an hour or so before Mama's special tea rendered her unconscious again.

She found her gun lying on the passenger seat beside her. They had returned it.

She needed to get home. Her stomach twisted as she thought of how upset Blair must be by now. She had told him not to worry, but she'd been gone overnight, almost an entire day. Grabbing her cell phone, she saw that she had no signal, no way to call him. Lucius and his people had just left her stranded out here.

'Bastards,' she repeated. She certainly disliked the Bastion's methods. Only desperate people would do that – truly frightened people who were afraid for their lives and for humanity. Or crazy people.

She felt in her pocket and found her car keys, which made her weak with relief. When she inserted the key into the ignition, she discovered that her whole body was trembling. She couldn't see straight. Lexi wanted to drive out of there, return to civilization, but she could barely keep her head up. With the after-effects of the drugged tea, she didn't dare drive, especially on these winding dirt roads. Too many sheer drop-offs to deep ravines.

Her head throbbing, she double-checked that the door locks were set – though surely any ruthless vampire could smash right through the windshield – and slumped back in a confused stupor for half an hour or so, just trying to recover, to get her head straight.

Finally, when bright early-afternoon sunshine streamed through the trees, she started the car, relieved to hear the engine come to life. Driving with painstaking caution, turning too sharply and then overcorrecting, Lexi crawled along.

It took her more than two hours to get back home. As soon as she reached the fringes of the city, she called home, talked to a frantic Blair. 'I'm all right, honest. Shaken, confused. Still processing. I promise I'll be home in half an hour.'

When she walked into the house, Blair was on the living-room sofa, obviously waiting for her. He lurched to his feet. 'You're safe! I'm glad to see it with my own eyes.'

'I told you not to worry.' She felt ashamed for what she had done to him, though she'd had no control over what had happened. 'I'm still alive, and I've got a lot to think about.'

Blair reached her in a few steps, threw his arms around her. 'You need to tell me everything. Don't lie to me.'

'Right now I just need to crash and process things. It wasn't what I expected at all. It wasn't Simon Helsing, but somebody else who wanted to tell me secrets.' She just stood holding him for a long moment. All the words had evaporated out of her head, and he didn't pressure her. She breathed into his shirt. 'Thanks for being there for me.'

'If I was *there*, then I wouldn't need to worry about you.' He stepped back. 'And I do expect to hear all about it – when you're ready. Can I make you a cup of coffee? I bought a French press for special occasions and I'm not afraid to use it.'

She squeezed him again. 'Rough night, rough morning, rough afternoon. What I need most is a shower, warm snuggly clothes, and a nap. I need to call in a free pass. No judgment.'

He repeated her own words to him. 'You always get a free pass from me. Oh, that detective came by to see you again.' Blair pursed his lips. 'Not impressed.'

She felt a chill. Had he somehow known she was meeting Simon Helsing? 'What did he want?'

'Something about the case. He said there's been another murder that you might be interested in.'

She felt a sinking in her gut. She hadn't been with Helsing, so maybe he had killed another person on his list. She groaned.

'You can worry about murders in a little bit.' Blair turned her around by the shoulders, marched her toward her room. 'First, you take care of yourself.'

The shower felt wonderful, as did her clean, warm sweats, but before she could crawl into bed for an afternoon nap, the phone rang – her parents calling for their weekly conversation. Lexi didn't know if she could face it. She couldn't even remember what day of the week it was.

She did her best to sound cheerful, normal. Her father said, 'We like to check up on you, especially with more murders in the news. Colorado Springs seemed like a nice place when you moved there, but it's just a dangerous big city after all.'

Before Lexi could respond, her mother continued, 'You'd meet a better group of people if you went to church. You haven't found a place since you moved, and it's about time.' Lexi could feel the lecture coming. 'Colorado Springs has plenty of good churches. Your father looked them up.' Perry Tarada considered himself quite an expert in 'the Google'.

'I'm sure there must be nice ones,' Lexi said. 'Churches are more common than Starbucks around here, one on every corner.'

Her parents paused on the phone. 'What does church have to do with Starbucks?'

'Never mind. I'll consider it. I've still got my Sunday church dresses – I was just looking at them the other day.' She hoped it would change the subject. 'I can't go this Sunday, though, because I'll be out late the night before. I've been invited to a fancy charity gala, very upscale and important.'

'Is it a charity for one of the mission organizations? I'm proud of you.'

'A different sort of charity. A philanthropist. He's a supporter of my site.' That turned the conversation around again.

'Be careful if you're out late. It's dangerous,' Perry warned.

Her mother asked, 'Are you still wearing the necklace we gave you?'

She fingered the gold chain and the small cross around her neck. 'Always, Mom. I promised.' It was a concession she had made to keep her parents from nagging her.

'We wish you'd come home.' Her father was getting that tone in his voice again.

'This is my home now. You should come and visit.' She cringed as she tried to imagine a week with Blair and her parents in the same house, but they would never make the drive.

'Those murders sound horrific. We've read all about them.'

'Oh, have you been checking out my website?' Lexi asked.

'Of course not,' Sharon said. 'But we watch the news.'

'The real news,' her dad assured her, 'not that fake news stuff.'

Since Lexi spent her days tracking down false memes and misleading stories, intentional misinformation designed to corrupt gullible people, Lexi had overwhelming evidence to show them about how their favorite news was extraordinarily biased, but she knew they wouldn't look. 'Thanks, but right now I want to get some sleep. I had a rough night.'

'It's almost time to start dinner,' her mother said.

'What did you do last night?' her father said.

'I was just working late. Goodbye now. Love you both.'

When she ended the call, Lexi felt tense in an entirely different way from what she'd felt after her experience with the Bastion. She closed the curtains and crawled into bed, ready for a long, deep nap. As she dropped off, she realized the irony of hiding inside a darkened house and sleeping during the day.

Thirty-Nine

The murder scene at the Rambler Star Motel was a mess. Yellow police tape sectioned off the room, the cement doorstep, and part of the asphalt parking lot. Crime scene techs combed over the site, gathering evidence. Dr Orla Watson looked down at the body with a calculating frown.

The victim lay sprawled on his chest, head turned sideways, his arms and legs bent at odd angles. He looked like a bug sprayed with insecticide, except for the mangled side of his face and neck.

'Busy day,' Watson said to one of the techs. They had spent most of the morning downtown in the tiny apartment of the decapitated taxi driver. That should have been enough work for a full week. But two corpses in one day?

'I don't get paid overtime for this,' Mel grumbled.

'Things are happening in Colorado Springs! Hmmm, maybe not a great ad for the tourism board.'

Mel pursed his lips, which made his thick mustache bounce. 'I don't get overtime for listening to your jokes either.'

'My husband's the comedian,' she said. 'But it does emphasize how necessary my job is. Can I count on your vote for me as El Paso County Coroner? The election is less than a month away.'

'I don't vote,' Mel said. 'Never have.'

Watson was shocked. 'It's your duty as an American citizen. Everyone should vote.'

'I don't want to be around all those people in the polling place. I'm not comfortable in a crowd.' He waved a hand to indicate the sprawled body and the blood that pooled across the concrete step. 'I prefer dead people.'

'We're in agreement there,' Watson said. 'But you can do a mail-in ballot.'

'I don't want to get on any lists. The government knows too much about me already. Haven't you heard about black helicopters and FEMA camps? I'm not signing up in the voting registry.'

She huffed. 'You have a driver's license. You're already on government lists.' She decided to give him a bumper sticker and a lawn sign for her campaign, whether he liked it or not.

Mel looked uncomfortable, got back to work. She squatted beside the dead motel manager. 'It's nice just to have a normal vanilla shooting. Wooden stakes and garlic-stuffed heads were interesting at first, but they're getting old.'

Nathan Dodge, the senior officer on the scene, joined Watson. While Detective Carrow was investigating the stake murders and warning other potential victims, Dodge had drawn the lucky straw for this run-of-the-mill homicide. 'Single GSW. Plenty of witnesses.' He glanced at the victim's head and neck, which looked like hamburger. 'Shotgun, obviously. Small-caliber shell.'

Watson scrutinized the shredded face and neck, the blood and skin fragments everywhere. 'Effective enough at close range.'

262

'Four fifty-one,' Dodge said. 'No doubt about it.'

Watson turned her head to look up at him. 'Are you the medical examiner now? On what do you base that conclusion?'

'Because the shooter had a four fifty-one reloading press mounted to the table in the room.' Dodge referred to his notepad. 'The witnesses heard only some brief shouting, not a prolonged argument. It escalated quickly. The victim, the motel manager, was standing in the door of room forty-one. Considering where the blast hit and the position of the body, the perpetrator must have shot him as he was turning to leave, possibly to flee. Maybe the victim saw something when he opened the door to the room?'

'I might hire you as part of my team if you're looking for a job,' she said. 'So long as you vote for me.'

'I always vote.' Dodge gave Mel a disapproving glance. 'But my vote is my own business, and I don't tell anyone who I plan to choose.'

'That is your right. Do we know the name of the room's tenant?'

'No records whatsoever,' Dodge said. 'There's something fishy here. All the other guests are carefully recorded both on the ledger and in the computer, but not room forty-one. No records at all. No clue who did this.' He scratched the side of his long jaw. 'Could be this was a drug den or headquarters for some other illegal business. From the supplies, clothes, and equipment, it looks like people lived in the room for extended periods, not just overnight. Could be the killer kept his base here, had an under-the-table agreement with the manager, but the deal went bad.'

Dodge clucked his tongue, continuing to muse as he stared through the open door. 'There was an argument. The manager tried to flee. The killer shot him, probably a wild impulse. This one's a crime of passion, someone surprised into shooting.'

Like a Hollywood reporter, Mel took pictures from every angle, not just the body but the concrete step, the turquoise door, which had also been splintered with spraying pellets from the shot. Other techs combed the interior of the room, bagging whatever they found, dusting for prints.

The shooter had been impulsive and clumsy, and Watson doubted CSPD would have a difficult job identifying him. The stake killer was something else entirely.

She got out her long tweezers and probed in the mangled skin of the dead man's neck. She plucked out pieces of the shot and dropped the bloody bits of metal into a small plastic container from her evidence kit.

As she extracted one fragment after another, she was surprised that some were square, some shapeless lumps, a few large, others tiny and jagged. They looked like pieces of coins, fragments of rings, even bits of chain. And they were bright. 'This doesn't make any sense.'

She stood up with a quiet grunt and turned to the turquoise door, looking at the spots where pellets were embedded in the cheap wood. She plucked out another piece and saw bright metal that was definitely not lead shot.

When Watson arrived at the scene, she had

assumed that the shooting victim had nothing to do with the stake killer, but now . . . 'Oh, shit.'

Dodge pulled out his notebook and paused, ready to take down her observations. 'What is it?'

Watson pulled out her cell phone and speed dialed Detective Carrow. She turned away from Dodge as Carrow answered. 'Hello, Detective? This is Dr Watson, the medical examiner.'

He huffed on the other end of the line. 'You really don't have to introduce yourself every time you call me.'

'A good coroner should follow every step of the process. I'm with a shooting victim at the Rambler Star Motel down on South Nevada.'

'Heard about it. Isn't Dodge there? I thought he was handling this one.'

'He's doing a fine job.' She smiled at the older policeman, remembering that he voted. 'But I'm afraid this case is going to fall in your lap as well.'

'Why?' He sounded harried. 'Got a dozen more names to chase down before a serial killer gets them. Isn't that just a routine shooting?'

'Shotgun blast, but it's connected to your other victims.'

'How? I'm heading back to see Alexis Tarada now. Anything that connects her to it?'

'I wouldn't know about Miss Tarada,' Watson said. 'But this was not a normal shotgun blast. It's very peculiar. Fascinating in fact.' She held up the bright metal fragment in her tweezers. 'The victim was shot with a silver bullet.'

Forty

After fleeing the motel, Helsing knew the police would be searching for his car. He tried to remain calm and avoid erratic behavior as he drove. He had a destination in mind – an escape route, a safe place. He headed due west through the city toward the mountains.

One of the witnesses surely must have identified the Honda, marked down the license number. He could have pulled into a parking lot and swapped plates, but that would delay him, and someone might see. He was drenched in blood. He needed to get out of the city and into the forested foothills without delay.

Helsing drove along surface streets, bypassing the Interstate until he reached the entrance to the sprawling, beautiful Garden of the Gods Park with its winding roads and spectacular rock formations, almost 1,400 acres inside the city limits. He had considered this escape route long ago. Sightseers cruised along slowly, gawking at the pocked red cliffs and strange hoodoos. Daring climbers dangled from ropes down the rock cliff faces, while crowds of photographers watched.

The tourist cars drove with maddening slowness, which only increased his panic. Helsing forced himself to inhale to a slow count of six, exhale to an equal count. One mile at a time, and soon he would be back in a safe hiding place.

He gripped the steering wheel, fixed his gaze on the languid curves of the road through the park, which butted up against the national forest. When a slow-moving station wagon in front of him pulled over at a scenic viewpoint, Helsing peeled around it, making his way to the western boundary of the park.

His heart hammered. Everything was falling apart. He had shot the motel manager right in front of witnesses! He had lost his base at the Rambler Star and left huge amounts of evidence there. He had never been so careless! Helsing still had his satchel, his weapons, and he had hidden other emergency bags – with stakes, mallets, another Taser, a machete – in three locations around the city, should it ever come to that. He would not be unarmed in his fight against the *lampir*, but he was being hunted.

Right now, the important thing was that the police would never think to look for him in Garden of the Gods, a tourist attraction with plenty of eyes and cameras, but it offered a back door to safety. At the edge of the park, past picnic areas and hiking trailheads, he reached the terminus of the Rampart Range Road, an unpaved thoroughfare that climbed steeply and ran along the spine of the foothills for sixty miles. From there, he would have ample access into the vast national forest and many numbered and unnumbered four-wheel-drive roads.

As soon as he began toiling up the steep switchbacks, the tourist traffic disappeared and the city dropped away. His best speed was no more than forty miles an hour, but once he crossed the national forest boundary, he felt a weight lift from him. No one would ever find him now. This was his territory.

He needed to find the Bastion again, at least for now. Lucius and the others would have to take him in.

To avoid hikers, hunters, or off-road vehicle enthusiasts, he diverted on to smaller forest roads, little more than logging routes. Helsing knew them all from when he had lived out here. Each member of the Bastion understood how everything was connected.

He spent more than two hours on the rough road before he found the right spot near an unmarked side trail. He parked the car out of sight at an unofficial camping spot with a ring of stones around a fire pit. The Bastion hid several emergency caches in strategic places, ready with food, clothing, and medical supplies in case any member needed it. Helsing could have taken what he needed from one of those, cleaned and resupplied himself without bothering to see Lucius again – especially considering that he had killed Daniel Gardon, one of their own.

Gardon had left the community, expressed doubts about the Bastion's beliefs, but he had remained loyal and helpful. Helsing had killed him – by accident, but he was still dead. Previously, Helsing had been so careful to kill only vampires, checking and double-checking his suspicions before making his move. But Gardon was an innocent, in the wrong place at the wrong time.

And that made Simon Helsing a murderer. He had a hard time wrestling with that guilt.

He and the Bastion did have the same goals, saw the same threat of the *lampir*, even though they did not share his methods. Now, distraught, he needed to go back to the people, a prodigal son. He had to find them again, had to tell them what he had done. Gardon was unintentional, collateral damage, a foot soldier fallen in a war for the human race.

Hours later, when he finally walked into the Bastion camp, exhausted and covered with dark, dried blood, he was surprised to see the people striking their tents, packing up the tables, folding tarps, and preparing their supplies for a swift move.

Lucius organized the activities while Mama tied down plastic sheets, wrapped up packages of preserved food. Teenagers coiled ropes, disassembled camp stoves, folded canvas chairs, latched crates and coolers. They spotted Helsing as soon as he approached, his footsteps crackling in the underbrush.

Lucius put his hands on his hips and glowered at Helsing. 'Our scouts reported you were coming from a mile back, but we couldn't wait. Too much attention, and we have to go deeper into the forest to hide. We've chosen a more isolated site.' He ran his gaze up and down the blood-covered figure. 'Oh, Simon, what did you do now?'

'I did what needed to be done.' Helsing looked at his red-flecked hands, holding the satchel that held his weapons and tools. They would find out soon enough about the dead motel manager, but right now he needed their help. 'Instead of hiding, I'd rather you came back to the city and joined me in my work. This is a war, Lucius!

I've exposed the vampires. With the whole Bastion working together, we could eradicate the *lampir*. Or at least fight back! I know who the king vampire is and where he lives. I plan to kill him on Saturday.'

The people paused in their work, and Lucius stood firm. 'You will have to do it without us, Simon. You've already endangered the Bastion. You draw attention to yourself, and you made the outsiders suspicious of us.' He leaned closer, drawing his heavy brows together. 'No one believes in vampires. They think you're crazy.'

'Alexis Tarada believes,' Helsing insisted. 'She's on our side. I've spoken with her.'

'So have I,' Lucius said, surprising him. 'I tried to convince her. She may help, but I won't rely on her. But what good could she do? Most people consider her a gullible fool, too.'

Children ran around the camp, packing their clothes into duffels. Lucius did not like to keep his people in the same place for too long, but this time they seemed more frantic about the transfer. They would flee deeper into the wilderness than ever before.

'I know the threat, Lucius. I'm helping to save the world. I've killed many vampires and identified others. But I never wanted to do this alone. I thought I was part of the Bastion, and the Bastion was part of the crusade. We can't just hide like rabbits!'

'The Bastion is about its own survival. That's why we were formed in the first place. I have to put my people first.'

Mama came up to stand next to her husband,

but she showed compassion for Helsing. 'You are welcome among us, Simon. Stay out here. It's too dangerous in the city. Your real mission is to help us survive – survive *with us*.'

'My real mission is back there.' He gestured east toward Colorado Springs. 'I'm a soldier, not a coward – like you all seem to be.'

Lucius said, 'The human race needs to survive. It is what it is.'

'I want to survive by killing the enemy.' Helsing felt rage. 'You and I have opposite philosophies.'

'That we do, Simon.' Lucius sounded deeply sad. 'If you stay here, you are welcome as a contributing member of the group, as you were before, but you have to follow the rules. If you go back to the city, you are no longer part of the Bastion.' He extended a beefy forefinger. 'Understand that. If you keep killing people, we can't have anything further to do with you.'

Helsing plucked at his sticky shirt. 'At least give me some clothes. I'll change and be away.'

Lucius remained silent, trembling with anger over the perceived danger to his followers. The big bearded man had been Helsing's mentor, someone who had helped save him and guide him after hunting vampires on his own as he crossed the United States. Lucius had been his ally, and the Bastion had been his army.

But not anymore.

Mama took pity on him. She went to one of the packs and sorted through clothes, pulling out a neatly folded shirt and an old pair of blue jeans. 'This is what we can spare.'

'Nothing more,' Lucius said. 'I did not want

271

this to end as it has. I'd rather have you here among us. I care a great deal for you, but if you are a threat to the Bastion, then I have to do what's right for my people.'

'Go ahead and run away. Vanish in the forest like frightened deer,' Helsing said with a sneer. 'I can take care of myself. I always have.' He snatched the shirt and pants from Mama's hands, then paused to look at her with more warmth. 'Thank you. You were always good to me.'

The Bastion pulled up stakes and packed two burly ATVs with full loads to go find their new camp. The vehicles rumbled off, engines buzzing in the peaceful forest. Deeply disappointed, Helsing swallowed hard and clutched the clothes against his chest as he watched them go.

Not wanting to stay as the rest of the camp finished pulling up stakes, he headed toward some old Army ruins where he could take shelter, change clothes, and rest while making new plans. He no longer cared about the Bastion. He didn't belong among them. He was alone in this fight against the vampire infestation.

Except for Alexis Tarada.

Forty-One

Lexi wasn't used to sleeping during the afternoon, and her dreams were full of strangeness – not nightmares about bloodsucking monsters, but fuzzy nostalgia of safe but monotonous high school days in Dubuque. She and her best friend Teresa were trapped inside a tiny bubble with a narrow horizon, both of them with aspirations to do more.

Maybe because of the after-effects of the Bastion's knockout drugs, she dreamed about Teresa now. She saw her friend in her bedroom discussing plans for the future, just like on that last night. Both young women were bright eyed, full of imagination and possibilities. Teresa seemed as real as her most vivid memory, but dreams always made things seem possible. Teresa looked as beautiful as always, young and with a full future ahead of her . . . even though Lexi knew that she was already dead.

Was a dream any less real than a ghost?

'You're doing it, Lexi,' Teresa said, 'just like we always promised each other. You and I both know that the world is full of mysteries. You'll find something. One of these days, you're sure to be right. We were going to do it together, but now it's up to you.'

'I want you with me,' Lexi said. 'You left me.'

Teresa just shrugged. 'It wasn't my call.'

She wondered if her friend had gained some great wisdom on the other side of death. 'I have to know. Were you really there in my room that night?'

Teresa used a seemingly tangible hand to brush long brown hair away from her eyes. 'Just as I'm really here now.'

'I'm dreaming.'

'That doesn't mean I'm not here.' She grew more intense. 'Don't give up hope, Lexi. You

273

and I know there are monsters in the world, just as there are miracles.' The young woman – the dream, the ghost, her best friend – frowned. 'And there are also disappointments.'

'I miss you, Teresa.' Lexi reached out for her, but the other girl vanished without responding.

After she awoke, she lay thinking. Were these just restless thoughts from her subconscious, or was it Teresa communicating with her again? At any other time, she would have doubted that, but now that she had heard the stories Lucius told, seen the dossier Simon Helsing had gathered, she wrestled with questions about the existence of vampires. Could Helsing, and Lucius, and all the members of the Bastion suffer from the same delusion? Some kind of mass hysteria? Lexi didn't know whether or not to dismiss the idea.

Was Teresa trying to make her remember her sense of mystery and wonder?

Blair made her a cup of coffee as soon as she emerged from her troubling nap. 'I don't care if it's late in the day. You look like you need it, Lex.' He handed her the steaming mug fresh from the French press. 'I know what it's like to have a hard night.'

'This isn't a hangover. At least not the normal kind.'

'I need to go to work, but we should have a chat when I get home. Free pass doesn't last forever.'

'I know.'

Blair kissed her on the cheek and headed off for the happy hour shift at the martini bar. Lexi sat at the kitchen table for a long time while her coffee got cold. She sipped occasionally, alone in the house.

Though it was sunset, the doorbell rang, and she was surprised to find a flustered Detective Carrow standing on her porch, still talking into his cell phone.

He scowled accusingly at her as he ended the call. 'You're finally home. We need to talk.'

She was immediately on her guard. 'Blair said you stopped by . . . something about another murder?' Lexi kept her voice cool, not in a conversational mood. She had promised to tell him if she had any other contact with Simon Helsing, but her long, strange meeting with the Bastion was something else entirely. She had never promised to tell him about the isolated community, and she doubted he would believe her even if she told him about the group of feral survivalists who feared a coming apocalypse, vampire or otherwise. 'Did the stake killer—'

Carrow cut her off. 'His name is Simon Helsing, as we both know.'

'I'm not disagreeing with you. And, no, I haven't been contacted by him again. I promised I would call you if he did.' She tried to keep a straight face, feeling disingenuous.

He seemed to take that as a small victory. 'Things change fast around here, Miss Tarada. I stopped by just before noon because another brutal killing occurred this morning – a man named Tom Grollin, stunned with a Taser and then decapitated. The coroner thinks it was done with a long butcher knife and a hatchet. Like Patric Ryan.'

The thought of the violence made black fuzz appear around her vision. Her stomach, already queasy, roiled with greater agitation. She tried to picture Helsing chopping the victim's head off, blood spraying everywhere. 'Was the mouth stuffed with garlic?'

Carrow gave her an annoyed look. 'You know it was. Grollin was one of the names in the file Helsing gave you, an identified target. And I know you remember that, too.'

'Yes, a suspected vampire. Is that how you found him? By checking names on the list?'

'I was trying to warn potential victims, but I was too late in his case. Yesterday, I went to see Hugo Zelm because I figured he was in the greatest danger. The king vampire.' His voice dripped with sarcasm. 'I messed up my priorities, left other people vulnerable.'

'And what about Tom Grollin?' Lexi pressed. 'Did you find anything suspicious on the body? In the apartment? Any hint that he might have been a vampire?'

Carrow's face flushed, and she could see he was genuinely sick and angry. 'Of course not! He was just a taxi driver, murdered in cold blood. Stop with your fairy tales.'

Now Lexi felt desperate. Her dream with Teresa had viscerally reminded her that there were indeed unexplained things in the world. She clung to her insistent hope that *something* had to be real. If vampires did exist, then Simon Helsing was fighting to save humans and saving lives. That would validate her interaction with him. On the other hand, if vampires *weren't* real, if

Helsing's evidence didn't hold water and he had killed an innocent cab driver – as well as those other victims – then he was just a madman and a murderer.

And Lexi was helping him.

'Could there possibly be anything unusual about the victims? What if that's the connecting thread among the cases? Similar blood test results, DNA matches, the presence of enzymes that would expose differences from a normal human? Helsing might have been obsessive, but he wasn't a fool.'

'You're sounding paranoid, Miss Tarada, and more than a little nuts.'

She remembered the look in Lucius's eyes when he told her about the vampire attacking their camp, slaughtering the honey woman. 'Haven't you seen any movies? The crazy guy who rails about supernatural threats always turns out to be right! *The Night Stalker*, *The X-Files*, *Invasion of the Body Snatchers*.'

'Those are just movies – fiction. You've been reading your own website for too long, and you're fostering his delusions,' the detective snapped. 'What if you nudged him over the edge by buying into that craziness? Convinced him to kill Grollin?'

Lexi lowered her voice and hissed, 'I didn't convince him of anything!'

Carrow lashed out, trying to startle her. 'So why did he kill the motel manager, then? Daniel Gardon. He wasn't on the list.'

The name meant nothing to her. 'Who's that?'

'Rambler Star Motel down on South Nevada. He was shot to death this morning, only an hour or two after the Grollin murder. This time it was a shotgun blast. At first it looked like an everyday killing, but the coroner just called.' He held up his phone. 'The shotgun shell was filled with silver pellets.'

Lexi's thoughts spun. 'I can't fault your logic, Detective. A silver bullet is too much of a coincidence. But why the manager of a motel? His name wasn't in the dossier, I'm sure of it.'

'The victim was shot at the door of a motel room where Helsing had apparently holed up. But he was out in broad daylight, standing in the sunshine. Helsing couldn't possibly have thought the guy was a vampire, but how else to explain the silver pellets? You can't buy those. He had to make and load that shell himself, and he's probably got more.'

Lexi had come up against too many strange theories, coincidences, and concepts that challenged her beliefs. The fact that Lucius and his followers also believed they had encountered vampires still strained her thoughts. She almost told Carrow about the Bastion, but she stopped herself. Lucius had been compelling, earnestly insistent, and Helsing so adamant. There must be some kernel of truth. All those people couldn't have been fooled.

Then again, countless people believed the government was using airplane vapor trails for mind control, or that the Moon was a hologram to hide an alien base.

Seeing her hesitation, Carrow demanded, 'Have you had any further contact with him? We need to stop him from killing again.'

'Helsing?' She felt disoriented. 'No, nothing.'

Her head still pounded. She had to know. What if there was an answer, and she was the only one objective enough to find out? Was that what Teresa was trying to tell her in the dream? There must be some connection between the motel manager and the other victims . . . or the other vampires.

'I honestly don't know why Simon would have killed that man,' Lexi said. 'He was so thorough, so meticulous with his evidence. I doubt it was just a crime of opportunity. There must be some link to the motel manager.'

Carrow glowered at her. 'Or maybe Helsing was just going for extra credit.'

Forty-Two

The murder of the motel manager was different from the others – which proved to be a good thing. In the previous killings, Simon Helsing had been meticulous, leaving no trace evidence, no fingerprints, no security camera footage.

But the shooting at the Rambler Star seemed impulsive. The killer had made mistakes. Witnesses had seen him, caught his license plate. The police were searching for his car right now.

By the time the detective reached the crime scene, the body had been taken away and Watson was getting ready to leave.

Mel showed off a big grin beneath his mustache.

'That room is like a supervillain's hideout, Detective. Lots of evidence.'

'He'd been holed up there for a while?' Carrow asked.

'See for yourself. Looks like a base camp – cans of food, a microwave, a cash stash, computer, lots of changes of clothes.' The tech raised his eyebrows. 'But here's the odd thing. It's women's clothes, men's clothes, kid's clothes. Either our killer has a lot of accomplices, or it's a whole crime family.'

Inside the room, Carrow spotted the shotgun-shell reloading press mounted to the table. A bloody trench coat had been tossed on the bed. 'We'll find fingerprints, hairs, DNA galore. We need to look at the motel records.'

'Already done.' Nathan Dodge stepped up to the splintered door. 'No records for this room. According to the books, no one has ever checked into it, but someone was clearly living here for quite a while.'

Carrow frowned. 'Somebody knew the killer was holed up in here. The manager must be connected somehow.' He gave Orla Watson a wry look. 'I'm pretty sure that Daniel Gardon was not a vampire.'

'There you go again, Detective – jumping to conclusions.'

'I'm not sure how Alexis Tarada's involved in this. She may just be collateral damage, duped by her own conspiracy theories.' He looked at the blood spilled on the concrete step, the pock-marked turquoise door, and mused to the coroner, 'Just to humor me, run thorough tests on the two new bodies. I want blood evidence that shows they were both human.'

Watson gave a sarcastic sniff. 'You think I have a vampire swab test in my medical kit? I wouldn't even know what to look for.'

'Gotta be thorough if you want to get re-elected,' he said, letting his own sarcasm shine through.

'As long as I have your vote.' She brightened. 'Some friends at the department asked me to invite you to our weekly margarita night. Interested in having a social life? Make friends, relax, have a good time that isn't work related?'

'That's what LeAnn was always bugging me to do.'

The coroner's face grew pinched. 'I promise we're much more fun to be around than your ex-wife.'

'I'm sure you are. I'll think about it.'

Mel returned with a report. His grin was even wider now. 'Plenty of prints, sir. If he's anywhere in the database, we got him.'

It was easy for Lexi to use her skills and slip through electronic back doors and access the CSPD case logs. She recalled much of the information in Helsing's folder, names of suspected vampires, surreptitious photographs of the targets. (And why didn't that raise a red flag with Helsing? Vampires weren't supposed to show up on photos, were they? What about mirrors? How many legends and rules were utterly false?)

Initially, Helsing's compelling arguments and unexplained coincidences had opened her eyes, but deep down she realized it was all just theoretical, names on pieces of paper. When Detective Carrow told her about the murder of Douglas Eldridge – a name she had just read in the dossier – the possibility suddenly seemed more real. And now Tom Grollin, another name from the list, horribly butchered . . .

If Helsing was right in his suspicions and investigations, then the victims were actually vampires. But did she really believe it? She wanted to believe, but that didn't make the idea true. *One of these days . . .*

Other people considered Lexi gullible, even ridiculous, but her impossible encounter with Teresa had taught her to keep an open mind. She *knew* that the visitation was real, not like ghostly typing on a disconnected keyboard.

Her recent dream *might* have been her subconscious speaking to her, like bubbling froth from the stew of stories she had been immersed in during a highly emotional circumstance, or maybe it was just the blurred after-effects of two different kinds of knockout drugs.

'Teresa, what were you trying to tell me?' Lexi whispered as she sat at her computer. She stared at the large screen, hoping that a string of keyboard characters would spell out an actual message this time, giving her the answers she needed.

But nothing was clear.

Slipping into the CSPD database, she found Detective Carrow's profile and had full access to the other murder files. Carrow wasn't thorough in his write-ups, and he had fallen behind on paperwork, but there were lots of documents submitted by the crime scene techs. The coroner added autopsy reports on the first three victims, and even a supplemental file about Douglas Eldridge's dead German Shepherd.

Dr Watson had performed careful analyses on the bodies of Stallings, Ryan, and Eldridge, finding no evidence of tainted blood or obvious physical or cellular anomalies, nothing to indicate that the victims had been inhuman. Surely a vampire – an undead creature with fangs to feed on human blood – would exhibit *some* clear differences. But the victims' teeth were normal and matched dental records.

She slumped in her chair and studied the high-res images on her screen, clicking from document to document. She had already seen some of the photos in her earlier work, had gotten over the initial shock, and now she reviewed the evidence until her eyes were blurry. Lexi was reluctant to admit what she already knew deep inside.

Maybe she was clinging to the irrational hope that vampires were real, because that would satisfy her hunger – or was it an addiction? – to prove that mysteries still existed in the world. Proving the existence of vampires, or ghosts, or Bigfoot, or anything at all, would demonstrate that such things were possible, really possible.

Instead, the deeper she dug for HideTruth, the more she suspected that those 'strange but true' tales were just crazy conspiracy theories and fake news.

If vampires were not real, then Simon Helsing was an obsessive and delusional murderer.

It was too soon for her to see any records about

the two most recent murders, but she began to do her own research on the motel manager. Why did Helsing choose Daniel Gardon as a target? And why switch to using a silver bullet instead of the more violent, more intimate killings with a stake or decapitation?

She found few details about the Rambler Star manager. The records seemed deliberately doctored. Helsing's other targets had been suspiciously reclusive, with no friends, family, or other human connections. Gardon had a wife, a nice, normal home. He was even a member of the Chamber of Commerce.

Helsing could easily have verified that Gardon wasn't a vampire. How could he have missed that? And if the manager was plainly not a vampire, then that meant Helsing had made at least one mistake. Gardon was an innocent man who had blundered into the wrong place at the wrong time.

And if Helsing had made such a terrible mistake, then he had murdered a human being, which cast doubt on all the other victims.

She sat back in her chair and stared at the screen without seeing it. Stoker1897 hadn't posted recently on HideTruth, but she was sure Helsing would contact her again. He would try to enlist her cooperation, cajole her with his supposed evidence, because he thought she was on his side.

But now she was almost certain he was truly a serial killer.

Forty-Three

Not surprisingly, 'Simon Helsing' wasn't his real name. Now that he had a full set of fingerprints from the crime scene at the motel, Carrow checked the criminal database for all fifty states but found no matches. When he went wider and searched all public records, including military service files, he hit the jackpot.

The story wasn't good.

As he read through the VA medical records and disturbing psychological evaluations, he shook his head. 'Crap almighty, this guy's life is a parade of red flags.'

Often after tragic massacres – school shootings, shopping mall rampages, crazed mail bombers with political agendas – the perpetrator's relatives and neighbors acted like drugged sheep. 'Gosh, he seemed like such a nice, quiet, normal person. Who would have suspected?' Then looking at the perp's history – psycho social-media posts, vitriolic blogs – it was painfully obvious that he was a hand grenade ready to go off.

The same was true here, but Helsing had fallen through the cracks, lost in an uncaring system. He'd been off the radar for years.

His real name was David Grundy, and he had served as a medical corpsman for the UN peace-keeping forces in Bosnia back in 1995. There, a perfectly normal young man had suffered some extreme psychological trauma, a terrible accident in an ambulance. Severely injured, he had survived in the forest until rescued by an isolated peasant family. He had never been the same since.

Grundy was diagnosed with PTSD. He had a psychotic break and suffered delusions about vampires. He was bounced from one VA hospital to another, psychiatric ward to psychiatric ward. He was finally discharged to fend for himself – at which point he fell off the grid, swallowed up in anonymity. No one in the VA had the resources, or inclination, to check on him.

Somewhere along the way, he had created his other identity as Simon Helsing, vampire killer.

Even though the information was a goldmine, it offered no clues as to what relatives or bolt holes Grundy might have in the Colorado Springs area. Had he come here on purpose, or was the city just a random stop? Did he start hunting vampires here, or had he been killing before that? In her original tip line posting, Alexis Tarada had mentioned other unsolved stake murders from years earlier in other parts of the country. Grundy's killing spree might not have started with Mark Stallings or Patric Ryan.

He printed out a copy of the man's photograph from his service record. Although the picture was twenty years old, at least it was a start. CSPD image-processing software could age the appearance, adding years and weight.

Carrow suspected the killer's next big move would be on Saturday at Hugo Zelm's charity gala. Something about the eccentric philanthropist set off warning bells in Carrow's mind, too, and he could see why an obsessive vampire killer might concoct a fantasy that the rich old man was king of the undead. Given that Zelm was so reclusive, Helsing couldn't pass up an opportunity like that.

Yes, Carrow had to attend the gala, and Alexis Tarada was the only one who had actually seen the killer face to face. He liked the idea of tagging along with her . . . to keep an eye on both of them.

With Grundy's photograph in hand, Carrow left the CSPD offices and headed out to see her.

Lexi greeted the police detective with another frown. He wore the same dark sport jacket, same white shirt, same tie.

'Detective Carrow, if you keep showing up on my doorstep, you better start bringing chocolate or something.'

He rolled with the comment. 'Matter of fact, I am here to ask you out on a date, of sorts. Police business.'

'You're not my type. At least ten years too old and with no imagination.'

'All part of my charm,' Carrow said. 'Hugo Zelm suggested I accompany you to the charity gala tomorrow. Armed and alert.'

She was taken aback. 'Why me?'

'You know Helsing suspects he's some kind of king vampire, and we think he might use the public event to make his move. Zelm has his own security, and I'll be there as part of a CSPD protective detail.'

Lexi considered. 'But you need a wingman?'

Carrow remained dead serious, all business. 'You're the only one who's seen him, Miss Tarada. But we know a lot more than we did yesterday. Thanks to fingerprints found in the motel room, we have his real name and some background, even an old photograph.'

Lexi listened as he spilled the details, unfolding Grundy's tragic story. She began to connect the incidents small and large that had helped him fabricate his belief in the vampire threat.

'Do you recognize him?' Carrow showed her the service photo of a young man, a normal man – thin, handsome in his own way, the eyes of someone who had seen little in life and had no idea what he was in for. Something about his face, the set of his mouth, his brow, and those eyes . . .

'That's him, but he looks different enough now that I doubt the photograph would help anyone else identify him.' He had sat right across from her, grabbed her arm.

'Zelm suggested that I quietly accompany you, blend into the woodwork, but you can let me know if you spot him. And I can help protect you, if necessary.'

Lexi felt a knot in her stomach. Even though she hadn't revealed the strange meeting with Lucius and the Bastion, she hadn't refused to cooperate with the police, though she hadn't been enthusiastic either, given his disparaging attitude toward HideTruth. Now, with her own doubts growing stronger after the shooting of the innocent motel manager, could she let Helsing try to assassinate the wealthy philanthropist?

Zelm was one of HideTruth's most reliable patrons. If he was a king vampire, why would he support a website that actively tried to expose the existence of vampires? Or was it a double fake? HideTruth promoted so many preposterous ideas, maybe that effectively made vampires seem preposterous, thereby increasing their cover?

'I've already got a date,' she said. 'Blair is going with me.'

As if on cue, her housemate came into the kitchen dressed for a late-afternoon shift at Rags to Riches. 'She does indeed, Detective, and I'm eagerly anticipating the event. A debut in high society.' Seeing Carrow's expression, Blair instinctively touched his cheek below his eye, where the bruises had faded.

'If I come alone, I'd stick out like a sore thumb, and Helsing might be alerted. I'll just tag along, like a third wheel.'

She was still uncomfortable to have Carrow hovering. 'Don't you have someone you can ask? Aren't you married?'

'Divorced, but it's been a while. Not quite on the dating circuit yet.'

'Big surprise.' Blair let out a sigh.

The more she thought about it, Lexi realized she could follow Helsing's train of thought, especially if he thought Hugo Zelm was the king vampire. 'I think you're right, Detective. Helsing might show up, but even if he did manage to slip in to the gala, he'd never get close enough to pound a stake through Mr Zelm's heart, not with all the security and all the guests. That means

Helsing would have to be more blatant, more extreme.' She felt a chill and caught her breath. 'Like using a silver bullet!'

Carrow was startled. 'That makes sense.'

'Bullets!' Blair looked alarmed and put a hand on Lexi's shoulder. 'Despite all my good intentions, I can't protect you alone, Lex.' He swallowed, clearly disturbed. 'If I were more of a fighter, I could have defended myself against Cesar. But I couldn't, so the detective better join us. I want you safe more than anything else. All right, Detective, you can be my pretend date.'

Forty-Four

Lexi was forced to consider Helsing's victims through a different filter, a rational filter – just as Detective Carrow always had. She struggled to find some irrefutable nugget of proof that would legitimize the vampire killer's mission. But no matter how much she wanted to believe, she still had nothing.

And she knew Helsing wasn't done. She shared Carrow's suspicion that Hugo Zelm might be the next primary target, but she wasn't sure Helsing could wait until Saturday to strike again.

Though Carrow had taken the folder with the list of targets from her, she still remembered a few of the names. One was a night ambulance driver, and it took Lexi only two phone calls to verify that the woman had been switched to the day shift. If Helsing came for her, he would not find her sleeping during the day.

The other name she remembered clearly was Frederik Lugash, the pizza delivery driver. She'd looked at so many photos while perusing the evidence folder that the connection hadn't at first clicked, but now she was convinced that he was the same creepy man who had hovered on her doorstep, asking her to invite him in. Something about Lugash had made her skin crawl. What if he *was* a vampire? Even if Helsing had made mistakes, did that mean they were *all* mistakes?

Of the names she remembered, Frederik Lugash seemed an easy target, a man living alone in a poor part of the city. With Helsing's accelerating cycle of violence, Lugash might be in danger before Saturday night. It took only a few minutes on the internet through her research resources to get an address for him.

Lexi had to go see with her own eyes.

It was nearly sunset by the time she reached the old residential district in the south part of town. Lugash lived alone in a one-story rancher. His Volkswagen Rabbit (complete with Checkers placard) was parked in the drive, which instantly confirmed she had found the correct house. Several of his neighbors had left garbage cans at the curb. One yard had a swing set that looked as if it hadn't been used in more than a decade. Several rolled newspapers were strewn across the driveway, one tucked under a car tire.

Theoretically, Lugash had to be at work soon, but the house was dark, the window shades drawn. His whole neighborhood was strangely quiet and subdued.

More than a block away she noticed an unmarked car parked at the curb with two men inside. At first she wondered if some drug deal was about to happen, until she remembered that Detective Carrow had assigned protective details to watch over the more likely victims. She drew a deep breath and let out a relieved sigh. Lugash was safe from the vampire killer . . . so long as he wasn't really a vampire himself.

Worried that the plainclothes policemen would be suspicious of her lurking around, Lexi pulled into the driveway of an obviously empty house from which she could watch the pizza delivery man's home. She shut off the engine, turned off the lights, and sat in the silent driveway, watching the house, the Volkswagen, the darkened windows. She sensed some eerie, dark presence lurking in Lugash's house. Was a vampire sleeping there? She quashed that train of thought before her own imagination could run away with her.

As twilight settled over the neighborhood, she began to relax. Helsing would never strike at this hour, when a real vampire would become stronger, more dangerous.

A light came on in Lugash's house, shining in the front room, and another light shone in the kitchen. She could see a shadowy figure moving inside. The man – the vampire? – was up and getting ready for work. Or to go on the prowl?

Lexi had seen all she needed to. She started her car, backed out of the driveway, and headed home.

Forty-Five

After washing off most of the dried blood in a frigid forest stream, then changing into the clean clothes Mama had given him, Helsing was ready to go back to the city to continue his work. The Bastion had abandoned him, abandoned their obligations to the human race. They were already gone, moved deeper into the woods. Hiding.

He was sure he could find them again, since he knew their ways so well, but he had no reason to. They were no longer useful. Lucius would keep monitoring the news and the police scanner with his own equipment, but he would never help. Simon Helsing was on this mission alone.

He intended to eradicate the king vampire, and maybe that would be enough. Ever since he began hunting *lampir* back in California, he had killed a dozen of them, and he took heart in knowing that he had saved countless human lives. No one would reward him for it, though. No one even knew what he was doing, except for Alexis Tarada.

Killing the king vampire might well cost him his life, unless he managed to escape through a combination of luck, audacity, and desperation. If he was going to sacrifice himself to exterminate Hugo Zelm on Saturday, he wanted to kill at least one more enemy before then. It might be his last opportunity.

Maybe Alexis would take up the cause once he was gone. Helsing had shared all the details with her. Surely she must be convinced.

Knowing that his car was still being hunted by the police, he found an empty vacation cabin on private property. A battered old pickup was parked by a woodpile, but it had current tags on the license plates. That was the important detail. Helsing swapped plates, which would give him sufficient cover. He had to remain unobtrusive for two more days.

If he did manage to escape after killing Hugo Zelm, he would leave Colorado Springs permanently. He could begin his crusade again in a new location. Vampires were everywhere.

To complete his work, Helsing needed resources, so he took all the emergency funds Lucius had stashed around the city. The Rambler Star Motel was blown, but every member of the Bastion knew where to find other caches. In two hours, he retrieved $650 in rolled bills, as well as two debit cards each loaded with five hundred dollars. *Take only what you need.*

Helsing needed it more than anyone else. So he took it all.

His next intended target was MaryJane Stricklin, and he knew where she lived. But when he observed the ambulance driver from a distance the next day, he was surprised to see her emerge from her house in broad daylight, dressed in her EMT uniform, showing no ill effects from the bright sunshine, not even wearing sunglasses.

He reeled. He had missed something! Even after his careful research and surveillance, he had been *wrong*. He had been about to make a terrible mistake.

Killing Gardon was already an impulsive accident. Though the motel manager had seen something he shouldn't have, he'd been fully human. If Helsing had pounded a stake through Stricklin's heart, he would have killed another innocent person.

That was not his mission! He was out to *save* human lives, not take them. The very idea that he had been misled – no, that he had misled *himself* – nauseated him. It blurred his crystal-clear resolve, and he couldn't have that. Vampires were the ones who clouded the facts, distorted the truth, warped the simplest answers into arcane enigmas. Killing Stricklin would have been a heinous crime on his own part.

About Frederik Lugash, though, he had no doubts.

He pulled up just before 11 a.m. the next day. The autumn air had a cool, invigorating bite. He saw the pizza delivery man's car in the driveway, the drapes closed, the rest of the neighborhood quiet. Most of the homes looked empty, their inhabitants at work in normal *human* jobs.

Lugash was holed up, sleeping.

Helsing parked his Honda two houses down and grabbed his satchel from the front seat. He glanced around, saw no movement, no kids playing, no adults strolling about. Several silent cars were parked down the street and in the nearby cul-de-sac. The neighborhood seemed to be holding its breath, as if Lugash had his neighbors under a spell.

Helsing strolled up the driveway, casually going about his business. He paused to look into the Volkswagen. Cigarette butts crammed the ashtray, and an air freshener dangled from the rearview mirror. Crumpled fast-food wrappers littered the floor. Lugash didn't even pretend to eat the pizza he delivered.

Helsing glanced at the front door, but slipped around the side so that he could work without being seen. He set his satchel on the lid of a metal trashcan, unzipped it, and took out the wooden mallet. He would break in from the side or the back.

He moved with furtive grace to the rear of the house, alert for any defenses the vampire might have put in place. A rickety gate in the redwood fence opened with a simple latch. At least there was no dog. He slipped into the yard, leaving the gate open as he scanned the house in search of the best way in. Two light wells in the ground were too small to let him work his way through the basement windows, and a narrow side window must have been for a bathroom.

A wide, sliding patio door covered by long curtains offered the best way inside. He jiggled the handle, hoping the latch would be loose, but no luck. The latch mechanism was held on with simple screws, though, and he could remove it in just a few minutes.

'Better stop right there, sir,' said a hard, confident voice. He spun to see a man stalking toward him, holding up a badge. 'Colorado Springs Police Department.'

Helsing froze. Had one of the neighbors called

to report a prowler? How had the police arrived so quickly?

'You don't belong here, sir. Please drop the mallet and the bag.' The cop slowly drew his holstered revolver, but he seemed to think his badge was all the weapon he needed.

Still holding the satchel, Helsing stepped away from the patio door, bracing himself to fight. The plainclothes cop strode closer, a thin man with a ruddy face, blue eyes, and sandy blond hair.

'I said drop the bag, sir. And the mallet.'

From the far side of the house, a second plain-clothes cop hurried into view, already pulling his weapon as he closed in. 'I got him, David.'

Helsing launched himself toward the first cop. He swung up his satchel which made him look large and dangerous. The cop aimed his gun toward the target.

Using the momentum of his run, Helsing swung the mallet with all his strength, not hesitating, thinking only of escape. The plainclothes cop fired, missed, and Helsing bashed the side of his head with the mallet. He felt a satisfying crack and a wet splash of blood.

The cop went down like a sandbag dropped from a balcony. The second cop fired a shot at Helsing as he ran, but Helsing was already bolting around the corner of the house and dashing through the still-open redwood gate. The other cop was right behind him, yelling threats. Helsing expected to be shot in the back at any moment.

But the second cop stopped by his fallen partner, and Helsing heard him shouting into his radio. 'Officer down! Send an ambulance. I need backup!' He rattled off the address.

Helsing bounded to his parked car, breathing hard as he clawed his keys out of his pocket. He leaped behind the wheel and started the engine. An instant later, the second cop charged through the gate, handgun drawn and yelling. He fired, and the bullet struck the side of the car. Helsing roared off, squealing his tires and racing down the winding residential streets.

The CSPD would respond within minutes, but he would be long gone. He didn't know if he had killed the police officer, but he had felt the skull cave in. If the cop died, Helsing would have murdered another unexpected victim, collateral damage, another innocent dead.

He hadn't even managed to kill the real *lampir*.

Helsing gritted his teeth as he drove away, but he forced himself to slow down as he fed into Circle Drive, merging with the traffic that ran past an endless succession of strip malls and shopping centers. He would have to abandon the vehicle and find another one. The Bastion had others.

While the avalanche of questions continued through his brain, his dismay only increased as he forced himself to accept the obvious answers. The police were protecting Frederik Lugash! That must mean vampires had infiltrated the police department.

But how had the CSPD known Lugash was even one of his targets? Why would anyone guess that Helsing had identified him as a vampire? The only other person who had seen the pizza delivery man's name was Alexis Tarada. He'd given her his folder, his list, his evidence.

But she was his ally.

Yet, how could the police have known about Lugash, unless Alexis had betrayed him? Why would she work to protect a vampire? Unless she had secretly been . . . turned.

He felt sick as he thought of yet another insidious example of how the *lampir* worked their way into society, herding the sheep so they could slaughter them one at a time.

The king vampire was more powerful than he had thought, and Helsing didn't have any time to lose.

Forty-Six

Lexi raised her arms and twirled slowly. 'How do I look?' The glowing delight on Blair's face already told her how much he approved.

'A vision of loveliness. Straight out of a fairy tale.'

Considering how formal the dress looked with its ivory silk trimmings, damask corset, perfect pleats on the skirt, and the scalloped wonder of lace at her neck, it felt *wonderful*. Not at all like the awkward dresses she had worn to church.

She ran her hands down her hips to her thighs. 'I never thought I liked formal stuff.'

'You're making *my* pulse race.' Blair walked around her, slowly inspecting. 'Did I do good?'

'You picked the perfect dress. I'll hate to return it after the gala.'

Blair ran a hand through his hair. 'I would not object if you wore it again. In fact, we should experiment with other fine garments. You're a beautiful woman, Lex, made for beautiful things. Not that you don't look perfectly fine in your everyday clothes, but this . . .' He stroked her shoulder as if touching a sacred object. 'This is outstanding. And now for the last detail.' He picked up the red velvet choker. 'Let me put this in place around that elegant neck of yours.' The crimson strip, so different from her usual necklace, embraced her throat. 'The precisely perfect counterpoint.'

She pulled out the white skirt. 'And you don't think this looks like a wedding dress?'

'You're perfect. Stop asking questions.' He smoothed the flared collar of his tuxedo jacket. 'You haven't said a thing about how *I* look.' He spread his arms and turned in a slow circle so she could get the full effect of his white shirt, cummerbund, cufflinks, glowing patent-leather shoes.

'You always look handsome and stylish, but tonight you are nothing short of dreamy.' She straightened his bowtie and gave him a wink. 'You do dress up well, Blair September.'

'We make such a stunning couple, no one will even notice Detective Carrow lurking behind us.' Blair positively glowed with satisfaction.

She studied his face and an edge crept into her voice. 'I need to touch up your make-up a little. You're looking pale, but the bruising is mostly gone. Don't let *anyone* abuse you again, and I'll be happy.'

He self-consciously touched his cheek. 'No, I won't.'

Carrow arrived on time in a charcoal gray suit, white shirt, and maroon tie. He looked awkward when Lexi opened the door. 'Feel like I'm going to a high-school formal.'

'Don't think of me as your date. You and I are more like, um . . . lab partners.' She allowed him through the door. 'Anyway, if you stop Helsing from killing Mr Zelm, this extra effort will all be worthwhile.'

Blair slipped his arm through hers. 'Lex is my date tonight, but you can be our driver.' He frowned at the detective with palpable disappointment. 'If *you* had been her date, you'd have told her how beautiful she looks.' His gaze rolled up and down Carrow's commonplace gray suit. 'You do know this is a formal gala? Everyone will be dressed to the nines. That's the best you could do?'

Carrow seemed baffled by the disdain. 'This is my good suit.'

Blair let out a long-suffering sigh. 'That's why rental places were invented.'

Ignoring him, Carrow glanced at his watch. 'We need to get going. Do you think there'll be food, or should we get something to eat on the way?'

Blair said, 'There'll be crudités and petit fours.'

'Good,' Carrow said, then repeated, 'Will there be anything to eat?'

'Snacks,' Lexi translated. 'But don't expect to pig out.'

As they drove toward the ostentatious Broadmoor district, Lexi sat in the front seat, while Blair commented from the back. When she pressed the detective about the two recent murders, he refused to tell her anything further, and she didn't reveal the details she had already learned.

'Your friend Helsing tried to kill someone else today,' Carrow blurted out as he drove along in the darkness.

'He's not her friend,' Blair objected from the back seat.

Lexi turned to the detective, but he stared straight ahead as he drove. 'Another attack? Who? When?'

'This morning. He wanted to kill a pizza delivery man.'

'The one from the list?' She didn't tell him that she had gone to the man's house just the night before. 'Frederik Lugash?'

'The same. Helsing intended to break in and kill the guy during broad daylight, but I had a protective detail watching the house.' Carrow gripped the steering wheel hard as he drove through the upscale residential area. 'He bashed one of our officers, Lieutenant David Amber, in the head. Cracked skull, brain hemorrhage, massive damage.' His voice wavered. 'Amber's in a coma, and we don't know if he'll pull through.' He glowered at her. 'One of our own! If only you . . .' His words trailed off.

Although horrified, she felt defensive. 'If only I'd what? You had the information, Detective. You took it from me. I haven't had any contact with Helsing since the one and only time we met at the coffee shop. He's dropped off the HideTruth discussion boards. I'm doing nothing to feed his delusions, nothing to help him. I'm sorry to hear about Officer Amber, but you're just looking for someone to blame.'

Blair reached forward from the back seat to give her shoulder a reassuring squeeze.

'Maybe I am,' Carrow grumbled. 'And you're right. I should blame Helsing instead. We'll get him tonight.'

The three rode in silence for the next fifteen minutes until they arrived at Zelm's mansion. To Lexi, it looked exactly like the kind of home a wealthy, centuries-old king vampire would have built for himself: wrought-iron gate, turrets, well-lit windows, and a grand entrance. A brick fence topped with cast-iron spear points encompassed the grounds. Cars waited in line as valets took each vehicle and drove it away: Mercedes Benzes, Porsches, Jaguars, even a Bentley.

When Carrow pulled up in his Ford sedan, the dark-haired young valet leaned toward the driver's window, not sure what to do. Carrow climbed out, left the car running. 'Not a scratch, you hear? I expect my car in the same condition when I pick it up.' He tipped the man a dollar.

Lexi climbed out of her side, careful with her dress. She didn't want Carrow to come around and open the door for her. Blair emerged from the back seat and hurried to offer his arm. As she stepped away from the car, she felt like a blooming flower.

Lexi and Blair walked together up the porch

stairs to the front entryway, while Carrow kept a safe distance. Private security men in dark suits stood like gargoyles at the corners of the house, at the entryway, inside the mansion. Several CSPD police officers were also in the area as backup, outside the property.

As the three entered, a swarm of paparazzi took their photographs. She clung to the sleeve of Blair's immaculate tux to make sure no one assumed she and Carrow were a couple. As a saving grace, Lexi realized that no one really knew who she was. The creator and site administrator of HideTruth? If it weren't for Hugo Zelm's patronage, she would never have been invited here.

She saw countless reporters, photographers, some of them with large cameras, others with small digital ones. Considering the sheer amount of media here, it must not be terribly difficult to get a press pass.

Lexi took in the sparkling chandelier in the foyer, the towering windows that looked out at the panorama of city lights below. Carrow sidled up to her, lowered his voice. 'Keep your eyes open. Let me know if you see Helsing.'

And her moment of warm glory dissipated. 'I'll look around.'

She scanned the faces. She had never seen so much make-up or jewelry in her life. All of these tuxedos and gowns probably cost more than her monthly rent. Straight-backed servers glided among the guests offering trays with glasses of wine so dark it looked like blood. A server extended a tray to Lexi. 'Pinot noir, miss?'

Lexi accepted one of the glasses, knowing it was more expensive than any vintage she had ever tasted. The first sip was delicious, though she wasn't enough of a connoisseur to appreciate its fine qualities. Blair clinked his glass against hers. 'Thanks for having me here, Lex.'

When Carrow took a glass for himself, she said in a low voice, 'Are you supposed to be drinking on the job?'

'I'm not drinking. I'm just holding it.'

A tray of hors d'oeuvres came by, spinach and ricotta puffs in phyllo pastry, another tray with tiny quiches. Carrow looked at the neat little canapés with toothpicks. 'Look at these tiny sandwiches!'

'Canapés,' she corrected.

Another server offered him a tray. 'Rocky Mountain oyster, sir?'

'What are those?'

'You'll like them,' Blair said, not offering details. The detective took one.

With starry eyes, Blair absorbed the crowd, and Lexi sent him off to mingle. Blair, the best wingman anyone could have wanted, had coached her, guided her, reassured her. Now he was in his own element, and she didn't want to diminish his excitement. He flitted about like a professional, introducing himself as a 'personal chemistry specialist' without explaining that it meant he was a bartender.

Lexi felt out of place. She knew no one here, didn't recognize a single face. She felt like an observer. With all the other fabulous gowns, even her lovely dress didn't stand out. She remained close to the wall.

A dapper old man glided up to her. He was bald, with an aquiline nose and close-set eyes. 'You must be Alexis Tarada? The creator of one of my favorite websites.'

She extended her hand automatically. 'I'm pleased to meet you. Hugo Zelm?'

'I am your host.' He clasped her hand, letting the grip linger. The man had a cold intensity about him, as if a hypnotist had just placed her under his spell. Self-consciously, she reached up with her free hand and adjusted the red velvet choker at her neck, feeling strange without the usual gold cross necklace her parents had given her.

'I'm glad to have a devoted fan, and such a reliable patron, Mr Zelm. HideTruth wouldn't survive without people like you.'

The moment he stopped to talk with her, reporters pressed closer, now curious about who she was. More photos were taken of her in that one moment than in her entire previous life.

'You make me want to believe. I am very, very pleased to support your work, Miss Tarada. You shed light on mysteries the world would rather ignore. I appreciate your efforts, and I fully intend to continue my support.' His grip lingered awkwardly, and she withdrew her hand. His flesh had never warmed. 'Thank you for coming.' Zelm turned and gave a curt nod to Carrow. 'I am glad you are here as well, Detective. I feel safer already.' He glided off into his party, followed by the flock of paparazzi.

At the front door of the mansion, even more guests and reporters were streaming in. Lexi feared it would be a long night.

Forty-Seven

Using the Bastion's cash resources, Helsing had bought a good second-hand suit, which would let him blend in. The gray tweed with felt patches on the elbows made him look more like an English professor than a reporter, the disguise he had chosen for the night.

After fleeing the home of Frederik Lugash, shaken by his near escape, he focused on his main task: destroying the king vampire. He was alone in his work. The Bastion had retreated into hiding. Lucius was a coward, failed as a leader. Alexis Tarada – someone he had considered an ally – had betrayed him to the police. For all he knew, Alexis was also in the thrall of Hugo Zelm.

He had washed thoroughly in a public restroom after buying necessary toiletries at a convenience store – ironically, the same store where Mark Stallings had worked. He had switched out his satchel for a large camera bag, also purchased at a thrift store, and stashed the mallet and stakes elsewhere, leaving nothing to arouse suspicions when his bag was inevitably searched by security. Doctoring a press pass for himself wasn't difficult.

No one questioned his credentials when he

307

arrived at the mansion, because Hugo Zelm basked in media attention, like a spider drawing in as many flies as possible. The king vampire wanted every reporter from every possible outlet to cover this event because it was part of his protective camouflage. The quirky philanthropist hid behind layers of security that merely disguised his true bloodlust. Zelm's web extended throughout the city, possibly across the state.

But Helsing knew who he was, and he intended to stop him.

Once he set the wheels in motion tonight, the chaos would explode. He had a vague exit strategy, but the king vampire had enough security to make every detail unpredictable. Many of the *lampir* were arrogant, and perhaps Zelm considered himself invincible, believing that no vampire killer would threaten him with so many people around at the gala.

Or maybe Zelm was just taunting him, daring him to make a move. It might be a trap.

Helsing stashed his car on a nearby street where he could retrieve it quickly – if he managed to get out of the house alive. Strolling ahead, he clipped on the laminated press pass and carried his camera bag, which received a cursory search by the guards at the gate and again at the main entry.

Helsing entered the lair of the monster.

The mansion was a flurry of perfumes, glittering jewelry, false smiles, and meaningless conversations. Helsing glided among them, wearing a foolish, star-struck smile that he had practiced.

So many other photographers scuttled about taking pictures that he blended right in.

The guests were dressed in dizzying couture, perfectly schooled in etiquette. People at this strata of society were accustomed to media attention, expecting it as if it were their due. And they were well practiced in ignoring it, paying no attention to the cameras in their faces.

Helsing felt like a wolf among the sheep as he looked around. No, not a wolf – the shepherd dog, the guardian. He would protect and save these people from inhuman predators. The real wolf was Hugo Zelm.

He had seen photographs of the king vampire and spotted him easily. The host was surrounded by cameras and sycophants. Seeing Zelm sent a shudder down his back. This man had a great deal of blood on his hands.

Helsing still had four silver-loaded shells. The king vampire would die.

He froze when he saw Alexis Tarada standing next to Zelm, beautiful in a lavish white dress. Smiling, she chatted with the philanthropist, and she had a strange dazzle in her eyes. Obviously, the *lampir* had used his glamour on her. Worse than that! Helsing saw the red choker around her neck, which surely covered fang marks. Alexis must be the king vampire's slave.

Not only had she betrayed Helsing to the police and likely to Zelm, she was also feeding him with her blood. Had the king vampire promised to turn her, to make her into a *lampir* like himself?

As anger sent a wash of heat through him,

Helsing opened his camera bag and removed the shell of the big Canon. He had to get closer.

While Detective Carrow was alert for an ambush, Lexi heightened her own awareness. She scanned the crowd to spot a man she had met only once, and he had been slouched, wearing a baseball cap. The paparazzi pressed close around Hugo Zelm, capturing photos and sound bites. The point of this gala was for him to be seen, and all those camera lenses guaranteed it.

After his perfunctory conversation, Zelm wandered off to chat with an older woman with an improbably lavish hairstyle. Blair was laughing with a dapper man who owned an art gallery in Old Colorado City, and Lexi smiled to see how happy he was.

Carrow came up to her. 'Anything yet?'

She shook her head, looking around the room again. 'I thought you were supposed to mingle.'

'Unlike you, I *have* been mingling.'

The detective hadn't even sipped his wine, but Lexi, unused to such large social situations, had bolstered her courage by emptying her glass, which she now handed to a server. Another tray came around within seconds, and she reached out to take a fresh glass.

Looking past the server, she saw a photographer in a tweed jacket making his way closer, raising a ridiculously large camera. Her gaze skated over him, then caught on his face as if snagged on a fishhook. She knew that chin, that cheek, those blue eyes. He looked up, and her gaze met his.

Simon Helsing!

As soon as he saw her recoil, Helsing lunged.
'That's him!' Lexi yelled.

Helsing smacked the side of his large camera with his knuckles, making a loud crunch. The lens and the camera housing broke open, the components separating, as if they had been held together with no more than tape.

Carrow began to move. 'Watch out!'

Hugo Zelm spun and ducked, moving as swiftly as a shadow.

The shell of Helsing's camera fell away to reveal a gun. As he dropped the outer pieces, he shoved the server aside, swung the revolver. The tray of wine glasses flipped, spilling blood-red pinot noir down the front of Lexi's white dress.

Other guests began to scream. Blair's mouth dropped open, and he pulled the art dealer out of the way.

Carrow dove for Zelm to knock the philanthropist out of the line of fire. Helsing fired with an explosive concussion, spraying a cloud of silver pellets that shattered wine glasses and tore into the sides and sleeves of nearby servers. One man fell to the floor.

Helsing fired his revolver again, then a third time. Shotgun pellets sprayed everywhere. Guests screamed and ran in opposite directions.

Lexi dropped to the floor among the smashed wine glasses and scrambled for cover. She touched her chest, pressed down on the oozing red liquid, unable to tell whether or not she'd been shot.

Zelm's security bounded in, big men in dark suits drawing their own large-caliber handguns.

Helsing fired one more time, and the blast shattered the magnificent main window that looked out on Colorado Springs. A rain of broken shards tinkled down, mixing with the screams. The gala turned into pandemonium. Many photographers fled, while some planted their feet and captured the fiasco.

His face flushed with fury, fixated on Hugo Zelm who had crashed to the floor, Helsing pulled the trigger again, but the revolver only clicked on an empty chamber. Still waving the weapon as a threat, he bolted for the door. Panicked guests and staff automatically dove out of the way.

'He doesn't have any shells left!' Lexi cried, but no one heard her.

The security guards closed protectively around Zelm like linebackers guarding a football. Helsing kept pointing the gun as he charged out of the room, scattering people like pigeons. He made a beeline out the main entrance of the mansion. As the shouting built to a roar behind him, he vanished into the night.

Forty-Eight

Carrow picked himself up off the floor, his ears still ringing from the loud gunshots, the shattering window, the shrill screams. Knowing Hugo Zelm was the target, he had tackled the man to the floor as soon as the first blast rang out.

The philanthropist felt like a mummified buzzard,

all bony arms and legs, and Carrow thought he might have broken the old man while shielding him from the shots – probably silver pellets, like the ones that had killed the motel manager.

After Helsing emptied his four shots and bolted, Zelm struggled away from Carrow and into a sitting position. 'I am intact, Detective. You are very, very effective as a human shield.'

Carrow frantically checked himself over. Some of the pellets had scored his arms, and his back felt like hamburger, but the low-caliber round hadn't killed him. He glanced about for Alexis Tarada, saw her drenched in red – wine, apparently – appalled but very much alive.

Like Secret Service guarding the President, Zelm's private security guards created an impenetrable wall of flesh around him.

The old man shouted, 'My guards aren't allowed to leave the grounds, Detective.'

Carrow nodded. Helsing had a head start. 'I'm going after him.'

As he ran for the exit, he could barely think amid the pandemonium in the mansion. Men in tuxedos fled like spooked cats in slippery patent-leather shoes, while women in cocktail gowns and high heels scrambled after them.

Carrow pushed his way through the front door. Standing on the porch, one of Zelm's guards assumed a shooting stance and fired at a figure that ducked and weaved in the darkness.

Helsing had discarded his bag and the pieces of the large camera that concealed the revolver. He hadn't had time to reload even if he had more silver-filled shells.

On the radio, Carrow called the additional officers in the area, preparing for full-on pursuit. Even above the sounds of panicked guests demanding their cars from the valets, Carrow heard another car start up down the street and peel out. That had to be Helsing.

He knocked people aside as he ran to the valet attendants. The first car was a sleek black Mercedes that was too expensive for Carrow even to look at. He waved his badge. 'CSPD! I need that vehicle!'

A dapper gentleman snapped, 'That's my car, and we're leaving.'

Carrow jumped into the driver's seat. 'Take it up with the police commissioner.' The dashboard looked like a space shuttle control panel. Giving a low whistle, he muttered, 'How do you drive this thing?' He realized the ignition was still running. Assuming that most controls were basic, he pulled the shift lever down and stomped on the accelerator. The engine roared to life, and he raced off as if afterburners had kicked in. He nearly ran down two women who appeared to be waiting for him, as if they wanted to hitch a ride. He swerved, overcorrected, scraped the passenger door against the open wrought-iron gates as he hit the residential street.

Many cars were parked along the road, narrowing the lane. Behind him he could hear the sirens of other police vehicles racing toward the mansion. Helsing's car was already around the curve and accelerating uphill, heading west out of the high-end neighborhood.

Carrow fought with the Mercedes. It purred

314

along smoothly, hugging the road, but he wasn't used to driving at high speed on such narrow streets. A few patches of ice remained from the early snowfall a week ago, but he skidded only a little as he pressed on the accelerator and whipped around hairpin curves up into the hills.

He shouted into his cell phone as he drove, calling for backup to follow him. Sirens continued to shriek behind him as he left the residential area and headed into the foothills. The sound of the road under his tires changed from asphalt to hard-packed dirt. The car rattled and bumped, and Carrow raced as fast as he dared while trying to control the car. In the upscale forest property, wealthy homeowners considered it quaint to leave the roads unpaved for the rustic ambiance.

At first Carrow thought Helsing was driving blindly, just trying to get away, but as he ascended deeper into the foothills, he seemed to have a goal in mind. Helsing drove at breakneck speed, anticipating the curves as if he knew the road. The dust of his passage made a smokescreen, and Carrow struggled to keep his eyes on the red tail lights, using them as forewarning for sharp turns. The powerful Mercedes could have closed the distance if he pushed it, but they were going over fifty on the steep unpaved road. The ruts rattled under the tires, making the steering wheel vibrate in his hands. The car slewed from side to side.

Ahead, the red tail lights zigzagged, but continued to accelerate. Somewhere in the rear-view mirror, dwindling sirens plaintively called for Carrow to wait up.

Gritting his teeth, he pushed harder on the accelerator and held on for dear life. The red lights ahead suddenly turned right, off the road, and plunged into deeper darkness. Helsing had turned on to a side road marked with a brown flexible post with white letters and numbers. Some obscure old forest road – the guy definitely knew where he was going.

Carrow fishtailed, and gravel spat under his tires as he braked and skidded, trying to keep control. He was unable to turn swiftly enough and nearly wiped out as he passed the turnoff, and when he stopped the car, the Mercedes was facing the opposite direction. His heart pounded.

He paused just a second to take a deep breath, then got moving again, turning into the narrow forest road. The killer must have some destination in mind, but Carrow felt that this track was a dead end. The ruts were deeper. He nearly hit his head on the roof of the car as he drove over a rock on the right side.

He shouted into the phone, 'Turn right up here! There's a forest road, hard to see. Watch for our dust!'

A voice came back from one of the pursuing police vehicles. 'That's F381, Detective. I've gone fishing up there. It leads to a reservoir.'

'Crap almighty, how do people know these things?' He followed Helsing's bobbing lights as the lead car continued to toil up steeper inclines. As he gained altitude, Carrow could see flashing red and blue lights and the piercing headlight beams in the rear-view mirror. The other cars were only a few minutes behind and below him.

Carrow almost missed a sharp turn, slammed on the brakes in time to avoid a fallen tree. Helsing's car disappeared up another switchback, grinding higher. Carrow backed, went forward, backed again, managed to turn the Mercedes on the extremely tight curve, and went after Helsing again.

The killer veered off on an even steeper track. It was unmarked. The forest was pitch black, the trees close enough that branches scraped against the car's windows and side. Carrow saw steep drop-offs to the right, a sharp slope dotted with rock outcroppings faintly visible in the light.

The tail lights flared red ahead, brake lights, and then Helsing halted his car, blocking the road. The door opened, and Carrow watched a figure leap out and run from the car along the edge of the steep slope.

Carrow slammed the Mercedes into park, tried to figure out how to shut off the engine, then gave up as he sprang out of the car in pursuit. Helsing, running into the underbrush just ahead, yanked off his tweed sport jacket and threw it behind him, as if it might fly into Carrow's face and slow him.

'Better freeze right there!' Carrow drew his revolver.

The killer dodged and crashed through the underbrush on the side of the road, working his way along the precipitous edge, barely able to keep his balance.

'I said freeze!' Carrow reached Helsing's parked car. It was so dark that he could barely see, especially with the bright headlights illuminating the fog of road dust that sifted through the air. He caught a glimpse of a figure melting into the shadows.

Carrow thought of the people Simon Helsing had killed, the men with stakes pounded through their chests, the butchered taxi driver, the motel owner blasted with a silver shotgun shell. Then he thought of David Amber, the young police officer assigned to watch over Frederik Lugash, now lying in a coma with his skull bashed in by Helsing's mallet.

'I will shoot!'

Helsing continued to plow through the under-brush, grasping branches to keep from slipping off the treacherous incline that plunged down the mountainside.

Carrow aimed at the shadowy form and muttered to himself, 'I'll fucking call it self-defense.' He shot twice. One bullet splintered a branch just next to the silhouette. The second caught the man in the shoulder, hurling him to one side. His arms flailed, and he tumbled down the steep slope, crashing and sliding through the impenetrable woods.

Carrow ran to the abrupt edge of the road and looked down into inky darkness. He couldn't hear any further sounds of a body tumbling down into the canyon. He didn't know how severely wounded Helsing was, if the gunshot had struck him in the back or just winged him in the shoulder. No matter – he was going to be damaged goods by the time he hit the bottom. It was a long way down, steep slope, thick trees.

How the hell was he supposed to climb down there? And in his good suit?

With an outcry of sirens, two police cars rumbled up and ground to a halt on the dirt road behind him. Car doors burst open and other officers ran up to join him as he stared down into the wilderness.

'Get flashlights,' Carrow said. 'I shot him, and he fell. Doubt we'll find anything in the dark.'

'We'll call in the Forest Service, bring dogs. He won't get away, Detective.'

'Damn right he won't,' Carrow said. He had been riding on adrenalin ever since the first shots rang out at the gala. It would probably be long after sunrise before they wrapped this up.

Forty-Nine

Branches tore at him like vampire claws as he fell through the trees, slid on pine needles and dry leaves, and crashed into hard outcroppings of granite. Helsing flailed for purchase, snagged and uprooted a small pine sapling, and rolled onward.

He smacked his head on a tree trunk and his ears rang as he tumbled. He was still too much in shock, in frantic flight, to feel the wound in his shoulder, but he knew he had been shot. His shoulder was bleeding. His arm flopped, numb.

He careened into a thicket of bushes that brought his plunge to a halt, lost consciousness for a few moments, then dredged his mind back to awareness. This was just like the ambulance crash in Bosnia, halfway down a mountainside. He couldn't stay here. He had to move.

He glanced up the slope toward the dirt road high above. He saw lights, heard voices. He couldn't let them find him. He would work his way through the forest, and he was far better at this than they were.

He had driven here intentionally, chosen this spot because he knew he could make his way to one of the Bastion caches deep in the woods, take shelter there. When racing away from Zelm's mansion, he'd expected to lose the other car in the maze of dirt roads, but the pursuing vehicle – no doubt someone controlled by the king vampire – kept on his tail. He had to stop somewhere or he'd be cornered on the dirt roads, but he could disappear into the national forest. Though the Bastion had ostracized him, he still knew where their resources were cached.

Take only what you need.

His right arm was useless, and he could barely bend it. Pain and blood screamed now from the ragged gunshot wound. The bullet had gone through. He could feel the large exit hole – a relief, he supposed, though it felt as if some werewolf had torn into the meat of his back.

Helsing dragged himself to his feet again and held on to the wiry bushes so he wouldn't fall farther down the slope. Blurry spots swirled around his vision, but the forest itself was pitch black. He fumbled along by instinct, keeping a grip, sliding ever downward. The base of the canyon was far below. The seasonal stream would be dry, but once he got to the creek bed he could follow it, find the tributary that would lead him to the distinctive rock outcroppings, a small cave where he would find supplies, food, a medical kit. His training as a medical corpsman would come in handy.

The bumbling police officers above would not find him tonight. He struggled along, knowing that his blood was leaving a trail for any real tracker, but he kept moving. It would take the cops hours to get the resources they needed to perform a thorough search. He couldn't let them catch him, not only for the sake of survival – Simon Helsing wasn't afraid of death – but because he still had so much work to do. He had used all his silver-loaded rounds, but Hugo Zelm was still alive. His mission had failed.

Clearly under the king vampire's spell, Alexis Tarada had helped to save the wealthy man.

Helsing had a lot more killing to do.

When he reached the stream bed, he stumbled over broken boulders choked with dry weeds. The dark and the dangerous forest reminded him of his terrifying night in the Bosnian wilderness many miles from Sarajevo. The *lampir* had hunted him then, too.

The police were pursuing him, but what if Hugo Zelm had also sent vampire minions after him? That thought gave him the strength he needed to fight his way along the ravine and thrash through thickets of willows. He paused to catch his breath while hanging on to a branch, but he couldn't afford to rest. He was losing blood drop by drop. He needed the medical kit in the hidden cache.

After what felt like hours, he reached the talus

boulders, looming outcrops of speckled pink granite far from any trail. His footsteps crackled and rattled in the underbrush as he felt along the rock face, pulled himself to the low point, and then up the other side of the slabs until he found the gap between two boulders. By now his eyes were adapted to the darkness, and he could see details by the starlight. He spotted a pale plastic sheet inside the small cave and brushed away the leaves and dirt to uncover the package.

With shaking hands Helsing fumbled until he undid the opening of the weatherproof bag. Inside, he found clothes, a Mylar blanket, emergency ready meals, protein bars, chocolate wrapped in plastic. And a first-aid kit.

He tore it open, looking for gauze and tape. Even though a deep chill had settled into his bones, he unbuttoned his shirt, pulled off the bloody mess, and set it aside. Taking a wad of gauze, he awkwardly reached up with his left hand and pressed it against the ragged exit wound. The small crater in his flesh felt warm and wet. He pressed hard to stanch the flow of blood, but he couldn't do much.

Now that he was in a safe haven, no longer fueled by adrenalin and endorphins, he felt the energy oozing out of him. Helsing began to shiver and knew he was growing weaker, in danger of going into shock. Even though he told himself he had to stay awake, had to treat himself, take the supplies, and keep moving, his body refused to listen. A black tar pit of unconsciousness dragged him down . . .

He awoke, still in darkness, to find a figure

standing in front of him with a flashlight. He lurched back to full consciousness, ready to fight, probably to die, but he would not go down without a struggle.

'Easy, son,' said a deep, familiar voice, masked by the bright light. 'You're safe for now.' When his vision focused, he recognized the big, bearded man as Lucius. 'I knew you'd go here.'

'You . . . came for me?' Helsing couldn't grasp the concept. The expression on Lucius's face was grave.

'I had to. I listened on the scanner and I know what you did. I knew you would come back to us, and made an educated guess you'd go to this cache.' He heaved a long, weary sigh. 'We'll take care of you, son.'

Fifty

After Detective Carrow raced after the vampire killer, Lexi stared down at her red-drenched dress. She felt no pain. Had she been shot? Was she bleeding? She touched the fabric, smelled the strong, rich scent of red wine. Not blood, then. She yanked the velvet choker from her neck as if it were strangling her.

Someone grabbed her shoulder, turned her around. 'Lex, you all right?' Blair's face was as pale as milk. 'I saw you fall.'

'I'm not shot. I think I'm OK.'

Screams continued in the background, and she

saw broken glass on the floor at her feet. She discovered jagged shards stuck in her arms, in the cloth of her bodice, from wine glasses that had turned into little razors. She brushed the pieces with her palm and knocked them loose to the floor. Oddly, even with the continued pandemonium around her, she could hear the tiny tinkle of glass. She began to feel the burn of multiple cuts, but none of them seemed deep.

Many guests had dropped to their knees, weeping, gawking at their shredded arms and chests. One woman looked like she had chicken pox with red dots across her cheek. Helsing's shots had been scattered and wild, unlike the close, concentrated blast that had killed the motel manager. The small silver projectiles had fanned out in a wide dissipated swath.

Blair checked her over. 'I was on the other side of the room, but I came as fast as I could.'

Instantly her thoughts sharpened. 'Mr Zelm!' Lexi pushed her way between two burly guards, trying to see the philanthropist.

He was touching his shoulder, running his hands over his chest. He sounded maddeningly calm. 'No serious injuries, apparently, but I could be in shock.' He touched his face, looked down at his hands as if he found the large veins and liver spots reassuring.

One of the guards, a man named Franklin, brushed off the front of Zelm's tuxedo jacket. He frowned at little cuts on the sleeves and collar of Zelm's jacket, but no blood. 'You are unin- jured, sir. None of the pellets penetrated the skin.'

The philanthropist looked shaken. 'Not a

scratch?' He drew a breath, then affirmed, 'Not a scratch!'

Hearing an odd undertone in Zelm's voice, Lexi asked cautiously, 'And what would have happened if you were actually injured with silver?'

He scowled. 'What do you think, Miss Tarada?'

She didn't know what to think.

A woman in a blue-sequined cocktail gown lay motionless near the shattered picture windows, her bare back ripped apart by the shotgun pellets. Lexi remembered seeing her talking with Zelm as if they were old friends. Another man huddled against the wall, his knees drawn to his chest; he moaned as blood ran down the side of his face. He had been caught with the scatter shot of another shell.

'We need to help these people, Blair,' she said.

He knelt beside the woman in the blue dress, propping her up by her shoulders, but her head lolled. He stared at her with a stricken expression. 'She's dead. The wounds don't look that severe, and the blast didn't go deep.' He cradled her, then gently lowered the cold body back to the floor. 'She was far enough away but . . . she's dead.' He climbed back to his feet next to the victim and looked around for someone else to help.

Numerous attendees had been cut by spraying glass. Lexi assessed her own cuts. 'I'll need a few bandages, too.'

Alarmed, Blair took out a white handkerchief and began dabbing away the blood. 'We should get you to a hospital.'

'Ambulances are coming,' said Franklin. 'We called them all.'

Lexi could already hear the sirens. She touched her ruined dress, and the smell of spilled wine nauseated her. Everything was a blur, and she didn't know how much time had passed. By now, Detective Carrow had probably brought down Simon Helsing.

Lexi leaned against her friend. 'Just stay with me, Blair, and help pick up the pieces.'

Fifty-One

Out in the forest, armed with flashlights, Carrow and the other policemen scrambled down the slope holding on to branches, slipping, getting scratched, cursing. He fell five feet before catching his foot on a rock and grabbing a tree so hard he almost dislocated his shoulder. The darkness blanketed them. Bobbing flashlight beams speared light into the shadows as the other policemen crashed through the branches.

'He went this way. I see some broken branches, skids in the pine needles.'

'Sure. Be right over,' Carrow said, holding on for dear life.

'A blood spatter, Detective. Looks like you at least winged him.'

That gave him great satisfaction. 'I didn't get him well enough because he's still moving.'

'He won't get far. This is rugged terrain and it's dark.'

'Even wounded he's better equipped for this than I am,' Carrow grumbled. He was dressed in his best suit and going-to-a-gala leather shoes. He needed hiking boots and ropes.

They worked their way down the ravine. Two of the officers took drastic tumbles. Carrow had cuts on his hand. The flashlight beams spread out, but Helsing could have gone anywhere in the dense forest.

Within an hour additional backup arrived. Cars and SUVs crowded the one-lane dirt road high above. More searchers probed the forest with flashlights, also finding nothing in the dark. He hoped they would apprehend Helsing before dawn.

Carrow said, 'Once we have the search dogs, we'll find him – or his body. How fast can he move? He's bleeding.' Even with the search party crashing through the underbrush and shouting back and forth, this place felt empty and isolated. He brushed leaves out of his hair. 'Thought I was just going to a fancy cocktail party. I doubt they'll ever invite me again.'

When Helsing woke, he was cold, weak, and angry. His wounded shoulder throbbed, and he lurched up, alarmed. Faint grayish light seeped like a poison mist into the thick forest. A big powerful hand rested on his shoulder just above the bandage.

Lucius said, 'Relax. You just drifted off.' The expression on the bearded man's face was paternal but sad, weary with responsibility. 'We understand what you tried to do.'

327

Helsing remembered the king vampire, the silver shells . . . Alexis Tarada. She had betrayed him. On the ground beside him, he saw torn packages of gauze from the first-aid kit.

'You were like a son to me, part of the Bastion. I always think of what's best for the Bastion and for our survival.'

Helsing's wound had been dressed and packed, the bleeding stopped. He felt safe for now, safer than he had been in a long time. Lucius was here. Lucius would care for him. Lucius would continue the fight, somehow, even if Helsing had to leave. Then bitter anxiety flared up inside him. The Bastion had also abandoned him. 'You left me! Why are you back?'

'The Bastion has found a new home,' Lucius said. 'You don't need to worry about us.'

Helsing ground his teeth together. 'You only think of yourself.'

'I think of the Bastion.' Lucius sounded calm and resigned. 'I know what you're trying to do, Simon. I even respect it. But the damage you've caused, the people you put at risk . . .' He shook his shaggy head. 'I remember when you first came to us. You'd seen more intense things than the rest of us even imagined. You made me understand the threat of the *lampir*. The Bastion had been on guard against so many disasters, but after what you told us about Bosnia, after the real encounters, you certainly frightened me.'

'I wasn't able to kill him, Lucius. The king vampire.' The extent of his failure deflated Helsing, yet also fired his determination. 'If you work with me, if all the Bastion joins together,

328

we could find a way! And if we kill Zelm, the vampire network will unravel. He's the key.' He reached out to clutch at Lucius, but the big man wasn't reacting. He simply looked forlorn.

'You try and you try, Simon, but sometimes things just go wrong. Do you remember Roland? Tall man, very hairy, simpleminded?'

Helsing nodded.

'Sometimes things just go wrong,' Lucius repeated, 'and it falls to me to take care of it. It's my Bastion, and you're all my people. It is what it is.'

Helsing detected something strange about the man's demeanor, a tension that set off his alarm bells. The pre-dawn shadows in the forest were still intense. He had crawled to this hidden sanctuary while the police hunted for him. They were inept, civilized oafs. It would take them a long time to find his trail.

Lucius, though, was something else.

The big man slid out a long hunting knife, not trying to hide it. 'I meant to do this while you were unconscious, but I wanted to see you, explain to you.' He swallowed. 'I have to protect the Bastion. You've made bad mistakes, Simon. You've alerted the whole city to our presence, raising far too many questions. I'm sorry, son.'

As the big man lifted the knife, Helsing kicked out with one leg, using all his strength to smash into Lucius's knee. The other man wasn't expecting it. The blow cracked his kneecap and snapped the cartilage, knocking Lucius off balance. With a grunt, he fell against the rock. Helsing only had a moment. Lucius could easily overpower him with strength and mass, especially while Helsing was injured. He had one chance.

With a primal scream, he threw himself against the big man, overbalancing him. Shoving Lucius sideways as he bent to clutch his torn knee, Helsing rammed the man's head against the rock with a hard muffled thud.

Lucius grunted. The knife dropped out of his limp fingers, and Helsing grabbed it.

He had the element of surprise, he had desperation, and he knew the reason for Lucius's hesitation: compassion. Despite all of his harsh decisions and stern warnings, Lucius didn't really want to kill him.

But Helsing *wanted* to survive. He had no choice, allowed no feelings to enter into it.

The bearded man lurched up. 'Simon, no!'

Helsing drove the hunting knife into Lucius's throat, faster and more effective than a stake through the heart. The point plunged into the back of his head, deep into the brain. One quick stroke. Lucius reached out, fingers twitching, trying to grasp him – or maybe to embrace him.

'Sorry, Lucius,' he said.

His shoulder was bleeding again, but fresh adrenalin had killed the pain. Leaving the big man dead in the cache of supplies, Helsing took the rest of the first-aid pack, paused long enough to finish checking his bindings. He found several pain pills and chewed them, not because he couldn't endure the pain, but he didn't want it to slow him down.

He kept moving.

Fifty-Two

'I am afraid the party is over, Miss Tarada,' said Hugo Zelm. His erudite manner held an undertone somewhere between annoyance and amusement.

Even though hours had passed since Helsing had fled into the night, an army of security guards still hovered around Zelm like a wall of impeccable dark suits, armed with bravado as well as handguns and muscles.

The mansion was in disarray, serving trays dropped willy-nilly, window panes shattered, wine glasses spilled. The serving staff looked discouraged at the prospect of cleaning everything up. It was long past midnight, and Lexi felt exhausted.

Beside her, Blair looked like a wrung-out rag, no longer able to prop himself up with mere enthusiasm and optimism. 'Not quite what I expected for my first high-society party.'

The media had captured every moment of the debacle, and Lexi was sure the footage would be sensational. Helsing had fired four times, the first blast directly toward Zelm, but the other shots had gone wild. The spraying silver fragments had caused numerous injuries, even killed the woman in the blue sequined dress.

Ambulances had arrived to tend the injured, including Lexi. Blair had already helped her wash her cuts, wiping away the blood with his hand-kerchief and some fine napkins taken from the dessert buffet. She found a small gash on his cheek from a bit of flying glass. She pressed a cloth against it, smearing the make-up that covered his fading bruise.

'Am I scarred for life?' he asked.

'It'll look dashing.'

When the paramedics treated her, one of the last in line because she insisted the others go first, they announced to her relief that she did not need stitches, only a few Band-Aids.

Colorado Springs Police filled the mansion, taking statements from all witnesses before allowing them to leave. Several of the backup officers in the vicinity had joined Detective Carrow in his pursuit of Helsing, while others helped secure the scene. Lexi had pressed them for a report but they would say only that the CSPD continued to hunt for the suspect in the deep forest.

By now, most of the attendees had departed, and the security guards had chased away the remaining reporters and photographers. Broad-shouldered Franklin encouraged the paparazzi stragglers toward the door, as implacable as a man made out of cement. 'Mr Zelm has all the coverage he wants for this evening, thank you.'

Lexi and Blair saw no reason to stay, but since Carrow had driven them here, they needed to find another way home.

Zelm addressed her, looking unruffled. 'This is not what I expected when I invited you, Miss Tarada. I hope you will allow me to make up for it at some point.'

She searched for her sense of humor. 'I had a fabulous time. Best party all year.' Right now, though, she was done. 'At least you're still among the living.'

Zelm seemed satisfied. 'When you are as old as I am, each day you remain alive is something of a surprise. We can all be very, very relieved once the police apprehend that awful man.' He snapped his fingers. 'Franklin, I need your assistance.' The security chief came forward as if responding to an attack. Zelm said, 'I believe Miss Tarada's ride has departed without her. Would you please arrange a car and make sure she and Mr September get home safely?'

'Yes, sir. I will take them myself, in case they need extra protection.'

Blair stepped up and extended his hand, speaking with no apparent sarcasm but rather respect, 'Thank you for a memorable evening, sir.' He followed Lexi after the security man toward the door.

'We will have to do this again,' Zelm called after them in a jovial voice. 'You can certainly count on my continued support for HideTruth. After tonight, however, we have more to fear from the vampire *killers* than from the vampires themselves.' He chuckled. She thought he might be correct.

During the drive home, she and Blair leaned against each other in the back seat, both of them glad that Franklin wasn't much of a conversationalist. Lexi's dress felt disgusting and sticky. Blair's tuxedo was stained. Neither of them cared.

She still felt flushed and dismayed. She couldn't

333

believe that the fanatical, murderous bastard Helsing had actually fired his gun in the middle of a crowd! Now she knew that his vampire fixation was nothing more than paranoia. Helsing saw vampires everywhere: hapless people like Mark Stallings, Douglas Eldridge, Tom Grollin, Daniel Gardon, and who knew how many others over the years? Everyday people who happened to have nocturnal schedules or odd social lives, even a pizza delivery man! Not to mention the poor cop who lay in a coma with a severe head injury. They were all victims of Helsing's obsession.

She felt disgusted and afraid. The man had been so convincing, both online and in person, had raised so many difficult questions. He had caught her in his web, infecting her with his delusions. *One of these days, I'm sure to be right.* Lexi had always insisted that she wasn't a fool, wasn't too gullible . . . and yet here she was. How could she have fallen for it? The embarrassment seemed almost as bad as the fear.

Blair seemed to know what she was thinking. He hugged her without saying anything.

She paid little attention to where they were going and was surprised at how quickly Franklin arrived at the house. One light burned in the front room, and the porch light was on. After Blair helped her out, she thanked the driver, but his acknowledgment was merely mechanical.

As they entered the house, closed and locked the door, Blair said, 'Quite the party. I can't believe how late it is.'

Lexi plucked at her dress. Her hair was

disheveled. 'And you wonder why I don't go to parties.'

He forced a reassuring laugh. 'You simply don't go to the right ones, my dear.'

She was exhausted from fear and confusion. 'Let's get some rest before the sun comes up. I'll face the shit storm tomorrow.'

Inside her room, she set her laptop on her desk, but she couldn't face going online just yet. The reports would already be buzzing around, but she wanted some peace for now.

Next time, she would let Detective Carrow hunt the killers by himself.

Fifty-Three

The watery first light before dawn did little to illuminate the forest. Carrow couldn't see where he was going, and invisible bushes grabbed at his legs and ankles. He was exhausted and annoyed. Tall granite slabs and outcroppings loomed, silhouettes against the trees and stars. The flashlights didn't help much. The other searchers crashed nearby with enough separation for a tight grid.

They wouldn't miss Simon Helsing.

Carrow didn't like the wilderness on the best of days, and he made up his mind never to take his girls on a camping trip for father–daughter bonding. Bushwhacking all night, sliding down slopes and wrestling through malicious underbrush made him feel like some surprise contestant on a survival show. Soon enough, he could leave this to the search dogs.

Carrow couldn't figure out why Helsing had made his way through this particular terrain on purpose. The man seemed to know the woods very well. Did he have a wilderness hideout? At least he was wounded, as confirmed by the fresh blood droplets along the trail.

Two of his fellow searchers were hunters, Colorado natives, and Carrow let them take the lead. One of the men said, 'I wounded an elk while bow hunting once, had to track him for two miles through terrain just like this. But that was in daylight.' He swung the flashlight around, illuminating a granite outcropping like a fortress wall in front of him. 'We'll find him easy enough once the sun's up.'

'The way he's bleeding, we might just find him dead in a ravine,' said the other searcher.

'Fine with me,' Carrow said. 'Save a lot of time and paperwork.'

They kept pushing through shrubs closer to the granite buttress, making as much noise as a marching army. The lead searcher held up his hand as he came around a corner of the tall rock. 'Talus cave, and the blood trail leads into it.'

'Obvious place for a wounded man to go to ground,' said the other hunter. The three of them stopped moving.

'Could be an ambush,' Carrow said. 'He's cornered. Gun was empty at the mansion, but no telling what kind of stash he has out here. My three favorite words right now are "Use Extreme Caution".'

The searchers stood outside the cave, sheltered by the curve of pale rock. Carrow shouted into the dark hollow. 'Surrender yourself, Grundy. We are armed and prepared to shoot.'

Only mocking silence answered them. Carrow drew his weapon, approached the edge of the cleft.

One of the officers shone his flashlight into the gloomy recess. 'I see a body. It's a man . . . and he's not moving.'

Carrow felt relieved, but wary. 'Be careful.'

The three moved forward, weapons drawn, shining their flashlights in a combined beam into the cave.

A figure lay sprawled inside the shelter of the rocks up against the back wall. The flashlight beams glinted off wet pools of blood. Carrow let out a slow exhale and moved closer, extending his revolver.

The light illuminated a man with a large hunting knife thrust into his throat . . . a big man with light brown skin, black hair, and a full beard.

Not Simon Helsing at all.

Fifty-Four

Lexi awoke from one nightmare into another.

She saw Teresa in the dream, her best friend coming back to her, no longer giving her quiet and heartfelt encouragement. This time Teresa's terrified face rose in front of her, screaming.

'Lexi, run! *Run!*' her voice commanded as her image dissolved. *'Run!'*

Lexi's eyes snapped open, and she found herself tangled in her sheets. Early-morning light seeped through a gap in her drawn curtains.

In front of her towered the silhouette of a predator, strong, sinister – a monster. Lexi lurched upright in bed, sucking in a breath to scream, but he pointed a weapon at her. She saw a burst of brilliance like a puff of lightning, heard a click, a whistling unspooling of wire. Then her body was entangled in a thousand electrified marionette strings.

She fell backward, jittering, in spasm. The snapping of stun voltage sounded like a rattlesnake, but she couldn't feel the fangs of the Taser, only a complete lack of control. Pain sucked all her breath away. She could barely gasp a breath, certainly couldn't scream.

This was worse than some vampire come to kill her. It was Helsing.

His attack was swift and sure, incapacitating her. As she lay paralyzed on the bed, Helsing yanked the curtains open to flood the room with blinding daylight. In the garish sunshine, his face was drawn and grim, his shirt covered in blood. His blue eyes were intense, as if he were possessed by a real demon, not just his paranoia.

Flat on her back, she struggled, but her muscles and bones had turned to water. Her thoughts flickered chaotically like a dying neon sign.

Helsing must have broken in, just as he had slipped into the homes of his other victims, just as he had tried to kill the pizza delivery man. She groaned deep in her throat, trying to reconnect the blown fuses of her nerves.

Helsing stood beside the bed and glowered at her, his expression inhuman. From the deadness in his eyes, Lexi knew that he didn't see her as human. 'You're one of them. You helped them.' His voice sounded bleak as he stared at the glare of morning sunlight on the bed. 'Damn you! Haven't they turned you?'

With great effort, she made her body twitch, her left hand flutter. 'Get . . . out!' Lexi watched her legs spasm uncontrollably. How long did a Taser stun last?

Helsing dropped a satchel on the end of her bed, opened it. To her horror, he withdrew a mallet, set it on the comforter, then withdrew a long stake, clean wood, freshly sharpened.

'Stop,' she said, and her voice sounded a little stronger. Her arms and legs remained uncooperative, but she could turn her head back and forth, and she could speak. 'Not a vampire . . . you *know* I'm not a vampire.'

Helsing leaned over her with the stake and the mallet. He seemed to be favoring the arm that held the stake. 'I'm doing this to save you. I saw you with Hugo Zelm. I know he controls you.'

'Not a vampire,' she insisted, intending her statement to refer to herself as well as to the eccentric philanthropist. 'Another . . . mistake.'

'You're tainted already.' His expression showed no sympathy. 'This is the only way I can stop you.'

'You . . . are . . . *wrong*!' She tried to fill her voice with vehemence, but it was no more than a sorry, pathetic plea.

He stood close to the side of the bed as morning sunshine washed over the sheets. Her bodily control was returning only in fits and starts. She couldn't fight him.

He yanked on the thin Taser wires, jerked the tiny hooks free, and pulled back the sheet to leave Lexi vulnerable. Helsing gripped the mallet, a brutal heavy tool. One powerful strike could drive the stake through her sternum and into her heart.

'No!' Her gasp was louder.

The half-open bedroom door swung wide, and Blair barged in, confused and wary. When he saw Helsing standing over her, saw the mallet and stake, his expression flared. 'What the hell are you—?'

Helsing spun toward him, and Blair charged forward, bare handed, without thinking. Lexi knew he was not a fighter, but now he dredged up some steel from his core. He let out a wordless yell as he threw himself on her attacker.

Responding like a viper, Helsing twisted himself, swung the mallet sideways, and smashed Blair in the middle of the forehead with a sickening soft thud. Blair reeled backward and dropped like a felled ox.

Now Lexi did manage to scream. Rage overwhelmed her terror, and she wanted to strangle Helsing, to *kill him* with her bare hands. Her arm twitched.

Leaving Blair crumpled on the floor, the vampire killer returned to her, grabbed the stake, and straddled her on the bed like some horrific lover playing a sadistic game. Her only weapon now was her brain.

'I am not a vampire,' she said. 'Think about it.

You know I can't be.' The words came easily. She moved her legs, tried to bend her knees to throw him off balance, but she had no strength.

Like a surgeon, Helsing pressed the point of the stake against the center of her chest. 'I showed you all the evidence. You *know* vampires are out there. You know that what I'm doing is necessary.' His voice grew louder, more enraged. 'But you betrayed me!'

'I gave you the benefit of the doubt,' she said. 'I listened. I believed . . . but you're wrong.' His eyes flared as she continued. 'Vampires don't exist. It's all in your mind.'

'Evidence! I gave you evidence. My reports.'

'*Circumstantial* evidence. There's a normal explanation for all of it. You already made mistakes, targeted innocent people. You don't have to kill me.' She pulled in another breath. 'You don't have to kill anyone.'

'I'm saving humanity. I am Simon Helsing!'

'No, you're not.' She raised one arm, lifted her head from the pillow. 'You're David Grundy, and *you* . . . are the real monster.' Lexi was passionate, too. She had her entire belief system on the line. She'd seen more than her share of gullible crazies, though she had thought at least for a while that Helsing could be right.

But he wasn't.

'The people you hurt were just normal people. The motel owner, that poor policeman.' Her voice came out raw. 'And now Blair! Just normal people.'

'There are real vampires! And the king vampire turned you. I'm saving—'

Behind him Blair somehow managed to rise up from the floor, his forehead bloody, his movements jerky. 'Leave her alone!' He snatched her laptop from the desk with both hands and crashed it down on Helsing's head. It was a weak blow, but enough to stun him, distract him.

Helsing jerked the point of the stake away from her chest, and Lexi managed to knock it aside. Blair collapsed again, still raising his hands to keep fighting.

Lexi seized the moment. With everything she had, she got control of her arms and reached into the drawer in her nightstand. She pulled out the handgun she kept there, the .38 Special revolver she kept against unlikely stalkers. She had trained, and she kept the gun ready.

Without thinking, she wrapped her finger around the trigger and swung the weapon toward Helsing. Point and shoot. He turned to her, raised the bloody mallet.

Lexi squeezed the trigger, squeezed hard, and kept squeezing, pointing the gun at his chest until the .38 fired. The explosion caught him in his body core, as the recoil slammed her back into the mattress. She nearly lost consciousness as Helsing's bleeding body collapsed on top of her legs.

She pushed him away and squirmed to one side. She raised herself on her hands just as Blair crawled to the side of the bed.

Helsing's mouth opened and closed, and blood trickled out of both corners of his lips. A big red hole in his chest bubbled, blood mixed with foaming air.

She leaned over him, hating him, but she saw

that his eyes were fixed on her neck, a smooth neck with no vampire bites. And the dangling gold chain, the delicate cross she wore because of her promise to her parents.

He gurgled, 'You're . . .'

'I'm not a vampire. You. Were. Wrong.' She pounded each word like a nail in his coffin. In disgust she shoved his bleeding body off the bed, and he tumbled with a thud to the floor.

Blair managed to haul himself back to his feet, swaying.

Though exhausted and terrified, Lexi managed to say, 'You saved me. Thank you!'

'I love you too.' He collapsed on to the bed beside her, groaning. 'Is it all right if I just stay here for a while? You were there for me after Cesar. My turn to comfort you.'

'Let's not keep score.' First things first, she dialed 911, called for an ambulance and the police, then turned to Blair. 'Just stay put. The paramedics will be here in a few minutes.' While they waited, she wrapped her arms around her friend.

Fifty-Five

When the ambulance arrived, the EMTs examined Blair's head injury, complimenting him on his thick skull. Though Lexi was a wreck herself, she hovered beside them as they worked, desperate to help and trying not to get in the way. 'Will he be all right?'

Lexi was surprised that the lead EMT was a woman named MaryJane Stricklin – one of the potential targets on Helsing's list. She was all business. 'We'll take care of Mr September. Severe concussion, no doubt about it, but he's responsive. When we get him to the hospital they'll run a lot more tests.' If Stricklin made a connection between her patient and the vampire killer who had targeted her, she didn't show it.

'First Cesar and now this,' Blair groaned as the EMTs wheeled the gurney to the front door. 'Lex, I've been battered more times since meeting you, than in my entire life.'

'Let's not make a habit of it, OK? We're done now.' Lexi clasped his hand, and Stricklin gave them a moment, though she was anxious to get him out to the ambulance. 'Thank you, Blair. Best friend in the world.'

'Shucks, it was nothing. I'd do it again in a second.'

'No you won't,' Stricklin said. 'Time to go.'

They wheeled him out the door and down the driveway to the ambulance. Lexi followed beside Blair, who was conscious enough to remark that one of the male paramedics was particularly cute.

Before going, the EMTs had checked her over for injuries and wrapped her in a blanket. The Taser had left no lasting damage, though she felt as if she'd been run over by a truck.

Detective Carrow arrived before they left, looking worse than she did, still dressed in his suit from Zelm's gala the night before. He was covered in dirt, shoes muddy, hair disheveled, face scratched. 'We chased him all through the night in the pitch-black forest, and the whole time he was coming for you.' He sounded relieved, even happy. 'Crap almighty, I could have just waited here!'

After all she'd been through, Lexi was not in a mood to celebrate. 'I wish you had been here. I was attacked, my housemate was severely injured, and I had to kill a man. I could have used some help.'

Carrow grew serious. 'I understand. Sorry. You did manage to stop a serial killer. Think of the lives you saved.'

She pulled the blanket tighter around her shoulders and heard the ambulance depart. She told herself that Blair was in good hands. 'Right now, what I think of is how he broke into my house and tried to drive a stake through my heart . . . and how it felt to pull the trigger and feel the weight of a dying man on top of me.' Her voice went hoarse, and she shivered at the recollection.

'I'll take your full statement a little later, if that's OK.'

The coroner entered through the front door, accompanied by an army of evidence technicians. Carrow sat beside Lexi on the sofa, awkwardly asking her basic questions, as Dr Watson reviewed the crime scene in the bedroom, studied the body on the floor. Displaced but with nowhere else to go, Lexi went into the kitchen, trying to ignore the bustle around her. Oddly, she thought of Holly Smith, how wounded she must have felt, how lost even after being rescued.

She found the French press and determined to

make the good coffee herself so she would know how to do it for Blair during his recovery.

Watson came out of the bedroom, her curly hair a mess. She pulled down the paper mask from her mouth and nose. 'Not much question about the crime, the victim, or the perpetrator. You'll fill me in on the details, Detective?'

'Once I get the full story,' he said. 'I know most of it already, just a few loose ends.'

'And it's all wrapped up before the election.' The coroner was actually smiling. 'That's good.'

Lexi slowly pressed the plunger in the French press, watched the hot water swirl around the aromatic coffee grounds. She closed her eyes, inhaled, blocked out the other sounds in the house and blanked the images in her head. She just breathed the coffee, in for a long breath, out for a long breath.

Processing the scene took hours even after the coroner hauled off Helsing's body. The evidence techs finished their work, and Detective Carrow hurried them along so Lexi could have a little privacy.

He had encouraged her to go to a hotel, but she stubbornly insisted on staying. 'It's my home. We know Helsing is no longer a threat.' She ran her hands through her hair. 'I just want something to be normal for a little while.'

The detective conceded, though she suspected he was bending a few rules by letting her stay there. By the time everyone else finally left, it was mid-afternoon. Carrow stood at the door, ready to leave. 'We've got the evidence we need. You can relax, Miss Tarada. I'm going to need to talk with you more, but we can do that later. I'll take care of everything I can.'

'Thanks, Detective.'

After he left, she went around the house and opened all the curtains, letting the sunshine in on a mess she couldn't face cleaning up. The bloody sheets and comforter from the bed had been taken away as evidence, not that she ever wanted them back. She was going to sleep on the sofa for the next few nights, or maybe in Blair's bed, since he would be in the hospital. Or maybe she would spend some nights there with him. She had slept in uncomfortable chairs before.

Right now she just wanted a hot shower, to let the steam open her pores and rinse out all the shadows and bad memories.

As she enjoyed the pounding spray and breathed the warm, thick air, she suddenly pictured herself as Janet Leigh in *Psycho* standing oblivious in a similar shower until Norman Bates yanked back the curtain to hack her with a butcher knife. Lexi climbed out of the shower, ran to the bathroom door, locked it, then went back to enjoy the warm spray again.

She had spent too much time chasing down crazy stories, monster sightings, bizarre theories. What she really needed to believe in were her friends. Blair had been her knight in shining armor, just as she'd been there when he needed her. That was all the faith she needed to have. She thought Teresa would approve.

She had fostered the doubts and fears of gullible people, making them want to believe. Some people were disturbed, and did not want their beliefs challenged. Lexi had needed a sense of wonder in her life, but maybe it was more important to foster a sense of *reality*. Sometimes the answer really was a stuck keyboard and random letters on a screen.

She decided to tell Detective Carrow everything, even explain about Lucius and the Bastion, though she was sure their camp would be long gone by now, moved to some other wilderness hiding place.

As she tried to wrap up the case in her own mind, she switched off the shower and let the warm water run down the drain. Lexi admitted to herself that there never was any evidence of real vampires. Only a blind fanatic would believe an impossible explanation when there were simpler, more rational reasons. The actual monster stalking Colorado Springs had not been a bloodsucking fiend, but a crazy man who thought he was killing vampires. With Simon Helsing gone, there was one less monster in the world.

Lexi dried herself off, dressed in comfortable sweats, and sat down in front of the desktop computer in her room. Her laptop, damaged when Blair bashed Simon Helsing in the head, had been taken away as evidence.

After phoning the hospital to get an update on Blair, Lexi called up HideTruth and began composing a new essay to post on the home page. It felt like a confession as she wrote out the details of recent events, telling the whole story. She posted her fears and suspicions, how much she had wanted to believe in vampires, how convincing Helsing's evidence had seemed. Then she confessed that she, Alexis Tarada, had simply been duped because she wanted reality to be something it wasn't, something more.

She knew she would receive a firestorm of comments from outraged believers. They would think she had betrayed them. They would rail at her, claim that she was part of the problem, not the solution. She might lose many of her regular supporters.

But she didn't care. After what she'd been through, Lexi had to take a different stand now. There was no hiding the truth.

Fifty-Six

Lexi called her parents when she was ready, but they had already seen the news. The crazed vampire killer had become more than a local story, and Lexi expected to get more coverage and exposure than she wanted. People would read, and mock, HideTruth, but she was used to that. She had faced and defeated a serial killer who believed in vampires. Trolls were nothing in comparison.

'First off, I'm all right,' she said as soon as her parents answered.

Sharon and Perry talked over each other in their excitement, but they said essentially the same thing, glad to hear from her, relieved she was safe.

'It's a long story. I'm not sure I want to tell all of it, but I'm OK. That's the important part.'

'We've been worried sick about you, dear,' her mother said. 'Your father was ready to get in the car and just drive straight out there. If it would help, we can come and stay with you for as long as you need us.'

Lexi appreciated the offer, but their visit would cause an entirely different kind of stress. 'I just need some peace and quiet. I'll rest here.' She suddenly realized how empty her house was.

As if picking up on her thoughts, her father asked, 'But your roommate – how badly was he hurt? Is he going to recover?'

'Blair saved me,' Lexi said. 'I talked to him this morning, and I'll visit him in the hospital today. The doctors say he should be all right.'

'I'm so glad he was there to help,' her mother said, 'though I'm still not sure what your relationship is to him.'

'Or if we want to know,' her father added cautiously.

'You don't want to know. I'm not dating him, but there's no better friend in the world.' She meant that with all her heart. Her voice cracked as she repeated, reassuring herself as much as her parents, 'He'll be all right.'

She told them the bare bones of the story about Helsing, enough to satisfy their curiosity, down-playing the violence. As she talked, she fingered the delicate gold cross around her neck.

'Just hearing about that dangerous man sickens me! We've told you—' Sharon's tone changed as she began a lecture.

Lexi braced herself, but her father cut in. 'Speaking of being sick, we got an unexpected report yesterday. We were going to call, but then we saw the news.'

'Perry, now isn't the time!'

He continued anyway. 'Your mother had more tests. The oncologist says that the combination of the chemo and radiation worked on her breast cancer. It's in remission.'

The news came as a complete surprise. 'That's great! I wish we had more surprises like that.'

'With cancer, you can never be sure it's completely gone,' her mother said. 'I'll still have to go in for tests every six months.'

'But it's gone for now.' Her father sounded happy and proud.

Lexi found herself smiling. Yes, she liked that kind of news.

Her mother didn't stay derailed from her lecture for long. 'I'll say it again, Alexis, and maybe this time you'll listen. You should come home. We still have your room. You can live with us.'

Perry jumped in. 'Rent free for now. It's dangerous out there in the world. You've seen it yourself.' His voice became stern, as if he were laying down curfew hours. 'Time to come home.'

Lexi drew a deep breath and spoke into the phone, clear and confident. 'There are dangers out in the world, no matter where you look. But I see wonders too, and mysteries. I have everything I need here. I am home.'

Her parents heard something in her voice and decided not to argue.

Fifty-Seven

When she arrived at the hospital to see Blair, Lexi brought more roses than she had ever carried before. Six red ones, six yellow, six white, six peach.

Seeing her at the door, Blair sat up in bed so quickly that he winced in pain. 'Lex, they're beautiful! Nobody brings me flowers.'

'Are you calling me a nobody?' She chuckled, but couldn't cover her dismay at seeing his bandage-wrapped head. 'I didn't know which rose color signifies "thanks for saving me from a serial killer".'

'You've conveyed the message perfectly. They're adorable, and you're adorable.'

She flushed, turned away while pretending to look for a place to set the bouquet. 'And I'm alive, thanks to you.'

'I was just in the right place at the right time. Take most of the credit for yourself.'

She cleared the countertop near his sink and arranged the roses in their vase. 'Are they taking good care of you?'

Blair lay back, his head propped on a stack of pillows and the bed tilted so that he could ignore the muted talk show on the wall TV. An IV bag hung from a metal tree beside the bed. 'Well enough, though not like the way you take care of me. I can't wait to get home.' He pushed his bed tray aside, shunning the half-eaten food on it. 'The meals here are abysmal. You could make better Jell-O than these people.'

'I'm from Iowa. Of *course* I know how to make good Jell-O,' Lexi said. 'And as an extra special treat for you, I'll even add canned fruit cocktail and Cool Whip.' Blair grimaced. She leaned close to kiss him on the cheek. 'I miss you. Get better. Come home soon.'

'If you keep hanging around with serial killers, I may have to find a different place to rent. Too much drama.'

She grew serious. 'I would never want a different housemate, Blair. Please don't leave me.'

'If you put it that way . . .' He sighed and became serious. 'I need you too. Can you help me with the paperwork here? The hospital is asking a lot of questions, and I like to keep my records as bare bones as possible.'

Lexi remembered he liked to keep his information private, which had posed difficulties when he'd first rented with her. He had insisted that all the bills and records be in her name, so that he could keep himself off 'lists'. She smiled. 'I'll answer what I can, but you've never told me why you keep so many secrets. Even from me.'

'There's a difference between secrets and privacy, my dear. You never know what somebody might do with that information. I don't share what they don't need.'

She clucked her tongue. 'The hospital will need to bill your insurance.'

'I have a well-funded medical savings plan that

will cover the bill. I don't want my records exposed and available for any hacker to steal my identity. No social security number, no scanned signature, no online bank accounts. I've gotten along fine so far.'

'Until you got whacked on the head by a mass murderer,' she said. She leaned on the bed next to him. 'Of course I'll help. If you do have a deep, dark past, I don't want to hear about it. I know what kind of person you are, and I know I don't ever want to lose you as a friend.' He clasped her hand.

Detective Carrow appeared in the doorway, shattering the moment. He wore his everyday gray sport jacket, which looked about the same as the good suit he had worn for Hugo Zelm's formal gala.

Lexi squeezed Blair's hand one more time and straightened, turning to the detective. 'I'm surprised to see you here.' She suspected he had more questions for them.

Blair frowned at the man. 'You're empty-handed. At least Lex brought me flowers.'

'I brought you my sunny presence,' Carrow said. He looked relieved and was actually smiling. 'I was here visiting Officer Amber and his wife, showing my support, you know. Prognosis is good. He's showing significantly improved brain activity. Doctors are keeping him in a medically induced coma, but the damage isn't as bad as they feared. Won't promise a full recovery but they're optimistic.'

'Optimism is good,' Lexi said.

He nodded slowly, still standing in the

doorway. 'I'll be optimistic for your sake, too, Miss Tarada. We won't be filing any charges, just in case you were concerned. There'll be paperwork and a hearing, but I'll vouch for you. When you shot Grundy, you were clearly acting in self-defense.'

'I can second that,' Blair said.

'You did help us out, even if you didn't exactly have an orthodox approach.' Carrow scratched the stubble on one of his cheeks. 'Maybe if I'd been a little more unorthodox myself, I could have put the pieces together faster.'

'I completely agree,' Lexi said. 'But then you wouldn't have needed me.'

'You make that sound like a bad thing.'

She shook her head, drove back the weight from the terror of the previous morning, of fighting Helsing, feeling the sharp point of the stake on her chest . . . pulling the trigger.

Blair shifted on the bed. 'You are not invited to go along with us to the next upscale party. Lex's dress is ruined, and I'll never be able to return it.'

She grinned. 'Hugo Zelm will pay for it. He already sent me a message.' She mused, feeling wistful. 'Maybe I'll keep it as a souvenir. I'll be salvaging a lot of things, but at least I'm alive and Blair is alive.' She drew a breath. 'And Simon Helsing isn't.'

Carrow came the rest of the way into the room and sniffed the huge bouquet of roses. He swung the door mostly shut for privacy. 'There's one more curious thing I wanted to talk about. When we were pursuing Helsing through the forest, we found where he had holed up, a small cave with some stashed supplies, first-aid items.' He skewered Lexi with an intense gaze. 'And another body. A large man, dark hair, beard. He'd been stabbed through the throat. Any idea who he might be?'

She felt a cold knot of dismay. 'Unfortunately, I think I do.' She hung her head, saw that Blair was also staring at her with intense curiosity. She had a lot to tell them both. 'His name was Lucius.'

It was long past time for secrets and assumptions. She explained in full detail about the Bastion community, the camp, how she had been lured out there with a promise of evidence, and drugged . . . all of it.

After hearing the tale, Carrow shook his head. 'That's a crazy story, Miss Tarada, but I'll surprise you – for once, I believe everything you just told me.'

His phone rang, and he pulled it from his pocket, turning away to answer the call. His expression grew disturbed as he listened, then spoke. 'No, nothing more, sir. We've wrapped up the case, withdrawn the plainclothes protection. Mr Lugash has nothing else to fear. We haven't had any contact with him in several days.' He listened again, then scratched his other cheek. 'All right, I'll have a look. But it has nothing further to do with the case.'

He ended the call and gave Lexi a questioning look. 'That was the manager of Checkers Pizza. Frederik Lugash hasn't shown up for work for the past two days, and his boss thought we had taken him into protective custody.' He paced the floor of the hospital room. 'I'll do a welfare check at his house, just to make sure. Too much of a coincidence.' He pulled open the door again to leave. 'Thank you both. I'll call if I need anything else.' He glanced at Blair in the bed, as if suddenly remembering he was there. 'Oh, and get well soon.'

'I'm going with you.' Lexi squeezed Blair's arm and set off after the detective.

Carrow frowned. 'No you're not.'

'Throw me a bone, Detective. I'm more a part of this case than anyone else. Besides, you must have more questions and paperwork for me. We can do it on the way.'

He sighed. 'Come on, then.'

They drove out of downtown and headed south, winding their way into the sad old residential area where Lugash lived. Lexi didn't tell Carrow that she had already snooped at his house. She followed the detective up the driveway. The Volkswagen with its Checkers Pizza sign was gone.

'Seems like nobody's home,' she said.

He pounded on the door. 'We know he's not at work.' He kept knocking, but received no answer.

'That's a good enough reason for concern, considering the circumstances,' Lexi said. 'Could Helsing have gotten him before he came after me? Is the door unlocked?'

'Why would he leave the door unlocked?' Carrow asked, turning the knob.

It opened.

Inside, the house was quiet and empty. 'Hello?

357

CSPD. This is Detective Carrow. Mr Lugash, are you here?'

No answer.

Lexi followed him into the front hall, adding her own voice. 'Anybody home?' She felt the emptiness, knew in her heart that they would find no one inside – no one alive at least.

The house was in disarray. Some of the drawers remained half-open; papers were scattered on the counter, as if hurriedly searched then left behind. She briefly thought the house might have been robbed, but this felt different. 'Somebody left here in a hurry.'

Carrow's brow furrowed as he walked deeper into the house, still calling out. Alert, Lexi moved cautiously. She didn't smell any blood, but that didn't mean the pizza delivery man hadn't been murdered. All the drapes were drawn, as she had expected. She looked around the front room, the bare walls above the sofa, poked her head into the small powder room and was surprised to see that the mirror above the sink had been removed.

'He must have been doing some remodeling,' she said aloud. Then a chill went down her back. She took another quick scan and realized that there were no mirrors in the house at all.

The bedroom closet was open, dresser drawers askew. A few clothes were scattered around, but most were gone. 'He grabbed what he could, packed up, and left,' Carrow said. 'Lugash is out of here. We're not going to find him.'

'Running from creditors maybe?' She knew it was a foolish suggestion.

'Why would he just take off? What was he afraid of? The vampire killer's gone.'

'He was afraid of something,' Lexi said. 'Maybe afraid that he'd be found out.' She felt gooseflesh on her arms. 'The bed hasn't been slept in.'

Following her instincts, she went to the mattress, pressed down on the bedspread, plucked at the corner. Her heart sank, knowing what she would find.

Lexi pulled back the sheets on the bed and found no mattress there.

Just soft dirt.

Acknowledgments

I have lived near Colorado Springs for more than twenty years. It is a beautiful place to live, surrounded by incredible mountain scenery and wild national forests that could hold many secrets. I have done a lot of exploring, but I still haven't found any vampires, though. I wrote much of the novel here, but the last chapters were written (by serendipitous coincidence) in Eastern Europe, in Prague and elsewhere in the Czech Republic, a place extremely appropriate for vampires.

This novel is even more special to me because just as I was starting to write it, a dear friend suffered a terrible personal loss, the death of her husband, and was struggling to pay funeral and everyday expenses. I rallied friends and fans and offered to name characters in *Stake* after anyone who made a donation to help her – side characters or victims – and the real name of the serial killer reserved for the person who donated the most. We raised over $5000 to help, and many of my friends and supporters are in this novel. Many of them, alas, meet terrible ends . . .

Special thanks to Steve Feldberg at Audible. com for giving the opportunity to write this novel. I've had it on my back burner for almost two decades, but timing was never right. Also thanks to Carl Smith at Severn House, my agent John Silbersack at the Bent Agency, Eric Williams at Zero Gravity Management, Brendan Higgins, and Diane Jones.